GODS OF LONDINIUM

GODS OF LONDINIUM

NATANIA BARRON

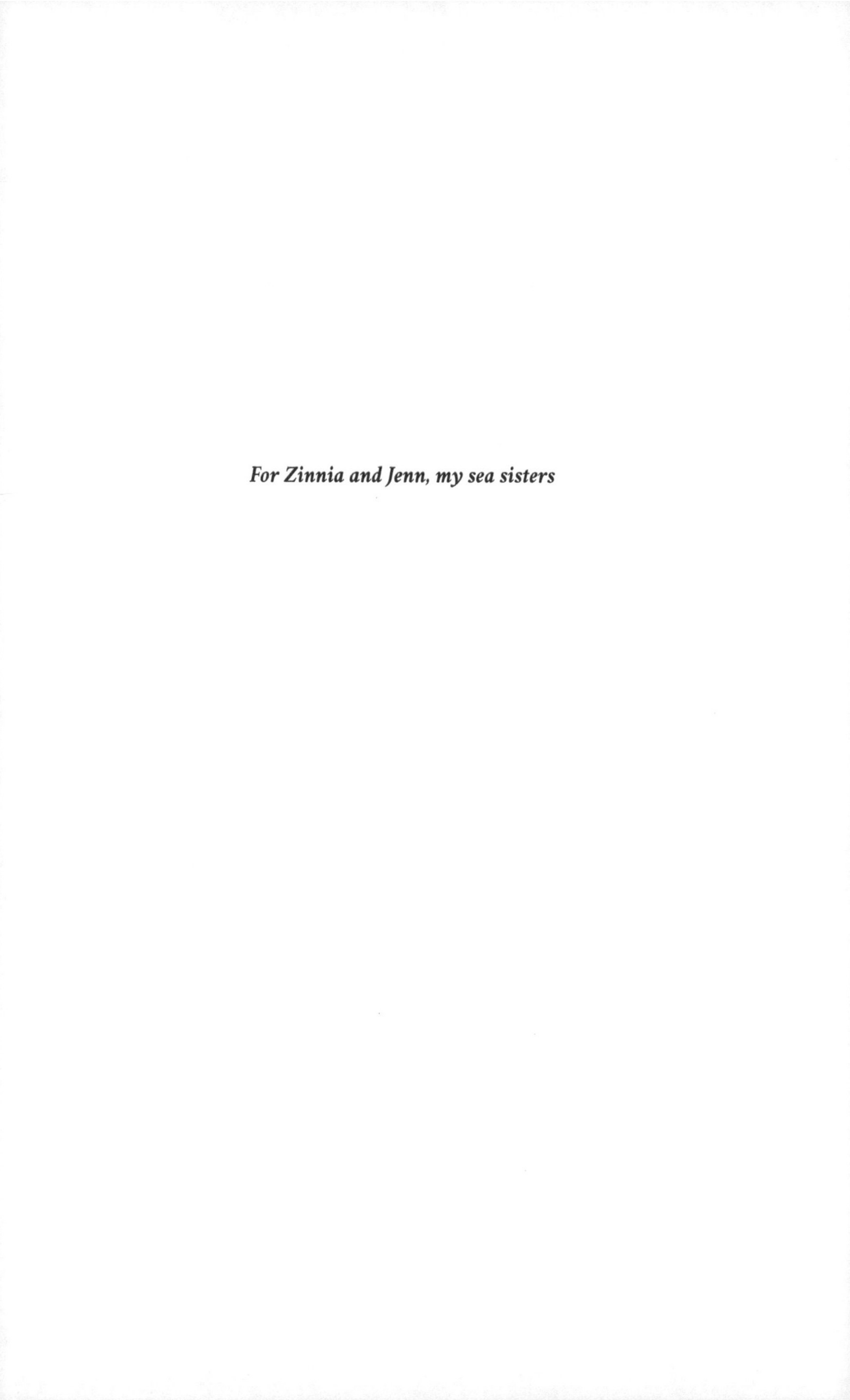

For Zinnia and Jenn, my sea sisters

Full fathom five thy father lies;
Of his bones are coral made;
Those are pearls that were his eyes;
Nothing of him that doth fade,
But doth suffer a sea-change
Into something rich and strange.
- Ariel, *The Tempest*

"I do not live in this world alone but in a thousand worlds."
— John Keats

PROLOGUE

It is true what they say.

I am a lord of the sea, of storms, and of thunder. I am the commander of waters, rivers, oceans, and all those trappings of old. I have transformed into titanic beasts and evaporated into mists; I have held lovers of the highest renown in my arms and made them quiver with pleasure; I have quaffed enough spirits to drown a small village and lived to tell the tale.

I have lived longer and wilder than most. I have laughed loud enough to shake the mountains and grieved long enough to watch babes live, grow, and die in the wake.

My life has spun stories, whirling eddies all about me. And I lose track of them now and again.

Yes, much of what they say about me is true.

But I was no wanted son, no cherished creature born to doting parents of high status. I wear my mistakes around me like a second skin of regret; I've a tendency to be a right coward and make enormously questionable decisions, and, at times, I'm dull as soft chalk.

How did I come to be? I was formed among the rocks and springs and rolling hills, my first breath of sweet mountain spring water, tasting of minerals and marvels. Rannerdale. Crummock Water. Home.

I wasn't born so much as I was made. For my father, too, was a spirit of the waters. A god of the deep, a rare being possessed of great power, but mad and corrupted by time and his own selfish pursuits.

He was old and weary. And when my mother, a sorceress brave enough to seek him out, waded into the clear water to summon him, he had no will to argue when she beckoned.

My mother was mortal, and he found her beautiful. With what little strength he still had, he meant to possess her. A final act. The last tide of desire.

They spoke.

She asked for him to come into her, and he did. And that is not a pretty story to tell. Laying with an old god like my father, grown strange and mad for thousands of years, is no easy task for a mortal woman, no matter how touched with magic.

Then it was over, the waters went still, and my father was gone. I lay in the mud, naked and new and small as a lamb.

I remember watching her fall to her feet, pale and afraid. She looked upon me with nothing but disgust and despair. I was an abomination. A horror. This was not the power she had sought. This was a curse.

I ached from being made, my skin was so tight I writhed. I called out for her in a high shriek that made the waters tremble.

My mother screamed and fell back. Oh, but I could feel myself beginning to grow, to change, to move and become something else. For a time, I was aware of nothing but the pain and wanted nothing else in the world but her touch. I wanted to be in her arms and feel her warmth.

I opened my mouth again to tell her in words of a language she could understand. For a moment, I thought she would take me to her breast, suckle me, and keep me warm. There were tears in her dark eyes.

But she threw me into the lake, anyway.

PART I

1

My life as a man begins in the great city of Londinium on the Tamesis River, in the year 1782. There are stories from before when I lived among the fish and bracken, but I won't relay them here. The language of fish is difficult to speak, let alone write down, you understand.

But know this: I learned a great many things as a fish. I spent time under the tutelage of a giant trout named Scale Bottom, and she imparted to me the wisdom of the ages, as she had done with my father. From her, I learned to observe human beings, to mimic them, and to do what most of them don't bother to do at all: listen. I learned that I was not like them, these people, yet they could mistake me as one of them if I worked to conceal my more unusual aspects.

I might have stayed a fish forever, but I was lucky, and I met a poet.

No, maybe it wasn't luck. Poets are, generally speaking, only trouble—though I never could have known it then. So maybe it was fate rather than luck.

You see, toward the end of my time as a fish, I became aware of a man who frequented my little lake, Crummock Water. I listened almost every day to his voice drift across the surface. He recited verses from the prow of a little rowboat while a woman watched him from the shoreline. The words lit something inside of me, a divine and shockingly powerful awakening, and I thought for the first time I could live among humans if they were more like this. That they were not so dull and slow as I had thought, and, perhaps they had some glimmer of the divine in them, after all.

At the time, I knew not what I was, exactly. Scale Bottom called me a brightling.

My poet guided me out of the water, I suppose you could say, though we never met properly. Years later, when I reached Londinium, I found a volume of his poetry and at last, I had a name: William Wordsworth.

Upon hearing those words, those lines, I became obsessed with the idea of poetry, with this creative spark of genius I experienced. I had to become human, as far as I could, to understand how their minds worked.

No, I was not a man, that I knew. I was also not terribly bright, and then possessed an unerring sense of optimism regardless of the situation. I would eventually learn to drown such optimism in sarcasm, cynicism, and whiskey, but I hadn't garnered such skills yet.

Still, I knew two things with utmost certainty: I was not a human, and there were other brightlings like me, though their numbers were fewer than the fingers on one hand, and none had as much raw power as I did. As to my proportions to humanity: I was bigger, stronger, and a good deal more dangerous than a human. I lived longer. I burned hotter.

The creatures like me, well, I called them whales, because I could feel them moving in my mind across large distances, a skill Scale Bottom showed me, based on the very same way fish locate one another. It is a part of the brain—basic and truly ancient—that is altogether scrambled in most human beings. With this ability, I felt three or four presences of these such celestial whales; once I felt a fifth, though it was slimy and far away and I didn't like the feel of it in my mind. Each whale was possessed of an unusual feature, a quality about them, like fires of different hues and heats or varietals of wine and spirits.

Scale Bottom told me that in the old days when the world was young, there were eight of these whales, and they shepherded over the entire world, each a ruler of their own domain. I, like my father before me, had a claim to my own: water, of course. But then I only knew oceans as vague promises in the distance and was quite confident to hold court among the trout. I did not understand the power granted to me, or even that I could use such power to shape the world. It didn't seem worth the time and effort in my younger days.

Yet, when it came to these other powerful creatures, though I knew of them, I was not ready to meet them right away. So I remained with Scale Bottom for many years, and I was content. Happy. I made that same egregious error common to humans and brightlings alike: I assumed happiness would follow me wherever I went.

Scale Bottom did not want me to leave. She warned against it. But once I had heard poetry, I grew tired of fish songs and fish conversation. She could not understand. I didn't believe I would be happy unless I knew more about human beings up close; she could never leave those waters. How could she understand?

Relenting and giving me her blessing at last, the ancient fish told me to find the brightest whale, who went by the name of Andrew La Roche. She said he was as trustworthy as such people could be, and he would take care of me and guide me in the world of man.

All I had to do was get to Londinium.

I HAD no need for roads, so I followed the current, swimming from little tributary to larger pond, brook, ravine, and waterfall, until I joined the larger rivers. I gathered what I needed from the water: clothing, language, and sustenance. I spoke to the swans often, who were haughty but helpful in their own way, so long as you brought them shiny baubles before you asked questions. They gave me tunes to sing. Bawdy and beautiful both.

As I went down toward Londinium, the waters changed drastically. And so, too, did the world around it. Since my communication with humans had been so small I did not yet understand their technological advances, their sprawling growth, crawling over the crust of the world like hungry ants. The water told their stories: the purulent, the holy, the profane. And everything in between.

Water brought me past vast cities, bustling townships, and advances I had never imagined in my dreams. I had thought carriages and chariots to be beasts of horrific creation. The close-cropped towns along the way reminded me of clustered mushroom colonies, and the people were little better. The vast aqueducts striating the landscapes confused me and often sent me in the wrong direction. How human beings could reroute water absolutely baffled me. They tore down mountains and re-shaped the land as they needed it, vast statues—some articulated with clockwork interiors—stood by every great town on my descent. Some looked vaguely familiar; others terrified me. I was particularly taken by Cartimandium, an ancient and resplendent settlement on the River Sabrinna. It had the largest homes I had ever seen, so large I could not comprehend they were homes at first and thought they must be massive hives. I later learned they were mansions and, once I saw Londinium, understood they were by no means unusual in Britanniae.

The aqueducts did not function in every city; some had figured out other ways to store and transport water. But the arcing elegance of the architecture was pervasive no matter where I went. Immense columns, wide spaces, pale walls, and wooden carvings. Even small houses, still echoes of their Celtic past on their decoration, spoke to the glory of a place I knew not yet: Rome.

I was planning to go into Londinium through the Tamesis, but when I began to plot my way, something truly astonishing happened: the rivers went underground. And then split. It was like going blind. Though I had gathered a great deal of what made up Britanniae, I had not prepared myself to fall. I was swept up in the filth that ran into Londinium and knew nothing for a time.

Then I heard a sound, a stomping above my head, and I was wrestled out of my stupor. It was the most beautiful sound, cold and clear and rhythmic. It filled me with more longing. Longing to run free and laugh, to feel the wind in my hair. To couple and dance and be wild like the buck I was.

They were, of course, horses. I had seen and admired horses before and had conversations with them. But I had never heard the sound of their hooves from below. I was in a sewer, and the noise they made echoed from the cobblestones above me.

When I emerged, blinking into the bright foggy morning, I knew I was at last in Londinium. Nothing prepared me for the smell, though. Not even those days in the sewer.

The narrow lanes and alleys of Londinium were filled with people going about their daily lives, those jobs that required little sunlight: the dung collectors, the street sweepers, the fishmongers. It smelled to high heavens, a persistent loamy must tinged with the high tang of urine and lye. Of course, at the time I had no words for such things, but I simply assumed it was the natural smell of urine.

And there were walls. So many walls! I was not surprised to learn it was called "the City of Walls" due to its meandering and often hilariously incomplete walls, owing to the prolonged "barbarian" rebellions occurring between the 6th and 14th centuries.

In Londinium, the aqueducts had their own unusual design: they were lighter in construction, often with pointed arches, and anywhere from two to four levels. In the better parts of town—not where I had landed, it's important to note—the third and fourth tiers were used primarily for transportation and, in some cases, were even inhabited. As such, even at a distance one could see the enormous boats, long and lean and painted brightly, moving across them, ghostlike and silent. Then, like veins, other tributaries passing all manner of items.

There were, as well, many guards on site to ensure nothing was stolen —at least not in the better parts of the city. For obvious reasons, they were called "ducks" though their technical nomenclature was the *miles aquam*. I always preferred the term ducks, personally, as they happened to wear green-plumed hats, and had about as much intelligence as a mallard in the breeding season.

Elsewhere, there were self-styled "water barons" who controlled the inflow of items to and from the poorer, or at least less patrolled, areas. It was a good way to make money in the short term, at least. The winding streets and waterways of Londinium, to say nothing of the miles upon miles of close together homes, temples, shops, and halls, invited a kind of surreptitious atmosphere to everything. Coupled with the pervasive fog.

That first time, emerging in Londinium, I was at the height of my abilities. The city rose around me like a great, living thing. I walked for hours on end, twisting and turning, looking to make sense of the water but always failing. It made no sense to me, a creature born on the natural flowing rivers of the north. So much human tampering left me baffled.

I had half a mind to sink back below and turn tail when I passed through yet another large gate, this one so thick with people and animals that I was scarcely noticed. Truth be told, I felt ill, like fetid water was seeping its way into my own skin. And though I'd heard horses, they were dead to me when I reached out.

Until I came to a large inn, that is, which I now know was called The Swan and Hoop. I had wandered farther than I had planned, following the sweet smell of hay and the perfect spicy aroma of horse skin and coat. In a rush of joy, I felt no longer alone, no longer sick. Something, a being of great majesty, called to me and so I came to it.

Knowing nothing of propriety, and only a vague understanding of customs, I decided to let myself into the carriage house and meet this great horse.

The carriage house doors might have been locked. I don't remember. A locked door did not matter to me, then. I would have just pushed it open. I was so intent on meeting the fine horses I paid no attention to details like locks or suspicious eyes. I was disoriented and confused, and really no better off than a beast of burden myself.

I came first to an old bay mare and she put her head on my shoulder as if I was her long-lost love. She spoke no words to me, but she didn't need to. My soul knew hers. So relieved I was to have her company that I stood there as the night deepened around me, unaware of the world, breathing in the bright, clean smell of the horses and wishing I were a horse and not a man-shaped creature.

I'm not sure how long I stood, listening to her heart and the rumble of her stomach and the fine churning of her thoughts, when someone interrupted me.

"How long are you going to stand there?" asked a high, soft voice.

With a sharp intake of breath, I pulled away from the mare and turned toward the source of the question. It was a young human woman, carrying a bucket, her dress hiked up over her ankles. I could see the fair curve of her calf, and I gawked like the buffoon that I was. Her form was very pleasing; she was healthy and buxom, her eyes and hair dark, and her lips very full. Unlike the mass of humanity out in Londinium proper, she shone like a new star in the firmament. I could hear the smooth whoosh of her heart, and smell the sweat on her brow.

Significantly better than a horse.

"Hmm? Have you nothing to say?" she asked. "I don't fancy having to call Father in. So you best just move. That horse is Captain Gaius's, and he won't take kindly to knowing you've been fondling her."

"I…no," I said, the words coming to my lips like breath through mud. I didn't want her thinking I was some horse-fondler here to steal these creatures. "Resting."

"Oh, *resting* on her, that's what they're calling it nowadays," said the young woman with a laugh. She put down the barrels and came a bit closer. She smelled of fruit and mountains and pure clean snow, and I wanted nothing more than to taste her.

No, I wanted to devour her, plain and simple. I wanted to bury my face in her breasts and take her from every direction, to make her cry and scream and wriggle. It all made sense in the moment, and quite the overwhelming realization to come face to face with an object of your desire.

As I said, I'd never been so close to a woman.

She knew. What playfulness there was in her eyes evaporated and she took a step back. "Sir, I am going to have to call the local battalion if you don't…"

I knew I had to leave. I had forgotten everything, every reason I had come here. To find poets, to meet the whales, to rendezvous with Andrew La Roche.

So, I did the most sensible thing I had done since arriving in Londinium: I simply ran away as fast as my legs could take me. Back the way I'd come, through the gate and beyond until I was utterly lost, decrepit buildings on every side, no sign of water, and voices everywhere. In my head. In the streets. Alone. Yet so many people in so many buildings and so much water and pressing in on every side… Everything leaned over me, the cobblestones whorled before my eyes, the pulse of the water below the streets. I stumbled over walls, tore through draped curtains and fabrics, upturned boxes of fruit and goods, and sent quite a few dogs running in fear away from me.

Then, it got even worse. The mist of fear and adrenaline lifted from my eyes and I looked about. I was in an alley; I stunk of rotten fish and sewage. And I had a trail of debris behind me akin to a small tornado.

"What do you think you're doing?" came a challenge from a side street. "You can't come in here and ruin our things."

The man's face was a ruin, his teeth but crags in his scarred face. But he was large. And he had friends. And they had clubs.

"I'm…" I tried, but again, the words were like heavy stones in my mouth.

"Guilty," said one of the man's friends. "Or at least this particular contingent says so."

"That's right," said the first. "Guilty."

"No," I said. "Lost."

They laughed at me, the sound of it cutting deep, goading me to fury.

"Wouldn't call it a fair fight with four against one in most instances, but you're something else." The ringleader swung his club with impressive speed, twisting it in a flagrant show. "Still, I'd say that pretty pale hair of yours might make a nice trophy. What say you, Burt?"

Burt spat on the ground. "I'm up for it if you're up for it, Ebzer."

They came at me fast, faster than I'd have expected. But I imagine it's what one gets for spending so much time around fish. I misjudged the air itself. It was not resistant to movements, of course, it wasn't. A hard lesson to learn for someone accustomed to hunting bugs and small lizards.

I took the first few blows with no reaction, and they stung on contact. One of the clubs had a nail in it, and it scratched my skin.

I didn't like that.

So I reached out my hand and slapped Ebzer. He flew backward, legs spinning up where his head should have been, and then collapsed in a heap, sliding down a wall of rusty metal and moldering wood. The attack was far more impressive than I'd intended, and everyone, including me, stared after him for a few breaths as he moaned and whimpered.

I was about to hit him again when I felt a hand on my shoulder and turned to see a visage that shone like the sun.

His eyes were the color of amber—even in the dim light I could tell they possessed an inhuman hue—and his hair was the same, a paler shade of rust. He had clever, curling lips and a wide brow, and his hair fell rather long, wavy down to his shoulders. For dress, he possessed a flair unlike any Londinium fashion I'd seen, a panoply of deep purple, crimson, and gold.

The man was no man, indeed. He was a brightling like me. A whale in a sea of plankton.

The brightling smiled, then, and it warmed me. I felt the heat from him rise up, a dry and welcoming sensation reverberated down to my toes. It made me shiver, and I realized how cold I was. How cold I had been my whole life. How there was nothing warm in the world next to that smile, and I had been living in darkness and dampness and sadness since the moment I knew my own thoughts.

"Let's run, shall we?" he said, as casually as if we were the best of friends. "I've fallen in with this sort of rabble before, and I assure you that we'll get nowhere with friendly banter or attempted mediation."

I had scarcely caught a handful of his words, but I knew following him was a better option than staying and fighting. I wasn't afraid for my own life; I was afraid for theirs.

The ruffians were too shocked at the state of Ebzer, who was bleeding profusely but was not yet dead, to pursue us as we made our way away from them and through the narrow streets of Londinium.

The brilliant whale ran faster than I could, a riot of crimson and purple before me, and had to stop every now and again to gauge my speed so I wouldn't lose him. I couldn't have lost him, though. Not once I found him.

At last we stopped, only deeper into the muck of Londinium but among large warehouses closer to the Tamesis, which, I realized, was not incarcerated like the other rivers in the city.

He was not out of breath at all but his cheeks burned bright. It struck me that he was enjoying himself.

With a wry grin, he gestured for me to show him my wounded arm. The puncture was already healing, but he looked at it puzzled.

"You leak," he said. "Mostly water. How curious."

"It hurts," I said.

"How astute. I am sorry to inform you, but you are merely *part* immortal, and not indestructible. Pain is inevitable." He took a step back, looking me up and down like a man sizing up an ox. "My, but you're enormous. I've never met one of *you* before. Your predecessor was rather elusive and wasn't much for playing our games. What shall I call you, though?"

I made a gurgling, grunting noise. It was how I communicated through water with my fish brothers and sisters, what they called me.

He laughed.

"Burble," he said. "That's hardly a name for someone like you."

I shook my head, spraying water in every direction like a dog.

Pressing a long-fingered hand to his chest, he said, "How about this? You may call me Andrew La Roche. La Roche is fine in a pinch."

"La Roche," I said, trying it out. "Yes. I was supposed to find you."

"Good. I'd sent some of my missives to your guardian a few decades ago. I wasn't sure she would hold to her promise."

"Andrew La Roche," I said again, not out of a need to be formal, but to double-check, I suppose.

"If we're being formal, though it's not my *real* name. I suppose you even know that's something we do not share unless we are prepared to be diminished in the face of our enemies. For who would want to know our true names but those who wish to destroy us?" He sighed, scratching the side of his face. "And here I sound so terribly cynical, don't I? It's not true what I just said, not really. Your name is yours to share, but the first rule is you shouldn't trust me. I naturally engender feelings of kinship in people, and it wouldn't be fair to coax it out of you. Even if I am curious about this son of Neptune."

I began to speak when he stopped me, putting up his hand.

"Keep your secret name," he said softly as if guessing my thoughts. "Once you relinquish your true name, you are forever ruined by its keeper. Only give it if you are willing to lay yourself bare."

Lay myself bare. I liked the sound of it, but I knew this was no time for such things.

I thought for a moment, listening to the sound of rain falling around me. Closing my eyes. Concentrating. Hearing what the water called me. What the river called me. She was not far, Tamesis. And she sang of the sea, even though it was so far from her muddied shores.

"Joss," I said, deciding it was a good enough name. It was the sound of a brook over sharp rocks. "Joss will do."

"Joss, then. Good. It's a place to start." He laughed, looking up at the sky as if reading a portend. "And it's a good thing you only came as far as the Isle of Dogs. I can hide you well enough here in one of the warehouses, but you're quite conspicuous. Like Poseidon come to life from stone! Ha!"

I didn't know what he was talking about, but I pulled at my beard self-consciously.

"Come with me, if you'd please. You need a bath. You smell of feces and marmalade."

I nodded and then my stomach growled loud enough for us both to notice.

La Roche smiled. "And yet, in spite of that rather heady aroma..."

"Hungry."

He let go a peal of laughter so pure and golden I had to laugh along with him, though I had no idea what was so funny. La Roche wiped at his eye and shook his head with amusement. "Good, good. I know just the place."

2

We walked together until he directed me to a large wooden structure—a warehouse among so many others—and opened the massive door with a flick of his wrist. We saw no other living creature of sentience, save a couple of clever rats too busy scavenging for their own families to take notice. It was a welcome respite from the noise of the day.

Inside the cavernous space was a table and two chairs, the pristine linens set with garish glass bowls full to bursting with fruit and cheese. My stomach growled again most indelicately, but I wasn't ashamed. I hadn't learned that yet. Some things have changed about me in the ensuing years, I suppose, but I was still a rather dim, sorry bastard then too.

I gazed at the repast: golden plates and ruby goblets filled with inky wine, four kinds of bread, and three kinds of butter. I'd never eaten such food before, having subsisted mainly on insects and worms, but I knew without a doubt I had been somewhat lacking in my diet now that I saw what was possible. Drool filled my mouth, salty and sweet, and La Roche handed me an embroidered handkerchief.

"Eat, please," La Roche said, looking quite proud of himself as I gawked. "It's of the best variety and vintage, I promise. And I will contemplate getting you cleaned and shorn."

I could have argued, but no dog set before a plate of fresh venison could be blamed for gorging himself. So I started to eat, glad to do so, forgetting my pain. The grapes tasted as if they'd been soaked in honey and warmed in the sun, the cheeses sweet and ripe and smooth, the bread still crusty and steaming on the inside. I half forgot La Roche was there while I ate, and only noticed when he draped a long cloak around my shoulders.

"We'll fix you up something better to wear shortly," he said. "But for now, this will do. I like to dine *au naturel* myself sometimes, but for now, we'll go by the rules of human propriety."

I looked at him, curious. "You talk passing strange for a whale," I said, not looking up but shaking my shoulders to indicate the cloak.

La Roche laughed. "Whales? 'Passing strange.' My goodness. Seven words out of your mouth and I am already lost. Though, I admit, I was worried you spoke only in monosyllables."

"I thought you were a whale." I didn't know half the words he said, so I just added a few more of my own.

La Roche looked offended, putting a hand on his chest. "I'm quite trim, I'll have you know. I look nothing like a whale."

"You swim like one," I corrected, tapping my temple. "In my head. When I close my eyes I can see you. That's how I found you."

La Roche shook his head as if warding off a bad dream. "What an unattractive descriptor of a godling." He took a deep draught of his wine and frowned down into the glass. "So, you can see me?" he asked, a little more hesitant than before. "Even if I'm not nearby?"

I nodded. "Yes. I felt you. Until things got too noisy up here. Everything stinks. And the water is in chains." I took a huge chunk of bread and stuck it in my teeth, reveling at the way the crust crackled beneath my teeth and the slippery butter coated my mouth.

"In chains..." he mused. "Well, I slipped beneath your senses, I suspect. How did you know I was a, er, whale, right away?"

"You're not like the little minnows."

"Minnows. Yes, well, we have another word for them: *humans*. But I suppose minnows are apt. Though I'd call them krill on most days. Few rise to the auspicious title of minnow. Have you never met a minnow, then?"

"Not really. Not as a friend. My mother was a minnow. But she threw me into the lake."

"Threw you into the lake? Rather unusual behavior toward a child."

"I was large. Very large. And rather ugly for baby."

"And you swam in the lake?" La Roche asked. "Just like that?" He leaned over, looking me as if I'd sprouted scales.

"Aye. Until I stopped being a fish."

"You—you were an *actual* fish?"

"I couldn't very well swim like this. Not for long, anyway." I gestured vaguely to my body.

La Roche looked at me as if I had an extra appendage. He was quiet for long enough that I was glad of it. The godling had a habit of filling every breathable space with conversation, and not being used to such tendencies, I found it increasingly insufferable. Besides, I was still famished, and I've always found it hard to fight hunger and think at the same time.

"You understand you are a powerful whale," he said, carefully. "Your father was a being of immeasurable power. A descendent of a true god. You may be the most powerful godling on earth right now."

"I call us brightlings," I pointed out. "But I am not sure what we are."

"Ah, quite. We use the term godling. Brightling is a far older term."

"I am old."

La Roche blinked a moment, unsure where to proceed in the conversation. "Fair enough. As to godlings. Minnows—humans—don't understand us. Rarely do they meet us—we are but few among their legions. Yet we are their protectors. If we choose, I should say. I work to mitigate their suffering when I can. They live short lives. A few dozen years if they're lucky. We live as long as we can hold on and then sometimes even that is vague."

"Scale Bottom died a thousand times," I said.

"Yes, and I killed her once," replied La Roche. "But humans don't come back like Scale Bottom. Or like we do. And even when we come back, we're not the same. Your long life and ability will forever set you apart from human beings. No matter how much you want to be part of them."

I sensed he spoke from true pain and experience. I could smell it on him, like sulfur on a sea tide.

"Tell me about the whales," I said, draining what was left of my claret. I liked how it tingled my tongue, and after four glasses it made my nose feel a bit numb too. It was like being on the lake, bobbing on the waves.

"Very well. I will tell you the story of how we began, and what we are. I would like you to learn from me, as Scale Bottom wished, but only if you decide that is right. And only if you take a bath."

I sneezed and shook, drawing water from the air and then casting it out again into the room about me. The resulting spray of fetid water barely missed La Roche, but it set him to laughing for a solid minute before he caught himself.

"Fair enough, fair enough. I should have known better," he said, admiring my much cleaner visage. "I will take that as a yes?"

I nodded and tucked in to more cheese.

Then he began to speak, and I could feel the waters of my life split. I stood at the delicate place where knowledge begins and ignorance ends. It is often a process fraught with pain. But it is a path worth treading. I suppose that day, in the warehouse, was but the first time I had ever experienced an outpouring of knowledge that would change my life and the very framework of my own journey.

This is what La Roche told me:

"Before human thought, there were eight gods and one world. They each had a number, a holy number that represented everything about them, a kind of divine mathematics. The gods, as the world was being created, began to take responsibilities. The eldest took to shaping the mountains, and the next to the sea; then came the light of day together with the light of the moon. After came the power to make the green things grow, and the font of knowledge and memory to keep them strong. Then came the last two, chaos and love. Two sides so often entwined. Neither good nor bad, but simply poles—North and South, East and West—giving direction to all.

"Human children were grown among the wastes, and with them other races. Some were proud and fair, some were quiet and lived in the shadows. But with more time, and with the gifts the gods gave them, they formed alliances. Then the gods themselves formed alliances. And war broke out.

"These poisonous conflicts gnawed down the Earth to its bones. The oceans spilled with blood. The gods raised new armies and threw them against one another until all that was left was darkness and shadow and the echoes of pain. Not even Chaos was happy.

"Earth and Water called together a meeting, and they all came: Light, Birth, Knowledge, Water, Cunning, Night, Chaos, and Love. They were tired of each other and tired of fighting. They agreed to sunder themselves in a great ritual, to split the world into eight and break apart their own souls, stranding the shards on the new earths, to be born again in human form, and to forget the pain and the sorrow and the loss. With great weapons forged from the hearts of stars, they each destroyed the next, a vast circle in the firmament. All fragmented—some say infinitely—into oblivion.

"Since that time, the eight worlds have entertained the eight godlings, born again and again. They are connected across these worlds, sometimes, across paths—waterways, secret passages, compasses—given to them by the First Eight. But they are hard ways to tread, fraught with danger. Death can only come at the hand of a mirrored one—a twain—and many take their own lives, or else vanish into the aether to be remade again. Sometimes the memories are kept, most times they are not. The knowledge of being set apart is always apparent. Some have died thousands of times over, each time becoming less god and more human. Others have lived only a few lifetimes. But all carry the same burden."

When La Roche finished speaking, I was changed. I felt as if I had been lying in the grass the whole afternoon with my eyes closed, facing the sun, and when I opened my eyes the world was in a new cast of shadow. My skin tingled. The world looked new. I felt sated and desperately sad at the same time.

"So," he said at last, "that is the closest to the truth I can give you. It was the truth I was given when I was taken under wing, and so now I grant the knowledge to you, our next generation. Should you agree to my terms of your apprenticeship."

"I don't know what an apprentice is."

La Roche grinned, the edges of his eyes crinkling a bit. "My apologies, Joss. An apprentice is a kind of student. A student of a master. And while I would not deign to give myself such an illustrious title, I'm afraid I'm the best you'll do right now in Londinium. No one else has the time or the inclination for teaching."

I thought about it for a moment before saying, "Yes. I would like to be an apprentice."

"Good! Well, my requirements are rather simple. Don't perform acts of magic without my consent until I've given you explicit directions otherwise. Don't commune with your power in the presence of humans, either. And don't pledge your allegiance to another godling, as tempting as it might seem. You can learn from them, and I encourage you to do so. But you will be protected by me."

"I'm bigger and stronger than you. I don't have to listen to you." Which I realize sounds like a moronic turn of conversation, I know. Except it was true. La Roche was older than I, but he had been remade dozens of times. I had only been remade a handful of times, and so my power was stronger.

But I was stupid, and he was the embodiment of intelligence. I could not outmatch him with wits, and I was well aware of my shortcomings among humans, let alone in Londinium.

"You don't *have* to listen to me. But I can teach you. And protect you. I can tell you who you are and what you mean to this world. I can shape you," he said.

"I am water. That is all I need to know, the knowledge Scale Bottom taught me."

He laughed explosively. "You are so much more than water. If only you knew."

"Then I agree to your terms."

"Really?" There was genuine astonishment in his voice. "It's that easy?"

"I don't think you're a bad whale. You're not all light. But not a bad whale."

"Who are the—no, no, don't tell me," he said, shaking his head. "If you agree to my terms you must hold out your hand."

I did, standing up across from him. My hand was much bigger than his.

"Repeat after me: By blood and bone this deed is done," he said.

I said the words.

For a brief moment the veins in my hands flickered brilliant yellow, and his an incandescent blue. Then it was done.

I didn't feel any different, so I continued our conversation, not quite knowing what I had seen and if it was power or just a trick of the light.

"Tell me what I am, then," I said finally. "Be my teacher."

"You are water, yes, it's fairly obvious. But not just a lake or a stream. You are ocean. Thunderstorms! Lightning! Quite thrilling, really," La Roche said, pacing away from me a moment and then coming back to wave his hands in the air as if trying to fish for the words he needed. "And yes. You are a great deal stronger than I am, which I'm sure you're aware of. I've been put through this world more times than I can count. But that's just part of my charm."

When I did not press him further, sitting back at the table and focusing instead into a fragrant cheese with a marvelous tang, he leaned across the rickety table, tossing back his hair. It glimmered gold in the light from the lantern, and I didn't need him to tell me who he was, which godling he had sprung from. He picked a grape and popped it into his mouth with a guileless grin.

"And who might I be?" he asked, almost teasing.

"The sun," I said without hesitation. I was unimpressed, uninterested. The food was so good, and I was not yet gregarious in any sense at all. "That's not even a hard question."

"Well, perhaps not," he replied, his smile fading around the edges. He straightened in his chair. "Sometimes we use the Greeks as our touch-point, since it's more familiar to us. They called me Apollo, and I've always liked the sound of that name. But Andrew La Roche is a bit less pretentious."

"You said us. There are more."

"Yes, and you shall meet them. Together, we are quite the merry band. Sometimes, in some great societies," said La Roche, "the godlings convene, all together, eight at a time. In Greece was one such place. My twain then was Apollo himself, or rather the figure who would be deified as such. In those days we were greater, stronger, able to propagate more easily—even with each other. There were demi-demi gods walking about, thought their bloodlines are significantly watered down these days."

Time was still a strange concept to me. I knew, without having to ask, that my father had been very old. The lake and mountain had been his resting place, a sort of hibernation, and my mother had sought him out after years of study. What had he been in the years in between? He could have been anything.

"My father lived for thousands of years," I said. "I don't suspect I'd want to live that long. He got old, and angry and strange." I hadn't thought much about dying, it was true. Time felt like a pool to me, rather than a river.

"Perhaps. Your father was oldest among us, having been born perhaps only once or twice. I'm afraid my line has a habit of living fast and dying rather young. Not necessarily by choice mind you. We cannot be killed by conventional means; our minds break before our bodies ever do, and it can be problematic. My sort tend to be a candle burning at both ends, you might say."

"So, we choose to die," I said.

"I suppose you can say so. But we live among humans. Have you had any dealings of note with them?"

I saw no reason to lie to him, so I said, "I've seen a woman."

"Yes, we have lots of them here."

"She was different."

La Roche grinned again. "Ah, yes. The *appetite*. Well, we really do have to do something about that. You know, before you go raping and molesting anything with a porthole within a ten-mile radius."

"I…I'd never…" I said. "I mean, I *didn't*… I just ran." Like I said, I was a right bastard but not so dim as to know there weren't rules. I thought of the woman I'd met at the stables. Of her ankles. I added, clearing my throat. "Though I wanted to. You know. Not run."

"Of course, of course. But we godlings have a habit of indulging our deeper desires when they go unsated, and as my protégé you cannot be allowed such egregious diversions," La Roche said with a lazy smile. "You cannot malign humans, you cannot intervene in their lives or deaths—no bringing back people from the dead."

"I can't imagine I'd ever want to do that."

"It is expressly forbidden. But the appetite, we can sate. For now, anyway."

He looked thoughtful a moment, watching me to see if I might respond. I just put more food in my mouth.

"No, I will not keep you to myself longer than I must!" he said. "I have a friend. Another godling. I was going to wait on the introductions, but seeing your current predicament…well, she will help in ways you can only begin to fathom."

3

We walked along the river, almost in a straight line. La Roche sang to himself and mostly filled up the silence between us with some of his favorite tales of Apollo. He also stopped to purchase me some clothing to replace the rags I wore. It did help with the remainder of the stink.

As we progressed west, a change came over the structures of Londinium. No longer full of sorrow and stench, the homes rose higher and higher along the banks of the Tamesis, in spite of the smell from the water which, I learned, was pervasive no matter where you lived. The buildings gradually became cleaner, the roads less strewn with shit of all kinds, the people less riddled with visible ailments. Marble shone on high buildings, their doors gilded with brass and ornately carved wood. The water smelled cleaner, too, and I became aware of enormous hanging gardens growing on the side of some of the aqueducts.

And, though the hour was late, there were more horses about the streets. Horses loved and cared for, like those I'd seen at the Swan and Hoop.

"I quite like the horses," I said to La Roche as a particularly fetching pair went by, huge beasts with furry feet.

He smirked, "Hopefully not in the same way you like women."

I laughed. It was a joke. A ribald, wonderful joke that I actually understood! And even if I was at the teasing end of it, I found it beyond humorous.

"No," I said, finally catching my breath. "No, not like that. It's only they remind me of fish."

La Roche raised an eyebrow at me. "You really were raised in a swamp."

"Not a swamp. A lake."

"It was cold and damp and full of mysteries, either way," he replied. "Why you would like horses defies my reasoning."

"It's their hooves," I said. "They sound like thunder."

He gave me a look that I later learned to interpret as meaning "you're right mad in the head, but I find you intriguing, so I'll let you to your moronic opinions."

"If you say so, good sir. But if you don't mind, I'll take your word for it. Ah, well, here we are."

We turned the corner and the buildings parted to show a truly beautiful sight: there stood an enormous statue of a woman, her hands raised to the sky, towering high into the aqueducts above and gardens besides. Her hair was made of long vines and blooming jasmine, and more greenery twirled about her waist and her arms like a great verdant dress weaving itself onto her. Her face was sharp-featured, her eyes curious and knowing. About her feet were innumerable candles and roses, many with notes tied upon the stems. And if my eyes weren't tricking me, the whole of the sculpture glowed a faint red, especially around the belly.

Between her legs was a narrow path, and beyond the path a door to a temple.

I must have gaped, for La Roche took my arm. "On we go," he said. "She doesn't like waiting."

I breathed shallowly, swallowed, then nodded.

We passed under the great statue's legs and the scent of jasmine hit me so strongly that I could taste it in my mouth. My eyes watered, and I sneezed at least twice.

Once I cleared my eyes, I took in the temple interior itself. It was painted bright gold and red and yellow and brown in places, but the carvings were realistic and done by a fine hand. I saw running fish and deer, goddesses dancing in long lines together, and many doves with entwined feathers and wings. I knew there was a story there, somewhere hidden within the design, but I couldn't make it out.

The thick lead glass windows showed little more than a hint of green curtains beyond, somewhat muffling the warm glow from within. It must have been a place of immeasurable beauty in its day, but in spite of the grandeur I could tell it was falling into disrepair; there was chipped paint and broken, hastily mended glass on the ground floor, and there was unsavory graffiti on the side someone had tried to cover up.

It was stunning to behold, yet tired. Sad. I could smell the change in the air.

"Welcome to the Temple of Venus," said La Roche.

"It must have been beautiful once," I said, running my hand over the crackling plaster.

La Roche nodded, looking for a moment as faded and chipped as the building. "Alas, all must pass away." His voice sounded different when he said it. Haunted, almost. Cold.

"It feels powerful, still."

"Good! It's a beacon of warmth and comfort in a crumbling city. They need her now, more than ever before, but as per usual those in Londinium cannot see past their own cold trousers. All this new love of chastity! It's embarrassing, that's what, when she lives right here. Truly, the cult of Diana is so boring."

Even before we opened the doors, I could feel the water in the place, old water, rising from the ground. Hot and warm and bubbling. I could smell the minerals mingling with the rose petals, the heady sandalwood and myrrh. It called to me as clearly as any voice and was a welcome distraction from the Tamesis looming behind me, grown more polluted and fetid as we approached from the north.

I turned to La Roche. "There is an old spring here."

He raised a brow at me and nodded. "Yes. Baths. I was hoping to give you a tour a little later this evening."

"It smells cleaner than the rest of Londinium's water."

"Though that is not high praise, necessarily, you are correct. The bathhouse here dates back to before the Romans, and it goes deeper than the source of the rivers, they say, and it remains unchanged by the aqueduct system, as far as I can tell. Though, far be it from me to speak as the expert. I am not the engineer among us."

Before I could ask who the engineer was, the doors swung open wide, and I almost forgot how to breathe.

I saw the most beautiful woman I'd ever laid eyes on, and I knew I would never again see her equal. I was right in that, by the way.

"Welcome to the Temple of Venus," she said. "You must be our great water lord. I am Verta. More properly, Verticordia. And we have been waiting a long time to meet you."

It's still hard to describe what I felt the first time I saw her. It isn't that she was simply beautiful, because without the power coming from her—heat and lust and beauty and love—I don't think she would have been far more than average. But I couldn't stop looking at her eyes, amber flecked with green, and her full, red-rimmed lips. At the time she was dressed in the Roman style, even though La Roche told me it was decades out of fashion, to give a sense of antiquity to the establishment. There was almost nothing about her left to the imagination in spite of the fact the clothing she wore was opaque. The silks clung to every line of her, sheer against her dark skin, as if someone had just sucked the air out between her body and the cloth. Her black curls fell in tight clusters all the way down her back, glossy and full, begging to be touched, fondled.

And that's to say nothing of the gold upon her. There were rings on all her fingers, bracelets draped lovingly around her wrists and ankles, chains on her neck and around her waist. But no jewels. Not a one. She was unadorned save for the purity of the gold about her, and she shone like the cabochon of a perfectly set ring.

Verta's eyes took me in, body and soul, and the edge of one side of her mouth lifted in a smile that nearly turned me into a puddle there on the floor. She made me ache everywhere.

"Pleased," I said. I'm sure there were other words I contemplated saying, but it was the only one I could fashion with my lips. Unfortunately, my trousers did the rest of the talking.

"We hoped you would attend the temple, but perhaps not so soon." She glanced meaningfully at La Roche. "I see the matter is pressing, then?"

"Verta, darling, this is Joss. He saw a *woman*," La Roche replied, rolling his shoulders. "I am only looking out for the safety of the people."

Verta laughed, putting a small hand on her cheek. "He is always making excuses to come visit me," she said.

"You wound me, madame," La Roche said.

"Andrew."

There was a chill between them. Even then, at my young mental age and capacity, I could sense it. I felt awkward, unwelcome. Verta straightened her shoulders and looked at La Roche, into him, through him. Like a wolf bitch quieting her mate, she bristled, and I saw him diminish and look away.

"She's correct," La Roche said softly. "This is not my demesne. As you may have guessed, Joss, Verta is like us. She is the embodiment of feminine intelligence, power, and sensuality. And, owing her respect, I do as she commands me in her place. But take note. Someday I may ask this of you. And it's a hard-won talent."

"I don't understand," I said.

"Think of Verta as a teacher in the short term. I trust her with my life, and with yours," La Roche said.

Then he shivered as if he had a terrible chill and I thought he was going to be ill. But instead of swooning, he held out his hands and his whole body contracted, twisted, and shrank upwards toward his head. Everything about him became cloaked in blackness until he hovered in midair, not as a man, but as a bird. Large, feathers oily black, and a gray face with enormous, beetle-black eyes. He had a single white spot on his throat and felt, for all I could tell, precisely as he had when he was more or less human-formed.

A rook, and a handsome one at that.

With a squawk, La Roche alighted on Verta's shoulder and she reached up to scratch him under the chin.

"For all his cawing, he speaks truly," Verta said, opening a thin curtain and gesturing me through. "He is a favorite among the lasses and the lads. But he's less of a distraction this way. For all his bright intelligence, the incessant conversation can get in the way of a truly intimate experience. And you are new."

I looked around dumbly, expecting to understand his transformation or else get an explanation. I found neither.

So I followed Verta down a flight of stairs, the walls smoothed by time and the passing of many hands, to another level of the temple. It smelled of the sulfur scent of deep earth water and was both familiar and disconcerting. I didn't like being in enclosed places, and though the water was cleaner here it filled me with confusion. I couldn't tell what direction I was going. As when I had been caught in the nightmare labyrinth below Londinium, I began to sweat and panic.

"No need to worry," Verta said gently, taking a large torch and lighting it in a brazier. It sputtered to life, sparks landing on the steps. "You are not the first, and certainly not the last, in need of instruction. And while Andrew will be your primary teacher, I, in turn, was his mentor. There are some things he simply cannot show you. Here, we have arrived. You see? Not such a terrible journey for a creature such as you."

Verta gestured ahead and had me go before her into a tiled room strewn with all manner of frilly pillows, dense with condensation and hot from the water below. Once I crossed the threshold, and she behind me, she turned and waved her hands over the doorway. The edges flickered, like the outline of a log still smoldering in the fire, and I stood back, admiring the door.

Verta went about the room lighting candles and incense, La Roche bobbing up and down on her shoulder, and insisted I sit down. It was somewhat difficult considering I was of such a height, but I was able to get into a more or less comfortable position on the pillows.

"Our impulses are part of who we are, as higher beings," Verta began, reaching for a long pipe that came out of an ornate urn made of ivory and etched glass. She drew on it with her lips, long and soft and without hurry. Every movement Verta made was measured, elongated, provocative. I could not stop looking at her.

She blew out a thin stream of smoke, smiling as the room darkened even more. The candles lit her skin like molten honey, and I wanted to taste her. To know her.

She laughed as if reading my thoughts, "Yes, your impulses are strong. But you will not be enacting them on me."

I nodded like a dumb mule and tried rather ineffectually to keep my eyes from her round ample, elegant body.

"Joss," she said softly. "It's a good name."

"Thank you," I said.

She put her hands gently on my shoulders, and as soon as I felt her fingers touch the skin of my neck—which she sought out as she started undressing me—it was as if I'd been hit by a pulse of errant lightning. The sensation went up my arm and right into my chest, making me cough. We both jumped back, and her cool demeanor was broken.

"Strong," she said. "I'll have to be careful with you."

"I didn't mean to hurt you," I said.

"Of course, you didn't. But we godlings hurt one another if we're not careful; and sometimes we can wound despite our care," Verta said, and even I wasn't daft enough to miss the double meaning. La Roche lowered his head in somber agreement. "The damage lingers far longer than that which is inflicted by the weapons of man. Swords and cannons can weaken us, slow us down, but not kill us. The power within our bodies, however, ever seeks to move away, to separate. It's a defense mechanism. A true wound lasts forever. Do you mind if I try again, perhaps a little more gently?"

She looked me straight in the eye, and I couldn't have denied her even if I wanted to.

Tenderly, she assisted me in removing my chemise, then put both of her delicate hands on my chest, palms down. The sensation of our skin touching wasn't as extreme before, but I could feel the ebb and flow of her own energy, feel the pull of air into her lungs. I could almost sense her thoughts, though they were distant from me. Like only hearing the high notes in a melody. She was not thinking about fucking, like I was. She was lost in a dark valley of her own.

Then she smiled and sat down across from me.

"Joss. How did you come by such a moniker? It's a good name," she said.

"A river gave it to me," I said, unable to think of anything else in response.

"Well, then, Joss, So Named by a River," she said, "tell me what you know of love and making, of the push and pull and great pleasure that befall creatures capable of such things."

I was embarrassingly uninformed, though my body said otherwise. I cleared my throat. "I know a little. From the fish. And the horses." I took my fists and pounded them into each other in a close approximation of what I thought it was. "It's only I don't know how to be gentle. And La Roche is worried if I keep listening to the water, I'll do unsavory things."

"Well, I doubt it," Verta said, rolling her eyes. "You're strong. And full of desire. But you don't understand. There is power in you, Joss, but a good deal of it is hidden behind a dam. I suppose you are aware. You're but a thimble of your full capabilities."

"I do," I said. "It makes me afraid too."

She gave me a sympathetic look, lips pressed together. "Love casts away fear. But to start, you must learn that love given is greater than love taken. And so, I've selected a special experience for you this evening. There will be two lessons. The first, Andrew will teach you; the second, I will teach you. You must learn to respect, and to joyously celebrate, the beings who wish to worship with you at the altar of Venus. Then, once you have cleansed your body of that most holy desire, you will be less afraid. But first, take some of this. I will help."

She offered the hookah to me, and I did as she had. I took in a long, shallow draw. It was not unpleasant, but it stung a bit on the way down. I shivered, holding back a cough, and then exhaled the sweet smoke. I liked the taste it left on my tongue, like honey and autumn leaves.

"Now, rest for a while in here, and I will prepare. I'll come get you when we're ready," she said.

I found myself delightfully relaxed, my head buzzing and twisting in a very pleasant way, and I leaned against the pillows and closed my eyes, falling into a half dreaming state. The last thing I saw was a flutter of La Roche's wings as he followed Verta deeper down into the temple. Their voices faded until all was soft, and silent, and lovely.

"Joss, it's time." Verta's voice was like a violin across a valley, waking me from my sleep.

Once I was fully awake, she took me to another pathway, and then through a stone arch to an enormous, pillared room carved right into some kind of bedrock—limestone, perhaps. I was good and soft in the head at that point, whatever she'd given me to smoke imparted a dreamlike mistiness to everything I can't deny was a relief.

I couldn't tell you how we ended up in an enormous room, but there was a pool in the center of it, steam rising and dissipating into mist all around us. Candles illuminated every corner and cast light on the tiles glittering like fish scales. I was filled with a sudden desire to go headfirst into the water and never look back again. Whatever reservations I'd had about the water dissipated entirely and I was as pliant as a lamb.

She steadied me with a soft hand, gesturing to the others in the room.

Sitting on the stairs leading down into the bath was a young woman, olive-skinned, with curly black hair down to her shoulders. She had a blindfold over her eyes but was otherwise entirely unclothed. Unlike Verta who was small and round, the dark woman was long and lean, the muscles on her legs and shoulders prominent against her oiled skin. Her breasts were taut and full, nipples large and erect. Around her neck she wore a simple jewel, a drop of amber the size of my thumb. As we entered the room she turned her head ever so slightly toward us, a smile on her lips.

"Andrew," Verta said, and the bird flew up to my shoulder, sinking his talons in enough to make me start. I felt pinpricks of energy sizzle down my arm in water. "You may begin."

"Let's walk to the water," he whispered in my ear, barely loud enough to hear. Even now, I wonder if he spoke at all or if he was communicating with me otherwise. "And I will guide you through. But first you must disrobe."

I swallowed on the driest throat of my life, and nodded, then complied.

When I was finished easing into the water, feeling more comfortable than I had since I first found clothing, Andrew continued. "First, Verta is here to measure you, to take stock of your soul. It is part of her vows to Venus, and she sees it as her holy duty. So fret not. I am only here to keep you reigned in." He flexed his claws into my shoulder again and I could tell what he meant. It stung like a thousand bees at once. I didn't make much of a note of it, though, as the woman was right distracting. "But understand you cannot harm these acolytes. Verta and I cannot kill you, but we can maim you. And we will if you do anything disrespectful. These priestesses give their lives Venus, to making their bodies and minds a living temple of the practice of desire. It is a gift they give you; it is not something to be taken."

"I understand." I barely croaked the words. I was terrified. But the fear was glazed with excitement, eagerness, and a willingness to learn.

Step by step I made my way toward the woman. She had been lathered in oil and scented with perfumes, little beads of water welling on her skin. Before I could touch her, the woman took my arm, her cool fingers impressing on my meaty arm.

"Hello, Joss," she said. "My name is Mirenne. I have come to lead you down the sacred path of desire."

We sank down onto the steps together and she began kissing me softly about the side of my neck, drawing her hands along my chest. She ran her fingers through my beard, shivered, and laughed low in her throat. I could tell that she was trying to see me without her eyes and she was pleased with what her hands were turning up.

"Verta ensures none of the women here are able to conceive," said La Roche. "So there's no need to worry. Just let her do what she needs to do, but for the love of the gods, put out your hands and let her know you're pleased."

"Aye," I said to her. "Aye, that's good..."

Her hands slipped across my skin, down past my navel, grasping for the length of me. It was only the bird's distracting claws preventing me from spending myself right there.

And I was glad of it. La Roche gave me the right cues, told me to kiss her back—on the lips—and to let my tongue reach hers, taste her, understand her. Something was building up inside of me, some impossible tide, I had never known even existed. And with each flick of her tongue and stroke of her finger, I became more and more aware of some cliff off in the horizon I'd soon fall off. Maybe it led to my death. In that moment, I didn't care.

When I entered her, my only thought was that it was slippery, like the skin of a fish. Familiar to me, as anything. She moved up and down my length, her muscles gripping and tightening, her head cast back and her arms aloft. I followed her rhythm, heard her cries echoing across the water.

And then, with the word from La Roche, I released. She sighed like the bellows, and laughed a deep-throated, jubilant laugh. We rode the wave together, our own waters mingling with the bath.

I fell back against the stairs, breathing hard and exhausted. Then I noticed Mirenne was being led away. Someone who I had not seen before draped her in a white gown and took her off, while two other women entered the pool. One was of a height to Verta, with soft, wavy black hair and brown freckles splashed across her skin. The other was tall, ebony, her hair wild and beautiful about her head like a cloud, falling down to her shoulders.

As soon as they entered the water I could feel them as if they were next to me. Could tell what they tasted like, which perfumes they wore, what they had last eaten. It was exhilarating.

La Roche flitted away and then reformed to his human shape, by the side of the water. He was naked and comfortable and smiling like a fox, stretching his head from side to side. "Now, Mirenne has given you a gift easy to take. She has commanded you to take her, and take her you did. But there is little challenge in that."

"Now, you have been born in the form of a man," came Verta's voice in my ear. I startled to see a swan, black as jet, floating beside me. She had a gold chain around her neck. She had changed, too. "These are my priestesses, Isabella and Colette, and they know some of the mysteries of our kind. They revere the first Mother of Love, and I help them know pleasure and visions. Though tonight, they will remember nothing but fragments of a fever dream."

She floated across me, rubbing her head against my beard. "Now, a man can be pleased a number of ways, but for most it is not a complicated business. You saw the way in which Mirenne was able to bring you to that most holy of places. With Andrew's help you contained yourself rather well."

I muttered gratitude. My brain was still singing with the reverberations of pleasure.

Verta smiled. "You may send Mirenne a bouquet of myrtle tomorrow to thank her. But for my part, I am here to teach you about the pleasures within a woman's body. Can you feel them through the water, Isabella and Colette?"

I could, indeed. And knowing Mirenne had made me far more aware of how a woman's body worked, and I wanted to know them both again. So I made to stand, to go over to them, to touch them.

"Ah, no, not like that," said Verta. "I want you to please them, but you may not leave here. You must use what you know to please them. If what Andrew tells me is true, and you can manipulate water, then it shouldn't be an issue. Long have women worshipped at the font."

The candles in the room brightened at Verta's command, and at first I was terrified I was going to fail. It was an unusual emotion; I did not want to let Verta down, did not want to hurt these women, did not want La Roche to be disappointed in me. Somehow that would be worse than failing to bring pleasure to these women. I did not want La Roche to see me as less than he hoped. I wanted to be great and powerful, I realized. Yet I felt like a child in an enormous man's body, and the imbalance of it all was beyond frustrating.

No, I couldn't reach across the water to them. I couldn't kiss them or put my hands upon them…

But I could feel them through the water. I breathed deeply, closed my eyes, and focused. The earthy, mineral-filled water was so like the lake of my childhood that without the burden of my vision, I could reach through and feel every crook and curve of their bodies. The language of water, it was one that I knew most intimately. The current, the temperature, the strength in such a seemingly simple element, was so much simpler than the world I'd found in Londinium.

I relaxed. I became one with the currents.

I began slowly, moving the water around their ankles and calves. I could feel the women move in surprise as I caressed their legs and entwined around their waists.

"Yes, softly, softly…" Verta said, watching and, no doubt, sensing, what I was doing. "My acolytes will not be broken. Though I do suppose you may have that inclination, and it is not always a soft, gentle thing. But today you will do as I command and rein yourself in."

I nodded, stilling my breath, eyes still closed.

"Begin like a trickle, and build," Verta suggested, her voice soft and low. "Time is irrelevant here. It is only you, and the water, and these women."

I put my hands out, hands floating just atop the surface, and continued after a few moments. The water began bubbling, moving with more surety. I could feel both of their bodies across the pool, reacting and moving against the jutting water.

But then they started to laugh. To giggle. It didn't infuriate me as it might another man, but it certainly distracted me. The water went flat, and I looked desperately over at Verta.

She reached out and drew her feathered cheek across my shoulder, soft and purposeful. It did not tickle in the least. "You see?" she asked.

Yes, I did. The women stood across from me and watched, eyes curious. Taking another great breath, I put my hands down on the top of the water, feeling the surface tension. I closed my eyes again and tried to follow Verta's advice.

They laughed again.

La Roche laughed. "Don't feel too bad, old chap," he said. "Some might argue that most men never figure it out."

But I wasn't listening. I tried again, and this time the women did not laugh. Instead of thinking of the water as an extension of myself, I thought of the water as something separate, wild, but willing. Every pool of water is different. Its mineral content, its story, its pedigree. This water was heavy, old, tinged with lime and salts. It had its own composition and mingled with the women differently than I might. As I understood this, and took my time, I began to change my approach.

The women responded, and I could hear them draw breath. I did not open my eyes again, did not let the sight of them distract me. I did not need to. As I grew to more intensity, caressing their backs and waists, moving deeper inside of them, I experienced their pleasure through the waters. Colette seemed to respond more to slower, yet more constant pressure. Isabella flushed brightly with a lapping motion. I felt elated to elicit such a reaction and continued to shift the flow of water to each woman.

"They are accustomed to strength yes, but you are unique to them—carefully, you can show them your power," Verta whispered. "But listen well to their bodies."

Instinctively, as if I had done it a thousand times before, I raised my hands—and with my hands the waters rose. They trailed around the two priestesses' bodies, twining about their hips and breasts and hoisting them up, water around them and inside them and though them. Their hearts beat with pleasure and excitement, and gently and purposefully I kept them on their own brink until Verta told me to release them to the complete and total moment of bliss.

"That was significantly more dramatic than I'd expected," La Roche said from across the pool. "If I were a sentimental man, I'd say that I was moved."

But his cheeks were flushed, I thought. Though I had not sought to pleasure him, he had been in the water as well.

When it was over, I was exhausted. I slunk deeper into the water, breathing shallowly, and thinking of sleeping—really sleeping—as I hadn't in ages.

Later, I was dimly aware of the women leaving, and of La Roche walking me back to one of the rooms. I fell straight asleep and dreamed and woke and fucked and laughed, all through the night. And it was magic.

4

Verta was right—as I learned she would be most often in matters of sensuality—that when it came to impulse and indulgence, for my sort especially, erring too far to the side of chastity would only get me in trouble. I needed instruction and constant reminding. She taught me to see beyond desire into connection. Otherwise, I would be a monster. Verta did not give me much in the way of details but told me stories of other godlings who had gone mad with their own pleasure, and how it was her duty to ensure such things never happened again.

Still, I did not sleep and fuck forever. La Roche began preparations so I could meet the other godlings in Londinium, and though weeks passed before I would make my first foray into town properly, I had work to do.

I needed knowledge. Reading came to me slowly, so for the few weeks I spent at Verta's temple, La Roche told me stories and then, eventually, gave me books to read. He discussed a great many things, the foundation of what it is to be human—for though I was not of them, I still had to live in their world. He gave me volumes of poetry, new and old, and stories of the Greeks and Romans. But poetry, he stressed, was the most important. He said, given his long life, that it was sometimes the only thing that gave him faith in humanity. They were so fickle and strange, he said, but their creativity—whether it was tied directly to his own divine inspiration or not—made him feel more alive than any other phenomenon. Even sex. Which, at the time, I found dubious. But I learned the way of things well enough later on, and I had been inspired by a poet, myself, and knew the power of such things.

By the time we were ready to leave the temple, I'd garnered most of the knowledge required for day-to-day conversation. I was feeling quite proud of myself, enduring La Roche's endless quizzes ("What does a haberdasher sell?" "How many dinars in a standard pound?" "Which fork rests to the side of your meal and which to the top of the plate?" among others) but I still struggled with societal details. People were simply minnows to me, still. Largely unrecognizable from one another save in a few instances—La Roche believed I could detect humans who still had godling blood in them, remnants from when we could procreate with one another and spawn demigods—and so it was difficult to wade into the day-to-day politics of Brittanic society without varying degrees of awkwardness. Being taller and larger than anyone I met did not make matters easier.

However, I could not stay in Verta's temple forever. As informative as it was, I longed to see more of the world, and reading was no cure. The more I read about the world, the more I learned of Londinium and its storied past, the more I wanted to make sense of the mire I'd stumbled into. To touch the old gates, to climb the Eye, the highest aqueduct on the Tamesis. To visit the Gaol of Londinium, where all the worst criminals had gone for the last four hundred years, and some of the heroes too. And of course, to cross Great Londinium Bridge, now crisscrossed by what was called the Feather Aqueduct and studded with some of the most beautiful homes in the city.

So when La Roche announced that I at last was ready to meet some of the other godlings of Londinium, I was filled with an apprehensive excitement.

That is, until La Roche told me where we were going.

"There are two kinds of holy markers of Londinium which predate the Romans: wells and pubs. Both provide water and community, but only the pubs are godling sanctioned."

"I'd prefer a well," I said, which was true. But then, I hadn't had enough pub experience to know any better.

La Roche laughed. "Ah, but you don't understand yet. Pubs appear, so I have noted, upon specific points across the face of the city, on invisible lines. Sometimes these are crossroads, which are holy in their own way; sometimes they aren't far from a church, or a river. Whatever the cause, there is a kind of magnetism associated with pubs."

"Must be all the drink."

"Ha! Well, certainly imbibing has its way of coloring the place. Generations of mead and wine and cider have certainly given them a gravitas, I will give you that. But pubs, like no other kind of structure — not even temples — can be manipulated by godlings. To provide us privacy, comfort, home, whatever we want."

"Doesn't make sense, though, since there are so many humans at pubs."

"Precisely. I have tried to tease out the matter from a scientific standpoint, but I surmise the reason we can hide has to do with the business. The latent, residual, and produced energy from so many beings in one place. We can weave ourselves illusions there. And my current favorite is the Swan and Hoop. It may be a livery now, but it was once the sole tavern at Moor Gate, and before then, a small gathering spot for the native Britons. The bones of the place run deep and we may be safe from prying eyes there."

I didn't need an explanation of why the place was special. I, too, had been drawn to it. To the horses, and to the woman in the stables. "I don't think it's a good idea to go there."

"How would you know? As far as I'm concerned, it's the greatest idea I've had all day."

"It's not that."

"I promise you, the drinks are delicious."

"I don't like wine much."

"Well, our compatriots can't wait to see you. And I know, I know, I'm being mysterious by holding back their identities, but it's so much more fun when there's suspense. You shouldn't be intimidated by them."

"I'm not."

"Then what is the problem?"

"That's where I saw the woman."

"Joss, you've seen quite a few women since you emerged from the Tamesis dripping in filth," he said.

"No. The woman. The *minnow* woman. The one I first saw when I got here. The one that found me near the horses."

It took him a moment, but then he understood. "Ah! Now it comes full circle. How curious. You must mean young Ms. Jennings!"

"She has large...eyes," I said.

"Oh, large *eyes* is it? Ah, well. But you're not the first mast she's risen. At any rate, I hear tell that she's near engaged to one of the tavern workers there, Thomas Keats. If you're really worried about seeing her again I can always…" He wiggled his fingers like waving weeds in the current. "Make her forget."

I winced, not liking the sound of it. "No, no. I suppose I should own up for my behavior."

La Roche raised an eyebrow.

"I did sneak into the stable and talk to the horses," I said. "Or tried to."

"You and horses. I will never make sense of it," said La Roche as he tried to suppress his smile, but as usual he wasn't very good at it. With him, even a smirk was like a sunbeam breaking through a raincloud.

"PEOPLE WILL HURT YOU, no matter how you try to avoid it," Verta said to me, fixing the tie around my neck so it didn't pinch too much as I prepared to make my way to the visit the Swan and Hoop.

I still hated clothing but understood it to be a necessary compromise.

"I'm not looking to be hurt," I said.

"No love between a mortal and godling has ever ended in anything other than sorrow and madness."

"She's much too small to hurt me," I said. I had told her about Ms. Jennings before, and she had advised the same.

"Ah, even the littlest frogs can carry poisoned darts," she said softly, patting me on the chest and smiling. "You look handsome. Though, I must say I still prefer you in your wilder state. This frippery is exhausting. Human fashion changes so frequently I prefer to stick to the classics." She twirled in her sheer silk dress and grinned.

"I do wish you would come with us."

"I only leave when I must, and the rest of the Rookery makes me tired."

"I suppose they're all birds, then."

"Well, Andrew is a rook. And they follow him like other birds, charmed by his everlasting smile and warmth. I used to be of such a flock. But I am more of a solitary swan these days. Andrew likes the term too. He says rooks are best in pairs and in flocks and have marked intelligence. I think he just says that to flatter himself."

"I don't see myself as a rook."

"Perhaps not yet." She took my hand and laughed lightly. "Oh, Joss. You're shaking."

"I'm bit worried," I said. "I can't tell if I want her to recognize me or if I don't want her to recognize me."

"I doubt anyone could forget you after seeing you. Not even for a second," Verta said. "Just remember that she's but a mortal. She is, in many ways, beneath you."

My eyes went wide at the mention, and she laughed her shimmering laugh.

"It's a figure of speech, Joss. She is but a minnow. You are a whale."

MY WORRIES WERE SOMEWHAT MITIGATED, however, upon entering the Swan and Hoop properly. The livery and inn was situated across from Moorfields, along the gate itself. As so much of Londinium, it was a confluence of old and new styles. Columns and narrow windows, painted exterior and dark slate roof. The facade was relatively new, blocky and hewn of granite, a contrast to the heavy round-windowed Moor Gate itself. I could smell the drink and people of the place, above the sweet stink of the livery.

The Swan and Hoop was filled with all manner of people, none of them particularly remarkable or extravagant in their ways. Far from the temple, we were squarely in a world of hard-working folk, all of whom were hungry for one thing or another. The door swung open and I inhaled an aroma of onions and yeast, tinged with a bit of sawdust. It was so busy I could scarcely tell one face from another as they swam past my line of vision.

"Through the door with pride," La Roche said, beckoning me forward.

We found a table toward the corner of the room and situated ourselves with our backs to the crowd. That didn't prevent me from craning my neck to try and get a better lay of the room. Someone played a lute in the corner while another made a half-hearted attempt to sing along, but it was drowned out with both an abundance of inebriation and a lack of skill.

"Verta didn't want to come along," I said. "She said she wasn't part of the Rookery."

"She keeps to her temple exclusively," he replied with a wave of his hand. "And that's hardly fair of her to spoil the name of our merry band."

"She said you distract her sometimes," I observed. "I'm not sure what that means, but I don't think it's just about the bedding."

My comment took the merriment out of his eyes. "Well, yes. Before she became Venus incarnate, She of the Immovable Feet, Verticordia was my wife. But she has since dedicated her life to the temple and to her girls since she believes the preservation of her holiness is more important than our union. We are no longer, as you say, intimately connected."

"She's very connected to her house on the river. I can't quite understand how, but it flows through her," I observed.

"It does. It always has been so. It matches her for its ephemeral qualities."

"You sound sad when you talk about Verta," I said, taking a glass of wine as La Roche offered.

"To be frank, Joss, I am starting to suspect she's simply waning. Fading. Giving up. Poof!"

I didn't need to ask what that meant. "So, she's old. For a godling, I mean."

"Indeed. Though, generally speaking, it isn't polite to point out such things."

"She wants to move on. And you do not."

For the first time since meeting him, I noticed I had upset La Roche. He cleared his throat and did not respond to me. Instead, he snatched a heavy flagon of wine and pair of thick green goblets, and poured them for us.

"To my protégé! And down with love!"

He raised his drink, brimming to full, and took long enough a draught to indicate he most certainly had not moved on from his relationship with Verta. I raised my glass and drank in response, watching him over the rim. When he drank, La Roche's cheeks flushed red, but not in the way mine did. His cheeks displayed the red of a youth, patchy and new. In that way his age was absolutely indeterminate to me. To a human, I suppose he looked no more than two dozen years old, but could have well passed for less. Yet the moment he opened his mouth to speak, his language and character defied classification or quantification.

In the moment of quiet, I examined the drink. Claret, he called it, and it burned all the way down and made my head feel a bit offish, like I was half my way to drowning. But not in a terrible way. Five glasses in—I'm a large creature, and a godling to boot, you must remember—and I was feeling as if my own concerns of my existence weren't too terrible in light of the world which, I was seeing, was too fast and fleeting for me to even bother with it.

La Roche was in the middle of telling me a curious tale of a dog and a donkey when he stopped and put his hand on mine. "Tell me. Can you feel them coming? My friends. Our other whales."

I nodded, grinning. "Of course." I had sensed them for quite some time but hadn't the heart to interrupt him.

He smirked in response, pushing open a door I had not seen before with a wide gesture.

"Here we are, friends. Welcome, Joss, to the Rookery."

A man and a woman stood talking together in the room, heads close in conversation, in great contrast to one another. The woman was of a height with the man, and her jet-black hair was braided and beaded and twisted about her head like a coronet. Her skin was dark as jet, her body corded with muscle and composed of such elegant lines I couldn't keep my eyes away. The angle of her eyes was feline, accented by thick brows dusted paler than her face. She wore a blue streak through her bottom lip that might have been a tattoo.

Yes, she was terrible and beautiful in a way I had never beheld. She was fear and power and strength of a sort beyond all reckoning.

She was dressed as a man, and I could see the subtle line of her breasts, though I figured they must be bound against her tightly, and her strong hips. But her clothing was the same jacket and trappings as I'd seen many men wear. Confusing to me, to say the least. I had begun to make up little rules about men and women to keep things straight in my mind, but it was quickly becoming apparent that every rule was made to be broken.

And the man was something unusual too. There was not a single hair on his head, but he wore a dark, close-cropped beard and mustache, both of jet. His skin was the color of sandstone and his eyes as dark and empty as a starless sky. He was dressed in bright gray and green, and carried himself with an air of authority, hand on a silver-knobbed cane. Nobility, perhaps, but not from this island. He felt foreign to me in a way I couldn't explain, and yet, as the woman, familiar.

"Ah, here we all are," said La Roche, extending his hands in joy. "At long last! The Rookery grows. My heart is simply pounding with excitement."

"You didn't exaggerate," said the woman, taking me in with her large, wise eyes.

The bald man frowned, narrowing his gaze at me. "You're broad as a workhorse."

"My friends, my brother and sister, this is Joss," said La Roche. "Commander of the air, rumbler of the earth, and tamer of horses." Before I could reply, he introduced his friends. "This bald-pated madman is Calvinius Pardo. And this magnificent creature is Trita Oya. She is older than me by a few centuries or so, but our dear Calvinius is the newest among us, not yet having achieved his first century. He is something of an alchemist, I suppose you could say. Though he does dabble in theatre, as well. I've no understanding for the craft, nor why they'd spend their time so frivolously, but so it is."

"Alchemist is a bit of an exaggeration. I make potions. Tinctures. Drinks to heal and to hurt," Calvinius said. "And La Roche is my teacher."

"I dabble. You excel." La Roche continued, "Trita is an actor, and a constant reformer. She has dedicated herself, body and soul, to art, justice, and passion. Though it is quite beyond me that she would waste her talent pretending to fight when she could be shaking the foundations of the earth with her spear."

"I have been performing in Londinium since before the walls," Trita said, slapping at La Roche's hand. "And that isn't to say I never use my spear. I am not retired, merely a bit less dedicated."

"And this is where she goes on a diatribe of how she fought sword to sword against Boudicca and prevented the retreat of the Roman army before dedicating herself to the stage," Calvinius said, yawning and pouring himself a drink from a seemingly endless decanter on the table before them. "So cheers to you, Trita, and your indelible experience."

"Enough banter, enough. This is where things get truly exciting," La Roche said.

"And he says I have a flare for the dramatic," Trita replied drolly.

La Roche ignored Trita's jibe and elbowed me in the side. "You must guess who they are. Trita first."

Yes, Trita.

There was enough moisture in the air that I could get a good sense of her. I could tell a couple of things: what she'd eaten before (honeyed pears) and what perfume she preferred (like sweet olive oil). But much of her was a mystery, inscrutable.

"Concentrate," La Roche said quietly. "You can do this."

I tried my eyes, then, focusing on her. She knew I was watching, but kept talking anyway. I listened to the way she spoke. A storyteller. But no words out of place. Precise and beautiful. Her nature was ever evolving. Because she understood deeply the power of learning, and how it means comes to naught if not applied.

"Knowledge. Wisdom..." I paused. I knew the word from my reading, and I had a guess from Calvinus's commentary earlier. But I didn't like saying it. "War." There was no doubt there. She somehow embodied all the wisdom and grace I'd seen in every sex, and made it her own. But it was tempered with great power. A fighting spirit I felt I needed to understand more. Cleverness. Calculating. Ruthless. She seemed embrace all aspects of humanity while remaining considerably a godling.

Trita smiled at me, rare and lovely. I wanted to make her smile more often, feeling it a challenge worth rising to. "Am I that obvious?" she asked.

"Every time you open your mouth," Calvinius said.

She shoved him playfully, and he almost smiled.

"Yes, Minerva or Athena would be appropriate for one of limited knowledge and lacking in a cosmopolitan view; however, she comes to us via the River Niger, far to the south, by way of the Kingdom of Yoruba. But that was another life. I am still trying to get her drunk enough to tell the tales," La Roche said.

Trita's smile faded, and she lifted her chin. For a moment I thought I saw lightning in her eyes. I knew that La Roche was no match for her, but I didn't have the heart to tell him.

"You could fill the Tamesis with wine and it would still not be enough, La Roche. Not all of us are open books," she said.

"And our Spaniard?" La Roche asked, shifting from Trita and gesturing to Calvinius with the enthusiasm needed for an abrupt change of subject. It was a good maneuver on his part. He always knew how to play his audience. Just enough tension and anticipation. "What do you think he embodies?"

As with Trita, I closed my eyes and reached out to the godling. I could feel him in the same way I sensed La Roche's warmth and Verta's heart, much easier than with Trita. I got the sense of a mind working overtime, experiencing a thousand different emotions at once, struggling to live in more than one place simultaneously and finding it impossible. A godling completely splintered, in some ways. He wasn't old, no, but he was clearly tortured, already. There was a tinge of the metallic about him. Flux and fire. Spice and whiskey. But ice, too. Cold and cracking. Things being made. Things being unmade. Then the pieces reforming again.

"Chaos," I said, which was not meant to be an answer. But when I spoke it, I knew it was true.

"You are correct, and I'm almost impressed," Trita said.

"Six godlings in Londinium, seven on the earth," marveled Calvinius, stroking his sharp chin. "We only lack the Hunter. Quite astounding."

"Seven, you said," I observed, taking a seat beside La Roche. "I can feel another I have not met, though I do not know her. She must be too far away."

Trita snorted, shaking her head. "Trouble, that's what he is. She who you sense is here, yes. She is the Mother—Miriam, we call her. She makes rules. She makes decrees. She pines for order and hierarchy and structure, and through those, peace. She drives me mad."

"The other is, or was, the Father, Achaemenes," La Roche explained. "We call him the Maker. And he and Miriam used to live as husband and wife; now they live as hunter and hunted. And I'm never sure which is which."

"They are older even than Verta, and have been at odds for longer than any of us can remember," continued Trita. "For centuries they've tried to recruit us to their war, but we have remained neutral. Or, as neutral as one can remain while in Miriam's demesne. Londinium is hers, and so, when it comes to our abilities, there are certain…limitations she can impose upon us."

"Godlings shouldn't have rules," I said, thinking the idea beyond preposterous.

"Well, it is our privilege as godlings, and a line we must respect. For, you see, we are each granted power over our *ken*, and so we can set down the rules and regulations if we use what's called a decree."

I must have made a face, for La Roche clarified. "A decree is an unwritten rule that binds us together. Our ken is our demesne. Our ruling passion. It is not always the same in each incarnation, and there are certainly shades of grey in between. Achaemenes is the Maker, the Mover. He is the great coordinator. It is he who has commanded friendship among us, who put together our system of teachers and protégés."

Trita continued, "Miriam is the matriarch, the compliment to Achaemenes in some ways—the Hera to his Zeus—but not always. They are both calculating. Powerful. Ancient. But Miriam's star is rising, and Achaemenes's is diminishing. They have been wounded by one another so many times, they have both decided to devote their remaining years to destroying one another."

"Miriam seeks worship," Calvinius said. "She wants no competition. We all remain out of her sphere of concern, but she has spent generations eradicating the existence of other beings—lesser whales. Dolphins, perhaps?" He chuckled. "In short, she has forbidden us to directly father, or birth, children made of human and godling. We are permitted our favorites, but we cannot directly involve ourselves."

"Which doesn't rule out copulation," La Roche was quick to point out.

"So Achaemenes rules we must be friends, family," Trita said. "But Miriam rules that we may couple with humans, but never allow our divine being released into them."

I thought about this. The priestesses in the temple had not born any children, not for all my attempts. Verta had said something about an herb.

"Verta gave her priestesses herbs," I observed. "That seemed to work."

Trita nodded. "Well, her priestesses are a complication, and one Miriam desperately despises. It is highly unlikely you would have engendered a child upon the priestesses because you must be taught to imbue your power, and you must not be restrained. Miriam gives you a draught of her hookah, does she not?"

I nodded.

"You are not at your full, heightened self, then, when you are making love to those priestesses. And you cannot allow your full self through."

"I could choose to, though," I pointed out. "If I didn't have that drug."

"And if you did, Miriam would curse the child, seek it out, and kill it," Calvinius answered sharply. "It is a risk none of us could endure. She cannot kill us individually, but the pain, I imagine, of seeing a child—a divine child—tortured, killed, separated—would be too much to bear."

La Roche stood up, shaking his head and holding his hands up dramatically. "Enough of this damned melancholic discussion. We are still allowed our games, the Maker and Mother be damned. I won't let her ruin everything."

"You've a mind for a game?" Calvinius asked, his eyes suddenly kindled. I had thought him quite drunk, but this turn of conversation had me doubting.

"A Boast," La Roche said. "A good, old-fashioned Boast." He held up a finger as Calvinius and Trita both made a movement to stand, or argue, or both. "But, first, we shall wait. But another day soon. Let us all rest, rebuild, and think of the challenges ahead. It is my *ken* to declare a Boast, and I do."

5

I retired to my bedroom and couldn't stop thinking about the horses downstairs, in spite of all the ideas running through my brain and newfound knowledge. You see how impressive my mind is? Instead of ruminating on my place in the world as a godling, or the decrees made against me, La Roche's Boast, and the subsequent revelations of my being, I could think of nothing other than resting my head against the muzzle of one of those delightful equine specimens in the livery.

Sleep would not come. So when the bed proved too small, I went to the roof and watched the stars move across the sky until I could no longer avoid the draw to the stables.

The smell of the stables was as welcoming as I'd hoped it would be, and I breathed in the sweet sawdust and grinned, feeling much of the stress of Londinium lift from my shoulders. The filth, the understanding, the noise, it had all be hanging on me like a yoke, and the minnows—the humans—hadn't helped. Aye, leave it to someone like me to prefer the stench of horse shit and straw to onions and spilled ale, but so it is. My world had expanded beyond my understanding so fast I needed to connect with something simple and true. And horses are nothing if not those qualities.

I walked the length of the stables quietly was I could, reaching my hand out to casually meet each beast in the dark. They were all soulful and strangely familiar, but it wasn't until I found a tall black stallion, the most stunning horse I'd ever seen, that I understood what had brought me here.

His coat was in great need of attention, and he had pulled so much on his trappings that there were sores at his mouth. But he was a king of horses. Proud and perfect, and so very far from home.

"Hush, now," I said, holding my hands out in peace. "Hush, hush, boy."

He looked me straight in the eye, shivered, and bared his teeth.

"You called me here," I reminded him. "I can help you, but you've got to be a gentleman about it." It's more or less something La Roche had told me many times when I resisted lessons on etiquette, and so I thought it an appropriate way to chastise the horse for his bad manners.

He bit me. Square on the shoulder. But I used the opportunity to shove my hand into his mouth and give him one world of a shock. He wasn't expecting someone of my strength, I don't think, and it brought him up short. All those taught muscles and jangling nerves began to loosen and he recognized what made me a divine kind of being.

At first the stallion didn't think too much of me, but after I sang him a bit of a song I'd been thinking about—something silly and sweet about fish and rivers—he calmed down and allowed me to do as I would to get him in better shape. He saw I would not hurt him, though he told me many had.

I discovered a bristle brush by his side on a stool. There were no attendants, as the sun had only just begun to light the sky, but I reasoned I was safe enough to begin brushing his coat. He didn't just need it—he was a mess of brambles and tangles—but I could tell that he *wanted* it.

Looking after the horse was more restful than sleeping: the feel of the beast's hot skin beneath his coat, the comfort of detangling his mane, the actions soothed me. It seemed that my brain worked out the challenges of the day while I labored, and I was so engrossed in the labor of working with the horse, again, I didn't hear Ms. Jennings coming up behind me.

"You again," said the young woman with a sigh. "You really ought not be haunting the stables. Hardly proper. As I said—"

In my surprise, I knocked over a leather pail of briny water, spilling over my feet and hers. I ducked down to clean it up and said under my breath, "Don't remember me, please. Just don't remember me. *Let this be the first time.*"

I watched the water run across her boots, and then let it run across the back of my hands, commanding it in a rudimentary way.

I then looked up at her, wincing. Waiting for her to recognize me and alert the guard. Even dressed as I was now, it would take a myopic baby to mistake me for someone else.

But that didn't seem to matter once she saw the stallion.

"He was in such a state," she said, walking over to him, looking at him as if with new eyes. "I'd scarcely believe it was the same horse if I hadn't seen him stabled myself last night."

"I'm sorry. I shouldn't have come here without asking."

She smiled, dimples deepening in her curious oval face. "You're right, but we'll forgive you Mr...?"

The stallion behind me made a sound. I liked it. I needed more than one name.

"Mr. Raddick. Joss Raddick," I said, taking the opportunity to add a little bow to the business. "I am a student, come to learn here in Londinium." It was true. At least I had that going for me.

"Well, I'm Frances Jennings, though nearly everyone calls me Fanny," she declared, as if I should have known the name. "And I work here. Though not with the horses, directly. I just like to check on them after a long night."

Frances smiled a little and gestured to the stallion. "This is Poetaster. Though I call him Potato. He doesn't like anyone. Let alone me. Though he belongs to our ostler, Thomas. Try as he might, Tom can't even keep him calm. Just a big, gorgeous waste of money." She turned back to me. "Are you studying ostlery?"

"No, not at all. Horses just like me, I guess," I said, as Poetaster nuzzled me from behind, sending my hair into my face as if from a gale wind.

"I'd say so. With talent like this you could make a pretty penny breaking horses for the gentry. What we get from the East is scarce, and they always have the hottest tempers."

"I'm happy to visit Poetaster whenever you need," I said, and that wasn't a lie. But I knew it wasn't up to her, and I knew I didn't mean just the horse.

"I expect a student of your sort is most assuredly otherwise engaged," Frances said, looking at my clothes. The way she was looking at me made me think inappropriate things and I took a little step back, feigning picking a burr from Poetaster's coat.

I cleared my throat and looked away from her. "There's always time to change one's vocation."

Without looking at her I could still see the shadow of those confounded dimples and hear the laughter in her voice. She found me amusing. And she found me arousing. I'd never been able to read a woman so easily but it was written on her skin, her freckled, flushed skin...

We stared at one another, the sound of the swishing of tails and the gnawing of hay around us.

"Well, Mister Raddick, I do hope to see you again, as you've offered. Since no one's able to calm Poetaster, I don't think that Tom will mind. He might even let you take him for a ride," she said at last.

"I'd never ride another man's property. But if Thomas agrees to it, I'd be glad of the work. It's relaxing."

We were talking about horses, were we not? Yet the way she looked at me spoke another harmony into the conversation. Thomas was hers too.

"Yes, taming wild beasts would have that effect, I'd imagine," she said. My heart, which on most days I took into no consideration, turned wagon wheels in my chest, and as I watched her go it took all my willpower to not glamor her into bedding me.

I swallowed on a dry throat.

"Good-bye," I said. And I left.

RATHER THAN LINGER around the Swan and Hoop, I made instead for one of the temples just to the Northeast that I had seen on a map during my study at Verta's temple. This temple was older, less in use than those deeper into the heart of the city, and was situated around an ancient burial ground. Interred were many founding Romans of Londinium, those relegated to the annals of history and so often politicized and sanctified, depending on which faction was in power.

Famed or not, I liked the idea of walking among the dead. At least they didn't make my trousers ache.

I passed through the soggy fields, noting the warriors and statesmen marked haphazardly. They had traveled over land and sea and given up their lives to a new Rome in this cold, miserable place. And it was not New Rome—it was something else. Britannaie was all that was left of the Roman Empire. Perhaps the founders never succeeded in conquering Eire or north of Hadrian's wall, but they did establish a remarkable society here. The Senate, I learned from my histories and from La Roche, was famed around the world, and still held long after the Persians had taken Rome itself and the Turks invaded Hispania. Gaul, Bohemia, and the surrounding Territories were more or less governed by smaller Senates who, in turn, sent their delegates to Londinium. Over them all presided the Queen of Britanniae, and Empress of the Holy Roman Empire, currently a woman by the name of Her Royal Highness Octavia Aurelia the Fifteenth.

I did not feel Roman, and I did not feel as if I were Britannic, either. I'd nearly been born above the wall. I had no idea of the politics, how the Scots were conspiring to supplant the current religion—which the Romans had once ruled the de-facto religion for all—with Marianism, which was growing with astonishing quickness out of Gaul. Which made me wonder what part Miriam had to play in all of this. I did not feel comforted by the manic tempo of Londinium. I felt as if I had been born out of time.

That night I reveled in the quiet. The tombs and stones were written in Latin, which differed from general Britannic conversational dialect considerably, but was far easier to work out. Reading each epitaph, I was moved by the meaning and brevity of their lasting effects, many already worn to nothing but stumps. Such short lives. Though I had not lived long above water, I still had a sense of how very fragile these mortal humans were.

To the Spirits of the Dead. Quintus Caedius Festus, son of Quintus, of the tribe Velina from Aquileia, a soldier of the sixth Praetorian cohort of Atilius. He lived 28 years, 4 months, and 7 days; and served in the military for 12 years.

Do not fear Lethe, for it is foolish to lose joy of life while fearing death at all time. For death is the nature, not the punishment of mankind; whoever happens to be born, therefore also faces to die.

Lo, beneath this marker are placed the bones of Soteris;
she lies buried, devoured by pitiless death.
She had not yet filled up twice three years
when she was bidden to enter the house of black Dis.
The lamentations which the mother ought to have bequeathed to her daughter,
these the daughter suddenly bequeathed to her mother

Lethe and Dis. Indeed. Myth and reality. There were plenty of statues to the gods, but they looked nothing like my strange new friends. There was Neptune, his head tilted up, his beard streaming down his chest, his bits just hanging out for the world to see, and rather unimpressively, I may add. I reckoned I should feel some kinship with him, except I had no stirrings. No moment of epiphany. That face might have been anyone's. Though there were shells strewn about his feet and horsehair tied in bundles, the stones were silent.

I was preparing to leave when I felt the presence of another godling, clear and sharp in my mind. I drew up behind the statue of Neptune just in time to see Verta, followed by three of her priestesses, walking bare-breasted into the temple carrying bouquets of myrtle, the flower she'd mentioned to me the night of the experience in the pool. There were veils on the women's faces, but not on hers, and try as I might I couldn't keep my eyes off of her.

She didn't seem to notice me, at least at first, but I had no doubt she knew I was there.

They vanished behind a curtain at the front of the temple; rather than leave I reckoned it wise to wait for them.

The evening deepened and I nodded in and out of sleep. When at last Verta exited the room with her dazzling retinue she looked tired, her eyes rimmed in red.

As she passed me in Neptune's shadow, she said, "You may escort us back to our temple, Joss, if you'd like. Or just walk with me a while."

"Of course," was my quick reply as I fell into step beside them. "I didn't mean—"

"No need to apologize. We have a way of finding one another, you know, we godlings; you do get accustomed to it after a time," she said. "I used to think of it as a happy coincidence. But other times it can be almost inconvenient." She gave me a disarming smile.

We passed through the graveyard quietly and the three priestesses were given leave to take the carriage awaiting them.

"Joss is more than capable of ensuring my safety," Verta said to her priestesses.

We didn't need to speak to connect in that mournful place. In silence we walked the rest of the tombs, our feet crunching against the gravel and sometimes padding softly on the smooth earth. Eventually, Verta began singing a low song in Latin. It began:

Dea sancta Tellus, rerum naturae parens,
quae cuncta generas et regeneras indidem,
quod sola praestas gentibus vitalia,

caeli ac maris diva arbitra rerumque omnium,
per quam silet natura et somnos concipit,
itemque lucem reparas et noctem fugas:
tu Ditis umbras tegis et immensum chaos
ventosque et imbres tempestatesque attines
et, cum libet, dimittis et misces freta
fugasque solesc et procellas concitas,
itemque, cum vis, hilarem promittis diem.

I mentally translated the poem as I listened. Latin was not spoken regularly outside of legal and church matters in Londinium, but I'd done enough reading to know the basics. Her song was an invocation to the Mother of the Earth. The keeper. Miriam.

Verta took my hand, and I could feel her thoughts. "You're singing someone else's song."

"Maybe I am," Verta said in her thoughtful, non-committal way. "Miriam and I have never had the best relationship, though none of us can claim to be her favorite, I don't think, but I find appealing to her vanity every now and again is a good thing. I think of it as a peace offering. There is nothing in the wide world I want more than peace, and though Miriam often sails under that banner, she is as warlike as her spouse."

"It's hard to imagine a mother as warlike."

"Ah, you have not met enough mothers," Verta said. "They are the fiercest warriors. But often blind to their acts on behalf of their aims. You heard she eradicated our progeny?"

I nodded. I recalled La Roche speaking of the matter, but he had not called them their own. They had felt old, mythological.

"I don't think Miriam would have done such a thing when she was younger, clearer. She grew more and more concerned that our inability to have our own children, together, was because we were spreading our seed too wide among human beings. And that our mixed progeny could rise up against us. And in a way, she was not wrong. I think she listened to men too much. She often had a retinue of worshiping priests. Too much time around human beings and we become so detached from our own hearts, our own beginnings… We change, and we cannot help it."

"Like La Roche, too, you mean."

"Hmmm," she said, considering her answer as we joined the main road toward Eald Gate. "Well, I suppose so. We had a time together, and it is over. But unlike Miriam who has shifted and changed to accommodate her new desires and state, he resists. He believes we should adhere to her rules, to never interfere with the life and death of humankind."

"He has never mentioned such a thing to me, only to say he will not teach it," I said.

"As if a lack of learning ever stopped anyone from raising the dead."

We were walking the old Virginal Way, and even then, I didn't miss the irony. While there were other roads, paved more recently and friendlier to carriages and palanquins, we walked the old path along the water. It was late enough that very few people passed us, just a handful of beggars and a few plebs. Verta stopped before answering me to give some dinars to one of them. Even I could sense the place was losing its power, but she gave it what she could.

"He loves you, you know. Down to his bones. If we have bones. I haven't decided whether or not we have bones in the way humans do, but..." I shook my head, seeing the amusement in her eyes. "I digress."

Verta took my hand once again with both of hers, holding it tight. She held me with the comfort of a sister. "He has been through a great deal. When we met, he was so young, and so full of passion and excitement. He made me rejoice again to be what I was, and I had forgotten that for a very long time."

"So, he made you feel young again."

"You rogue. I am eternal."

"I extend my apologies," I said.

"No need. I will tell you: I came from the East. My father was a Shah; my name was Harit. Like you, I am of questionable parentage. But it became clear rather quickly that I was no typical child. My father used to say my mother was a daeva, but I do not know for certain. But as all things with us, I soon outgrew my family. My friends. My relationships. I did not age. I could do unexplained things. I could not die.

"I helped win Rome for the Persians, once, and they have yet to win it back. But I can no longer live there. Instead I found myself drawn to Londinium, drawn to La Roche. Strange that I sit in my enemies' capital and contemplate my end."

"That doesn't make much sense."

"Sense rarely has anything to do with our hearts. The heart of Persia changed, though. My people left the gods to worship of the One; the Father. Achaemenes. And He grew powerful. He was my teacher, my lover, my companion. But I could not live in the world he built in Persia.

So, I bound him with a spell I knew would keep him occupied for a time, and then I left."

"I doubt he liked you leaving."

She brushed back her long, dark hair, retwining her long braid and letting go of my hands. "He had no time for me. He only wanted to seek out those who would worship him. To build cults and sacrifice lands. I wanted to know other godlings, and I could feel them awakening in the world, I wanted to see the oceans and trek across the frozen wastes."

"But then you met La Roche."

It was odd. Usually she was veiled to me. But that night I could catch glimpses of her thoughts. I couldn't have told you her story if you'd outright asked me, but I knew what she was thinking just a moment before she spoke. And her feelings generated images in my mind before she explained herself.

"Yes, indeed." Verta calculated on her fingers. "That would have been in the year sixteen and twelve. Right after the Third Plague, not long before the Fourth. Like me, he was born to a mortal family. But they were all killed in that deadly disease. I had lived three lifetimes before we met, and there he was…standing on the pyre, unable to burn, mad and alone; the image still makes my heart ache. I had never been so moved, never so broken by the plight of another…"

That was something I'd never heard before. "Surely we all burn."

"Not he. How can the Sun burn? He burns always. I'm not sure what he remembers of that day, as we have rarely spoken of it. But I know what I saw. He had carried every member of his family, and a hundred more besides—children, women, babies still in swaddling clothes, all swollen and covered with pustules. And he lit them afire. With his own hands. Hoping to die along with them. He had been standing in the flames for so long when I found him, his body was charred black, and the hair was gone from every inch of him. But I could not let him torture himself. Eventually, I convinced him off of the pyre and we began our life together. He was a bright, strange boy."

"He's a bright, strange man."

I thought Verta might laugh, but she looked gravely at me. "Yes, I suppose he is."

"And you taught him to control it."

She nodded, taking my hand again. I could feel the sorrow in her, distant but still palpable. "And we lived together for many, many years. And we loved each other. But he…"

I could hear her words, so I said them aloud so she didn't have to. "He doesn't want to let you go, and you want to leave."

Verta's eyes filled with tears. "And I linger because I have been the one constant in his life. There is a war coming, Joss. Not a petty, human war, but a true war, between the godlings. Miriam has been keeping herself from us, in part because she wishes revenge on Achaemenes. That is why I prayed to her tonight. Achaemenes is ancient, but unlike me, he only wishes to cling to life. At any cost. To fight the fading, to live on. Meanwhile, in this city, Miriam only gains power. Her followers shun me, and my priestesses, they laugh in the face of Neptune and Apollo and Minerva and Mars. They will trample us. In a way, it's a miracle we've held on this long..." she trailed off, her eyes far away after she wiped her tears. "I cannot endure a war."

I could smell her tears, and in them the scent of frankincense, a touch of sandalwood, memories of a thousand thousand days. She didn't appear old to my eyes, no, but I could feel the weariness in her soul like a funeral shroud. I could see how bleak everything now seemed to her, and knew, too, her priestesses, her temple and those who depended on it, were all she had left. They were the beloved emissaries of what she'd worked almost a thousand years to achieve.

"I drink this draught," she said, pointing to a flask at her hip, "because it allows me peace. You know it, I can tell. The pressing rush of people, and their thoughts, how it drains you. We are connected, you and I, in many ways. It is the same I give you to smoke when you lay with my girls."

Reaching over, I wiped her tears gently with my fingers. They were bitter.

As if she caught me rooting around in her thoughts, she continued. "Heart and sea. Home and thunder. The Greeks say Aphrodite sprung from waves, and it makes sense, I suppose. But the moment I saw you, I knew you were different. Tell me, Joss, what do you think of the Rookery?"

"I think I like them. I feel as if I belong. Almost."

"It is good to have friends. And it is good to know those who make us feel a sense of belonging, but understand: in this coming war—a war with the godlings and not with man—you will be used as a pawn unless you choose your own path. Miriam will want you. Achaemenes will want you. Andrew will want you. If anyone has the power to change the course of the world, it is you, *oh savior of ships*." She spoke the last epithet in Greek, and yet I understood it.

"But *you* do not want me."

If she caught my double meaning she did not show it. "Andrew wants me to fight. With him. He believes if we can work together—five of us—we can bring Miriam around and stave off a war. But to do that, he may need to fight. And I am so wearing of fighting, Joss…"

I sighed because she shared her thoughts so readily with me. "But you love Andrew. Still."

"Ah, alas. I suppose, even though the centuries have scarred my heart, when the fog lifts from all the memory and pain and regret, he will always be the truest love I ever did have. Even if we no longer share as we used to. Yes, I would rake my own soul over the cinders of Hades for him, if he asked, if he begged." Verta paused and laughed for the first time during the course of our conversation. "Though, come to think of it… I have been to so-called Hades, and it is hardly unpleasant. Though the food is rather terrible, and it stinks. Garum as far as the eye can see."

"If you love him, then I will continue as his student."

"Yes, of course. There is no other godling more suited. But do understand, Joss: just because he teaches you does not mean you owe him allegiance. In the end, I have found among our kind, we can only claim fealty to ourselves, else risk all."

6

I returned that night and slept fitfully upon the roof, finding it more comfortable than the beds at the Swan and Hoop below.

I could not stop seeing the gravestones in my mind, nor tasting Verta's bitter tears. To make matters worse, I could feel Frances Jennings sleeping just a few rooms over. It was a constant point of irritation for me to have to endure her breathing, even if it was a floor and seven doors away. I didn't want to think about her, what she might look like under her frock or what her skin tasted like or how her breasts would feel in my hands. But that's all I could do when I was in the building itself. The roof was far more manageable. Somehow it tied me better to the sky and cut off the constant thoughts about Frances. I liked the stars.

In the day I'd been gone, La Roche had not left a message. And I did not see the rest of the Rookery. So, the next morning, I visited the stables again to check on Poetaster and hoped to see Frances. That was when I first met Thomas Keats.

He was far shorter than I, a compact man with a head of dark hair and curious hazel eyes. He was one of those men who never seemed to stand still, who had a constant, restless energy about him, always grabbing a brush or fixing a bridle or fiddling with odds and ends in his pocket.

And to his credit, he was not afraid of me. Nor was he angry when I entered the livery.

"Ah, I suppose you're the giant who's tamed Poetaster, my good..." he said to me, somewhat conflicted about how to address me. He finally added: "Sir."

"I'm no Sir," I said, extending out my hand to shake his. "Joss is fine."

"I'm Thomas, then. Thomas Keats. My fiancée, Frances, told me about you," he said.

"Mmm," I replied, nodding. "She found me with the stallion. Claims no one's been able to tame him."

"Indeed not. And I've been trying my hand at it for the better part of the season and was preparing for despair. Was going to sell him for glue."

Poetaster snorted ruefully, as if on cue. I couldn't help but laugh.

"Well, he seems rather calm again."

"Oddly enough, he's best when he's with you. And I wish I could say it pleased me, save that I was hoping to ride him myself."

I stroked Poetaster's chin. "Well, I'd be pleased to show you how, if you'd like."

"I'd be indebted if you think it possible. Where did you learn such skill with these beasts?"

"I suppose I just have a natural inclination."

We spent the rest of the morning discussing Poetaster and his requirements. I tried not to make it sound easy, but I knew what the animal needed and wanted without having to say a word. I touched him and felt it. He didn't like wet oats, for one, and preferred the dry. Apples made his stomach turn. He preferred to see outside if possible. So bit by bit we got Thomas more comfortable with Poetaster, and the horse responded in kind. It would take a while, I think, to build the right trust, but I found a real joy in teaching Thomas to see the animal more clearly. I had never been a teacher, myself, and though I'd had some instruction from La Roche and Verta, it was not anything I could consider formal.

And I liked Thomas, which was especially odd considering I'd spent the majority of the evening before contemplating spreading his fiancé's legs and just what sort of noises she might make if I touched her pleasingly. Thomas was hard not to like. He was simple, straightforward, and without too much complication. I suppose, on more than a philosophical level, he was more like me than my colorful, divine, magical Rookery friends. Thomas Keats spoke simply and without pretense. I enjoyed listening to him talk and, as we went about feeding and watering and caring for the rest of the animals in the stables, I hardly said a word. I didn't have to. We had a comfortable silence, and I knew even then that it was a treasured thing.

When I finally left the stables—because Thomas had other duties—I decided to take a walk around Moor Gate and familiarize myself with the area around the Swan and Hoop. Londinium still frightened me with its noise and captive waterways, but I figured if I could start with this little corner I could expand my knowledge street by street, aqueduct by aqueduct. Familiarity might breed a better sense of calm, for I was so restless.

I hadn't walked half a block from the inn, though, before I found La Roche. He was waiting for me. Verta was right. We had a habit of running into one another.

Andrew La Roche was leaning on a post, hat down over his eyes, with that offensively red scarf around his neck, lackadaisical and handsome. He smoked a pipe, long and white and elegant, his shoulders hunched in comfortable concentration. As I got closer, he turned and looked at me and smiled. And the world seemed to smile with him, golden and resplendent. I felt warmed from the inside, filled with comfort knowing that he was my guide in the world.

After all these years it's that pose, and that moment, I remember clearest. After all we went through, after all we lost. His smile was mine.

"*You* look pretty," he said as I approached.

I'd taken the time to plait my beard, which grew out no matter how hard I tried to shave it, and had finally put away my tiresome jacket and trousers for the clothes La Roche bought me.

"Pretty enough, I suppose. But I'm afraid I'll never pass in genteel company," I said.

"Not such a bad thing, Joss my friend," La Roche said, clapping me on the back. "Though I hear you've been making tracks all about Londinium these days."

"Hardly. I ran into Verta in the fields across the street." I gestured toward the old cemetery.

"Ha! No one 'runs into' Verta. She's a thousand years old. Everything she does is calculated down to the very, most perfectly infinitesimal measure of time. She must have wanted to see you, for she does not make a habit of leaving unless something truly intrigues her. My guess is she was curious about the Rookery. Did she ask after us?"

I nodded.

"Well, was your discussion enjoyable?"

I didn't appreciate his making light of our meeting, which had been serious indeed. But it was his way, and I had to remind myself his japes hid the sorrow. "She was helpful. Filling me in."

He gave me a scandalous look, and I understood his assumption.

"No. No, it was a discussion of godlings. And alliances. And histories. And life and death."

"Ah, gave you the tragic comedy treatment of our long and harried relationship, now did she?"

He started walking, and I started following. It seemed as good a time as any to talk about it.

"She told me she wants to leave the world, and you don't want her to. And that you should teach me about life and—"

"Of course, I don't bloody want her to leave! What a stupid observation," he snapped, then caught himself immediately. "No. I'm sorry. That was rude of me. It is but a sore subject."

"You love her. I understand that much."

"I loved her *differently* once," he said, a weary tone to his voice. "It has all gone topsy turvy on me, and it maddens me to think she's done with this world when there is so much more yet to see."

"We all must leave in our time," I said, recalling the epitaphs. "Even godlings."

"Not if I can help it," he said. Then he put away his pipe and took a deep breath.

"She said I should learn about raising the dead and..."

The look on his face was ice, utter fury. "Out of the question. Joss, do not ask me again. To do such a thing would mean calling down the wrath of Miriam to such a level you cannot comprehend."

"I don't understand."

"You don't need to. You just need to trust me. Do you trust me?"

Slowly, I nodded, feeling a knot in my stomach.

"Now, we have an appointment to keep with Trita. Don't want to leave her waiting."

"I didn't know of any appointments."

La Roche's anger was over, and he laughed brightly. "I didn't tell you, which is part of the lesson. Life, Joss, is unpredictable and ever-changing. It's the only thing you can truly plan on."

La Roche and his appointments; he was on his own time, ordering the rest of us to move and orient ourselves as he needed. Like a great solar clock, orchestrating the movement of heavenly bodies. Perhaps it was a trait in his ken, I do not know. But especially in those early days, before I developed a spine, I did not question him. There was no doubt that being in his presence, even under his command, felt comforting. La Roche had a way with people, and I ever felt the greater when I was following his suggestions. I felt taken care of, swept up, and important.

We made our way through the worst parts of Londinium, east of the Swan and Hoop toward Aldgate, and the landscape became only more doleful with every step. I was not afraid to be in such places, but they did make me feel uncomfortable. I knew Fanny and Thomas were not well-to-do, but they eked out a living as they could and seemed happy and healthy. Here, though, the aqueducts crumbled and the water smelled of death.

"I consider this to be the more unsavory corner of the city," said La Roche, "but Trita finds it inspiring. She likes to excavate the most sodden piles of refuse to uncover any possibility of enlightenment. I quite believe she likes the challenge."

The homes here could only be described as shacks, barely standing and often cobbled together from weather worn planks of wood, shipping containers, and old cloth. Children ran about, snot-nosed and pale, faces smeared with soot. Wild-eyed women peered out at me from ragged doorways, angry and hopeless men lurking in the shadows behind them.

I took in the ramshackle landscape. "It's a sad place. Sadder than I've ever seen. It hurts to look upon it."

"Yes, it does," La Roche said, twisting the scarf on his neck a little tighter. "But they could be worse off. I've seen it. At least here, in Londinium they have guardians after a fashion."

He did not elaborate, but not two blocks down—if this sort of place could be measured in blocks given its state of degradation—and just in view of the Tamesis, two young children came up to La Roche with their eyes bright, calling him by name.

"Look, it's Jane and Mary," La Roche said, reaching into his pockets and pulling out two little sweets, the rose-flavored candies he so favored. "There you go now."

"Thank you, Master La Roche!" the eldest said. She was pinched and worn in a way such a young child should never be, but when she smiled, I saw hints of a strong, bold woman she would grow to. If she could survive long enough. Murder was rampant in these streets. "Trita's waiting for you."

The youngest's eyes grew wide, taking in my stature. "Are you friends with a titan, Mr. La Roche?" she asked.

"Perhaps someday he'll let me be a friend—but yes, this is my acquaintance, Mr. Raddick. Quite impressive, isn't he?" La Roche said without casting an eye toward me. A strange choice of words.

"Jane, don't stare so. It's rude," the eldest said.

"But he's so big!" Jane exclaimed, holding her tiny hands under her chin. "He looks like he could move aqueducts all by himself!"

La Roche laughed and said, "You have no idea what he's capable of, do you, darling? I wouldn't be surprised if he could, indeed, move the very waters above."

Little Jane marveled at me, and my size brought her joy. I had never spent much time around children, finding them small enough to be unsettling. Yet here, this one, she felt different. Brighter. Her sister, too. I could see why La Roche spent time with them.

Then Jane held out her hand, her other behind her back, her stomach leading the rest of her body. Her big brown eyes regarded me with a mix of fear and challenge.

I need not have asked what she wanted.

Kneeling down, and hunching over some more, I held out my hand to hers, palm to palm. Her skin was cool and clammy and her hand so small it could have been closed completely in mine, engulfed. For a moment I thought she would scream. But then she just giggled and marched her fingers up my palm and then poked my thumb.

Both girls ran away, cackling, shouting, "A titan! A titan!"

"Little miraculous things," muttered La Roche, gesturing toward a long, low building before us. "I'm quite certain if they didn't exist and give me a constant sense of hope, I'd have burned this city down to its bones ages ago."

THE EAST SIDE building had once been a fish market, before the great fish kill of 1780. La Roche explained that, while the numbers of fish were closely approaching sustainable levels, it took a long time for the industry to regain its foothold in Londinium again. For two months, dead fish littered the shores of the Tamesis—and then some more. Giant squid, bloated whale carcasses, enormous clams and mollusks never seen by Brittanic eyes. It seemed some had simply been dropped, as if from a great height, rather than navigate from the sea. It was considered by most in the city to be a sign from Mary to turn their ways from Roman gods and the Great Deva.

Although, he pointed out, most recently there had been a noticeable increase in the presence of marine life in the Tamesis, much to the joy of local fisherman.

Regardless of the history, the market—where I stood with La Roche that day—had fallen into considerable disrepair, shabby even in contrast to the dilapidation surrounding it. Once the center of employment and pride for the scrubbier East, it was now widely used in crime rings as an organizational center. Which, I quickly learned, was the point.

Trita strode from the shadows to meet us. I could hear people inside the ramshackle warehouses talking to one another, chairs scraping on the floor. She had a finger to her lips, though, and moved with the calculated ease of a seasoned warrior.

"You look like you disapprove of this place," Trita said when she got close enough. She wore men's clothes, as she often favored, made of dark leather. But more buckles, and hanging off the buckles, knives. She smelled of flux.

"It's a sad place," I said. "It's hard to feel otherwise."

"Sadness is in your perspective," said Trita, nodding somewhat sympathetically. "And yours is not yet set, young as you are. Hasn't La Roche taught you the long, fraught history of humankind? If there's one thing they're good at, it's finding new and creative ways to torture one another, century after century."

"I'd read about it. I'd never seen it. It's different," I pointed out.

"Well, my saintly friend, the good news is I brought you here to help, if you consent to administering your considerable girth to the issue. Within these walls are some unsavory individuals I've been tracking for some time. Their crimes are many, but it's particularly the defacing of the Globe two weeks ago that has me moved to action. In addition, you can add vandalizing, extorting, and murdering a prostitute to their long list of ills. I am not typically in favor of frightening them and have no intention of killing. But seeing as I have asked nicely, and their response was to call me a slur so offensive I will refrain from uttering it in your presence, I have asked you two along."

"So, you want me to hurt them," I said, not guessing.

She rolled her shoulders. "If the situation calls for it. Perhaps just seeing our combined grandeur will convince them otherwise, though I doubt it. Wisdom and war are both part of my ken, you see. And I work very hard to ensure the second is only used when absolutely necessary."

"I don't like hurting people," I said.

"Such candor, my heavens," Trita said.

"It's part of his charm," La Roche said.

"If you say so," Trita replied doubtfully. I liked the way they bantered. Their minds working against one another in a most riotous way. I hoped to one day be as sharp. "Yes, you are correct to go slowly into the fray. These human beings are more than the sum of their actions: they are fathers, some of them. Providers. Citizens. Husbands. One, Heb Marcullis, even worked for me at a time at the Globe, cleaning up after our shows. I blessed his daughter when she was born." She sighed sharply, disgusted. "But I have learned that some human beings addle their wits so fully the only way to get through their heads is by breaking them."

I felt La Roche's hand on my arm, warm as if he had been sitting by the fire. "This is your ken, as well, Joss. Battle. Justice. You know, all the grit and brawn and big explosions. Godlings' strengths often intersect, as you may suspect. And Trita is the right one to guide you in this direction, rather than say, Calvinius. Violence is not for the faint of heart, nor is it to be taken lightly. And it certainly is not my ken."

"Neither of you have to help. I'm perfectly capable of dispensing with these roaches," Trita said, shouldering one of her weapons. "But I do entreat you to watch. You might even learn something."

Trita pointed to our left. Decrepit crates lined the side of the building, but they were not simply refuse. They covered a ramshackle entrance, either unguarded or unapparent to the thieves and ruffians within. I crouched down low, then realized I would have to crawl on my hands and knees.

"I fit better this way," said La Roche, flying by my head and into the space between the walls in his rook form.

"We're not all so lucky to sprout wings," I muttered.

We were quiet, the three of us. Quiet in the way I suppose human beings cannot be. Especially Trita. Watching her move, her feet never on the ground longer than absolutely necessary, her spine and her body angled, prepared. It was remarkable to observe. I kept pace behind her, but not with as much grace. Just because I was quiet didn't mean I was terribly effective at the approach.

We skirted our way behind crates and boxes, walls erected behind shabby sailcloth. The voices got louder, and Trita held up her hand to keep me quiet. La Roche took up his favorite spot on my shoulder, his talons a little less brutal now that there was fabric between the two of us. I had a moment of modesty, thinking about our evenings at the Temple of Venus, but it passed quickly.

"There were supposed to be two bodies," came a voice from deeper within the compound. Sharp. Assertive. Used to giving orders, used to not getting what they wanted. But then, I reasoned, also used to giving orders impossible to meet.

"One of them got away. The boy," said another voice, rough and low.

"Got away?" asked the first voice, incredulous.

I craned my neck and was able to get a better view of what I couldn't sense. There were four figures crouched around a pile of bodies in burlap bags, their stench beginning but not quite obvious. They had been dead just a short time. Something smelled off about them all the same, and I couldn't place it.

Another voice: "The boy was sick."

"What do you mean?" asked the first voice. "Sick, like a cold?"

"No, sick like—coughing. Didn't want to be near 'em."

"Sounds like a cold."

"Coughing *blood*," the rough voice explained. "Didn't want to get mixed up in that, you reckon? Londinium is a shit place, but it's not a sick place. Not until recently."

Initially I thought little of the revelation, but I felt La Roche tense, hiss. Every feather fluffed, and his head went down. It meant something more to him. Trita signaled to keep listening.

"The All Father has long kept us free of such illnesses," said the master, but his voice was shaken. "You must have been seeing things."

"I know what I saw," said the man. "I *know*. Didn't want to touch him."

"Probably dead, anyway," said another, shorter

"Now, gentleman!" said Trita, leaping forward. "I told you if the vandalism didn't stop I was going to take matters into my own hands."

"Ah, the fucking Moor," said the shorter man. "We're not afraid of you."

She laughed at the lie.

It would make a much better tale if I said I was a masterful fighter from the moment I stepped forward with Trita, and my moves precise and effective and impressive. But that would be a significant lie.

I froze. And gaped. And did nothing.

Trita, now. She fought in a brutal, smart, measured way. I believe full well she knew I'd be little to no help, and La Roche had no intent of fighting either. Trita knew, without a doubt in her shrewd mind, she was fully capable to taking all those men and rendering them unconscious.

Here's about how the fight went.

Early on, after I stopped staring, I got caught up watching Trita move with her weapon, a long staff of some kind, and metal-tipped. La Roche flew up and away to the rafters, leaving me to gawk after the woman as she slipped deftly into the cluster of stinking men and chopped away at them with the agility of a serpent and the strength of ten. They did not have time to react to her, for they were so surprised. One had just enough time to call her a name, something to do with the color of her skin, as I recall, but she shut his mouth very quickly and freed him from the burden of his clacking, mossy teeth.

Trita Oya fought with pure discipline, her movements never wasted or exaggerated. She waited more than she attacked, sizing up her opponents and then taking them down with practical speed and precision. When the most oafish of the fellows found their way toward her, I was certain she would have a challenge. But he was favoring one foot—even I could see that—and it took just a twist to the left for the man to come crashing down on his knee. She clocked him about the head with a long board, and he fell, unmoving, to the dirty ground.

I did not notice the man coming up to me until I felt a pinprick of pain below my rib. I had been standing there for quite some time, an enormous spectator too dull to even notice a knife sliding through his skin.

Reaching down, I pulled out the knife and examined it, confused. A small trickle of blood ensued—I had never cut myself badly enough to see actual blood—and then a gush of water.

My assailant might have been sixteen years old, judging by his gait and the look of his face. He was briefly surprised at my action and, likely, my lack of response. But he was worn, tired. He had not been nourished physically or emotionally. His eyes had the look of a man beyond hope.

Still I did not attack him. I did not see the need to. He was no real threat to me.

"I'm sorry," I said, though I wasn't sure why.

He came at me again with another knife, but I turned it away by twisting his arm with my hand. I felt a snap, a bone popping out of place, and he fell to the ground whimpering like a babe.

You see? Far from poetry in motion.

La Roche did not fight, not even in his bird form. He perched high above us and watched.

Trita finished the hard work. I stomped menacingly behind her and propped up the unconscious or moaning thieves as needed, tying them up with rope she threw my way. When all was said and done, I'd broken a young man's arm and frightened a few others with growling. Truly spectacular.

We tied the leader to a chair and made sure he was conscious enough to talk.

"You're good with knots," La Roche said, coming down upon my shoulder to observe my work. I shivered as he flexed his talons. "Makes sense. Nets and oceans and all."

Trita wiped at her mouth. A trickle of blood stained her hand behind and she scowled at it. The man remaining was tall and wiry, perhaps thirty years of age. He squinted and trembled in our presence, looking back and forth between Trita and me as if we were going to devour him to the bone.

Pressing one finger into his chest, Trita growled at the man. "Humphrey Migdal."

He nodded before the name was even out completely. "Yes, ma'am."

"What did I tell you the last time we crossed paths?"

Migdal's face blanched and he spared a glance at his fallen comrades. "That—that you'd reach so far…so far down my throat you'd pull out my—"

"Yes…" Trita pressed. "Your what?"

"My—y-yellow liver," he finished.

"You are a bully and a thief. You've apparently considered my warnings to be merely empty threats and no more. But I promise you, every word I utter—every curse and blessing—is pregnant with promise."

"I'm sorry."

"You're sorry? You're *sorry?*"

"I am! I swear!"

"Ah, you're not sorry now. But I'll make you."

Migdal shrieked, falling to his knees. I saw snot spew from his nose as he began to sob.

"Let's not kill him if we don't have to," I said.

Trita gave me a warning look and I decided it best to keep my opinions to myself.

But she didn't kill the captive, and La Roche just clucked a bit at my ear, almost like a mother hen might to her chicks.

"Do you know what that word means, *sorry?*" Trita asked Migdal, though it was clear she wasn't anticipating an answer. "It's an old word from the Saxons and the Angelisc. Originally it meant riddled with sores. To be sore. To be hurt. To be in *pain*. I do not think you are well-represented of this now, but you will find, in the weeks to come you are overwhelmingly sore in your ass. Every time you sit down, it will hurt. And until you give the majority of your fortune to the Globe Theatre, anonymously of course, you will be in pain every waking moment."

She leaned forward and pressed the metal tip of her staff to Migdal's forehead. His eyes rolled back a moment, and I was sure he was going to begin frothing at the mouth from some sort of seizure. But then he blinked and looked around.

"Now go," Trita said. "You've a donation to give."

Migdal frowned, pain registering across his face, and then nodded. "Yes, I do."

As he hobbled away, he never looked at me or at La Roche. He didn't even take care for his wounded friends. One by one, Trita pressed her staff to their foreheads, too, and most of them fell asleep.

7

We reconvened at the Swan and Hoop the next evening to discuss our first adventure, and though I was full of observations I waited until Trita had her fill of food before I started in on it. I was learning to be polite, I suppose, though I think I've lost my manners in the ensuing years.

At last sated, Trita pushed back from her chair and leveled me with her round, intense gaze. "There, now you may ask your questions."

"More like critiques, really," I said.

La Roche snorted into his goblet.

"Then critique away, good sir." Trita did not smile, but her voice lost its sharpness.

I leaned toward her, thinking myself important, imposing. "Seems like taking vengeance into your own hands is something of a habit."

She grinned. "I did keep a vow of peace for two hundred years, but I grew tired of it. War is part of me, deep in my bones, and I can only ignore the clarion call for so long. So now, I keep the streets safer than I leave them, and while I could devote my entire life, such as it is, to these endeavors, I find that just enough havoc works best. The rumors of me are just as powerful as my own actual presence."

"But no one remembers you," I pointed out.

"Precisely. A least, not clearly enough for incrimination."

"It's your spear. You do some sort of magic with it."

"It is," she said with a shrug. "It was a gift to me, from long, long ago. In plain terms, it muddies the memory of the mortal who comes into contact with it. And so, I remain, for the most part, incognito."

"An essential component to her heroics," added La Roche, "considering her current run at the Globe."

"Which is almost at an end," she pointed out. "I have had my fun. And the revolution needs a little more of a push than what I can provide from the stage. The Marians, Miriam's followers, are not in line with public performances of a political bent. So, I'm afraid I'll have to discuss matters with her directly."

La Roche and Trita exchanged looks in an uncomfortable silence.

"I haven't met Miriam yet," I said.

"No, you haven't. But that may change soon," La Roche said. "She's invited us to dine with her at Marmor House, where she currently resides, to meet you."

"I'd much rather just fight things," I replied. Nothing I'd heard about Miriam made me anxious to meet her.

"Well, I can't guarantee you'll manage to keep avoiding Miriam, but I can help you learn to fight more effectively," Trita said.

"Aye. A good idea."

Trita smiled more deeply this time, and I could tell it was just what she had been hoping I'd say.

So Trita taught me how to fight. She was glad to see I had some propensity with basic weaponry but didn't feel as if I'd need it much. While she implied I had far greater reserves of power, she wanted to be certain I knew the basics of defense so I wasn't sloppy. She called me a natural learner. I just didn't find it particularly difficult, and admittedly it felt good to do something with my body that was a challenge.

She told me the way she fought was taught to her by a master in the Far East, but the style wasn't suited to my form. But there were many other approaches she knew, and she drilled me for hours in the early hours of the morning on the Globe stage for weeks.

La Roche was glad to hear of my hobby, but he only sometimes came along. And always as a rook.

I felt myself grow stronger, my head clearer, as I absorbed Trita's lessons. I liked fighting against her, but I liked fighting with her the most.

I could feel and anticipate her movements. It was more like dancing than fighting. We dispensed with ruffians when we could, and though we could never tackle every crime, I learned more about people and Londinium through our good works.

But then came the inevitable.

"If there was a way around this, I would have found it," La Roche said as he entered my room, holding out a new suit for me. "Miriam sent this along. In your exact measurements."

"She's paying attention, then," I said.

"She's always paying attention. We've spent mountains of energy trying to worm our ways out of the summons, but it is her right to do so."

I put the suit on the bed and looked it over. It was magnificent. Steel blue wool, embroidered silver cuffs, and a sailor's hat like the one I'd been wearing about, but this one made of an expert hand. Brushed beaver pelt. She'd even had a pair of boots delivered.

"I don't like formality," I said.

La Roche laughed. "It is a place where you and I cannot disagree more. My friend, at very least, you will have the opportunity to see one of the stateliest homes in all of Londinium and its surrounds, eat the most delectable food the island has to offer, and have a chance to size up Miriam. To decide which side of things you are on."

"I'm only on my side," I said, thinking back to what Verta had told me in the cemetery so many weeks before.

I could tell that stung a little, and La Roche cleared his throat, looking busy by arranging the clothes on the bed.

"Well, however you view yourself, there is no doubt you will need her at least on the better side of neutral. She is powerful, and she is waxing. Like a great moon in the heavens, building power and magnetism. I've never seen the city like this before. The Marians are ushering in a new age of propriety." He half spat the last word from his mouth and shuddered. "But if we can't see what she's doing we won't have any recourse."

"I feel a bit like bait," I admitted. "Dangling there so she'll have audience with you."

"We are not on bad terms, Miriam and I…we are just at a stalemate. And we are all attending. Even Verta."

That got my attention. "I thought she never left."

"As I said, Joss, Miriam is growing in power. We all must learn to live with it."

Marmor House was, in a word, doleful. Amidst the blooms and blossoms of a deep Brittanic spring, Miriam's house stood as still and bleak as a mausoleum, under the shadow of newly built aqueducts, set upon a large field. Situated in this way, the three-story home rose like a tooth, white and stark and unwelcoming. All the natural landscape about it had been beaten back to manicured lawns, and though the intent was probably well-meant, the result was a rather foul-smelling view of the Tamesis.

What I noticed immediately was the utter silence of the place. How strange it was to me that I had become accustomed to the loudness of London, the ever-present din of human beings, and the thick press of water, blood, bile, and the dozens of other substances found in cities like it. We weren't far from the city, really, but it felt like a thousand miles away.

La Roche squinted up at the mansion and then looked back at me, a rather apologetic look on his face.

"If I could avoid this, I would," he said, straightening the lapel of his jacket.

He had dressed us both with care and expense; admittedly, he did cut an impressive figure in his satin-lined jacket and bright, bold burgundy hues. I, on the other hand, looked like an overgrown ape stuffed inside a blue sausage casing. The collar was the worst part, tightly tied about my neck so it was impossible to get a full range of motion.

"Stop pulling at your collar, Joss. You are a gentleman."

"I most certainly am not. I'm an irascible old godling of the sea who doesn't like dinner parties," I growled.

"You have made your distaste well known," he replied, walking ahead of me and swinging the ornamental cane he wore with ease and poise. He made everything look easy. "But when it comes to Miriam, I'm afraid there just isn't another option. You must look the part. She will seize on any opportunity to discredit you, to make you appear less. It's her way."

"I'm not sure why we're giving her so much of our time," I grumbled. Dressing in frocks has never been a favored pastime of mine, but it was far preferred to company of a pompous godling with a superiority complex.

"Because it's polite."

"Polite is overrated."

"My friend, polite is a best first line toward progress. We play her game, do as we're expected, and then in time if she does not work with us, we dispense with the nicety."

VERTA HAD GONE AHEAD of us, and her gilded carriage—chipping paint in places, but still rather impressive—remained outside the house. There was another, as well, no doubt the one that had carried Calvinius and Trita, sleek black and silver.

Inside, the house opened up in the current fashion, all staircases and doorways, a line of maids draped in high-collared robes greeting us. They each carried roses in one hand, some crimson and others a deep purple hue, and did not meet our eyes.

"Miriam's acolytes," whispered La Roche, likely replying to my confused expression. "It is a bit over the top, but part of her charm."

I smelled the sharp tang of blood and noticed the acolytes were clasping the roses with their bare fingers, the thorns piercing their skin.

"I'd hardly call it charming," I said to him. "I'd call it brutal."

"She calls it *discipline.*"

We were ushered down a long corridor, the air smelling faintly of sawdust, the plush carpets meticulously woven. I had the sudden desire to take off my shoes and run the bottoms of my feet across the warp and weft, but was self-aware enough to think twice.

I could smell dinner cooking as we approached the grand dining hall: at least three kinds of meat, Persian spices, grilled fruit, dark bread, and lots of wine.

The grand dining hall was open all the way to the roof, light streaming in through a kaleidoscope of stained glass in a rose pattern above us. It was easy to miss the rest of the room with such a view, and it was a good thing that there was so much light. The furniture was all staid, without embellishment, but polished with precision. The deep red linens matched the roses, and the flowers on the table were red and white roses, spilling from an enormous vase across the tablecloth. I think it was meant to look whimsical, but it felt incongruous with the rest of the room.

Miriam—there was no doubt it was her, for though I sensed her dimly, I knew her impression on my mind—stood at the head of the table, her eyes drinking in her new guests. She was not as large a woman as I imagined; indeed, she was almost half my size. Broad across the shoulders and forehead, she had a kind of sturdy symmetry I found impressive. Nothing about her could be considered beautiful, exactly, and yet she was well-made. Her hair was tied back in a severe, smooth bun. Like her acolytes, she wore billowing robes covering her neck and down to the very edge of her wrists. All black. No adornment. Well, save the stern look on her face, which was cold as any silver.

On her left sat Verta, a vision in saffron and bronze. A perfect contrast to Miriam's considerably more conservative appearance, every line of her body pulled close to the saffron material, a kind of sheer silk. Her dark brown skin was a gorgeous contrast, her long hair spiraling down her shoulders in thick, twin braids spun with floss.

Trita looked as Trita always did, but this time her masculine attire was a little smarter than usual. And Calvinius was clean-shaven and wore a brown suit with a wide lapel and neck scarf not unlike my own.

"Well, La Roche. For once, you did not exaggerate. My heavens, he's a veritable giant."

Those were the first words Miriam spoke in my presence, the timbre of her voice causing a strange sense of dissonance in my ears.

"Miriam, it is my pleasure to introduce you to Joss Raddick," La Roche said with a grand sweep of his hand.

I walked forward and bowed to Miriam as La Roche had shown me how to do. When I stood again to my full height, I saw her gazing up at me in what I can only describe as awe.

"Well, I'm glad you finally decided to assent to my invitation," Miriam said, gesturing to where I would sit. At her right. "La Roche has kept you busy, or so I hear."

Whenever she spoke, I could feel, or hear, a whining in the back of my mind. I glanced a little nervously at La Roche, but he did not indicate anything was amiss. So, we all took our seats and began to eat.

"I have been studying," I said as the plates of the first course came out. Raw venison with pickled berries. "La Roche has been very kind to take me under his wing."

"His wing! How clever," Miriam said, cackling to herself. No one laughed, and Verta looked very intent on her food. Now that I had a better look at her, I saw the makeup on her face. I hadn't seen her with any kind of enhancement before, and it took me a moment to focus back on the conversation at hand.

"He is a very good teacher," I said.

"You flatter me," La Roche said in his easy way. "I am no such thing. You are a talented, driven student."

"I can't imagine Londinium would make you happy though," Miriam said, off-handedly. She took a tiny nibble of the raw venison as if making sure it was edible. "Someone of your talents would be better served in the wilderness, I would think. How do you manage without water?"

"There is plenty of water here, ma'am," I replied, unsure at what she was getting at. She had a way of twisting the words in everyone's mouths, and I couldn't quite understand how she was doing it. "The aqueducts fascinate me, in fact, and I was thinking of spending some time learning their ways, to see if I can be of any service in their building and maintenance."

"How amusing," Miriam said. "You're fond of human architecture."

"I am," I said. "I've not been long among humankind, but I find their innovation inspiring."

"Inspiring," Miriam echoed. Her eyes traced my face and then down to my plate. "You do not like venison? It's from my own wood."

"He doesn't eat meat," La Roche said. "A particular quirk I find a bit amusing. But occasionally irritating."

"Well, I would have preferred you mentioned such a detail to me before I went through the trouble of making this meal, La Roche," Miriam said, though it was clear she didn't make it. "It is rather inconsiderate given the circumstances of my hospitality."

An acolyte took my plate and I saw the deep scratches on her fingers where thorns had dug deep. It made my stomach churn.

I didn't know how to respond to Miriam and I looked desperately across the way, hoping Verta might rescue me. But she was intent on her food. Calvinius had that lopsided grin on his face, curious at the events.

Trita was my savior. "We've tried everything," she said, trying to break into a smile. Instead, she looked strained. Stressed. I could not imagine that anything had the capacity to make Trita Oya stressed. "But he somehow keeps his build with bread and fruit and vegetables. Though he is quite fond of cheese. The saltier the better."

"Then I will bring out more bread and fruit and vegetables," Miriam said uneasily. "And cheese. We have an aged Gaulish céadar just in."

We fell into silence as we ate, and I took more than my share of bread to make up for the unintended offense. The cheese was quite good, though I preferred the local fare at the Swan and Hoop if I was honest. For all Miriam's pride, it was a bit hard to chew.

Part of the way through our meal, I began to find myself aware of music playing. Between the clinking of our silverware and the ever-present sound of people chewing meat—truly abhorrent to me, still—I recognized a far-off melody, not unpleasant, but strange. I tried to look to La Roche for confirmation, but he was seated on the same side as I was between myself and Calvinius. Strategic on Miriam's part, I suppose, but wholly frustrating for me.

It was not until dinner's end when Miriam began speaking again. This time, she was purely rehearsed. I suspected there was something in the wine; La Roche had warned me time and again of Miriam's power. I simply had a hard time believing she was stronger than me. Certainly, she was more experienced, I had no doubt. But I had believed, in my rather naïve state, that on raw power she would not light a candle to me.

I was wrong.

We were in her demesne. Literally and figuratively. The home, the house, the table. Her power was at its apex, here, and though the Tamesis was not far away, the captive water of the aqueducts did little to bolster my own power.

"I have, of course, brought you all here for a reason," she said, standing to her full height and raising her glass. "It is not lost on me that you all have plenty of other engagements you would much rather attend to at the moment, but I would like to remind you we are family. You may not much like me, or each other. But we are the gods of Londinium, and we are its beating heart. We, together, have kept the memory of Mother Rome alive, have weaned and fed her over the centuries. We may not be a complete pantheon, but we are growing in power."

I heard La Roche clear his throat, but he said nothing else. Verta was looking at the contents of her wine glass rather than at Miriam.

"That said, there are two matters we must speak of this evening. One is a large matter and one is a smaller matter. I will begin with the former," Miriam said, leaning forward on the table. The wood strained with the pressure, groaning like the planks on a ship. "Most of you are well aware war is coming. No, war has commenced already. My enemy has sent forces as far as Gaul, now, crossing our sacred border set apart decades before. He has amassed an impressive following in the Persian strongholds to the South, developing new technology where he cannot make headway with his own power."

"Gaul," Trita said, the news clearly a surprise for her. She looked across the table at La Roche, a line between her eyes. "We have heard nothing of this, Miriam. It grieves me to think of forces so close to our borders."

"As it should. My acolytes have a reach far and wide and have retrieved not a few captives from the fray. They, for now, have come only so far as Lyon. Trita, my general and my warrior, it is time for you to take up again the spear and the blade, I fear. I will need your tactical mind and your influence to help guide me."

Trita nodded. "Yes, Miriam. Of course."

I could not believe she was so straightforward about it. So willing to comply. I knew Trita did not like or trust Miriam, and yet, she was not even offering an argument.

Both Trita and Miriam raised their glasses to one another and drank.

"And Calvinius. La Roche tells me your prowess in recreating the potions and apothecary advances has led you to some fascinating research. I would ask you share any such recent work you believe may help us. In fact, it may be time to send a few of you to Ancyra, where I know there is a trove of such recipes waiting to be found."

"Of course," Calvinius said, raising his glass and sipping, as Miriam did in reflection.

"Verticordia," Miriam continued, smiling tightly at her next prey. "Oh, what to do with a waning god? I have thought long and hard on this matter, have measured all the possible contributions you could make. But given your history with my greatest enemy, I do not think you are best suited to any roles of action. And given your clear health struggles, it would not be a kindness to put you in such a place, either. So I only ask you one thing: to not meddle. To remain in Londinium, in your temple, with your acolytes. To avoid converting new followers. And when the time is right, using what influence you have left to guide more followers to the Marian cause."

I felt the blow of Miriam's words, even though Verta remained ice-faced through the barrage of insults. I knew Achaemenes had a history with Verta, but I would have thought her a benefit, not a drawback, in this fight against him. And she was capable of so much more than keeping to her temple! She was not waning so severely, was she? I had seen the power of her, time and again, had learned from her gentle ways.

It occurred to me this tension it was deeper than it appeared. Hera and Aphrodite. Ancient grudges come to a head after centuries: the marriage bed and the courtesan's palette. She wanted Verta out of her way.

"Of course, Miriam," Verta said, without hesitation. She raised her glass, sipped, and watched Miriam do the same. Unflinching.

"And now, we come to our giant," Miriam said, turning her gaze to me.

I could hear that infernal music rising around me once again, twisting through my brain. I pushed against it, felt my temples throb with the pain. Sweat beaded on my back, under my eyes. "What are we to do with you? I have to admit, I'm not even certain I know *what* you do."

"He is…" La Roche began, but then fell silent.

"Capable of speaking for himself," Miriam said.

I cleared my throat. "I am still yet understanding my abilities," I said, even though the music had made its way to my teeth, rattling against my skull. "But I command water, most of the time. I can sense things, especially in humans, related to the balance of their humors. Whether or not they are ill, for instance."

"And can you heal them?" Miriam asked.

"No," I said. "I don't think so."

She did not look impressed. "Can you perform minor illusions?"

"Sometimes," I replied. "Though not consistently."

"And combat?"

"I am learning."

"Not very promising," Miriam said, looking to Trita, who gave her a shrug. "But I suppose you are still young. In this, then, I will ask you to work closely with Trita Ora. I am aware you already have found yourself of use in the seedier districts, and I am not opposed to such behavior so long as it continues to be covert. We may be the gods of Londinium, but we are not, my dears, intended to live among humans as saviors."

I raised my glass to her and sipped, knowing she had not created for me any significant challenge, compared to the other godlings present.

"And Andrew La Roche," Miriam cooed, tilting her head in an almost girlish way. "My shining sun. Our Apollo." She let the words linger a moment more before continuing, dragging out the suspense. I felt ill at ease, again. I didn't like the way she spoke to him. "You have a strange habit of finding loopholes, of manipulating situations for your better purposes. I would like you to remain as Joss's teacher, but I also implore you to look after yourself."

What a strange thing to say. I thought little of it, but La Roche apparently did not; he paled as I had never seen him do so before. He sipped, nodded, and said nothing. The idea of anyone rendering Andrew La Roche mute was a perplexing thing, indeed.

"Now that we are all settled, I must remind you of some lesser matters. You are free, as is your right, to inspire, to boast, to enlighten the streets of Londinium as you wish. You are all gods, after all, and I cannot prevent you from meddling at all.

"However. Oh, however, my dears. Let us not meddle with human beings. We may save them from eminent danger, of course. But we do not deal in life and death. This means we do not change the threads of their lives. We do not twist the will of Fate. We do not procreate with them, even if we could, and we do not twist their lives to our desires. We may guide, we may inspire, but we may not—and I reiterate—do anything forceful."

Her eyes lingered on La Roche a moment, and when we all raised our glasses and drank, the music finally stopped, and dinner came to an end.

"Do not hesitate to find me," she said, as we prepared to leave. She took my elbow, and I felt a warmth go through me, entirely unexpected. I had anticipated a sense of revulsion when she came near, but it was not. "I know it is a difficult world in which we live, Mr. Raddick, and you are learning quickly. You have a few good friends, here, but you must remember, we are each the potential ruin to one another. We may wound with more than weapons. I have seen ages come and go, and I look forward to our friendship."

WE RETIRED to our homes and rooms, then, full of the strange enchantments Miriam laid upon us. I found I did not want to speak to the other godlings; I needed time to think.

Of course, within a day, La Roche sent an elaborate message written in his looping hand, declaring we all should meet at the Swan and Hoop for an important discussion on Rookery business.

We found La Roche sitting at a table laden for three, full of all our favorite things to eat—none of which were actually on the menu, but which he always managed to procure for us. It was an elegant departure from the meat-laden nonsense of Miriam's house.

I thought La Roche looked tired and I wanted to ask him, but Trita seemed unconcerned entirely and sat down, pouring herself a flagon of claret and dispensing with it swiftly.

"Delightful spread," she said after downing half her drink. "To what do we owe this pleasure, Master La Roche? I had thought we'd all remain stunned and frustrated and alone after Miriam's last enchantments."

La Roche tightened his scarf and smiled his sunbeam smile; for a moment I could not believe I'd been worried about him at all. "Oh, Trita. My darling. You know it takes much more than that irascible old witch to get me down. And truly, she got me to thinking. I am inspired."

"Oh?" Trita asked. "This doesn't usually end well. What crack scheme have you found yourself burdened with, La Roche?"

We all had to laugh at that.

"No, no, Trita, dear, please. Have you no faith in me?" La Roche asked.

"It depends on the phase of the moons," she said, half-joking. "Just like your moods."

"I am wounded, truly. But it does not matter in light of this discussion. Miriam is right: we are called, nay it is our duty, to participate more fully in the culture and art of Londinium at large. I believe it is time for an important discussion. First, some privacy," La Roche said. He twirled his fingers in the air and I was aware of the world shifting slightly as if a veil descended. He saved this kind of magic for important moments.

"As it so happens," La Roche continued, "the last thing I would want, after all the careful work we have done with our most impressive cadre, is to out ourselves to the general public. Such theatrics would be disastrous. However, it doesn't mean we can't have a little fun." He grabbed a pear and took a delicate bite of it, then made a face and put it down. "As I said, Miriam is fully in support."

Trita sat stiffly in her seat, the merriment gone from her face. This was not what she was expecting, I didn't think. I didn't know what La Roche was getting at either, and didn't like the constant discussions of Miriam. After her antics at the dinner, I was surprised to hear him saying her name over and over.

Still, I said nothing.

La Roche waved his hands again, gesturing to some invisible horizon only he could see. "It is in our natures, you see, to give more back to the world, to usher in a season of enlightenment with the powers granted to us. None of us will live forever, even if we try, and as you might have seen, I have a certain dedication to the arts, and poetry, in particular, to engender. It's a compulsion. And, well, if I'm honest, a bit of curious competition."

"Poetry, now?" Trita asked. She rolled her eyes. "Oh please, continue. I am beyond thrilled at the prospect of more doleful verse in the world."

"You scoundrel. I know you enjoy an elegiac stanza every now and again. And, besides, you can blame Calvinius for the inspiration; I merely took his happy circumstance and adapted it," La Roche said.

"If Calvinius inspired you, it must be quite the story," I said.

"Yes, Joss. It is! You see, he fell in love with a woman here in Londinium who was pregnant. He was distraught at this woman's status in life, and came to me full of sorrow and fear for her well-being. So, I let him in on a secret: we could, as godlings, bestow some of our power to mortals in the form of blessings. I had worked the spells myself, long ago, but was thrilled when he was capable of the same—after some practice and guidance, I am happy to report the woman's son is indeed a marvelous poet. He is full of the madness and brightness of poesy. I have never seen a mind like this young man's before in my life." No small words from La Roche, whose demesne was poetry itself.

"A mad poet, indeed, to be blessed by a godling of Chaos," I said.

At La Roche's words I was beset with a kind of anger, a jealousy, I could not understand. Calvinius? *He* had sired the greatest poet of the age? It was asinine. How could a child blessed by the mad alchemist know anything about what poetry truly meant to humanity and, indeed, to godlings too.

Trita, for her part, looked equally uncomfortable with those outrageous claims.

"Joss, just because something is chaotic does not make it less artful," said La Roche. "But what is more important is that Calvinius has since declared he has blessed the greatest poet of his age. Which, while rather adorable on his behalf, made me think about ushering in our own golden age of poetry with bit of a competition."

"A poet competition," said Trita.

"A boast," said La Roche, and I knew he was using an older word than the one he spoke. "And it has already begun. You see, before bringing anyone else into our little game, Verta and I decided to bless our own children. It has never been a challenge for me to find such willing minds. And for Verta, well, she had many compliant friends in the gentility who loved the idea of a literal fairy godmother."

He drained his glass and called for more, and we all topped off again. La Roche cleared his throat. "Verta was more fruitful earlier on in the progression, siring her first in '87, whilst my child is somewhere about two at the moment. Ideally, given the lengths and memories of humankind, we have a specific deadline: the year 1800. All others blessed afterward will be out of contention."

"Your child must have a name," I said. I needed to know details. "A country. A temperament. You can't have just chosen him from nothing."

"He is scarcely two summers, as I said, and he likely has more brothers and sisters on the way. I do not desire to be a part of his life directly, as I believe what I have bequeathed to him is enough, though detachment is not required. For my part, I wish him a childhood of fancy and flight, of fishing and hunting and natural things, while being taken care of. His parents will cherish him, and he will do great things. Poetry will always be at his heart because, as I am aware you all know, it is my greatest gift."

I was disgusted with his confidence, but his spell was working. This jealousy, this sense of competition, writhed inside my heart like a hooked fish. He awoke a part of my godling mind that had been dormant my whole life.

I muttered louder than I meant to: "You wouldn't know good poetry if it fell from the skies. I was *awakened* by poetry. It's in my blood."

La Roche grinned. "Oh, Joss. You are but a pup of a godling. It is quite the claim you make."

"As if either of you could compete with the poesy of battle, of wisdom," said Trita, eyes dark and contemplative.

La Roche burst out laughing, hands over his head in triumph. "You see, you can't *help* but be offended. Isn't it marvelous? It's part of who we are. This stirring, this Great Boast, is part of who we are. The oldest game in the world!"

We both looked doubtfully at him, mutually ashamed of our behaviors. I rubbed my eyes as if clearing sleep. It didn't help, but my fury somewhat abated.

"I feel like you're controlling us," I said. "Enchanting us."

"Joss, you wound me. I am simply arousing a most ancient power in you. How do you think the Greeks raised generation after generation of warriors, poets, scientists, and royals? They interfered. They blessed."

"What of Miriam?" Trita asked. "She is aware?"

La Roche continued, somewhat ruffled at her mention of Miriam. "She practically gave us permission at dinner, but of course there are rules." He spoke the last word as it tasted bad. "You may not attempt to sire a child upon another godling or directly upon a human, nor may you participate in any unkind procreation—no ravishment, confusion, potions, or spell-making under any circumstance. This is forbidden by Miriam's own ken, and she has promised to wreak havoc upon the child and its family. You are *blessing* the child. Not making the child. Though that doesn't mean you have to restrain yourself from consensual bedding. I would never forbid such a thing. So long as the child is not yours. Also, you may not prolong their lives nor harm the lives of the other children of the boast."

"And what of our bond to the child," I said, feeling as if he was leaving something out. "Surely with the blessing we will feel a connection."

La Roche seemed surprised by the question. "It is up to you. There are some complications with such a relationship, yes. If you decide to depart the world you will find it more difficult while they yet live, as those blessed are connected to us by holy forces known only to the First Godlings. For some, simply living near their blessed could be disorienting or distracting, and there is no guarantee either way. For others, it is powerful, intoxicating. Exciting. But no. It is not without risks."

I looked at La Roche and he met my gaze only briefly. He did not need me to say what I surmised. I was certain he liked the idea of a new golden age, but I knew even more certainly that this was the thorn between he and Verta. She had blessed a child and it was keeping her here, making her eventual departure even more painful. Clever, cruel La Roche.

Clearing his throat after we both were silent for a time, La Roche asked, "Well? What say you both?"

"I will take the challenge," Trita said before I could add my agreement. I wouldn't have, but didn't want to appear a coward to her.

"Aye," I replied. "I suppose, with the right teaching and guidance, I could do the same."

La Roche's smile returned, and he pulled out an exceptionally old coin from his breast pocket. Upon its head was a lyre, and on the other side the unmistakable face of Apollo in relief.

"It is an ancient piece," he said. "Discovered upon the ruins of Rome. Let it seal our pact and begin the Boast here, and then toast, as Miriam has taught us."

We held our hands over the coin and agreed to the terms, then drank ourselves into oblivion.

8

I knew right away who I would bless. Fanny Jennings was set to marry Thomas Keats. Though we had managed a few cursory conversations, I had yet to truly befriend her in the way I hoped. It was a considerable frustration, and yet I could think of no other family more deserving of a great poet. They worked so hard, Fanny and Thomas, yet money was always out of reach.

Admittedly, I was afraid of what would happen if I got too close to Fanny. If my passions overruled my emotions.

"I was thinking of asking Calvinius about a potion," I told La Roche one night, a few weeks after we had agreed to the boast. It was a gnawing concern, persistent and unyielding. I could scarcely think of anything else. "To see if maybe there was something I could take to quiet my mind."

La Roche and I sat together on the banks of the Tamesis, as we often did, throwing rocks and discussing the finer matters of being godlings. That day we had spoken of secret words—like the word for boast—as powerful as our own names if applied correctly. He was dressed warmly for the weather, a thick scarf around his neck, and I thought he looked a little pallid. Like a dimmed sun.

He laughed at my suggestion, and I felt a mix of shame and anger.

"I need help," I said.

"She's just a woman," La Roche continued. "And she clearly fancies you."

"I don't need assurance; I just need a bit of something to settle my nerves. When you shake, you're small enough no one notices. When I shake it's like an earthquake. I want her to trust me."

"You helped with their horses. They've told half the city about it," La Roche pointed out. "Don't you think you have enough clout with them already?"

When I did not reply, he sighed. "Well, there is Verta's tea. You've used it before, when you first visited the temple. Opium is not my preferred method of dulling the senses, but it did seem to work for you while you needed it. And now you've all manner of trysts, and I do not think a single one has complained. You're as gentle as a kitten."

"Not always," I said.

He cleared his throat, fiddling with the edge of his cuff. "Well, perhaps a tamed lion, then. I would recommend good, strong opium tea. It will dull your other abilities a bit, but ultimately you'll be safer for it, I think."

VERTA WAS MORE than glad to supply the tea for me, and, sure enough, I slowly became more integrated into Fanny's life. Primarily, I befriended Thomas, who was an easy man to like. We had a mutual love of horses, and Poetaster was always on his best behavior when he was around me. I spent my afternoons at the ostlery with Thomas, and Fanny would bring us food. She would sit in the hay, her dress hiked up to her knees, and nibble on the sandwiches—always cucumber for me—and nuts and sausages that she brought out, regaling us with stories of her patrons and discussing all manner of mundane human life. We cared for the horses, we delivered foals and fillies together, we built a better stable and a firmer financial situation for the family.

I loved it.

I was not accustomed to friendship in such a way. Yes, the godlings were my friends, but we had an intense, sometimes transactional relationship. We had a long time to get to know one another. I knew I would live centuries more if I wanted to, and they would as well. But Fanny and Thomas were young—so young—and already starting to fade. Mortality is like a shroud I see on human beings, and it grows ever more opaque as they age.

They took me into their home and served me dinner at least twice a week. When I wasn't working on drills with Trita, or taking lessons with

La Roche, I became a regular fixture at the Swan and Hoop. And I think I was happy. Simpleton I was, dulled with opium, I did not think the story would be anything but a celebration. I would give their firstborn gifts beyond their imagining; his talent would support them. And I would win the boast.

Ah, to be so dim-witted again.

I first noticed Fanny was pregnant when she came to bring me water one afternoon in the stables. Thomas was out on errands and, as he was wont to do, he trusted me with the day-to-day upkeep inside.

She looked pale and had a subtle scent of vomit on her. Still beautiful, her dark eyes took me in.

"Evening, Fanny," I said, straightening up and bowing low.

"Oh, Joss, don't," she said, dismissing my formality with a wave of her hand. "It's embarrassing."

"The horses don't mind," I said.

She was breathing fast, shallow. Her dark eyes continued to drink me in, to move across my face, my chest. I was in my working clothes, stripped down to just my trousers and a loose chemise, yet I felt very naked, indeed.

"Fanny. You are unwell."

It took me a moment to understand everything happening, for many occurrences clicked into place at once. I understood there was a child inside of her, and the child was a boy, the very child I had hoped for. I also understood she and Thomas were not yet married, their relative poverty and work strain making the formality unattainable.

Above all, I was aware of her lips upon mine. How she was suddenly, gloriously, in my arms. Her head smelled of hay and sandalwood, her skin sour but not unpleasant. She slipped her hands purposefully down the sides of my hips.

"Please," she said softly against my chest, "Joss, there won't be much time. I need to know the feel of you before my life is decided."

"Shh," I said. "If you want me, there is no shame in it."

"Joss, I need to tell you—"

"You're with child. His child. I know."

I wish I could say I had better judgement than to take a man's fiancée in carnal lust.

But I didn't.

We didn't need words. Yes, Thomas was my friend, but he was also my competition—if one can consider such a thing between a godling and a human.

And she wanted me, utterly. Even through the dullness of the opium, I could feel her desire rippling off her body in whorls and eddies, her heat and her power impressive. Though I do not doubt some human beings possess their own arcane abilities, others have it in other measures; Fanny Jennings power was in her surety, her pride, her awareness of her body. And heavens above, awareness of *my* body.

Unlike the trained acolytes of Verta's temple, Fanny devoured me with a curious, but less methodical, hunger. She undressed me swiftly, trembling fingers exploring the broadness of my chest, the slope of my shoulders, the roughness of my beard. Her cheeks flushed bright when I met her with a smile, and she kissed me again, so hard I caught my breath. Kissing her was an art in itself, a game of push and pull as ancient and powerful as the oceans themselves. Her hair fell around my groping hands like a dark, silken waterfall.

I felt myself entirely lost to her. The heat of her sex blazed against my leg as she arched her back to come closer to me, her small fingers finding the buttons on my pants and freeing me.

She gasped, then gave a sultry giggle, and ran down the length of me with her hands, exploring with confidence.

Oh, how to put it into words. I had known pleasure before in Verta's temple. I had learned how to please my partners, how to measure their responses, and respond in kind.

But I had never tangled such a way with a mortal. I had never been wanted, so purely and nakedly.

When I entered her, I felt as if my body had been turned inside out. My head spun and I uttered words that may have been words of power but were in no language I knew. She groaned in pleasure and we slipped to the ground, she atop me, half-undressed, one bare breast displayed between the long strands of her hair. Looking up at her I wondered if I had been mistaken all my life about godlings and humans, if she was not, perhaps, a goddess herself.

Then she began to move, gripping me with her thighs, and I reached up to take her breasts in my hands. She was so small but so powerful. Demanding, in fact. And I did not mind. Verta's acolytes provide pleasure as a service; Fanny pleasured me out of a deep need, and my body made no argument.

When we were finished, we lay together as the moon moved behind the clouds.

We did not speak.

And it did not happen again.

I did not go back to the ostlery in the same capacity as before. The winter turned to spring and between the mud and the boom of customers, the Keats family was simply too busy. At least twice a week, I worked with Thomas on the horses, but it was with more silence than before. I was unsure whether or not Fanny had told him, but she certainly did not seek me out. Oh, when we crossed paths, we were ever polite and on good terms. But as she became more heavily pregnant, I knew—and she knew—too much attention would be unwelcomed.

Samhain night, the locals called it. The night where the old Celtic tribes, so long beat back or else integrated into Roman society, believed the veil between the real world and the world of the dead was the thinnest. I never much believed in their kind of religion; as far as I knew there was no world beyond death, unless you were a godling.

I was in my rooms upstairs when I heard a knock on the door.

There was Thomas Keats, panting and restless.

"It's Fanny. The baby has come," he said, shaking his head. "The midwife can't come fast enough, there's a Roman woman in greater need. And I thought since you'd helped with the foals..."

There was no need for him to continue. My blood boiled with fear, thinking Fanny was in peril.

We rushed together down to Fanny's quarters, where she was struggling against the pain in her bed. There was a young servant girl, one of Fanny's cousins if I recalled correctly, standing rather uselessly to the side with strips of cloth and fresh water.

The room smelled of blood and urine.

When Fanny met my eyes, she looked away.

"Fanny, listen to me," I said to her, putting a hand to her brow, gently. She was too warm. I took a nervous glance at Thomas. "I'd like to examine her if you don't mind."

"Of course," Thomas said, his trembling hands raking his hair. "She started this business early tonight. Her legs..."

Her legs were swollen terribly, purplish, and almost blistered. When I pressed into the flesh at her ankles it left an indent for a moment.

"Tell me when you first noticed something wrong," I said. I was no midwife, but I knew I could read the waters inside of her. I could feel the wrongness. In the back of my mind, I worried her condition was due to our coupling, but I pushed the fear away.

"Two days ago," Thomas said. "The midwife came by and said all was well, and then Fanny got hot to the touch and wasn't making much sense. Then, when Sally went to check on her, she started with the apoplexy."

"We need to get the child out," I said. "Thomas, I need you to pay attention to me. Have Sally boil water. I need to check how far along the child is."

A stillness came over me then. I had not had any opium to drink in a few days, and the crispness of the world was both stark and unforgiving. I saw these humans in all their sad, mortal truth. Fanny's body was failing her. It was rejecting the child as if it were some strange, alien interloper.

I had seen similar things in horses, but never to this degree. The child was turned slightly, and as I tried to examine more fully, Fanny's waters erupted. They smelled sweet, strange. I could sense the child within her even before I saw him with my eyes.

Had I been a more calculating godling, I would have begun the blessing there. But I could not think of the boast.

Fanny was dying. The woman I loved was slipping away.

"Fanny, you must heed me," I said, willing my voice to reverberate with certainty. "We must deliver the child now. You will die and he will die."

"I can't." She spoke with finality, that clarity I knew so well. "I'm sorry, Joss. I'm too tired."

"Fanny, you must. I cannot—we cannot live in happiness ever again if you leave us."

"Please, love," Thomas said, between his sobs. "Please, listen to Joss."

Sally came over with the hot water and I dipped the strips of cloth in them, imbuing the water with my own power. It was not something the mortals could see, but it was a risk. I put each strip across her belly, whispering spells to bind strength to her, to keep her safe.

She pushed for almost an hour before she died.

It happened so suddenly. I saw her, like a star in the heavens, burning bright, and then... nothing. There was a squalling babe in my hands, sticky and covered with caul and blood, the cord still connecting him to his mother throbbing in time with his screams.

"Gods, Fanny!"

"No..."

Death and life.

I could not. She could not die. Blearily, I handed the child to his father and then turned to Fanny.

I was not trained in any such magic; I had no business doing such a thing. But she was made of water, was she not?

Putting my mouth upon hers, I breathed into her lungs. I called forth life and rebirth; I felt my own consciousness enter her body, felt the knitting together of her burst blood vessels, the weary heart and limbs, the purging of contaminated waters.

Still, she was not alive. Her body was woven back together, but she was not alive.

I had to find her in the mists.

"Joss," she said to me, "you should let me go."

"I can't," I said.

"Perhaps it's better this way."

"Your son needs you."

"He'll have you."

"No."

I found Fanny Jennings in the mist, and I froze the air around her, pulling her through the chill of death and back into her body. It was done, but she was broken. Something inside of her was missing. I screamed, knowing what horror I had brought up on her, what my selfishness had wrought.

I was thrown back to the hot, dark room once the deed was done, falling into the wall behind me and cracking the plaster, winded and drained.

Outside, thunder clapped.

Fanny Jennings opened her eyes, tears falling anew.

"What did you do?" she asked.

"I'm sorry," I said.

"Fanny!" Thomas was at her side.

I stumbled, standing.

"I don't know what you are, Joss Raddick," Thomas said weakly.

"The child." I looked at the bundle in Thomas's arms, dread coiling inside of me.

Thomas pressed the babe into my hands. "His name is John."

"It's a good name," I said, looking at his small, pinched face. I had almost forgotten about the boast, the fear of breaking Miriam's law crawling up my back. The wrongness I saw in Fanny Keats, the veil of mortality hanging over her like a funeral shroud.

Thunder again, closer and louder. The room shook.

I blessed the child, my tears falling on his face.

"He will be a boy of genius," I said. "Soft and kind, fond of claret, his heart and mind capable of greatness heretofore unseen. A true poet. A philosopher. A child whose name is writ on water."

WHEN I ARRIVED at Verta's temple I was weeping, and so, too, were the skies. The storm had intensified, and I could not rightly understand how I got to the temple so fast; I knew Miriam would find me. I had broken her law. And La Roche would not understand.

Verta was there to greet me as if by some magic portent, and her eyes were filled with tears. She took me in and held me as I wept, sobbing like a snuffling horse in the middle of the winter. I could scarcely breathe at first, but as she held me, I felt the comfort of her rise around me, calm me down, just as I had once done with Poetaster.

When at last I could open my eyes, I noticed there was no one in the brothel to speak of. The priestesses were gone, else dismissed. Like La Roche, Verta had a habit of being able to set the stage before she even knew the scene.

"Miriam cannot find you here, not yet," Verta said. "This is yet my demesne and I will keep her away while I can."

"I couldn't let her die," I told her. "I should have, but I couldn't."

"Hush. You need to rest. You performed great magic tonight; the Tamesis itself rose over the banks, rising to your power."

She brewed tea, chamomile and lavender, and had me bathe in the pool. Then she wrapped me up in blankets and sat me down beside the fire.

We did not speak. We did not need to. I dozed in and out, watching the flickering flames move about the hearth. For a moment, I thought I saw a face hovering above mine, shadowed and dark, and startled. I rubbed my eyes and saw nothing.

"You snore," Verta said, going to the fire and gently stoking it with the bellows. It was a few hours before the dawn.

"I'm tired," I said. "But it's a weariness sleep does nothing for."

She sighed, her round shoulders going up and down beneath the thick velvet on her blanket. Her dark hair was completely loose, falling to the back of her knees in corkscrew curls. I'd never seen her dressed so, casual and yet refined. Verta's face was paler than the last time I remembered, and she wore none of her precious bangles.

"I don't know what got into me," I said, feeling the weight of it upon me again. "I didn't think I was even capable of such things."

"It's Andrew to blame for this. He should have been there to guide you, to help you."

"He said I wasn't ready to learn such magic. Such a thing asking for a catastrophe. I felt the wrongness, but I could not help myself."

"You did. And you will do more terrible things, Joss. Even when you believe with all your heart you are doing the right. Such is the struggle of our kind. We have power, but so often our humanity gets in our way. As it did for me, with Noel."

"Noel?" I asked.

Verta closed her eyes and held out her hand. In an instant, there was a flash of green, and then a star, eight-pointed, hovering above her palm like a great gem of immeasurable worth. Before I could ask her what it was, the image shifted, and the face of a young boy, perhaps seven or eight, appeared. He was smiling, remarkably handsome, with dark hair and eyes.

"My blessing. My curse. I could not help myself. Andrew had conspired, of course. He felt the strain of poetry on their line; he knew he needed but a little more to be truly great. And so, he introduced me to the woman. I blessed the seed in the womb of a very sad, madwoman. I have been watching him grow, now."

"The Boast," I said. "La Roche thought if you sired a child you would stay."

"I do not want to stay, but I still love Andrew, even though it aches every day as my body fails me. I see ruin in Noel's life, Joss. I do not think the Boast helped."

"I could help the babe, the Keats' child."

"You could. But it is a precious, fickle magic."

"Miriam will find me."

"Yes. And she will seek revenge. While you are here in Londinium, she can wound you deeply."

"I do not want to leave."

"Save yourself. Leave the boy in the care of his parents, and I will watch over him for you until Miriam has cooled. She has a war to run, after all. There is so much you have yet to do, but I fear Andrew never prepared you. He may have been jealous or else…" She trailed off, looking away. "I hate to think he was setting you up for ruin."

I did not want to believe such a thing. "He'd rather you live, and hate him, then not live at all. He's done this for love."

"Yes. I know. I'm no fool. But at what cost?"

It did seem a heavy one.

"I don't know where to go."

"Go where your power is greatest, where you've always been drawn. Go to the sea where you will be healed. Let time will heal the wounds you've already endured so much. Flee and ruminate. Forget mortal troubles. I promise, if you are required, if the war comes too far and we are in need, I will find you. You know I can. Better than anyone else." She held up her hand and the compass flickered for a moment. "But do not dally. Miriam will find you soon."

PART II

9

I no longer knew how to be a fish, but the idea of the sea no longer terrified me. I couldn't very well build a boat, and I didn't relish stealing one. So, in the middle of the night, coward I was, I simply plunged into the Tamesis, filth and all and began my voyage to the sea.

Though the water was not clean, it was still magnificent. As soon as I felt the water move over my head, every concern I'd had started to wash away and vanish in the tides. All the worries and stress felt inconsequential as I breathed in water for the first time since passing as a man in the world of mortals.

But this salt water tributary, this was different than Crummock Water. I had never been in a body of water so large, and in that connection the world opened up before me. I felt tied to the entire earth's surface, my consciousness splitting and snaking across every hill and dale. The continents themselves became black masses before my eyes, while the waters, they illuminated and formed into roadways only I could travel.

Years later, I would use those roadways to travel between worlds, but as I felt my body sweep away from Londinium, I let go of part of my mortality and focused on the encompassing feeling of power and of belonging. I saw how lost I had been, and time stretched out before me, free of the ripples and concerns brought about by the rigid lives lived above, the machinations of the godlings of Londinium.

I didn't need to breathe, though when I first encountered salt water on my way past Gaul, it did take some getting used to. I could not turn into a fish, but my body was suited for the water—my lungs adapted, my skin toughened. What nourishment I needed, I got from the plants growing on the reefs. And sometimes I managed a meal of clams or shells of kelp.

I could still sense Miriam in the vague distance, a burning coal of fury. But the deeper I plunged, the quieter her ire. Eventually, I did not sense her at all.

I didn't think about Thomas and Frances Keats. I forgot about La Roche and Trita and Calvinius and the filth of Londinium. Their presences faded farther away with every stroke. I floated on the currents; I spoke to the creatures of the deep. I vanished unto my own self, and it was bliss. Ignorance, of course. Selfish, absolutely. Cowardice, entirely and unequivocally. But Verta was right. I was safe. I was hidden. And more than anything, I could learn again. Not from La Roche, who had never truly taught me what I should have known, but from the depths themselves.

Time slipped and twisted, and it was only the sea and me. Only the rising tides and the falling tides, the song of the whales and the cry of the birds. It was life and death and life and death and the very cradle of the world. There was so much there, so much to know and to hold and to remember, and most of it has left me now. Even if I tried to write it all down, or even tell it, I'm not sure there are words to describe it. The world below the earth is a wild, raw place, full of danger and wonder. There are more stories in the seal's cries than in the entire cycle of human civilization. We godlings, but strange hybrids made human in our form by some trick of the Eight Worlds, rarely remember that the simians are but one refrain in the great story of the world.

Perhaps I lived and died a hundred lives in the deep. Perhaps I fell in love and truly lived. I will never know. I was not myself. I was a deeper, older, stranger thing. I was raw, irrational, and bestial. And it was necessary.

The tides ran through my veins, and the rains wet my hair, and I rode the waves with my staff, conjuring up horses where no one could see because I still missed them. I found joy racing in the light of the sun, even if I worried sometimes that a stray albatross might be a rook in disguise.

Each year, I ventured deeper. Time lost meaning. I lost meaning. I became, again, a fish. A lost whale, beholden only to the currents and the tides, blissfully unaware of what passed above me. I sank into the sunless realms, buoyant and solitary, oblivion coursing through my veins and the rushing waves in my ears.

But La Roche did not come looking for me, and Verta did not call me back. And Miriam was extinguished from my thoughts entirely.

So, I went deeper still.

Then, ten years after I fled Londinium, the deep began calling to me.

They were not pleasant noises, not the sort of call a sane person would heed. But I, being neither sane nor a person of the regular variety, felt the compulsion to follow it.

I knew where I was, or close enough to it, and I knew land was not safe. Greece was no longer the stronghold of Roman forces, as the Turks had long ago allied with the Persian forces and taken it over, to the delight of Achaemenes and the constant ire of Miriam.

So, I swam south, toward the cries. They were at times high and at times low. At times pained, at times filled with loneliness. The deeper I swam, the more I began to understand the language, the words. It was a beckoning, calling to me.

Yes, she had sensed me as I had sensed her. Old and ancient and wise, she reached out as only she could.

Darker went the water, darker and fouler. Thicker, colder, full of glowing masses and other whispers and wails. It was alien and calm, hectic and familiar.

I ought to have been afraid, knowing as I drew closer to her there was some great power pulling me far beyond the reach of the sun. I didn't feel her the same way I'd felt the godlings, but rather as another tributary. A change of current, temperature, direction.

All light was gone, but I didn't want to risk adding anything to it. I could make my staff phosphorescent if I desired but felt it unwise to disturb the creature with it. It wasn't simply that I sensed her presence, but I, too, could sense her power. She was the sort of being wound from the same arcane fabric as the godlings, but yet still a threat. She called me "brother", but she could have named me "snack" as well.

"I am thinking you may turn on your lightish thing if you wish," she said, her voice ringing all around me.

I couldn't see her; the blackness of the water was so complete even my blessed eyes could see nothing. I hesitated and she said:

"It's been many a thousand years since I looked upon the face of your kind, brightling. I am thinking you will want to be afraid of me."

"I'm sure I will," I replied. We weren't speaking in any human language, but her thoughts still came across to me, jumbled and strange.

I felt something brush across my waist—by now I had nothing but a few rags clinging to me—and it was like being grazed by a living tree trunk. Out of fear, and admittedly surprise, I held aloft the staff and it kindled in my grasp, green and blue and white. For a moment I truly thought I wasn't going to see anything at all because the light took a moment to diffuse through the cold water, thick with particulate.

At first, I mistook the creature for part of the ocean floor, but then I truly beheld her. She was crusted in eons of growth, ruddy and red, flaked with debris. Massive. A world unto herself. Each arm, eight all told, rising from her enormous body, was as thick and corded as the trunk of an oak tree. I could smell her in the water, a deep, green scent, tinged with fishiness and a heady, almost musky note. Her eyes were each larger than my head, quivering in the glare of my lamp, but still curious. Old though she was, she was not yet ready to relinquish her own light.

When she coiled one of her arms around me, I did not fight her. Knew better than that.

"The brightling with a bright thing," she said, turning me so I floated sideways. My hair streamed across my face for a moment, lit to near white in the phosphorescence. "He swims from a long, long way. Running away! I am thinking he should be asking the questions of me. I am thinking he is very small."

I tried to tell her my name, but she laughed. Or else, I felt her body tremble in amusement. "Names are dirt. Are sand. Are like the taste of foul, dead fish. I am thinking I do not need your name! So small. So fishy!"

"I've come to learn. From the sea," I said, trying to make it sound nobler than it did.

"I am thinking it is wise. To come to me. To Khasma. I am thinking that is not my name, but the brightling wants to know something. To remember something. And his brain is too small to know the truth. I am thinking that, yes."

As she spoke, I could feel what power fueled her moving through me, a subtle electrical current. The suckers on her arms pried at my body curiously, like strange tongues tasting my flesh. It made me, rather uncomfortably, remember the touch of Fanny. And with the dislodged memory came the rush of everything else: La Roche and his sunshine smile, Calvinius and his potions, Verta and her tears.

I almost forgot I could breathe the water, and for a moment began to panic in her grasp. Was it on purpose? Could the creature have known? It seemed plausible. And cruel.

"I am thinking the brightling needs rest. Swimming for so long. And yet so young! Still, I am thinking his mind is elsewhere, while he ought to be asking of me. Ask of me, brightling! I am thinking you will forget."

"Khasma," I said to her, bowing my head. I wanted her to know I respected her. "What can you teach me?"

"I am thinking that is not the right question!" She shook me, her arm tightening to the point of discomfort. Khasma's whole body trembled, sending vibrations through the water from little finials all up and down her massive, knobbed head. "You are not thinking right, not to be coming here, where for the thousands of years Khasma has been left in quiet. In peace. In tranquility. And now you come to ask of me like that! I am thinking I should feed you to the hungry ones. I am thinking you would be a small meal, but a tasty one."

The hungry ones. I had never heard them called by name, but as she spoke of them, I could sense them. Shadows in the deep. Monstrous creatures formed by godlings or gods or both, forged in fires not meant to make beings with thought and speech. Fueled by hatred. They were the children of Khasma, she told me so in her touch, she had adopted them. Protected them. Fed them those she found wanting.

I didn't want to be found wanting, as you probably surmise. The threat was enough to put a little more lightning in my spine. This was not just her realm; it was mine, even if I was new to it. This was my inheritance.

"Will I be a fish again?" I asked her.

The question delighted her, and she flushed green. "Mmm, yes. I am thinking you will remember to be a fish again. Not for some time. You have much human business, brightling. Years you have been in these waters but still, you smell of them. Until you no longer smell of them, you will be no fish. Perhaps, if you decide, you could even be fish as I am. Great, best, most wonderful fish."

I didn't want to tell her the truth of her existence, but then wondered if she meant something broader by the word. I certainly never felt lacking when I was a fish, for all those years. And surely, if there were any other creatures of the deep, they could scarcely be larger.

"Now ask real question. I am thinking you have not much time," she said.

"Will I ever see Fanny again? And her son?" I asked.

I was worried the question would anger her. It was personal, and something entirely out of her power. But she did not get angry. She continued to turn darker green, and her skin got a translucent quality about it. Staring down at the arm about my waist I could spy the thousands of tributaries running through her: veins, arteries, capillaries. A great map.

"I am thinking when you leave your hearth home, yes. You will also see much more pain. And much more love. Your woman will have changed when you see her again. Oh, there is to be more blood, brightling. There is always blood. Your blood, her blood, their blood. So much blood the seas will run with it. But then, in time, maybe I am thinking when you are great fish, you will forgive yourself. You will make the good things, and the bad things. But it is what you are, storm child. Waves child. Horse child."

She let me go. I tried to swim back down to her as I felt myself being lifted bodily. I had never had a difficult time, not even in the greatest of currents, maintaining my direction.

"Wait! I have to ask you about La Roche!" I called to the water, as bubbles rushed up around me, obscuring the kraken from view. "Did he know? Did he manipulate me?"

"He is just a minnow, ship savior. Just a minnow… I am thinking that, yes. His scales will shine bright in the light of the sun, and then slip into shadow."

"No, wait!"

"Tremble, child. Tremble, little fish. Awaken."

And at that moment I realized I was at the center of an earthquake, and someone was calling me. *Joss Raddick. Joss Raddick. Come out of the sea.*

I was breaking apart. I was changing, trembling, shifting, at Khasma's word. The water turned brackish and, for the first time, I felt the power of the earth rise around me. That unsaid ability, shaker of the earth. I could not fight it, for it was larger than I was. I was too young, not strong enough, not clever enough, to tame it.

10

It was upon one of those damned islands in the archipelago, blissfully unoccupied, where I finally washed up, sixteen years after I left Londinium. My questions answered, my power drained, I no longer felt as if I could swim as I had before, no longer could avoid Miriam. I knew Khasma had taken something from me in return for her answers. I could feel it, just as I felt what I had taken from Frances when I brought her back from the dead. I wasn't angry about what the creature had done to me, but a little disappointed. I had thought I would return from the sea with more of me, not less of me. And from what I could tell, I had become more human than godling after the experience.

But I could tremble. She had showed me how.

I was just contemplating what it would take to make a vessel for my escape, when I saw, in the distance, explosions of some sort on the horizon. They lit up the sky, bursts of colored light, and the reverberations echoed for some miles.

I did not want to risk going there, but the current was too strong to fight. I began to swim in the direction of the boat. By dawn, the explosions lit up but the waters I found myself in were littered with boats and sailors, mostly soldiers.

"Verta," I whispered, trying to reach out to her. But I could not sense her. I could sense no one. Perhaps it was because I was on the open sea, or that my earthquake had addled my wits, but I was altogether adrift.

War had come.

The flag of Gaul was prominently displayed on one of the sides of a particularly impressive vessel, and I figured sooner or later I would have to try my chances to get back home. John would be a strapping lad by now, and perhaps the rumor of my ill deeds would be passed over by Miriam. I had, at least, stepped on land and she had not destroyed me.

I squinted at the ship. Gaul was an ally of Britanniae, at least there was that. It was better than being adrift on my own, so I made for the boat with great, powerful strokes, skimming the top of the ocean.

One of the shiphands spied me first and called something out in muddled Breton. I got the gist of it but replied in heavily accented Latin, nonetheless.

"To whom do you swear allegiance?" asked the man from the top of the ship, staring down at me. He had a ladder in his hand, but he wasn't ready to relinquish it.

"I'm a citizen of Britanniae," I said.

The rope ladder came down and I made my way up, my staff slung to my back. As I ascended, I tried to think of what I should say, what background I should give myself. I was thinking an exotic alter ego, a world traveler perhaps. An explorer. I'd need something that took me out of the conflict for long enough while remaining plausible.

I needn't have worried, though, because the first face I saw when I put my foot on the wide boards of the deck was Andrew La Roche, looking fresh and fine and fancy. Wind in his hair, cheeks pink, amber eyes wide with wonder and, if I was not mistaken, a little fear.

"Joss!" He was as surprised as I.

"La Roche," I said.

Then I punched him straight in the mouth.

We had quite a brawl until they separated us, though I don't think he'd intended to continue fighting. In his defense, I did throw my entire weight at him and, if not for having lost something to Khasma, I might have smothered him into the waves entirely, and all in front of the baffled mortals.

It took four men to get me subdued enough, and when I was dragged to the ground I stared up at La Roche and spit at his feet. They put irons on my legs and arms and my strength slipped away.

"Fair enough," he said, wiping a thin stream of blood from his nose. He looked at his handkerchief as if surprised, his fox-fur eyebrows rising under the brim of his hat for just a moment. "But you'll hear me out, Raddick."

"I don't need to hear anything from you," I said, my fury still stoked. I'll admit I was furious he'd found me in the first place. Out in the middle of nowhere, to boot. I was outraged, embarrassed, furious. All the emotions stewed about inside of me and made me want to retch. "You didn't warn me. You didn't prepare me!"

La Roche indicated he was fine to one of his men, a fellow festooned in bright orange pantaloons and a fine blue waistcoat, and waved his hands about to let the rest know to get to work. They'd tied me to the mast with rope studded with iron links—something they seemed to have no shortage of on board—and had thrown my things at La Roche's feet. I noticed for the first time his hat was larger than it used to be, though his clothes were relatively the same shades of gray and of black. And he was wearing a pistol as well as a saber, not to mention his ever-present scarlet scarf.

He saw my eyes go to his hip as if I sensed the threat in spite of his neutral hand position.

"Much has changed, Joss," he said to me, and I caught the weariness in his voice. I caught the familiarity. It had been so long since I'd heard speech, godling or otherwise, it was jarring. I almost teared up, but I looked away. "And things aren't exactly as you thought they were when you left. You made an error, but there is a way forward."

"I made no error," I said. "You didn't trust me, and I ruined her."

"There's been war, my friend. War on the waves and in the mountains and on the roads, from John O'Groats to Constantinople."

"Fuck your war."

La Roche pulled on his goatee, shaking his head at me with all the pedantry of a schoolmarm. "When you're ready to hear me out, I'll untie you."

"I have nothing to say to you."

He grinned. "Good, then you'll give me plenty of time to do the talking, which is my preferred configuration. We're sailing North, then we're going to make port in Paris. Then Londinium. Then, I'm not sure. But for now, you're my prisoner, and my men will do what I say, and there's more iron where that came from. When you decide to parley like a man of character, I'll be glad to entertain you in my quarters."

I spat at him again, and he almost kicked me. But he didn't.

Always the gentleman, Andrew La Roche.

IT TOOK me three days to give up, more for the discomfort of the iron than for the pride. La Roche came by to talk to me three times a day, always bringing wine and food, and me always refusing. I didn't sleep. I didn't talk. But eventually, I got too tired to fight.

Yes, at a point, even my stubbornness has an end.

"I'm ready to talk to La Roche," I finally told my guard on the third night. He looked up at me, surprised to hear near-flawless Breton. At a point, you do get familiar with a language. I've always been better at it than most. My lips were cracked and dry, and my limbs hurt so much I began to wonder if I'd have the strength to hold them up of my own volition. But I needed to. In case I had to hit La Roche again. Sadly, they exchanged my ropes for iron shackles.

I'd never had the pleasure of seeing La Roche's home in Londinium, but I was not surprised at the state of the cabin. As captain, or whatever official title he had on the boat, he commanded the most impressive quarters. Garish for my liking, but not at all like the deep, sultry garishness of Verta's brothel and temple.

La Roche liked shiny things, gilded things, silver things, the sorts of things with corkscrews and curlicues on top for no purpose at all other than to draw the eye. Staggering in, I had to shade my eyes from it all. There were too many things to look at that it made me dizzy. Shaking my head, I was able to parse out the individual parts of the room—the elaborately carved bed, the thick, stuffed chairs with gilded embroidery, the many books and scrolls tucked away on shelves.

And in the middle of it all sat Andrew La Roche, smoking a long, narrow black pipe, one leg crossed over the other and staring at me intently. He wore a striped black silk robe lined with fur about the neck, and in his other hand he swished a bit of brandy.

"Leave him," La Roche said in Breton, waving off the two men who'd brought me down.

They both hesitated and he rolled his eyes. "I'm quite capable of taking care of myself. If I require your intervention, you'll know."

The two sailors reluctantly let go of me.

When the door was closed, La Roche offered me a seat. I didn't take it. I'd balled my hands into fists and was trying very hard not to slap him across the face, shackles be damned.

"If you'd have told me you were fucking Frances Keats, I might have helped steer you in the right direction."

In a burst of fury, I swung my shackled hands at his face and connected, hard. The brandy glass tinkered to the floor, but he held on to the pipe. He didn't even make to hit me again. He just looked resigned and a little flustered. But the speed at which he gathered his composure was truly impressive. One bit of his hair had gone out of place and he calmly moved it to the side as his cheek flushed red with the impact.

"Well. We'll see if I really deserved that. Suffice it to say, I'm aware of what went on," he said. "Since you've clearly demonstrated your opinion with your most deft punch, will you please take a seat? You're smaller than you last were but still damned intimidating."

I wasn't sure what he meant by smaller, but I took the seat anyway. I did feel better for striking him. My ears still rushed with fury, but I was prepared to hear him out.

"It's the iron making you sick," he said, gesturing to the shackles. "I hedged my bet on it, just in case. Doesn't bother me quite so much, but apparently does the trick for you."

"Enlighten me," I said.

He cleared his throat, dabbing at his sore cheek. "I shall do more than enlighten. As a gesture of faith, I will undo them for you."

I held out my hands, and felt the ground rush to me as soon as the shackles were off. I felt light-headed but ignored his attempts to give me more to drink. I found my way to a chair, breathing deeply.

"Now, before we get into the raunchy details, I'd like to hear what you saw that night, in Londinium, when you left so hastily," he said, rubbing his jaw.

"You know," I insisted. "I don't need to tell you a fucking thing."

"Indulge me, Joss. I'm weary. It's been a long war, which I'll be glad to inform you of sooner or later. But if you're going to be of any help to me, I must be on the same page."

"I was going to bless the Keats' child. But Fanny died in my arms. So I made her not dead--but I didn't know how because you would never teach me. I broke Miriam's law--she would destroy me." I took a deep, shuddering breath. "So I went to Verta." Every word was like being pierced in the side. I wanted to break the world with my grief.

"Oh." La Roche paused, momentarily at a loss for words. He had not expected my response. "To Verta. What part of her *convincing* had you running out to sea?"

"She told me to lie low. Considering I had broken Miriam's law. She didn't think your treachery was surprising."

"I'm sure she was quite prepared to cast me as the villain. Any reason to rid herself of my perpetual company..." he trailed off and batted the air. "And while I'd like to take credit for deception when it's due, none of it was my style. I would never, Joss."

What he said made no sense, so I told him as much. "You didn't teach me enough. And I broke her. I tried to heal her, but I broke her."

"What you did was not healing. I will not apologize for neglecting to teach you necromancy. Such practices belong to the desperate and invite corruption."

"I could have fixed her properly if I had the skills."

"Even so, I find the practice diametrically opposed to my very being. I am the sun. I am warmth. I am occasionally distracted by shiny objects and the round backside of a departing figure, but I'm most certainly not capable of raising the dead. Come now, man, surely you understand. I thought you were just at the ostlery doing your work. Not breaking the rules of gods and man. It's bad magic, Joss. Bad magic."

"Verta doesn't think so."

I thought for certain he was going to argue with me, but he didn't. He got rather somber at the mention of his lover's name and sat back down in his immense chair, defeated. Holding up the glass of brandy, he watched the liquid move about in the light, swishing to and fro by his own volition and the movement of the ship.

In the distance, I heard a thunderous boom, the sort I'd heard from time to time during my travels. It didn't distract La Roche at all, and so I figured it wasn't anything to worry about, in spite of the fact I could hear rushing feet above us.

When he looked at me again, there were tears in his eyes. "If only I were capable of speaking to Verta."

I felt my stomach turn its own riptide. "She's not—"

"No." His voice broke again, and just when I thought he was going to break down into sobs, he downed the entirety of the glass of brandy.

I frowned at him. "You don't look well."

"Nothing is bloody well, Raddick. The whole world's going to piss, and I've been able to do virtually nothing to stop it. And now I'm floating in the middle of the Akdeniz with a vessel full of Bretons and Quakers, preparing to go to war with another godling. All because of Verta. And you."

He let out a mad little laugh.

"Ah! Before you slap me again. I'll tell you that your blessed poet child is very well. He goes to school, he has siblings. He is relatively happy, though he suffered the death of...well, Thomas Keats died when little John was only eight. Thrown from his own horse, Poetaster."

"John is a good name." Poetaster.

"Yes. John Keats. Short. Succinct. To the point. He's a sturdy chap with his mother's looks. But a little lackadaisical. The best of us are."

At that moment, someone began banging on the door and shouting rather unintelligibly from the hall. La Roche let loose a string of curse words, looking conflicted. Finally, he made up his mind about something and went to his desk, a marble-topped piece of furniture with legs like carved wings, and threw something at me. I caught it. A book.

He started pulling on his clothes, talking to me at the same time, but not making eye contact. "It's all in there. You should be able to backdate it. It's my personal journal. I'm allowing you to read it. It's a gesture of trust..." His eyes met mine, amber brown and intense. Deep and unfathomable, old beyond the smooth face. The world stopped a moment as he said the word again. "Of *trust*. Ask yourself if anyone else among our number would do such a thing."

He hopped into his trousers and then went to fetch his boots which were strewn around the room. Miracle he could find anything in the room to begin with.

As things went in the room, however, the book was slim and plain. Green leather, laced with a long, braided cord. It could have been new or a thousand years old, it held a sort of strange, ageless quality to it. And oddly it felt warm to the touch, like it had been in La Roche's lap the entire time, though I knew it hadn't. It was living.

"Read. I'll be gone for a bit," he said with a sigh. "War's a nasty, ugly business, and I've fought enough to know there's never a right side. Just one with a fewer body count, in the end. And they tell the stories that follow. I'd prefer to be on your side in such an instance."

"Always with the self-preservation," I said.

"So says the godling who flung himself into the sea rather than deal with Miriam's wrath," he said with a roguish grin. He secured his hat on his head and laughed through his nose. Then he ducked out of the door.

I heard his boot-steps retreating, and more scuffling above deck. I stared at the book, opened the first page, and did not stop once I began.

11

The journal began rather simply. It was written in a strange ink that was neither brown nor black, and yet seemed to change as I read it. There were hundreds upon hundreds of entries, and yet as I rifled through, I often found just what I was looking for. Certainly, some godling trick, but intriguing nonetheless.

"I'm writing this because Verta has told me it's good for my heart, my being, my soul," he wrote in the first passage. "Though I much doubt I will keep it up long. I rarely do, with these sorts of things…"

But in spite of his predicted failure, he did not stop. Almost day upon day, he wrote passages. Some a few words long. Sometimes just one. Memorably, on June the 30th , 1709, he wrote: "Bliss." There were reams of personal things, admissions of infidelity to Verta, his own hopes and dreams and failures. Orphans he'd raised, people he'd let perish. All written in his very characteristic script and tone.

1794: "The water chap is so much larger than I had expected. From my research, I've discovered he can't be more than a third or fourth generation, and I have to admit always thinking Verta was teasing me when she said we used to be larger. He's a veritable giant, though he's got a very calm, gentle nature about him too. Notwithstanding the underlying current of power. Saints and martyrs, I can feel it from miles away. It's like wading into a warm current and following it.

"He dresses as he can, and I've given him some allowance for better weeds. He'll have to find a tailor. And as to his feature and face, why, he doesn't look like any man of Britannic descent that I've ever come across. More like a wandering Norseman. His hair's a hue akin to pale flax, and his skin is somewhat ruddy though most is covered under a rather impressive beard. I'm told the moment he tries to shave it, it grows right back, though he tries to keep it from going unkempt. His eyes are what unsettle me, though. There's no denying he's a handsome man—his cheekbones are well-placed and his mouth full and easy to smile. But those eyes are dark brown. And speckled. Like the belly of a trout."

Belly of a trout, indeed.

1795: "Miriam has gathered us all for dinner. Verta and I were up late into the night arguing again. She perplexes me, with her desire to teach Joss the darker arts of our kind. Miriam has forbidden it, and due to my previous experiences with such things, I have to agree.

"Verta often tells the story of how she found me, burning on the pyre of my dead family. I have told her the events leading up to the scene, but she seems to forget it, believing that ending life and resurrecting life are essential to our existences as godlings. I have refused to teach Joss these skills, even though I am best suited. Perhaps that is folly, but so far, his talents do not seem to align themselves with such tendencies. I wish I had more time to teach him, but Miriam keeps me perilously busy.

"My family died, one by one, of pestilence. The whole village I grew up in followed suit. And I, numb and terrified, resurrected them one by one over a series of days. They would live for a while, relieved and grateful, and then the sickness would come again, and they would die. I gave up, eventually, on the rest of the village, but my mother and father, my sisters and brother... Each successive resurrection changed them, warped them. Broke them.

"At last, I knew I had done the unthinkable: I had created monsters. They hungered for blood. They clawed at their own skin, and bit each other. It was madness. I could not kill them, then, except by fire. Then I tried, wracked with guilt and fury, to burn myself. But I, like the sun, could not. Verta found me then, and I told her what had happened.

"We had a child, Verta and I, a godling foundling when we were young. His name was Castius, and we had a mind to raise him, bless him, since we could not have children of our own.

"I once recounted his story in another volume, but I burned it. I will tell the story again as I remember it word for word. Here follow my entries on the matter.

'1742: We have made great progress, Castius and I, since his accident. I think he's trusting me more, at least, which is a start. Again, I found him with a blade, contemplating ending things. He relented, and I promised we would do more traveling together if it would help ease his mind.

'1744: The African Continent did a wonder for Castius. He was at home with the greater kingdoms, there, and while he was aware that making long-term relationships with non-godlings was likely not in the cards, I do feel he is coming to a better understanding of respecting human life. And he is coming quite along in his studies in regards to alchemy.'"

Respecting human life. The words had a strange feeling to them, and I ran my fingers over the page, contemplating. What was La Roche trying to say about Castius's respect for human life? The details of the outer world were often left to the peripheries of La Roche's journal; he was not a chronicler of history, but rather one of emotion. I wished I'd had more context.

"'1745: I am distraught. We left the North after staying scarcely six months. I thought he was ready for the power of that place, but it did nothing but muddle his wits more. I feel stupid for having a mind to bring him there, I realize now, but he was doing so much better. I am always struggling with how to bring him more solidly into a moral mindset. He sees the patterns in everything, the networks and connections he tells me, but he flounders in the chaos. His incident with the King's wife means now that two more kingdoms are at war, and this one likely to be long and bloody. I think I will take him back to Londinium where I can keep a better eye on him. I had so hoped that seeing the world would be a benefit.

"'1753: Thankfully, Londinium has been a help. I am weary, truth be told, and even though I believe that Castius can rehabilitate himself, there are days I have my doubts. As of yet, he has not caused irreparable damage, other than that which is already broken in this damned place. There are more murderers and rapists in one square mile than in all of Gaul combined, but perhaps that's why Castius can blend in so well. His errors are…relatively easy to cover up. I hate the city. And it means I must be closer to Verta. But for the good of Castius, I will endure it."

"1756: I lost him for a time. He claims to see the future in their entrails and so help me. Maybe he does. Maybe I have become too human. But the grief on my part is horrible, and there's nothing for it.

"1759: "We have kept him for almost four years, and he is a misery. He will not recant his behavior and claims that we will all understand when the years wear on.

"I am tired, and unwell again. I need to rest but cannot find the strength to do so. I regret everything in the dark.

"1760: Castius escaped this evening. I awoke from a strange slumber to feel my heart twisting about in my chest. I rose to my feet and ran, finding Verta at the door. She had a look of knowing on her face and tried to stop me, but I could feel the pulse of Castius's frantic presence not far, and I had to get to him.

"When I reached the tower, he was standing at the top, his hands extended, one on either side. In the dead of the night, only the guards were awake, but they did not seem to take notice.

"He called me, saw me. Told me I was his false father. That he scorned the earth upon which I walked, that all my words were lies and I was to blame.

"Then, he leapt. Into the Tamesis. We found what was left of his body the next day. My heart will never heal. I have broken the world, broken my boy, and I will never see joy again."

The book fell from my hands to the wide-planked floor, just missing the elaborate carpet. I could feel the pain La Roche had endured. No wonder he sided with Miriam—and Verta, how could she still want such magic in the world?

I picked up the book again, running my fingers over the words. He had loved the boy, and he had broken him. An inconsequential human being, perhaps, but one that wrought havoc upon Londinium nonetheless.

It took me a moment to realize that La Roche was coming down the stairs again, and I attempted to look presentable, though my eyes were red and raw from crying.

When he opened the door, the left side of his face was bandaged. A small trickle of blood escaped.

"No need to worry on my account," La Roche said, going to his vanity and checking the side of his face. He gave an exasperated sigh of disapproval. "Just grazed me. But it might leave a scar. Funny thing about iron."

Then he seemed to remember what I'd been up to. His eyes fell upon the journal in my hands. "Did you find it riveting?"

"You could have told me," I said. I decided not to try and hide my emotions, so I wiped my eyes.

La Roche's face fell, and in that instant, I could see just how old he was. Nigh on four hundred years, though he hardly looked past his mid-thirties, the weight of it all was like a yoke around his neck.

"Perhaps I should have. Perhaps I worried what you would do with that knowledge; I have never told anyone the whole story," he said.

"But Verta knows, and she still supports the necromancy."

"Indeed, she does. She believes it is a gift given to some of the godlings, and ought to be used, wielded, correctly. Except that I'm unsure that it can be done so. I have never seen it succeed; it has only ever led to ruin."

"And Frances Keats?" I asked.

"She is…changed," La Roche said slowly, measuring his words. "I wish I could tell you, Joss, that she was happy. But the life you rebuilt for her was incomplete."

"I loved her," I said.

"Miriam doesn't care about love. She cares about rules. And though there are a dozen rules I cannot abide by when it comes to her, this one is utterly immovable. It is too dangerous," he said with a sigh. "Especially now."

"The war, you mean."

He nodded. "Their war, yes. We have joined up in hopes of bringing an end to the fighting, and perhaps gaining favor from Miriam."

"I broke the rules," I said. "Even if it was by accident. How can I ever find my way back to Londinium again?"

He gave a bitter laugh. "If that is your will, there is a pathway there. Allegiance. We have been forced to pick sides, to fight in a war waged by humans for the sake of godlings. Miriam brings with her the Marians and the Quakers, while Achaemenes brings a promise of the old ways, the native ways, letting all worship as they will. But it's a small force. And a tired force. Though their pyrotechnics are most impressive. If Miriam falls, so too do her protections."

"And curses."

La Roche frowned. "Perhaps."

"So, you need me to help win this war," I said. Outside I could feel the water shaking against explosions, feel the tension of the men on the ship. I had missed most of their fear earlier, so engrossed I was in the book, but reality was coming fast upon me.

"If we do this for Miriam, she may forgive…the mess," La Roche said. He needed no elaboration.

There was more he was not telling me. "You mentioned being ill," I said. "In the book. What's wrong with you?"

Another explosion shook the boat. La Roche swallowed. "There are yet things I need to tell you, but now is not the time. I must describe the events of the current war, demonstrate what I think you can do for us, and then you can decide. Your choice is yours alone. Should you wish to leave, I will let you go, no questions asked. I will understand if you never wish to speak with me again."

"No, it' s not—"

The boat shook again, and I stopped speaking and just watched La Roche. I knew that he was in pain, I could sense it flowing through the water in his body. Not just from the injury to his cheek, but something more. Deeper. Rooting around inside of him.

His eyes brimmed with tears, and he shook his head. "I am many things, Joss, but I am not a liar. Not in matters like this. It was my idea to involve you in the Great Boast—and yes, initially it was for selfish reasons. But I owe you a way out."

I took a deep breath, the air still feeling too warm in my lungs. I nodded. "Show me what you want me to do, then."

Most of the war had already been won for Miriam. In the last three hundred years, her brand of Marianism had run rampant throughout the Continent, attracting near zealotry in places like Hispania and Gaul and even parts of Constantinople and Persia, though that was nested deep in contentious territory. For decades they'd been encroaching, and Britanniae had always kept a tenuous alliance with them. Until shortly after my departure, when a fleet of Egyptian ships sank half a fleet outside of Corsicae, which had been the one remaining Roman stronghold for centuries.

What no one knew was how firmly Marianism had been growing in the remnants of Rome itself. It seemed to have come from nowhere, according to La Roche, and when the forces began to pull back toward the Akdeniz, they were met by a united—and federally supported—Marian force, sails festooned with images of the Virgin Mother, and yellow and green and red banners floating all about them. They crushed the world-renowned Egyptian fleet, and only a handful of survivors lived to tell the tale of supernatural strength, a ship moving three times natural speed, and wonders above the waves.

Then came similar stories from the East. A rider, heading a horde of unearthly cavalry, decimating troops in the heart of Constantinople, not far from Thrace. But that didn't last long.

Walking to his writing desk, La Roche took out a roll of parchment and set it out, putting heavy weights on the corners. The boat shifted as if in response, but the map stayed in place. He studied it for a moment, then pointed to the Akdeniz, just to the west of Sandalion, the island to the north of Corsicae. He waved his hand over the map again and not only did our own ship, *Hoel*, appear but so did the rest of the fleets. The Marian side was a mass of gold and green, denoting different ranks, and the Persian side was represented in an odd purplish-black ink that seemed to move and waver on the page.

"Impressive," I said.

"Is it? I suppose I never was as flashy with you before. Perhaps I ought to have been." He sounded regretful.

"It's helpful, seeing it in this way. I'm used to the terrain below, not above."

"Yes, I forget how little of the world you've seen. It's a shame, really." He paused and looked me square. "You've been missed, you oaf."

"I haven't decided yet if you have been."

La Roche tried to suppress the smile, but it failed. If he'd been in bird form, he'd have ruffled his feathers in glee. Turning to the task, he pointed, "Here. This is us. Our sweet little ship. We are currently holding the blockade across the rest of the Akdeniz, you see? Food, supplies, anything coming from the Northern African states or the southern part of Hispania, these are all prevented. Which puts us in a good position. Now, there's a good part of our fleet somewhat engaged here, near the Straits of Gibraltar, and support coming out of Malaga. But if we can hold out a few more days here, and if the weather is amenable…"

This is where he wiggled his eyebrows at me like a catfish awaiting its prey.

"You mean for me to mess with the weather," I said, stroking my beard. I was suddenly more conscious of my looks now that I'd read La Roche's thoughts on the subject. I could only imagine my state now. What glimpses I'd managed in the general shine and shimmer of La Roche's room weren't encouraging.

He snorted. "Well, calm down now. It isn't as if you're the sole hinge on which the entire venture swings, as we have some other contingency measures. I knew where to find you; I always do. But yes. Essentially, I went out of my way to drag your seaweed-sodden self from the bottom of the depths to help 'mess with the weather' as you so eloquently put it," La Roche said. "If you think you're up for it."

I hadn't practiced much in the way of weather alterations in the last few years, and even when I had been able to work it, it wasn't exactly in my control. I didn't want to lose face in front of La Roche, but it was hard to have confidence in something I had so little experience with.

"And you think I'm capable of it," I said. "Even after all of…everything. I haven't told you what happened in the Deep."

"And I haven't told you my whole tale. Even I'm not stupid enough to write it *all* down. But you came when I called, and that's all the encouragement I need."

"I thought it was Verta. Calling to me."

He sighed at her name, wrinkling his nose. "You heard what you wanted to hear. It was me," he said, poking at his chest with his thumb. "Since you left and Londinium erupted into war, that woman has been nothing short of impenetrable. Mentally or otherwise. She spends all her time holed up in her little temple looking after Noel and John in her scrying glass."

"I'm sorry," I said.

"I know. But she did give her blessing, if that helps. We've reconciled as much as we can, mostly on account of you. "

La Roche began adding elements to the map. A typhoon here, a bank of fog there. The illuminations on the parchment moved and swirled and tempted me. I liked the look of it; I liked the thought of it. Momentarily I saw myself standing on the prow of the *Hoel,* my hands outstretched, commanding the waves like some god of old. The vision was crisp and clear, and I was only wrested out of it by La Roche's hand on my shoulder.

"And no one else can help you, I suppose," I said. "No one else. To work the weather."

"Well, we all have our strengths. But most of us are too weak or else too tired and distracted to be of any real use in the matter. Trita is fighting, and Calvinius has disappeared."

"Disappeared?"

"I haven't had time to find him, and he's the one godling who can vanish, untraceable."

"I still don't see how I can be of help."

"You don't quite realize your potential."

"Oh, I know my potential. That's the whole problem," I said, moving my finger across the map to the area where the bank of fog rolled. The movement ceased when my finger made contact, then darkened and began storming even more. "But there are people involved. And sides to be taken."

"If you're with us, we can't lose. We *won't* lose," La Roche said, his voice almost to a whisper. He knew something I didn't.

He was getting agitated and swiped his hand across the map. All the figments and illusions evaporated into purple smoke and he stood from the table and strode across the room. He took a few minutes to shuffle through his collection of coats before picking a dark green one with silver floss about the collar—really, rather extravagant—and putting it on. He pulled at the cuffs and tightened his belt, checking himself in the vanity again.

"And you're so sure," I said. "Forgive me if it all seems a bit odd."

"Well. It does seem that way to you. But to me it's quite clear."

"Nothing with you is ever anything less."

La Roche dragged his hands down the side of his face, sighing at me, exasperated. "I deserve that. Alas, we haven't the time to cover the last three thousand years of history. All I know is if you help us, we will *win*. Most likely. I know this because it's one of my..." he waved his fingers around while he searched for the words, "my abilities. My powers. I see patterns. I can predict them. Much like you can sense an oncoming storm, I can often times sense what is going to happen. Or what is likely to happen."

"Convenient."

"It isn't something I can control. Heavens, it would be more than lovely if I could summon it up at will. All I know is that I know if you fight, Miriam will win."

I said nothing.

"Can I at least appeal to your sense of adventure?" he pleaded.

He was right. I wanted the adventure. The sea had left me wanting, grasping for something more. My heart was cleaved in so many pieces already, and here I stood at the edge of the next grand calling. Yes, I was angry, and I was tired. I still had a thousand questions.

As if he could hear my thoughts. "And your desire to protect your blessed one; if Achaemenes finds his way to Londinium, no one will be safe."

I held his gaze again, waiting for him to say something more. When it was clear he wasn't going to try and fill the space with more words, I said:

"I've got only one requirement."

"Hmm?" he asked.

"You come with me. I won't do this alone. Not this time. If I get out of hand, it's on you to control me."

A whisper of fear came across La Roche's eyes, and then he shook his head. "I will do all that is in my power."

12

And that's how I entered the war. Because, no matter how deep my anger, being in the presence of La Roche was a welcome reminder of friendship and kinship. I had found no real answers in the deep. I had not found redemption. I had only found more self-loathing and continual loneliness. I was not a fish; I was not a man. I was a monster in between, and La Roche understood better than anyone.

At night, while we couldn't be detected by the crew, we slipped off of the *Hoel* and into the waters below. I rejoined the water, both glad and skeptical, and La Roche chose one of his own familiar forms, the dolphin, and I marveled at the ease of his transformation. There was a bright blue spot just below his throat, and I thought it strange and beautiful. I had noticed a similar patch of white in his rook form and noted it was where his scarf was. I almost asked him, but he began moving fast.

We had some miles to go between us, and only the stars to guide us. When our first approach proved too slow—he was a faster swimmer than I was—I fashioned horses from the waves, and together we rode them west. That, at last, impressed him.

I pulled fog around us to obscure us even more, worried there was a chance we'd be sighted by boats patrolling the coast.

Dawn was rising when we reached the first location. La Roche explained that this particular fleet, positioned about twenty miles off the coast of eastern Gaul, had been engaged in the slaughter of six Marian-controlled towns in Constantinople. They had fled this way and, after leveling some of the local towns on the coast, had set up a small barrier preventing the townsfolk from fishing, essentially forcing them to restock the fleet. So much of the area's population of Eastern Gaul was already engaged elsewhere on the continent, and the majority of those left behind—women and older fishermen—hadn't been able to do much to prevent the ships and sailors from their deeds.

And while it sounded as if La Roche's plans were entirely humanitarian, I knew well enough how fertile those grounds were. Not to mention their location. The ships there were impressive, some of the strongest in the Persian fleet—black and high-sailed with cannons not to be reckoned with.

"Besides, they're right in the middle of our escape route," he added as we began our descent under the ships. The idea was to stew the storm closer to land, as La Roche insisted it would keep the coastal folk safer.

I got into a good current and started planning what I would do. La Roche indicated that he wanted more than just rough weather — a little damage to the ships wouldn't be terrible. We weren't talking about a high loss of life, just some good punctures. Ships could be filled with more people, after all, but their entire loss was irreparable. The Persian fleet may not have taken the same route technologically speaking in many aspects compared to the rest of the world—at least in terms of clockwork and research into drugs and essences—but their ships were stronger, faster, and more deadly than anything the Marians could boast. It was that strength that had kept control of the Akdeniz for as long as they had.

"I don't think it has to be a storm," I mused to La Roche as we gazed above us, the ships arranged like tiny, shadowy fish over our heads.

"What are you thinking?" he asked. He didn't speak the words, but I heard them in my head the same.

"Scare them first," I said. "Then we can consider the storm."

"By all means. Be creative," he said.

I closed my eyes and held out my arms, feeling the sea around me. The waters were cool, morning cool, and it felt marvelous to be surrounded by them again. In my mind I could feel the entirety of the Akdeniz, arrayed like La Roche's map. I knew every island and crop, every rise and fall, the cavern of every creature in the deep.

I didn't want to put my ocean friends at risk, for they had given me so much. I already felt their hesitancy, knowing I was once again in the waters, reeking of human filth. But there were parts of the ocean that were stronger, more dangerous, to ships, which didn't include the beings beneath it. There was, after all, weather below as well as weather above.

I told them this was an effort to rid their waters of warring humans. But in my heart I only did it for my godson, the child I had brought into a cursed family. My guilt goaded me forward.

I looked at La Roche and he nodded to me.

Below, far below, the water moved dark and cold. So cold it didn't take much to bring the temperature down even more. I reached myself down into it—which is the only way I can explain the feeling to you—and sent every frigid thought I'd ever had. Then I made it colder still. I concentrated in one localized area, and began building the crystals, knitting them together as I'd done with ice in a glass back in Londinium. But bigger. Much, much bigger.

"You might want to swim inland a bit," I said to La Roche. "And think warm thoughts."

The icebergs rose from below, the water currents cooling before they broke the surface. I hadn't expected them to be so large—I ought to have considered it, but I wasn't exactly practiced. I was weaving spells, theoretic spells, oafish spells that weren't precise in any sense.

Not that it mattered. La Roche spun out of the way just as the first passed by us, churning the water in mad, sharp frenzy. It was jagged and harsher than I had expected.

I started to move to the surface but was turned around as the great masses of ice careened by. The currents were disturbed enough I lost my place in the sea entirely.

Then something pierced me, sharp and cruel. I gasped, tasting my own blood in the water.

Tremble, child of the deep. Taste the blood, taste the rime.

Khasma and her madness. La Roche and his faith in me. The slight chance my godchild would be spared a life of suffering.

My mind fractured. Fury stoked. I felt chains burst in my mind as I pulled at more and more of the power of the ocean, unable to curb my appetite for it, the ancient ice feeding me with reckless abandon.

In the distance I heard La Roche calling my name, begging me to stop. I felt feathers on my face, jellyfish stings, but it did nothing other than cause me more anger. I became furious, engaged deeper and deeper, confused.

I fell into blind rage. A darkness in me shattered, broke, and was born.

How many ships did I destroy? How many lives did I take? I'm afraid I can't count them. I don't know the names of the boats, let alone the men and women aboard them. It was not the last time death came at my hands, but it was without the regret that I'd come to know later as a matter of direct choice. I expanded on every side, like a god of old, strong and sure and wreaking vengeance. Like a shark, the blood egged me on, fueling my ire and hatred and anger and sadness. While I moved mountains and shook the earth beneath the waves, I even forgot my name.

I might have ripped the bottom of the Akdeniz clear to the burning core, if it hadn't been for her.

I heard her rippling across the water, and I stopped my rage, just long enough for Miriam to subdue me. I'd never seen her in her power, and in my fury, she looked like a pillar of smoke and fire, roiling toward me, arms outstretched. When she reached me, I could do nothing else other than breathe her in, and slip away into the blackness that bound me, even as pain seared through my brain and through my body.

When I awoke, I was aware of an immensely drowsy feeling and knew instinctually that I was on land. The solid emptiness of rock between me and the heart of the earth was unavoidable.

I heard voices around me though I could see nothing and felt the presence of two godlings: La Roche, dim and distant, and Miriam. I didn't have to open my eyes to see her, as her presence—before only vaguely attainable to me—burned into my mind. But it was hard to focus. On godlings or anything else.

I burned. Most noticeably the area from my scalp to my chin and my side, down around my ribs. When I moved my mouth, I could feel my skin stretch unnaturally, puckered and pinched, the wound still raw, and not healed.

I went to move my hands to find they were entirely restrained, and I lost my mind for a while again while I raged against the chains. They were iron, thick and well-forged. Pure iron, not like the shackles from before. My strength was a thousand times diminished, and I fell back, exhausted, heaving breaths between the sobs. I only had a vague idea of what had happened, but I couldn't forget the smell of all that blood in the water. I had called the sharks to me, and they had dined on anything that had passed their gaze.

And I had fed too.

The sash across my eyes allowed nothing through but watery, wavering light, and the pain coursing through my body was difficult to bear. I stained the sash with tears and called out La Roche's name a thousand times, but no one came to my aid. I only felt their silent shadows in my mind, reluctant whales.

It felt like an eternity as I screamed and let the poison leave me, the rage. La Roche told me I lay a whole week there, shouting obscenities at the sky and cursing everyone I had ever known, promising to raise a tsunami and drown them all. Even then, though, I knew I wasn't capable. Part of me was spent, gone, used up. I began to hunger and thirst like a human, to feel the sunlight on my skin. To feel anything other than the continual gnawing at my flesh.

Finally, I fell silent, and made only prayers in my mind, and wept no more.

AT LAST, Miriam came to me. I heard her voice, deep and hushed, before I knew she was close. My sense of other goslings was much diminished; I had lost that part of me.

"And here we are. Joss Raddick. Our child of the deep," Miriam said.

I groaned.

"It is a wonder we were able to subdue you in the first place," she said. "Andrew had quite a time of it I briefly thought he would give up the ghost in the fight. You wounded him. And he wounded you. And in the end, it took a very large quantity of opium and Trita's spear to your head to get you to stop."

She removed the sash from my eyes, and even though the room was only lit by a small fire in the corner, I had to squint to make out anything. My eyes streamed tears, burning my chapped face.

My eyes wandered to the rest of the room. It was stone, for the most part, though bits of the details were cut from wood. For the first time, too, I realized just how cold it was. Perhaps it was Miriam. For her part, she wore a thick velvet cape that whispered as she moved. She sat comfortably on a small stool by the bed—or torture contraption—where I lay.

"What happened?" I asked, my throat like saltwater across a wound when I spoke.

Miriam laughed—a high, strange noise in her throat that was oddly girly, like some young belle at a ball trying to impress a lad. "We were briefly outplayed. Achaemenes knew you were in the waters, somehow. And he pierced you with an ancient weapon, filled with a poison known to stoke the fires of godling power and transformed you into a shark in the waters. But he miscalculated."

I didn't know what to say to her, but I could hear the note in her voice of pride. She was proud of herself and somehow proud of my accomplishments too. Dark and sordid as they were.

"Granted, you destroyed quite a number of my ships, and even killed one of my most prized captains. Which is unfortunate—yet in light of *everything* else, rather insignificant. It's one of the truly redeeming qualities about the human race—they proliferate rather impressively. You mow down a thousand, and two thousand more are waiting somewhere else..." Miriam said, reaching over and wiping my forehead. Her hands were like fire, and I winced.

"Where am I?" I asked. "Where's La Roche?"

"He'll be in shortly to help you through the last stage of your healing process. We fended you off with Trita's spear, and some is still lodged in your skull. To say nothing of the talon in your side. There is no human healer capable of doing such an operation, and so we've had to keep you in a slumber while Andrew heals himself. As I said, you *wounded* him. You understand that, don't you?"

"A bit," I said, clenching my teeth as the area at my temple began pulsing with pain again. Buried iron. It stood to reason that's why it hurt so damned much.

"Forgive me," she said, though I knew she didn't mean it. Every line of her was flashing impatience. Disappointment. "I know this is not the story you want to hear."

My side. That's where La Roche had gotten me. Somehow, even before she told me, I knew. It felt like the sun had crawled in there and was rooting around in my ribs.

"I suppose you're in quite a remarkable amount of pain, and I am truly sorry. But the risk was worth the reward. You have destroyed what is left of Achaemenes's ships, and he has agreed to meet with me to discuss the terms of his surrender. As much as I'd like to be angry at Andrew for his schemes, I cannot. He behaved as he should. And you did, as well. Though it may be some time until you're able to move the waters. A few thousand human bodies are just larger plankton in the grand scheme of things, you know. Every mother knows that for new children to be born, they must feed on the blood of those who have died."

"Miriam, I…"

I began to weep, and she sighed.

"I will not wound you," she said. "It seems as though you have done that to yourself well enough. As to your ultimate absolution, we shall see what the next days bring."

13

When La Roche came to see me, I was startled at his appearance. His long hair was shorn short, and there was a bandage around his head similar to mine. He wore a plain robe of simple brown wool, up past his neck, and much of the vivacity I'd come to know in him was diminished. La Roche's skin had gone sallow, and there were fading bruises around his face and around his wrists. Miriam was not exaggerating when she indicated he'd taken a long time to heal.

He met my eyes but didn't speak for a long time. I could feel the tension rippling off of him, and strangely, I could sense his emotions better than ever before. There was an air of confusion about him, a sense that he was trying to make up his mind about something. La Roche hid it by trying to tidy the room as best as he could, pulling the drapes closed, and fussing with a handful of instruments he'd brought with him.

At last he said, "It's a strange sensation, isn't it?"

I wasn't sure what he meant, exactly. "The wound near my lung, or something else?"

A quizzical, almost curious look came over him then. "You really don't remember a bloody thing, do you?" he asked. He was speaking in Breton, and I'd almost not noticed. Languages were becoming harder and harder for me to tell apart, though no one noticed when I spoke that I was anything other than a native tongue. Miriam had been speaking in Latin.

"Not much," I admitted. "Not after the first bit of our adventure…you could tell me the rest."

For the first time since meeting him, I saw in La Roche a true expression of pain. Of guilt. He put his hand on his mouth, and his shoulders slumped forward, as if he was going to retch. I realized, then, that he was trying not to weep.

"I feel responsible," he said, at last, wiping his eyes with the back of his hands. But the tears were falling quicker than he could keep them.

This was not the La Roche I had known before. The concern in his eyes was genuine. When he touched my chest, I felt the wave of remorse he did, knew how truly he grieved. He couldn't meet my eyes, so instead he started rooting around my side, checking the wound that he had inflicted upon me.

"I knew you seeped saltwater," he muttered, reaching into his robe and pulling out a small silver disk. He removed a waxy substance from it and began slathering it over my side, making a face when he lifted up the bandage. "But eventually you bleed blood. And it goes from red to deep blue. It's disturbing."

"Not much of a difference. Just a different color."

"Hmm. You'd think. Except salt water has a bloody difficult time clotting over. I have to keep rubbing this pesky stuff on you to prevent you from withering away altogether."

"But you still must shackle me." I'd given up against the shackles, but it didn't mean I had to be pleased about it. Even if I thought it a wise choice.

La Roche took a deep breath and gave me a glance under his foxy brows. As he took his hands from me, I could feel him disconnecting, sense something else clicking into place in his strange brain.

"I can at least tell you how I did this to you," he said. "I will leave enough details out of it, but you may find it relatively amusing."

"I could use a spot of amusement. I remember roiling water. Blood in my mouth. Bones…horrid things. Just, no faces. It's a bit like the entire human race became nothing but plankton," I said, trying to explain to him exactly what it is I was feeling.

La Roche smiled, the edges of his lips upturning impishly. "You were a *Kraken*. Immense. It was terrifying and amazing, and nothing like I'd seen in my life. I didn't know exactly what to do—so I went to my griffin state, which I hadn't achieved in some centuries, and never without Verta's help. I used my claws to get you down to size, at least. One of my talons lodged in your ribs…"

He held up his hands to me and I noticed for the first time that his heart-finger was gone, entirely. The base was black.

"It's still there," I said.

La Roche nodded, then showed me some of his instruments. They were all gold of the highest purity and studded with gems. Scissors, knives, pliers, and a long set of tweezers. "I am here to take it out. And the bit of iron in your head was Trita's doing. When I couldn't subdue you, she cut you down to size. You almost…" he shook his head.

"Her staff," I said.

"The same one. Iron isn't as dangerous to all of us as it is to you, apparently. I've tried to inform Miriam it's dampening your powers enough to render you practically human and that the shackles aren't needed, but as usual she's not listening that closely to me. She's rather ecstatic over the crushing victory and has been going on and on about the Synod."

"Tell me the details after this blasted thing is out of my side. I can feel it grinding against my ribs," I said.

"Well," he said, after a moment of deciding over which instrument to use, "let's see if it's bone or talon. I doubt I'll be able to affix it again, but it's worth the effort, isn't it?"

What proceeded was pain to a multitude of anything I'd endured before. La Roche was trying to be kind about it, but the fact was the talon was lodged between ribs and curved in toward my lungs. Man or godling, such surgery required a kind of courage I couldn't muster, seawater in my veins or no.

The pain changed from a steady heat to a constant, sharp, impossible noise that riddled my body. My ears filled with the rushing of the waves; my heart threatened to leap from my chest with the force of it all. Through my temple and down to my toes, I felt everything. After what must have been half a day, La Roche finally removed the talon—for it was still very much a talon—with a great gush of fluid and a scraping of flesh and bones. Immediately I could breathe better, but La Roche had to fret about the room to get more towels and blankets to soak up the mess.

I saw him stagger and fall to his knees, and just as he did so, three veiled priestesses entered the room and helped him stand again.

"Get him more opium," he said, his voice wavering in and out. "Let him sleep. I shall have to finish…much later."

I DREAMED OF CRUMMOCK WATER, of Scale Bottom, of the look in Frances's eyes when I took her upon the floor of the stables at the Swan and Hoop. I wept in my sleep and was certain I'd awake again swimming in a sea of tears.

Then, Verta returned.

She now looked like what I imagined the original goddess would have. I had never seen her in the daylight, always in the dark of her temple or the evening when we strolled the old cemetery. Her long hair was down, falling to her thighs, and was strewn with small, white flowers. She wore a simple gold diadem, intricately etched with the image of gamboling swans. Her clothes were somehow less revealing yet more alluring, a combination of hanging silks and iridescent fabric that fell down to her feet. It was quite chilly, and so she had a thick cloak of ermine and a pair of white leather boots to keep her warm.

She said nothing at first, but simply unfastened my shackles with nothing but her bare fingers. Leaning down, she kissed each wrist, and the pain subsided significantly. My head was still sending tendrils of pain down the side of my face, but with the talon removed from my ribs I could at least sit up with less pain. My body protested the action, having been prone for so long, but as I was learning, I was made of strong stuff. Stronger than the strongest man alive.

"You grew *scales*," Verta said, pointing to my wrists.

I sat on the edge of the bed, and we were more or less of a height. She gave me a sad smile.

"La Roche?" I asked.

"Resting," she said. "The surgery was long, and he was able to remove all but a shard of Trita's spear in your temple. He was not able to reattach his finger, and the effort of removing the talon from your body without harming you even further drained him. He is very distraught."

I stretched, feeling my body flush with strength as it finally was free of those shackles. My back still hurt, though, to say nothing of my head. I rubbed the area by my temple, trying not to disturb the bandage, but it itched worse than nettles.

Verta brushed back her hair, ringlets cascading down her forearm before falling into place. She had a way of exuding such beauty in the simplest of movements, it near broke my heart to watch her. In the light, her skin was luminous.

"There's to be a meeting. A Synod. As soon as Andrew is feeling better. We are all here, gathered on this island, for what is considered to be a first in more than two thousand years," she said softly, as if she hardly believed it herself. "I didn't want to come. But I knew I had to, especially after what happened."

"Why did you unshackle me?" I asked.

She smiled lovingly, head tilted. "You are no harm to me. You are no harm to anyone. Not right now. Miriam is nothing if she isn't cautious. You transcended, somehow, in the war. You channeled the Source. But the shard in your skull will prevent you from doing that for the meantime."

That seemed simple enough. I didn't want to transcend again. I didn't want to know what was so bad La Roche couldn't even tell me, he who'd slept with thousands of people and lived as ribald an existence as anyone. Morality was a footnote to him, and yet I had shocked him to silence.

"Then I don't want it out," I said.

Verta blinked at me, surprised, her mouth falling open to reveal her pearly teeth. "You can't be serious, Joss. The pain would drive you mad."

"Perhaps. But so would doing that again."

"Joss, you didn't choose to do it. You were poisoned."

"Does it matter? I've won this sodding battle for everyone else, but the cost is so great I feel it in every breath I take. I left, Verta, because you told me to. I learned. I met creatures of a like I never imagined to be. And I was taken too. I left a part of me down there," I said. The scales at my wrists, which had apparently grown in response to the chaffing of the manacles, were flaking off. The skin beneath was mottled and pink and new.

Swallowing hard before she spoke, Verta put her fingers to her throat. "I'm sorry," she said. "I know Andrew blames himself, but I blame myself, as well. I judged him before I knew the truth. And once I found out, we were up to our necks in bloodshed, and you were gone."

"Tell me my child is safe," I said. In the moment, little John was all that mattered. "Tell me you watched over him."

"Even better, I can show you," she said, her eyes full of memories and tears. "He is safe. But his life has not been easy."

Verta walked to the other side of the room and took the washbasin, a copper bowl in the shape of a seashell, and filled it with water. Then she placed it beside me on the bed and took a seat across from me. I had to move to face her, and my legs protested, but the pain was becoming easier to ignore, especially in light of what she was going to show me.

"Miriam would not approve," she said, glancing to the door, "but I will be brief."

Casting her hand across the water, the surface turned slick as ice but as reflective as a silver mirror. She wiggled her fingers and her star emerged from her hands, the same she had showed me before when she let me know she could find me wherever I was. She breathed a few words in a language I didn't know, yet understood—I caught the word for child and life—and the surface began to ripple as if she'd thrown in a handful of stones.

At first, I saw nothing save my own reflection, distorted in a thousand ways and sadly bruised and battered. But then it started to change, and the streets of Londinium came into view. They were streaked with rain, as always, but it was a late evening and the skies were turning crimson. I longed for it, strangely.

The view shifted and came upon the Swan and Hoop, but then swung back, out of place.

"He is not there," Verta said softly, "though he visited recently. His mother is ill."

I said nothing to this, choking back the memories threatening to send me sobbing again. I'd had enough tears, I'd have thought, but seeing the Swan and Hoop brought the memories of that horrific evening swirling back. We went north, and the view opened up upon a brick building, impressive in stature, with many lit windows.

To the windows we went, one by one, until Verta showed me the face I had longed to see. He was not a large boy, but he was strongly built. His hair was a handsome auburn, his eyes a pleasant hazel, and he bent over his book with a rather lackadaisical concentration. Every few moments, his gaze flicked up off the page to something else in the sparse room. The chair, the window, the single painting on the wall of a seascape.

He was the most beautiful child I had ever seen.

"It's enough," Verta said. "He is safe. He has two brothers and a young sister. He will apprentice in a few years to the apothecary's school, if he can manage to keep his grades passable. His teachers are concerned that his performances are somewhat unpredictable."

I didn't dare to ask, but she answered for me. "He has the soul of a poet, and though he adores learning—and history in particular—he has a certain difficulty containing himself in the light of all of that. All the music and poetry is in his blood, running through his thoughts, and yet he doesn't have the power to make it sing, yet. He has yet to learn to tune his lyre, you might say."

"He's beautiful," I said.

The vision changed and she showed me a young girl, perhaps ten, standing in the middle of a room with her hands behind her back, reciting something to a group of adults. Her eyes were large and luminous, and her dark, curly hair was tied in a neat braid down her back. As she spoke, her chin rose and there was a fire in her eye that reminded me of Trita.

There was a grizzled man among them who smiled most.

"This is little Mary Godwin. Trita's scion," said Verta. "She is almost ten, if I have my calculations correct. She lives not far from John."

A wave of her hand again, and the setting shifted to a shadow darkened hillside with a small young man running down it, carrying a parcel of books. He was birdlike, his hair almost crimson, and his cheeks splattered with freckles. He kept looking behind him, and then stumbled and fell, only to be overtaken by a group of other young man who took his books and scattered them in every direction.

Verta sighed. "And so it is with Percy Shelley. He would go so much farther if he could learn to keep his mouth shut. But his godfather never does, so I suppose it is in vain to wish otherwise."

Then, with a moment's hesitation, she showed me one more. Her own scion. The location could be no more different than what I had seen of the rest. No Londinium home, no boarding school. It was a sprawling converted temple, now dotted with years upon years of high-arched Persian inspired architecture. The old temple could be seen off to one side, but the rest was quite Eastern in its presentation.

In one of the rooms, sitting by the fireplace, sat the handsomest lad I'd ever laid eyes upon. His face was akin to the sculptures I'd seen of Adonis, though his hair was jet and curled delicately at his forehead. He sat in the chair, a glass of mead in one hand, staring into the flames with a look of near disgust. There were littered papers nearby, splattered with ink and crumpled a thousand times. And there was plenty of half-eaten, discarded food. A dog was gnawing on a ham bone that he had thrown in the corner.

"And this is Noel. George, by right. He is, I suppose, my Achilles. That foot, though..." she sighed. "Gods help him, he is as indulgent as I was in my youth." She almost smiled when she spoke of him.

But then she disturbed the surface of the water, and it was over.

"Those are our four," she said. "Mistakes, blessings, curses? I do not know. But they are...purposeful creatures."

"As are we, I suppose."

"Joss?"

I was fading fast, and she could tell. "Yes, Verticordia."

She paused at the use of her full name. "I'm very sorry for all of this. If you had only come to us a little earlier, perhaps you would have known how beautiful it all was once. When we were in our Eden. You would have been more at home."

"You and La Roche, you are my home," I said.

I could tell she was crying even though my eyes were closed. I could smell her tears.

She smoothed my brow, and her hands were deathly cold now. She gave me something to drink, bitter and sweet, and I fell back to sleep, dreaming of La Roche cutting John Keats from my body.

14

La Roche recovered more quickly than Verta expected, though I didn't see him until two days later. In the mean time I was allowed—or rather, nicely asked—to remain within the temple premises and to alert Miriam's acolytes of my comings and goings. It was as it had been in Marmor House: dark robes, clutched roses, dour faces.

Outside the confines of the temple I could fell the press of the ocean surrounding us, but it did not call to me as it did in Londinium. Now I was afraid of the waves, afraid of the secrets they kept in their depths. I breathed the air and tried to forget the horrors below the waves and the memories in the brine.

It was difficult, with the wound still fresh and the iron lodged in my skull, but as the days passed the pain lessened somewhat. There were times in the day when the pain was worse, primarily when the moon appeared, but it was tolerable with opium which Verta administered most expertly.

I found Trita dining with Miriam on the third day after Verta's visit, sitting together on one of the mosaic patios by the main temple. A slew of servants were in attendance, mostly men clad in little more than loincloths in spite of the chilly weather. The sun was out, and it was tolerable, but far from warm. The wind coming off the water was enough to make me gasp.

Trita looked vastly different than the last time I'd seen her. Like La

Roche, she was wearing simple robes but cinched across the middle with the pelt of some speckled beast. Her hair was beaded and coiled up about her head, and it gave her a queenly appearance as if she were holding court. Miriam was still in the same black robes, eating olives out of a glass bowl, held aloft by a young boy with black curls and a dimpled chin.

When Trita spied me she stood up as if to fight. Then she sat back down, slowly, as Miriam put her hand out to still her.

"He is subdued, Verta assures me," Miriam said when Trita looked to the other godling in concern. "And he remembers virtually nothing."

"You didn't mention that he..." Trita trailed off, pressing her long fingers to her lips. "Was given free reign of the island."

"Far from it. My acolytes know his every movement," said Miriam.

"I'm sorry," I said.

"That's Trita's spearhead lodged in your temple," Miriam said casually as if commenting on the quality of the olive oil. "I see you have not yet had it removed. Though I'm glad to see you are well enough to be walking around."

"The gift of Mnemosyne," I said. "Perhaps that's why I can't remember."

Trita gave me a tight grimace in response. "I would have killed you if I could. You know that."

"I would expect no less of you, Trita Oya. We've fought enough beside one another for me to trust your judgment to the last," I replied, my heart sinking.

"You're smaller than you were," Trita muttered, almost half to herself. "La Roche told me as much, but I didn't expect it to be true. I suppose you look less of a threat, but that would be a good cover for one who has become more poisonous."

A flutter of wings followed and La Roche himself flew down, in his bird form, onto my shoulder. In the light, I could see what a magnificent bird he made, though there were still signs of his injuries. One of his talons was wrapped in an odd silver mesh, and there were feathers missing on some of his sleek, black wings. The white spot on his chest looked larger than it had before. Or perhaps it was a trick of the light.

"Have we not moved beyond all the feather pointing?" La Roche asked Trita. "I can vouch for him. Considering I was rooting around in his ribcage earlier, I do think I'm the foremost authority on the matter."

"I hate when you're a bird, Andrew," Miriam said. "It's dishonest."

He squawked in my ear. "Dishonest? It's a necessity. If you remember,

I had a Kraken's arm to the head a week ago or so. It's much easier to conserve energy in this state. It's a simple matter of mass."

Miriam scrunched up her face like a spoiled little child tired of her mother's lessons. "Don't start in with the science again, Andrew. It hurts my head."

La Roche dug his good claw into my shoulder, and I knew without asking that he was trying to keep his mouth shut, which was challenging even when he was feeling at his best. I could imagine the strain of illness made it harder to concentrate, at least it did for me.

"At any rate. In the last three millennia, a meeting of this sort is unprecedented," Miriam said, rising with the help of one of her servants. She wiggled her fingers and another servant brought her a glass of steaming mulled wine; I could smell the spices from where I was.

"Achaemenes's forces crumbled," she continued, "His ships have been scattered to the ends of the earth. And with the setting sun this evening, we shall gather here on my most treasured island, Menorca, where my cult first began so many centuries past. Today we shall witness the passing of the savage age, and onto the age of enlightenment, carried on the backs of my acolytes who bear the words of my ancient predecessors and the Gospels of my followers.

"Today," Miriam said, raising her glass and looking up to the skies, "we usher in an age of peace, of prosperity, and of progress. And all of you shall receive your due."

And so began our gathering, our Synod. At last we would see this Achaemenes, at last we would join together—all save the Huntress, who was not yet upon the earth again, and Calvin's, who had not heeded Miriam's call.

Before the Synod began, La Roche informed me that my personal state left much to be desired. Miriam claimed I looked not only as if I'd been dragged up from the depths but had also been dragged along the bottom for good measure on my way up. Which was, more or less, true. Verta was already in her finery, and both she and La Roche agreed to take me in and put me in better clothing, suited for one of my stature.

I followed La Roche—now in his human form; after the sun was at its pinnacle, he seemed far healthier than earlier in the day—to one of the smaller, stucco-style buildings away from the waterside. He paused before we walked in and turned his face to the sunlight; for a moment, his short hair kindled with the brightness of the sun itself, and then was out. His skin was flushed, and he even smiled as we passed through the threshold.

A simple joy. An uncomplicated joy. The godling and his element.

Then it was gone when he opened his eyes and saw Verta.

She stood by a large bed with her hands crossed over her chest, three of her own acolytes surrounding her. I recognized the cut of their clothes and their bearing, but not their faces. They were going over swaths of cloth and comparing them, showing them to her, while she shook her head or nodded. She even rolled her eyes at one point.

"Is this truly the best we can manage?" she asked the tallest acolyte, a redhead with a comely form.

The red-haired acolyte saw me pass through the door, and then replied to Verta. "You understand, her Ladyship prefers black. She finds it more respectable."

The two other acolytes looked shocked at the redhead's criticism. I liked her pluck right away. And her voice. It was deep, soft, tinged with just a bit of roughness around the edges. And she had an accent, too, though I had no idea where from.

"Ah, Shanna," Verta said, waving away yet another bolt of cloth with dismay, "You'll need to learn to curb your tongue a bit, my dear. Her Ladyship prefers her girls to be of gentle countenance and demure manner."

Shanna glanced at me again and grinned. She had a dimple, damn it all, and that about sent me into a fever. She was the sort of woman I wanted to curl up with by the fire, to bury my face in her bosom and feel her hair between my fingers. And damn the woman, she knew it by just looking at me.

The other two women, both smaller and slenderer than Shanna, giggled a bit.

"All of you," sighed Verta, throwing up her hands in consternation. "We are no longer in Londinium, and this is not a temple to Venus. Chastity! Is it so impossible for you to behave?"

"I have that effect on people," said La Roche, taking the lead and making a large bow to the group. "You mustn't blame their gentle, demure hearts."

Verta looked less than pleased. "We've made an agreement, Andrew. I'm trying desperately to turn courtesans into vestal virgins for a few days, but I might as well be passing off tin for gold."

"Ah, now that's not fair," I said. "Shanna at least is passable for copper, she shines so."

"Hm. She does," Verta had to admit. "But that isn't the point, is it?

Miriam is calling for unification. And I have promised to stop recruiting for now. And to help my daughters become more...Joss! Please. Stop staring. You're only making matters worse."

"Our apologies, darling," La Roche said, sitting down on a large fluffy pillow. He fed himself from a small bowl of almonds, pausing to crack each one in half between his teeth. Birdlike, indeed. "You've just got the best taste. We can hardly be blamed."

"Clothes?" I asked after a moment had passed.

Verta didn't grace me with a response, but instead went behind a screen and came out again with her arms full of fabric. She rifled through them on the bed and then finally picked something out and held it up to me. It didn't look like clothes. It looked like cloth.

"I'm thinking something Classical," she said. "What do you think?"

Shanna giggled.

I walked to the fabric and took it between my fingers. Soft, yes. Blue, yes. A color I liked. However, what Verta showed me looked more like a curtain to hang in a window than a vestment to wear.

Then I looked at La Roche. He was wearing robes, as he had when I first met him after I'd awoken on this island. The finery was gone, and its place was a kind of simplicity.

"Like that?" I asked her, jutting a thumb at La Roche.

"More or less," she said.

"Do I get trousers?" I asked, for it seemed a sensible question. There was plenty of fabric to be had, but it begged the question of my bits.

Shanna giggled again, trying to hide it. I kept finding my eye straying to her. Most people would feel embarrassed by such a show, but I felt quite the opposite. It had been a long time since I'd even contemplated taking a woman—and having her take me—and I was sure Shanna was of a mind.

Verta grabbed my chin, her touch electric. "Focus, Joss. You don't need trousers. Just rudimentary undergarments."

"It's cold out there," I said.

"You are the godling of the sea, my sweet," she said. "Don't tell me a little chill will be the death of you. But I was thinking that this seafoam blue, with the ivory floss, would suit you best. Joss!" She pinched me.

In the end, she had to dismiss the girls and had some rather sharp words for me. Though the glint in her eye indicated she wasn't half as angry as she made it sound. It was, after all, her ken.

She had two manservants come in and wash me first, using a copper tub in stages since I couldn't fit in the whole thing myself. I liked the process, which included being rubbed with an abrasive salt to get my skin soft and remove the excess scales which had grown about my wrists and ankles.

When my body was clean, they draped me in a blanket and brought me to the window, where they oiled my hair and plaited it. Then they trimmed my beard, perfecting the end to a nice little point. I felt a bit strange without as much of a tangle on my chin but glancing in the mirror I had to admit it did make me look better. In the years since I'd left, my hair had dulled from soft flax to a kind of silvery white. It aged me but keeping the beard short helped me retain a bit of youthful vigor.

Then came the clothes. There were, as Verta had said, a variety of undergarments. Wool leggings, and a sort of halter over my chest. Then she wrapped the robes, cinched it with a silver hammered belt made to look like fish scales, and clasped a thick wool cloak of darkest blue around my shoulders. A simple torc around my neck was all that was required.

When I looked in the mirror again, I could scarcely believe the sight.

"I take it you want me to make an impression," I said to Verta as she stood back to observe me. "The only piece that doesn't look right is the bandage up here."

"I think I have an answer," La Roche said. "If you'll permit me."

"Just don't stain the robes," said Verta.

La Roche stood to my side and put two feathers, laced to a leather thong, in my hands. They were his, from his rook state. "Hold these gently between your teeth. This may sting."

He lifted the bandages from the side of my head and clicked his tongue. "Indeed. As I thought it would. The shard has nearly surfaced. It won't take much to remove it."

"But I don't want—" I tried to argue, but he was quick.

"Shh, give us a moment," La Roche said.

I didn't feel much different, just a little disoriented. I watched, still biting on the feathers, as he handed the metal shard to Verta. She took it in her hands, and then went to the fire, holding the metal over the flames with her bare fingers. I could see her working it as if it were simple as clay. When she came back to me, the shard was shaped into a small heart, hollow in the middle. This she laced around the leather thong, and then slipped it—and the feathers, which she instructed me to release—around my neck.

My headache was gone, but there was a heaviness on my chest. I tried to reach for the charm and touch it but found my hand oddly repelled.

"It has wounded you, and so you are bonded to it. The feathers help keep it grounded, as they are a reminder of another wound," said Verta, putting her hand to my chest. "You may not be able to remove it, but should you need us to…either Trita or La Roche or, perhaps, I may be able to."

I was shaky, and nervous. The charm made me feel off-balance and I had to walk about the room to get my bearings.

"Achaemenes will need to see you like this," La Roche said. "You see, your wound is already healing. He may feel that you are wounded, but you will not be weak. Simply reined in."

"And why do I want to impress him in the first place? To show him Miriam's got more of us on her side?" I asked, loathe to involve myself in politics.

"Exactly," said La Roche. "He is alone, now. We have all allied with Miriam, and the war is nearing the end. He needs only admit his defeat."

It made less sense to me than ever, and it must have shown in my face because Verta took pity on me and described it in simpler terms.

"Your spectacular performance on the waters demonstrated he was weaker and older than he'd imagined. The new godling beat back the old. Now it's simply a matter of words and the exchanging of weapons. He will be given the concession prize…"

"Concession prize?" I asked. "What in the depths would that be?"

"The New Land. So-called America…" La Roche said, and I could hear the longing in his voice, the wistful desire.

15

The Synod took place in a large, circular building at the very center of Miriam's island. It seemed to have been built for this specific purpose, as it contained the precise number of seats—eight of them carved from old stone—arranged in a semi-circle. It was open to the air above, and the walls were polished bright as mirrors. About the floors and on some of the walls depicted mosaics, as well, mostly images of the sea and fish and what one might expect of an island culture. But there was not much left to it, really. While I couldn't have quite called the place a ruin, it was not long for the world. A remnant, perhaps, of the golden age Verta sometimes spoke of, the pinnacle of godlings.

I was brought in behind La Roche, in a particular order deigned by her Ladyship. Miriam was very specific about how we would walk in and oversaw each and every detail. I was to come last since I was the youngest. Trita went first, carrying her broken staff, followed by Verta.

It was hard to concentrate on anyone, however, once I became aware of Achaemenes's presence. Later, La Roche told me Miriam had him in a lead and iron-encased room, which is what kept him out of range for me to sense before the event. But once he was released, the very air around us became charged and almost tangy, metallic odor. The air felt robbed of moisture, or else tainted with something which made it more difficult for me to breathe. He was the eldest among us, though Verta wasn't entirely sure on the exact count, and he was powerful in strange and dark ways. Mad, weird ways. It was a flavor of power that I had never known. A true dragon of a godling. Fierce and brimming with magic. But old too. Dying.

The doors to the other side of the room opened up and two rows of red-robed guards came, each carrying a length of iron chain. There were eight guards on each side, huge men of a variety of ethnicities but of the same basic bulk. And right in the middle came Achaemenes, his head up, but his body bound with chains.

Miriam was more afraid of him than she was of me, it seemed.

When his face came into view, I was surprised at how young he seemed. I had imagined him a compliment to Miriam, who was weather-worn. His hair was slate black, his eyes followed suit, angular and bright. His skin was pale and his cheekbones sharp; he was beardless, which was strange to me, and appeared no older than twenty summers or so. He had been stripped of his clothing and carried with him only a sarong. He looked like an impetuous young man and not the wizened old godling I had expected.

Miriam clapped her hands and all the guards dropped their chains, making a most terrible noise upon the marble floor. Achaemenes raised his head and looked upon all of us, one at a time, and it spoke of more strength and power than any of Miriam's hollow words.

Still, she made more of them.

"I welcome you all to the gathering of the Six," she said, raising her hands to the sky. "A momentous occasion, and a gateway to peace."

Achaemenes said nothing, but stood, close-lipped and defiant. I knew all too well the pain of iron, and the charm around my neck was boring down into my chest as I watched him.

We all stood and waited for Miriam to continue. She was gloating, reveling in the silence.

"You are all witness to the culmination of two millennia of strife. The loss of human life, the changes to the course of history… This thread is finished. Here, we have come to an agreement, Achaemenes and I, at very long last. He will abide by my terms.

"In exchange for peace, he will be sent to the New World, where he will fade into the end in no less than one hundred years. So, it has been decided."

Achaemenes said: "And so it will be done." His voice did not echo, did not shake the ground. It was a strong, sure voice, an easy voice to listen to.

"Who will carry out the deed?" asked Miriam, looking to each of us. "The Wounding pact?"

My heart went cold, for even without knowing precisely I knew what she was asking. She wanted one of us to wound Achaemenes—wound him beyond the realm of return. I could not do it, but I contemplated what that would be.

"Not you, earth-shatterer," Achaemenes said as if he had read my thoughts. He tried to laugh but he was too tired. "You have already spilled enough blood to fill the rivers of the world. You do not need to add to that tally."

La Roche made to speak, but Verta held out her hands, shards of light blinding us. I shouted, the talisman at much chest burning hot against my skin. I fell back.

"This is my right," Verta said, her voice ringing from every corner of the room.

The rest of the godlings, disoriented and confused, broke into a cacophony. But it was too late.

Verta stepped forward toward Achaemenes. She spoke a word that was beyond all language, a promise—a threat—an oath. I can't say what the word was, because it was like the earth moving. Or the call of a distant star. Or the thrumming of the deep. She had committed herself.

She took one more step forward, and as she did a bright blue border rose up between us and Achaemenes, transparent enough to see through. It crackled with energy and filled me with sorrow and dread and fear. Touching it was the last thing on my mind.

"Verta!" La Roche shouted, trying to move toward the barrier, but falling back in a spray of white and blue sparks, tossed like some child's toy. "Verticordia! You can't survive it!"

I leaned down to get him and helped him to his feet. He thrashed in my arms and then went still as we watched.

Miriam's haggard face lit with the blue fire, and she smiled and smiled and smiled.

Verta was visible, like a great dark shadow, through the barrier. And then she opened her arms wide. All of her seemed to grow and lengthen, and while I at first thought it was to make the shape of some strange animal, I realized that she was becoming a twisting vine, a thorned rose of some kind. She twisted herself around Achaemenes, over and over again, and sang as it happened, an old song in a long-forgotten language. His song reverberated about the building, tearing into my ears as each sharp spine made contact with his flesh.

Miriam watched with glee, her small hands clasped beneath her chin. She had waited for this moment for longer than I could fathom. This victory was to be savored.

Achaemenes's voice grew and grew, deepening in strength and building until he was silenced, crunched by the pressure of so many vines. In one burst of light the wall fell, and where the two of them had been now grew a pillar, rising through the roof, of blue and of crimson. It twisted and coiled, like two fighting snakes, until the red propelled through the sky like a comet, and the blue reformed again in the prostrate, naked form of Verta. Her hair spilled down her shoulders and on to the floor, and she did not move, not even when La Roche came to her, sobbing, and put his arms around her.

I looked to Miriam for an answer, but she appeared concerned.

"That was *messy*," Miriam said at last, bending down to inspect Verta. She brushed Verta's hair from her brow and then put a finger into her mouth. Sticking out her tongue, Miriam then nodded. "She has not given up her ghost yet, but it will not be long, Andrew."

"*I* was supposed to wound him! We'd *agreed*!" La Roche shouted. He was getting angrier, the heat from him burning when I touched his shoulder. Trita was beside me, doing her best to comfort him, but the look on her face was both grave and without much hope.

Miriam stood above all of us, her hands folded. "She will survive," Miriam said. "But she did not follow the *rules*. Again. Which none of you seem to do, anyway. Do you find them amusing? Do you mock my demesne?"

She was talking to me. She knew what I had done to Fanny Keats.

"It can wait," I said, half growling at her. That Verta was in such a state brought me so far out of my own sorrow that I could think nothing else.

But Miriam was not about to listen to me. Her eyes flashed at my direction, shocked at my impudence. Yes, she knew I was powerful, but she had also gotten me to swear my allegiance. To attack her—especially after all she'd endured with Achaemenes—would be an act of war.

La Roche looked about to faint; his lips were white, and his eyes unfocused.

"Not now, Miriam. Please," he implored. "Just give us a moment to gather ourselves before..."

"This is my demesne. I am done with you all for now."

"What about absolution?" I asked. "You said..."

"I said I would not ruin you, wound you, Joss." Her eyes flashed and Miriam drew herself as tall as she could. "I make the rules, I do not control the outcomes. Your choice to raise that woman from the dead has cursed the entire Boast. I curse it. Here and now."

"They are just innocents," said Trita.

"I set the wheel in motion. And the wheel doesn't spin unless it's been pushed. Regardless of your intentions, oh earth-shatterer," she said, with as much mocking as anyone had spoken to me in my life, "the motion was made. Boasts are sad little distractions from what truly goes on, and I'm afraid no amount of talk or deed of allegiance will ever change that."

She clicked her fingers and two of her priests appeared and ushered her from the room.

I watched Verta's face, still and empty, heard La Roche's bestial cry, felt Trita's hand on my shoulder. There was no side of truth. There were only mad godlings, grasping at power, and we between them.

16

That evening, Verta changed to a dove as she dimmed. I kept vigil with La Roche, alone.

We told ourselves we were lucky to watch her leave the world.

La Roche did not leave her side. He put her small, white feathered body upon a bower twisted with hawthorn and thistle, flowers out of season but nurtured by the magic within his own body. The light had left his eyes.

I stood silently by him as the night deepened. In silence. It made me itch to say nothing, but I knew the man's pain. Though mine was great, his was greater still. Verta's fragile bird body breathed in and out, rhythmically, but there was no improvement.

"La Roche..." I finally said.

"Shh," he said. "Let us keep a silent vigil. For her. There is yet more to do."

He took the small body of Verta in his hands and looked down upon her, whispering something softly. Immediately she flicked her wings and stood up, looking curiously at him. He brought her to his ear, and he listened. I could not hear the words they spoke, for it was in a language other than which we can make with our mouths.

Then, La Roche turned toward the Western window and let her fly out of it, into the setting sun.

We stood again in silence until all was dark.

Then La Roche turned to me, his eyes blazing like starlight. "She will fade tonight. She wants to make a final flight, and then she will return to me."

"La Roche…"

"Saints and martyrs," he said, his eyes glowing bright for one heartbeat as he looked upon me. "Enough with the stupid 'La Roche' business. It means only 'the Rock' and it is far from what I feel right now."

"Andrew." I tried, relieved beyond imagining that my friend had rekindled his spark. Somehow.

"Merely a perversion of the name I was given," he said with a sigh.

"I'll call you friend."

He smiled at me, and his eyes filled with tears. "I would like to tell you my name."

"That is not wise," I said. "You said as much."

He shook his head. "No, Joss. You had reason to mistrust me before, and my guidance has led you down paths of darkness I had not foreseen. I cannot give you anything else than this to show you I will never deceive you again."

"Did Verta know your name?" I asked, a strange sense of jealousy rising in me.

"No," he said. "I kept it from her because…because it was the one thing I had that I knew was mine alone. The one part of me she could not have."

"But you loved her."

"Do not mistake love and trust, darling," La Roche said softly. "I sometimes saw Verta and myself reflected in Miriam and Achaemenes. To my doom."

He rose slowly, staggering, like a man drunk or weakened to the point of frailty.

I caught him, the heat of him blazing against my hands.

Yes, I was smaller than I had been before. La Roche was a tall man by human standards, but now I was only a few inches more. I looked into his face, feeling his look of pain pierce me utterly.

"Aneirin," he said, placing a hand on my chest. It warmed me, stilled me, calmed me. His name brought with it the same sorrow I'd felt when I'd read his journal, but more it was the power of connection. The name filled me with an understanding, a bond. "I would like you to call me Aneirin. I feel as if we have earned that, now. We have crossed through the flames and stand here now."

"I might never sleep again," I said, wiping my eyes. "Knowing what I know now."

"Then you have truly become my heart." He touched my brow with his fingertips before releasing me, breathless.

WE AGREED to leave for Britanniae in the morning. Trita greeted me in the best way she knew.

She held a cold iron dagger to my back. I didn't fight her. I could tell her anger blazed and seethed and there was nothing I could do. So I stood silent and waited for her to speak.

"One of the best of us gave up her life for this fucking war," she said, emphasizing her language by twisting the knife.

The pain gave me a strange kind of clarity into Trita, who had always been difficult for me to read. While the blade seemed to erase some of my abilities, it enhanced our own connection somehow.

"I can't apologize for what I didn't mean to do, Trita," I told her. "But I am sorry it has cost us so much."

She let go of me, pushing me in reaction. I let her. I could have fought back, even in my weakened state. That moment, when she'd connected with me through the knife, I'd learned a great deal about her. I felt things, sensed things. Her incarnation had been born a thousand times, her lifetimes filled to the brim with sorrow and disappointment and anger. Her knowledge, which filled her to bursting, had so often taken her to the brink and beyond.

Trita growled in frustration. "You have no right to have done what you did."

"I know," I said.

"You have the gift of Mnemosyne now," she said, sitting down upon one of the stone benches and cradling her head. She gestured to the talisman. "But I cannot forget. I don't know if I can bear looking at you. And it breaks my heart, Joss."

"It seems to be the sole purpose of godlings, as far as I can tell. Shattering hearts and slowly going mad with time."

For a moment she looked like she pitied me. Then she said: "Then I suppose that's all we have between us. Time. In time, I hope we can fight together again."

"As do I, Trita."

Before I left the island, I did what I had done so many nights in Londinium. I took a walk. The island was a great deal smaller, that was true. But there were fewer people to interrupt me, and I still felt distanced from all the beings upon it. No longer did their presences come to me unbidden. I was left alone, almost, to my thoughts.

It was then I found Shanna wandering around the night garden, wrapped in silver furs, shivering. When she looked up at me, there were tears in her clever eyes, and I ached for her. It felt good to grieve for someone else, and I welcomed the tears.

"She won't come back for us," she said to me, picking at the withered rose bushes. "She won't. She told us…we knew. We knew what it meant."

I was afraid to be near her as she approached me. Afraid that I would lose myself again, even though my powers were much muted. I backed up, and she looked hurt.

"I wish I could help you," I told her. "But I'm a danger."

"You don't have to be," she said. Her hands were like ice on my skin, and she trembled so much it made me worry. "It is my practice. I am a Priestess of Venus. We can heal each other."

"You were. But you are promised elsewhere."

Shanna frowned and then dropped her head on my chest. She smelled of salt spray and green grass. Her curls corkscrewed out in a thousand directions, and oh, by every god holy and profane, I wanted her.

The moonlight skittered across the water and I sunk down next to her in the cold sand. I warmed it because I could. Just a matter of heating the water just so. She sighed, sniffled, and smoothed her hand down my face.

"Verta told me you were a visitor of her temple in Londinium," she said. "And that it was full of springs of water, drawn from deep clean wells. And how you were known for certain…talents."

"Shanna," I said. I begged. I could barely swallow my throat was so dry.

"I kept a temple in Eire for her, but it burnt after the Marians came. I am so sad, Joss. Let me worship, one last time," she whispered, her fingers tracing down my stomach, then up my thigh and to my mast.

I gasped. Of course, I gasped. There was more to the woman, I knew, than a mortal soul. She was fire and water and joy.

"Please," she said, her fingers tracing knot work across me, delicate and intricate. A spell.

In my youth I would speak every detail to share, and spare nothing.

But with Shanna, it was no initiation as before in the Temple of Venus. It was not a simple conquest. It was desire, on her part, to commune with her goddess through me. Oh, she knew what I was. There was no hiding it. But I was aware that I was her conduit, and nothing more. The iron and feather heart about my neck bore down on my chest and kept me subdued, though I cannot say the experience was unwelcome.

I let her take me and lost myself in it all. When the sun rose, we walked together to the water's edge. I was less afraid.

In the distance, I could see the boat where Aneirin awaited me, the *Hoel Reborn,* fitted with bright sails and freshly painted. And now, as I looked upon the ship, dark against the crystal waters, felt the call of the waves and yet, I found I could resist. As before, Shanna had taken something from me while she lay with me, but it was something I had given willingly. Fear, perhaps. The act of love given for the purposes of healing, of worship. Maybe there was magic in it even if Verta was diminished and dying.

I went to speak to her and turned, looking first at her eyes. I startled to see them flash green as grass, rippled like a tide pool. She was naked and yet her body shimmered with scales.

"Thank you, Joss," she said.

"What are you?" I asked.

"I am a daughter of the sea, one of the very last," she said, raising a hand to my cheek. Her fingers were wet, dewy, as they traced the wound at my temple. "I will return to the waters and sleep silently until I am needed again and my sorrow is quenched with the waves. Perhaps then, we will meet again, oh tamer of horses, oh savior of ships."

"Shanna, I…" What would I say? There was nothing. No promise, no oath. Our time had come, and then it was gone.

Shanna cried out, a wail from deep within her spirit, and melted into the water, the tide sweeping her out to sea. For a moment her hair was visible, a great red blot like blood upon the waves, and then she was swallowed up by the sea foam. I stared after her for a long time, no words in my throat save the whispering wind.

17

"I didn't say it was *impossible*," said Aneirin said later aboard the ship, filling another snifter full of brandy in his cabin. He'd listened to my story of Shanna rather politely, quaffing as much alcohol as possible. "But it is highly unusual. It's not that I don't believe you, exactly. I just need to point out that you're still reeling from grief and self-loathing. Much as I am."

"La—Aneirin," I said, stumbling through his rightful name.

"Though, I wouldn't doubt if it was the kind of company Verta kept. If anyone could attract a naiad, it would be her. Or you. And I suppose you both did." He laughed, hollow and cold.

While his old ship had been destroyed, this new vessel had been in Miriam's fleet and was an even stouter ship. But he hadn't had a hand in it. I did not know if his journal had been lost at sea, but his chambers were clearly not his own design. The decorations were all wrong. It was well-appointed and high quality but not garish or embellished. It was very much to my liking.

He wore the colors of the most senior of Miriam's guard, argent and deep blue. The colors did nothing to dim his appearance, as even though his hair had been shorn short it was still a most vibrant red-gold. As agitated as he was, he still had the bearing of a most comely soul.

"She vanished. I swear to you," I said. "Her feet turned to water and simply slipped into the water. Like ice melting."

Aneirin sighed, fussing over his maps. "Well, at the very least I will agree there are some left in this world. In the Golden Age, when we were allowed to breed whenever and whyever we so chose, the world was rather filled to bursting with their sorts. So, it makes sense some linger."

"Though it is a shame she didn't have any sisters to share," I said.

He looked oddly at me, as if I'd said something unexpected. "I suppose."

I put a hand on his shoulder. "Will you be alright?" I asked.

"Of course. I have been preparing for this, after all, a very long time. Verta was right."

"If you need *anything*, please," I said.

"I need forgiveness. But I'm afraid I'm the only one who can provide that to myself, and damned if I've sworn never to let it go."

"Aneirin..."

His eyes brightened just for a moment at the use of his true name. "I must get some rest, Joss. You understand. I'm weary to my bones. And if I don't rest, I'm afraid I'll evaporate, myself."

I slept deeply and darkly, in a chair across from Aneirin's empty bed.

Then someone was shaking me awake. A young man with a scar through his bottom lip, as if he'd been fished out of the water and someone had torn out the hook.

"Sir—the Captain..." the man said, pointing over to the other side of the room. "He's ill, and he's not talking right, and I didn't mean to wake you from your slumber."

Aneirin was slumped over in a chair in the galley, drunk beyond belief. Drunk to the point of hardly breathing. For a man, that might take a few glasses of brandy. For him, it was likely a barrel. I was amazed he was still upright.

"Thank you," I said to the sailor. "Leave us. I will send for more help if I need it."

He nodded, left, and shut the door behind himself.

No words he spoke were even remotely coherent, even when I pressed him with questions—even when I sought to speak to him about Verta. He wouldn't move of his own accord, and so I decided I'd have to move him bodily. It was less trouble than I imagined; he was not a heavy man. Dead weight though he was, it did not take me long to take him in my arms and place him in him his rather expansive bed. Maybe he did have more to do with the boat's construction than I thought. The quality of the fabric was beyond compare. Silk.

I pulled over a bucket in case he was going to be sick. It wasn't often that a godling was made so ill from liquor, but it wasn't impossible, either.

Thinking him simply drunk, I took the chair and dozed on and off while the ship plowed on. Then I heard his voice, thick with tears.

"Joss."

He was pale. Lips pale, tinged with blue. In the dim candlelight that blue made me afraid, knowing it was warmed by fire and yet so cold.

And his eyes. Still amber but starved of joy.

He held out his hand. "I need to tell you something. To show you something."

I stood and took a few steps over to him, kneeling by him.

The closer I got the more I realized that he was not drunk. Oh, there was a measure of alcohol in him but no more than I'd seen him take before.

He was sick.

"There is a reason there has never been another plague. Why sickness and pestilence remain rare," he said. "Do you remember I told you I was born amidst a plague?"

"I do."

"And you now know what I did. What I was when Verta found me."

I nodded.

He swallowed and winced, his pain palpable. When I, at last, took his hand, it was searing cold. He shook from the violence of the pain he was in, his missing finger flaring bright blue for a moment before extinguishing.

I looked on in question.

"Verta taught me old magic, magic given to her by Achaemenes. Wherein I could exert a great deal of my power and absorb certain curses. To make up for the horrors I wrought bringing back my town from the dead," he said, shaking again. "It seemed a righteous exchange."

"I don't know what you mean," I said.

"We are not gods, but we are god-like. Calvinius's potions and tinctures have kept me stronger these years since I have made recompense, but he has been missing and the fight against you, and the loss of my stores aboard the *Hoel* have left me weakened."

"And Verta."

Aneirin nodded. "I can scarcely feel my arms. Joss, untie my neck scarf. I'll show you."

My hands trembled as I carefully undid the scarf at his neck, the material so light I was afraid I might rip it in my clumsy fingers. I brushed the skin on his neck and felt compelled to look him in the eyes, to watch him as I followed his directions. He had a calm expression, near curious. I stopped a moment to help get his head more comfortably arrayed, and then I had the knot undone.

As I had noticed in his dolphin and bird forms, he had a blue spot. But on human skin, the effect was more frightening. It looked as if he had swallowed a shard of glowing ice, and it pulsed under his skin. A source of pain. A thorn.

With a surprisingly strong grasp, he took both of my hands and stared at me. "I took the sickness of the world. I swallowed it. Verta helped me cast the greatest spell I ever learned, and I took all the plague and the pestilence, and I have kept it all this time."

My throat thick was with tears. "It must be torture."

Aneirin grimaced. "Most days I can push through it. I wanted to grant the people of this earth a season of health, freedom from the plagues that took so many lives. I thought without illness they would become peoples of culture, learning."

"Which is why you got so upset. When you heard of the sickness in Londinium."

He nodded. "Calvinius and I were working on a potion recipe that would help, but now I'm falling apart from grief and the pain is so great. So great."

"Hold on, Aneirin," I whispered. "Please."

"Oh, Joss. I do. I will. I know the moment I expire will be the death of many more. But I weaken every day. It's falling apart around me."

He began to weep silently, burying his face in my hands. His tears were hot, and they evaporated quickly on my skin. I drew him closer.

I had never felt this way for another godling, but this moment was many years in the making.

When I kissed Aneirin it was soft at first. Fatherly. A kiss on his cheek, grown so unnaturally cold in his sickness. I ached to heal him; my skin burned with need. Verta taught me intimacy could heal, that the touch of another could mean so much more than simple pleasure. What was it she had said to me? "Pleasure is but the messenger of intimacy, the assurance that what we do has meaning. It is in the afterglow where the true resolve rests."

But then it grew more intense, not just in the attraction between us, but in the movement of our own powers. I could exchange more than an embrace. I could love him, and I could give him some of my own power if I chose to do it.

I did find him beautiful. I always had. His charms were difficult for anyone to ignore and I was not immune. But that night aboard the *Hoel Reborn* was significantly different than if I had simply lain with him during our first year in Londinium. My experience in the deep brought me closer to my own mortality—for godlings are mortal, only in different ways—and so, too, it brought me closer to pain. To know what to give and what to take and how to comfort another.

His eyes opened wide when I pulled away to look him in the eyes, but not in fear or surprise, exactly.

"Joss," he whispered.

"You won't weaken while I can help it," I said.

"You don't know what you're doing," he said. "You're confused."

"Far from it. You, of all people, should understand."

He nodded. "You have seen things, I know."

When I took his hand again it was blazing hot, trembling. I reached my other hand up to smooth his fair cheek, cut so sharp and fine. When I had first awakened his beauty had arrested me, but it was more now I knew him more fully. Now I could feel the way his body responded, the heat of the center of him drawing toward my cooling waters.

In my arms, he blazed.

"There is no one else who can help you in this way," I said. "You know it to be true."

He nodded, and closed his eyes as if gathering his thoughts. He breathed shallowly, measuredly. "I will admit to having played out a similar circumstance in my mind many a time, Joss, but I hadn't imagined…"

It was enough talk from him. I showed him just how well this would play out, and we came together atop the waves, and I gave him pleasure and understanding and strength. Where his body was smooth and fair, freckled and fine, mine was rougher and stronger. It took some time to find the right way of it, but then we were complete, and there were no questions. It was all touch and sensation, pleasure and discovery.

When we finished, he lay spent upon my chest, silent, his hand gently moving the silver hair growing there, avoiding the charm still around my neck. The chattering rook was without words to describe. I was tired, too, but stronger somehow. It was a new font of knowledge, a deeper and truer connection to another soul, the greatest understanding there is.

I will be the first to tell you it is almost never like that; with Aneirin it was unique in ways I will never be able to put into words.

"Do you feel better?" I asked him, at last.

"I am warmed to the cockles," he said, and I could feel him grin against my skin.

"I mean, your throat," I said.

He put an experimental hand to his throat, and took a deep breath. "The pain abates some. I feared I might vanish without a trace." Aneirin propped himself up, looking me in the face. He touched the bridge of my nose, trailed his finger across my eyebrow. "You must not expend yourself so. Else you will diminish as well."

"I have plenty to spare."

"Would you sing to me?" he asked, putting his head back down. "I would like to hear some music."

"I'm not much of a singer."

"I will not judge."

As we sailed on, half asleep, I started to sing the water songs I'd learned as a trout. They were songs without words, the notes bubbling up from the depths of the earth and finding their resonance among the streams and tributaries of Cumbria.

At last, he fell into a deep sleep, cheeks flushed bright and clear. Perhaps my songs had made him forget. The dreams of godlings are strange and haunted, but there is magic in our music more powerful than the ghosts of our imagining. I like to think I kept those unwelcome spirits at bay for a while.

And eventually, I fell asleep too. But it was not long until someone was at the door, and I woke to the feeling of the ship rising and falling at an alarming rate.

Aneirin didn't stir, even when I left the small bed. I thought at first that I should do what I could to rouse him, then decided against it. Whatever sleep he was in, there was peace there, and I didn't want to disturb it. As a godling, he was perhaps the only one on the ship who didn't have to fear for his life.

I found the first mate, a man named Nathaniel, standing pale-faced at the door.

"It came out of nowhere," he said to me, breathless. "We knew not to disturb, but I wasn't sure what the Captain would do in a situation like this. The seas are full of horrors."

Nathaniel was a sailor of some two decades, and he'd been through wars and storms as the most seasoned on deck. Perhaps he had seen my destruction too. He looked afraid of seeing what he knew to be possible, and with the knowledge of how fragile a boat would be in such a situation. The *Hoel Reborn* was a sturdy ship. She was one of the sturdiest, most lovely brigs on the fleet, pieced together in Britanniae and sent to Akdeniz. She was swift, but not impervious.

I tried to reach out my mind to sense more, to see if it was one of the godlings—had Verta come back? Was it Achaemenes?

Without a word, I followed Nathaniel abovedeck and felt a chill upon me as I met the fresh sea air. It was snowing all around us, akin to a blizzard of the northernmost reaches, but the sun was shining brightly. The clouds weren't causing the snow, it was the icy wind shaving off the tips of the waves, casting ice at us sideways.

Everything was encrusted in ice, and the deckhands struggled to keep from falling with every step. I could hear the wood crack and strain as the hot and cold temperatures made war with the frame of the ship. The *Brittanic eels* moaned as the ice grew about her like the quickest lichen, crushing her from the outside.

In another time, I'd never have missed the change in the waters. But I had never been so otherwise preoccupied as I had been with Aneirin, either. Coupling with a godling was nothing short of transcendent.

The hair on my neck stood on end. There was magic in the air. Old magic. And fury, fighting. I wished that Trita and I had not parted on such difficult terms.

"Call all the men belowdecks," I said to Nathaniel.

The first mate gave me a perplexed look. "But sir—"

"There's some things which I prefer to keep to myself," I said. "You understand. Everyone needs to be kept safe. Huddled down. Out of sight."

I felt the fear in him ebb away somewhat, and he put his hand on my shoulder.

"Can you keep…contained?" he asked. I hadn't had to tell him, but it was likely there were rumors among the men.

I clasped the trinket at my chest, feeling the bite of iron sharper than the cold wind. I nodded to him.

Some of the men hesitated and tried to go to work against the first mate's wishes, which was surprising to me. My guess was that not all of them were used to working their stations, and there were stories to tell on the ship that, alas, I had no time to hear. But the wind picked up, and when shards of ice began pelting the deck and skidding around like glass sabers, the men picked up their feet.

For my part, the ice caused me no problems. I have seen mortals and godlings slip across the surface, but it has never been an impediment for me. I simply walked, using the moisture aboard the ship to keep myself rooted, stalking toward the stern.

It proved easier than I imagined, though the wind was making quite an attempt to throw me. I went higher and higher until I was above the storm below, and it was a strange view. The boat was wreathed in mist and snow, the ice and frozen precipitation glittering in the sun. Once past the main-topgallant sail, I was even warm. The ice that had gathered in my beard and hair melted, sending tickling drops of water down my back and chest.

That was what I needed to see.

Shanna.

18

She floated on a bower of ice, naked and pale, her red hair streaming out around her like blood seeping from a wound.

And she was being pursued.

"Ice dirae!"

Aneirin had made his way abovedeck, impervious to the cold. He was handsome and bright as the sun, his captain's carb gleaming, his hat staying on his head only by virtue of his hand.

"What the blazes does that mean?" I asked.

"Furies. Horrid things. They'll tear her to shreds."

At last, through the ice and snow the furies came into view. Their faces looked like drowned, frozen women, grimacing and gnashing their teeth. As they writhed, their feathered bodies glistening in the sunlight cast colder and colder air all around them. Ancient creatures, to be sure, but not without power. Something had awoken them from a slumber, I could sense that, and they were frenzied. Their voices reverberated across the frozen waste.

Shanna wouldn't be able to hold on for long, and she had already been grazed by their talons. But I couldn't simply jump into the water to save her; I was too afraid. Now, I could feel the temptation of power rising in me, an uncontrollable urge pulling at every desire at once: I lusted for it, even though I feared it.

"I don't know what to do," I said, watching as the furies began dive bombing Shanna, trying to swipe at something that rested in her hands.

"Heaven's fire, it's Verta!" shouted Aneirin, and I saw it to be true. The tiny dove, unmoving on her priestess's body.

My heart sank.

Aneirin moved out of the corner of my eye, and then I saw him plunge over the water, changing to the form of his rook. He was flecked with amber and gold and met the waves just as one of the furies was about to clasp its cold talons around Verta's body.

The ice encasing the entire ship began to fracture, threatening to rend it asunder. I couldn't let such a thing happen, knowing such damage would certainly lead to the demise of our crew. That thought was enough to keep me from fearing the worst.

So, I turned my mind to the ship. Aneirin would be safe, though I worried he would sustain damage by the furies. But I had given him some strength back. Shanna might die, and we might lose Verta forever.

Sliding down the foremast, my feet hit the deck with a thunderclap impact. I had no shoes and curling my toes downward to feel the boat as it shuddered beneath me. The wood spoke to me, every burl and knot, each braced beam and arch. I closed my eyes and felt myself at the very center of the ship, filled with all her knowledge and strength and experience. And I felt, too, the men aboard her, clutching one another belowdecks, weeping in fear of their lives. Some had lived through our cruel war, and more besides, only to find themselves here in this most unbelievable of circumstances. Their lives might not have been important to the sea, but they were important to me. I had to keep them safe.

Aneirin was becoming larger and fiercer. The rook sprouted silver feathers and grew a longer neck, his talons sharpened to razor points. With a great cry, he buffeted the furies—four of them by my count—keeping them away from Shanna and Verta.

I had to focus on the ship. In this way I bolstered the weaker points with my own powers, digging deep and preventing the temperature from changing too quickly where the ship could not withstand it. I glazed ice on the rafters and slowly brought the metal nails and braces to a comfortable balance without letting them snap. For a moment, I felt the very fingerprint of the shipwright who had made her and understood her more deeply and perfectly than I had almost any other living thing. Which isn't to say she wasn't living. Perhaps that's a large part of it. I came to understand just how alive she was.

If one can love a ship, I did.

Nathaniel later told me they could see nothing but the mist, though the waves lashed the ship and they froze, huddled together. They could hear rumbling, but no words intelligible to human ears. While he knew what I was on some level, he never bothered me for the details. When I returned belowdecks to tell them it was safe to return to work, they emerged into the sunlight, shading their eyes and pale-faced. Many had not expected to weather the storm.

With the ship steadied, I turned my attention to Aneirin. He was failing and failing fast. I had to do something but dared not risk going into the saltwater myself. I would never return.

But I could command the water, especially now the ship was steady.

Slipping forward to the starboard side, I took a deep breath and reached out across the waves. The furies needed the cold weather, and I knew from experience how powerful ice could be in such a situation. But if it warmed, they would not be able to sustain the attack. Aneirin had done a good job of keeping them at bay, but they were still on the offensive.

Boiling water would put Shanna and Verta at risk.

But I could command horses, the steeds of the deep.

With a roar like the wind, I pulled at the waters below, shaping them and twisting them into my steeds, those I had ridden in happier times before I had gone mad with the power. They rose around the icy bower and tossed their dewdrop manes, seashell eyes rolling in their noble heads. Whether they were true hippocamps or else simply extensions of my own ken, I will never know. Aneirin later told me they were disturbingly lifelike.

As the furies came down, up reared the hippocamps. They buffeted the talons and gnashing teeth and slowly swirled around the icy bower, building a kind of wall of water between the horrid creatures and their unconscious prisoners.

Together, Aneirin and I fended them off until, at last, I was able to take Shanna's limp body, still cradling Verta's dove form in her hands, and lay her on the deck. She was living, but barely. There was a great wound near her heart, puckered and still seeping blood. But she yet lived.

"The bird is dead," said Aneirin, his voice hollow.

I had become, indeed, a savior of ships. Though it had come after so much destruction. Perhaps it was a small penance on my way to redemption. I do not know. Through my long life I have learned that some get repaid for their madness and malice, and others do not, no matter how many centuries they tread the earth. It is an unfairness shared with humans and godlings alike.

But it was not enough to save Verta.

We could not pry the bird from Shanna's hands, try as we did, without harming her. An hour after she was taken from the sea, the bird, all that was left of Verticordia, turned to dust.

I THOUGHT it would be difficult to return to Londinium, but as we approached, I could feel the Tamesis, and it smelled sweet in spite of the stench. It was a smell of home. Of familiar rivers and lakes, of the sound of voices speaking the language I had first fallen in love with. Of La Roche and Verta and Calvinius. Even of Frances. Of innocence. Before deception. My youth, if it can be called so.

"You are thinking so hard there are practically storm clouds gathering at your temples, man," I heard Aneirin say softly from beside me.

"It smells so sweet," I said.

"Of course, it does. They're celebrating Marymas," he said.

We were coming down the Tamesis, and it was nighttime. But the edges of the river were lined with lanterns and candles. Every bridge and aqueduct was illuminated by the glittering lights of men and women standing vigil.

I looked at him questioningly. "Such festivities for Miriam, already?"

"While you've been away, Miriam's cult has taken fire. Quite literally. As you know, the whole cursed island has always been rather affixed to Diana, as she's always had a character of virtue and chastity which somehow speaks to the Britannic mindset. It was only a matter of time before Miriam's cult made it here, and...well...yes. The stench of the lilies makes my eyes water."

I looked down into the water and noticed that it was strewn with flowers, lilies and roses mostly, in spite of the cold weather.

"Lilies," I said, pointing to the flowers. "It's December. In Londinium."

"Yes. The second of her feast-days. Superimposing Marymas over Yule was clever. You know, ever-burning fires in the winter and all that rubbish. She's made it so that the roses and lilies bloom on this one day alone."

"How?" I asked.

He shrugged. "Some artifact? Some trick? A secret greenhouse? I haven't a clue nor a care. It's always theatrics with her. She has tried my patience and broken me beyond caring."

"They're calling out to us," I said, after listening for a moment. Voices on the shore.

"Yes. The ship. It was under these sails that Mary herself appeared as an apparition upon the sea and drove the usurper from the depths and won this terrible war."

It took a moment for me to understand his words. "But she didn't."

"Of course she bloody well didn't, Joss. It's a myth. It's…fabrication. But you'd rather they knew the truth?"

No. I did not.

THE SUN barely crested the horizon when we reached Londinium at last. The outline of the city had changed, the great cathedral of St. Paulius no longer the only monument of note: now, too, there were new aqueducts, made for travel and, it appeared, as residences. Decadent homes, draped in hanging gardens, stood out among the aqueducts like beads on a necklace.

We traveled by carriage to Aneirin's home, which was not in the city proper but some distance north, in a district known as Suthringa. It dated to before the Roman presence, according to Aneirin, but had retained some of its original charm in spite of having a decidedly Roman form to the streets and building placement. It was at the southern side of the Queen's Bridge and was sometimes called Southwark by the natives.

"It isn't much," Aneirin said. "But it is home."

Aneirin's residence, which he had dubbed High House, was in a row of townhouses, all crammed up next to one another, high and lean and new. He told me that there were a cluster of older, Roman wooden buildings until a few years ago, until they were taken down by a rather curious fire. I needn't have guessed who'd been there at the heart of the arson, but I chose not to weigh in on my accusations.

A woman answered the door when Aneirin rang the bell, tall and willowy with clever brown eyes and long, white hair. It was braided a bit haphazardly down one side but was of a most impressive hue. Otherwise she was a rather typical woman, though there was an astute intelligence in her features that kept me rather captivated.

"Welcome home, sir," she said in a deep, rich voice.

"Penny, there's a good girl," Aneirin said. "Would you please send Amos to the carriage? Our friend is ill, and I need to take her to the sick room."

Penny nodded, as if this had happened a thousand times. She took her candle down the hall and vanished in a swirl of robes. When she returned, there was a dark-faced man beside her. He was nearly as tall as I was and dressed as a gentleman, in spite of the late hour, with a physician's coat atop his other clothes. There was a large golden hoop in one ear.

Aneirin explained, "This is my assistant, Amos. He's an aspiring apothecary, and quite talented. But also rather strong, and careful." He leaned over and whispered something to Amos, who nodded and made for the carriage. "Which comes in handy in situations as this. I'm still not feeling myself."

"Let us get inside," he said to me, putting one hand softly on my shoulder. "We could all do with some modern conveniences, I think."

SHANNA WAS STILL UNCONSCIOUS, in spite of our attempts.

"She's probably dead anyway," Aneirin muttered, "and a traditional healer is best suited to her situation." Then he shook his head and directed me to where I would stay.

I was shown to my room, which was on the third floor and had a balcony, to my relief. A manservant named Stephen drew a bath in the basin for me, but it was scarcely enough water to cover me to the waist, and try as I might, my own powers remained dormant. I did the best I could given the circumstances, and enjoyed the hot, mineral-filled water. It sloughed away the salt and grit that had accumulated for so many miles.

Finding clothes for me—being not so large as I once used to be it was not so difficult—I gladly put them on, feeling myself more of a man than a godling or a sailor.

Stephen escorted me to the main dining room when Aneirin called for me, and I followed him down the narrow stairways and passages—all decorated in Aneirin's odd style, which is to say never a corner without a painting, a sconce, a bauble, a mirror, or a statue. We came into the main dining room, which was set with a meal in spite of the late hour.

Aneirin was at the head of the table, and Penny beside him. She was still in her nightrobe but was eating beside her master as if an equal. I had seen the servant class like this—often Saxons or Jute long kept as servants as their forefathers had, with the help of the Roman army and conscription. There were few servants in Londinium, or all of Britanniae, who did not stem from the same ancestry, purportedly descended from some obscure king.

Aneirin looked well, in spite of what we had just endured. For all the worry about Verta, the gnashing of teeth and deception, somehow, he was more or less his usual self.

That certainly concerned me. But I agreed to play his little game, regardless.

There was a place-setting for me, and I sat down. Aneirin, remembering my preferences, had arranged for vegetables, bread, cheese, and fruit. The fruit was dried, and had a rather stale taste to it, but I was thankful nonetheless. I had done with far worse during my travels. I declined the wine, but Aneirin poured me something I had only smelled before.

"It's an obscure alcoholic spirit," he said, as he poured me a small amount of amber liquid into a tiny cordial glass, etched to within an inch of its life. "It's all the way from Eire, if you'd believe it, and it comes only once a year during Marymas. I suppose, with the tensions ceasing—oh, they do so love their Marymas in Eire—it will be easier to come by."

I sniffed it, and it smelled of peat and life and memories. "What's it called?" I asked.

Aneirin poured himself a bit as well, then downed the entire shot. He smacked his lips and explained, in his usual overwrought way. "While the Romans never could get a foothold in Eire, they did meet quite a few times with their chieftains over the centuries. They were given this drink, which the Romans rather boorishly simply called what they called everything distilled and alcoholic: aqua vitae. The water of life. But apparently the Irish liked it so much, they reversed it into their language, calling it uisge. And now we call it simply *whiskey*."

I didn't think a shot would be enough to do any irreparable harm, and so I drank it. It tasted so much more delightful than it smelled, though the scent was a part of it. It set my mouth afire in the most pleasant way, like when I had kissed Aneirin. Then it warmed me from within, sending a smokey, sweet flavor across my tongue.

One did not seem like enough, but Aneirin was wise and kept the bottle from me.

"Strange considering you lived so close to the Antonine Wall too. Had we made peace with the Scots, you'd have had barrels of their whiskey. Which, in my humble opinion, is even finer," he continued.

"It tastes of a summer field, green and fresh; it burns like the sun and yet it's sweet, and familiar," I said.

"You'll welcome it, I'm sure. May it serve as a poultice to your soul. I know it does for me."

We ate in silence for another course—leeks poached in butter with a honey garlic sauce—and then Penny excused herself.

Then Aneirin was called away, and I finished my food.

When he returned, he looked as if he'd seen a ghost. And I knew, in that moment, that grief had come to him at last. So unpredictable. So strange. I braced myself.

"I can't understand it," he said. "I can't accept it. I am certain that if she was truly gone, I would *feel* it. But Joss, it's like…" he grimaced. "It's like she is in the other room, just waiting for me. Except I saw the bird with my own eyes. Dust."

My heart sunk and I thought of Verta, and of Aneirin's denial. "Perhaps it is just like the dew evaporating from the grass. It is there one moment, and then…"

"No! It cannot be. I will not allow it!" Aneirin shouted, banging his fist on the table so that the glass of wine wobbled almost to the point of spilling. He took a deep breath and calmed himself. "I'm sorry. I am…tired and confused."

"My friend, please," I said, reaching for his hand. He blinked down at it and then slowly pulled it away.

I felt my insides go cold. The sun turned away from me.

"What of Shanna, then?" I asked, looking away from his face. "Is there hope for her?"

"She has been gravely hurt. She is strong and uncanny, but no godling, she. And yet…"

"May I see her?" I asked.

"If you wish," he replied, shoulders slumping. "I can show you the source of my most inelegant hope."

19

We departed the lavish table and went down a level of the house, and then down yet again. The temperature rose. I started to feel the waters again, akin to those in Verta's temple. My ears rang with it, and I felt short of breath. I had to stop in the spiral hall to steady myself.

"There are hot springs down here," Aneirin explained as if I couldn't feel the growing presence of the water. "I had the house built strategically. I've kept it up, but we've taken over most of the other houses in the area, as well, though much remains uninhabited…it's just easier that way."

"I'm still not sure what we're doing," I said. "Is Shanna this way?"

"Yes, but there is more. You restored me," he said, in the tone that made me feel as if I were stupider than a stump of wood. "What's inside of you is unprecedented power, but it has its limitations—you cannot continue to give yourself away to every godling you meet."

"I hardly plan to," I argued, feeling an unexpected wave of shame. I was glad for the beard and the dim light, else my cheeks would have given me away.

"My mind, it is ever working. Working and working, moving like vast clockwork," he said, half-singing it. "Through the grief and all of this I have felt myself reach deeper and wider than ever before. And I think I may know a way for you to control yourself without that stupid talisman around your neck, too."

"Aneirin," I whispered, confident we were alone, and I could use his name. "What's this to be?"

He knew what I meant; using his name always got his attention. There was power in it, more than I knew.

"This is to be true friendship, Joss. This is to be my promise to you." He squeezed my hand and then beckoned me forward. "But for now, the gears in my mind are turning."

I felt that sick feeling again in my gut, like worms finding their way through a midden heap.

The room Shanna slept in was filled with steam from the hot springs. The walls were weeping from the moisture, but they were carved of porous stone. We were at an intersection of limestone—white and gleaming—and another darker stone that I couldn't recognize. The room was half in and half out, the top bright and clean, and the bottom half rather dark and flecked. Like moss.

Shanna's skin had healed somewhat in her slumber, though there were still scabs darker than the crimson of her own locks visible through the growth. She was stripped entirely and had a damp gauzelike material draped over her. Someone had drawn markings and divinations around her, as well. Etching in the limestone, hot rocks and crystals placed around her body. I noticed a large basin of water at her feet, water from very far away. Water I didn't know.

"She is a naiad. A child of the rivers. Her name, you know, is from where she was born. The River Shannon, in Eire. We were just speaking of the water of life, were we not?" Aneirin said. "Strange I didn't connect it then. But, no matter."

He squatted beside her and drew his fingers down the soft curve of her cheek. She drew a breath as if she'd touched something hot, but then went still as soon as his fingers left her skin.

"I'm a healer, Joss. It is one of the three fundamentals of my being. We all have them, we all find them. I heal. I burn. I see. Oh, I've other talents. But these three are the strongest in me. My truest ken. And I have tried to heal her and tried to heal myself—but I fear my powers too weak, even with all you have given me. I am too human, in the end. But you...you are not. You are more alien to humanity, and much of your power—for good and for ill—is just below the surface."

"I helped heal you," I said. "Even before..."

He nodded. "If there is any creature alive capable of purifying the waters within her, it is you. There is a kind of pestilence beneath her skin, keeping part of her body in a kind of rigor mortis. I suppose you don't have to even heal her so much as make the water flow again. Within her."

"It could hurt her. And I'm not sure I can bear it," I said.

"I will assist you. And why not? We have exchanged wounds and more besides," Aneirin said, holding up his four-fingered hand. His left. The heart finger was the one that had lodged in my ribs.

I went around to the cot, examining Shanna. It was only a few feet off the floor, but the white material had gone dark brown in places—especially around her head. She had bled for a while. I could smell poultices and herbs, those both familiar and strange to me. Aneirin had not rested since we arrived.

Kneeling down, I got a better look at Shanna's face. Her once plump cheeks were sunken, and her beautiful eyes were rimmed in wrinkles, dark puffs beneath them.

I was about to say something to her, something soft and gentle, when she put her hand through my chest.

It was a strange sensation, feeling her fingers slice through my chest and bones and innards. Of course, there was a great deal of pain, but it was a distant and curious pain, more like an incessant pressure, like swimming down below where the glowing creatures lie in wait. And indeed, I was reminded of them, the voices below Khasma.

I gave a helpless glance at Aneirin whose eyes were wider than teacups, clearly with no concept of what was happening.

"Joss!" he cried, coming to my aid. But her arm was caught firm.

Shanna sat up, her body flushing pink and filling in. I had to twist along with her, gritting my teeth against the pain.

Then she pulled and took something out of me. I knew immediately it was also something she had given me, left inside of me for safe keeping. But it hurt. I had kept it so long inside of me, this tangible power, that it had felt no different from the rest. I coughed, gasped, staggered back, and watched her.

Taking the thing, some strange shard of blood and light, Shanna stuffed it in her mouth and swallowed hard. Her head tossed back, and she threw her hands over her head, rising a measure off the plinth and then lowering again.

Then she was quite restored. Her wounds healed, smoothed over, vanished. Her eyes were clear and bright, her cheeks smooth and free of blemishes.

"Joss, oh, heaven's fire…" Aneirin whispered, then looked at me with utter confusion.

"I'm not dead," I said.

I felt around my chest. The talisman remained, and there was not even a hole in my shirt. I felt no surge of power, no desire to do harm. But the wound at my head throbbed anew, and when I looked at Aneirin, he had gone pale

"Some naiad," I said.

Shanna shuddered and then began to shiver. "Get me something warm to drink. And a blanket," she commanded. Then she stopped and said more sweetly: "If you'd please, Andrew."

Aneirin blinked, and shook his head. "You see, Joss," he said softly. "I told you. She was just in another room."

That's when I realized what had happened.

It was not Shanna.

It was Verta.

Her body was entirely different, but she was knit into it as surely as her last form. There were places where I could see her face changing as she looked around the room, the nose widening slightly and her eyes moving to the sides, but all in all, she still held the general appearance of Shanna, the naiad. Every now and again the skin about her shoulders shifted, as if a school of tiny silver fish flitted below the surface, then went still again.

It made me feel sick again, not the least of which was due to the idea she was inhabiting another creature's body. Shanna had not been a human, not in the sense of other mortals, but she was something beautiful and rare. That Verta had used her as a means of resurrecting her body, even in brief, was shocking and surprising to me.

Aneirin went to the cupboard and grabbed a thick wool blanket and then presented Verta with a glass steaming with water from the hot springs nearby. His hands shook as he held the drink to her, and he watched with tear-filled eyes as she drank.

Neither of us had words. I felt rooted to the earth. Even though I wanted to leave, to forget what had just happened and lose myself to the sea, I couldn't. There was a part of me within Verta, now, connecting me to her, making me unmoored. More than even before. She had wounded me. And she had not asked. She had simply taken it. I was some godling vessel for her, and it infuriated me though I could not put words to it.

"I could not leave yet," she said. "But wounding Achaemenes hurt me too much. Still, I had contingencies in place."

"Where is Shanna?" I asked.

"She sacrificed herself for me. She had dedicated herself to my service for a hundred years. This was done of love, and Joss, you helped her along."

I did not like the sound of that.

"And the furies?" I asked.

"They are vicious beasts. Miriam sent them. She knew I was breaking her rule," Verta said, holding out her arms and looking at them. She marked the freckles there and wrinkled her nose at them. In a moment her skin was smooth and free of markings. "But you kept them at bay for me, and now Miriam is in Rome, settling in to rule. She will not have the reach, now. If she can even detect me in this form."

"You could have told us," Aneirin said, teeth clenched.

"But you knew I wasn't gone, Andrew. Didn't you, my love?" she asked, all innocence.

They gave dagger eyes at one another, and then they both softened. He would forever be in her nets.

I finally found my feet. My chest ached. I had to leave. I could not watch Aneirin gaze upon her with pain and love and confusion one moment more. I needed air and I needed the stars.

20

When Verta came back into our lives, I lost Aneirin.

I intended to leave them and stay at an inn, unsure I'd want to live under their roof. Verta was tired and ill, coughing up blood and trying to accommodate her new body. It was an old, dark magic, and I could see that Aneirin was afraid of it—afraid of her—and yet torn. But he would not leave her. His soul was knit to hers.

"I'll be back," I told Aneirin when he caught me on my way out, bags packed. I hadn't even stayed one night in his house. How could I now?

"Don't do anything you'll regret," he warned. Gods, but he looked so tired.

I wanted to touch him, but I refrained. "How else will I have any fun?" I said darkly. "I'll make sure to steer clear of any of your concoctions."

"I mean the Keats family. You'll want to go there, to see him, but you may not be welcomed. You may have saved his life, but I do not know if the family remembers you so well."

"You don't need to remind me."

"Joss, please don't be angry. I was trying to make light. You're dampening the mood. We should be glad."

"Glad? *Glad*? You saw what happened. That magic…" I dropped my voice even lower. "It makes me sick. It should make *you* sick."

Aneirin licked his lips, looking over his shoulder as if she were there to see him. "I don't know what I feel. But she has come here, to be with me. I cannot turn her away."

"With you? You *really* think that?" I asked. "The last time I tallied the sums, the very last thing she wanted was to linger a moment longer. You're deluding yourself. This whole thing reeks and you know it."

"The war changed us," he said, icily. "You weren't there. We've all done things we regret."

"Yes, and it hasn't stopped. We dragged her body from the dregs, a body she took. Then the moment I get back, what does she do? Does she apologize? Does she ask after me? No. She rips out my *fucking heart*. And I'm not being metaphorical."

"No, you're being obtuse. It wasn't your heart. It was an essence, a bit of power."

"I don't fucking care what it was. It was wrong. She did not ask."

He calmed himself, smoothing the front of his crisp shirt. "I think you're a bit jealous, now. And you must understand..."

"You're blind. Fucking blind."

We were close. A breath apart. I wanted to punch him square in the jar and I wanted to hold him and run away at the same time.

I kissed him, instead.

"Joss." Aneirin whispered my name against my neck. I put my hands on his back, feeling his quickening breath, knowing we needed one another.

He melted under my touch, moaning into my mouth, and we burned together against the wall in the foyer, fumbling and mad and beautiful. It was insistent, short, and powerful love-making, fueled by anger and loss and hurt. We bit back our cries and blazed.

Spent, I re-buttoned my trousers and took his face in my hands.

"I can't stay," I said.

"Even now?"

I smoothed his check with my thumb and he closed his eyes.

"Especially now." My voice was scarcely a whisper.

"Just come back," he said, desperation in his voice. "When you can. Joss, I need you."

I WENT to the Swan and Hoop, thorns in my heart.

So much of Londinium had changed under the New Marians, but I've always had a habit of missing those kinds of details. By and large, Londinium looked more prosperous than I remembered. But the shadows looked darker to me. Maybe there weren't the kind of brigands there had been during my days fighting with Trita, but I could sense sneakier fish in the shallows.

I'm never one for the details in politics, either, but it bears note. The prosperity was largely due to the Senate reluctantly allowing Marian representation in court; since then, the New Marians made a remarkably peaceful, yet powerful, sweep. As it came to light in the papers, there had been an underground Marian revolt steeping for decades, and it was through Her Mercy—as they claimed—that they were given the strength to finally reveal themselves and raise Londinium to its true and most remarkable glory.

The cobblestone streets were familiar, and the fog, too, though the new buildings rose, and gardens twisted about me. I breathed in and out, in and out, trying to taste and sense what used to be so easy for me. When I was younger, unwounded. But everything smelled different. The food cooking in the home fires, the flowers under the dirt, the drinks in their glasses. With new trade routes opening up they now began steeping tea and trading silk and eating spices heretofore mostly out of reach. People were making a great deal of money. And Brittanic eels, apparently, were all the rage.

The Swan and Hoop was freshly painted, the stables full, the company rowdy. I didn't feel the presence of my godson, didn't know what to look for, really. I suspected I'd feel him before I saw him, but standing outside the inn in the shadows I sensed nothing but the crush of drunken men and women, the baking of bread, and the pouring of spirits. I could not bear to be a guest, not after what had happened with Frances Jennings.

I found myself dropping deeper into melancholy but pressed on.

Of course, I went to the stables. The horses, fine as they were, beckoned me first. That and my cowardice. I both wanted to see Fanny again and didn't. I knew I shouldn't. She was still alive, but she was broken. Could I bear it? I hoped the horses might put some sense into me, calm creatures as they were.

I had hardly made it halfway through when I was interrupted.

"What are you doing in here?" asked a frightened voice. Not Tom's. Not Fanny's.

"Just visiting some old friends," I said.

The man walked over to me and scowled. He couldn't have been much older than his mid-teens, but he limped fiercely. Not a limp from a club-foot or deformity, either. I could tell by his gait that he was a man suffering from the wounds of war. His hair was flaxen, his hair pale. A Saxon, perhaps, freed in the war. There were many of those, as Miriam had called in every last man to help in the fight against Achaemenes. Indentured servitude defined their entire culture, but he had no torque or ring in his ear and dressed as an ostler might.

When he looked up at me, I could see his expression, searching my face for something familiar.

"Old friends?" he said, his voice softening. The horses turned their heads toward his voice, and I felt them calm. He noticed as well.

I felt, too, my old friend. Poetaster.

"There was a horse," I said, "I used to spend time with him. Oh, years ago. He'd be ancient now, but..."

A look of amazement came across the Saxon ostler's features and he blinked at me a few times. "You must be the Tamer," he said. "And Goddess strike me, but you're here. It's like you knew."

I closed my eyes, and opened up to the room. And I could feel Poetaster, knew even which stall he occupied.

And I knew he was dying.

"Heaven's fires," I whispered. "Of course."

"I'm Aelfric, by the way," the man said, a little uncomfortably. "I didn't know if you had a name, so I'm sorry if—"

"Joss."

"Mr. Joss—"

"Just Joss."

"Yes, sir. Yes. With the horse, with Poetaster. He just hasn't been the same since Mr. Thomas passed. He threw him, you know. No one's sure exactly what happened. That was well on five years ago, though. Then right after, Mrs. Fanny, she up and takes the horse. Where she went? No one really knows. Not even the children, poor little ones. And little Fanny, just a babe..."

I tried not to show my emotions. Frances was gone.

I walked beside him as we proceeded down the center aisle. He was talking faster than I could make sense, but he was a projector—one of those people whose words spun more pictures and sensations than average. As he spoke, I could see the children, all four of them, and poor John the eldest with all the pain of his parent's failures and troubles on his shoulders.

"We told young John to stay at school, but he'll be on his way in the days to come to help with the matter of his mother. But the horse, he came back this way. Can you hear it? It's a sound like the rattling of Hades's chains," he paused and made the mark of Mary, pressing his fingers to his lips to ward away the evil. "My pardons. I'm still adjusting."

"How do you know me?" I asked him.

"The Tamer of Horses? Well, it was Mr. Keats's favorite tale to tell," he said, full of pride. "That, and how you delivered Mr. John. Though you're not as big as he always claimed. The children do so love the story."

He was going to say something more, but I could hear Poetaster's labored breaths, now, and I could no longer focus on the man's prattle. Horses have short lifespans, far shorter than the average human. The horse I had left years before was at the peak of health, a shining paragon of what a horse ought to be. The finest horse I'd seen or would see again. What I saw crumpled in the corner was a pitiable beast beyond recognition. He was wracked with spasms from coughing yet pulled against his chains in defiance. The metal had cut into his face and hindquarters, cruel but self-inflicted. I could feel the rage coming off of him.

"Are the restraints so necessary?" I asked.

"I didn't know what else to do. He was throwing himself against the side of the stall, damned near broke through the wood. Made a racket as to bring down the stars, and the Master wouldn't have none of it," Aelfric explained, rubbing his chin stubble. "This is what I was told to do. Though I don't like it. I only wish I could ease his passing."

"What are his symptoms?"

"He spits up blood and froth and all manner of terrible things," said Aelfric. "I worried it might be something to do with Mrs. Fanny's state..."

I looked at him, questioningly, and he added weakly, "Excusing me, sir, but I know you're a friend of the horses, but not sure if you're a friend of the family. I mean, I remember Mr. Thomas speaking of you, but I never heard a word from Mrs. Fanny, and I worry I'm running my mouth too much. I get in trouble for that."

"It's quite alright," I said. "I will stick to the horses for now."

Poetaster saw me, and his eyes rolled back in his head. At first, I thought he would lunge at me, but instead, he folded down on his legs and turned over, showing me his belly like a dog would. His breath came in rasps and there were pools of dark hay on the ground littered all around him. He had let watery shits all over the place, and stringy lines of mucous came from the sides of his mouth. His once magnificent chest was sunken, barely more than bones stretched across a dull, black coat.

The air turned sharply and became tinged with blood and filth, that sweet and strange harbinger of death.

This was part of the price, I knew. Everything I had touched in the Keats family would wither and die.

"It's time," I said. "Do you mind if I help ease him?"

Aelfric, tears in his eyes, nodded.

I sat down beside Poetaster and he lifted his head and put it in my lap, his tongue darting out for a moment. I wished I'd had something to give him, some tasty morsel from his too-short life, some token of kindness, but I had nothing. So, I simply sat with him while he breathed in and out, each attempt to gather air weaker than the last. His eyes were crazed sometimes, but toward the end simply calm and waiting.

With nothing else to do, I sang to him. I sang a song of the lake, wishing him a cool and weightless rest in the lands to come. For him, at least, there would be that. For me, it would be torture and then another life to live, my consciousness always on the edges of living and death. I would never find the sort of peace Poetaster did. Part of me envied him that. He would be free of memory and loss and wanting, and I would be forever in its thrall.

There was no bright sunset to wish him home. Poetaster, the finest horse of my knowing, fell into a lasting sleep in the thick of the night as the rowdy inn's noises rose around us. All the horses beside him fell silent, too, as in recognition of the passing of this king among horses.

21

Well, what do you mean she's *sick?*" asked Aneirin the next morning.

While I wanted to stay away forever, Poetaster's death had cut me to the quick. I needed to sleep beneath the stars in my balcony, to feel the presence of the other godlings.

To his credit, Aneirin said nothing when I came downstairs the next morning for breakfast tea; he did not tease me or goad me, he simply wished me a good morning and asked what I had found at the Swan and Hoop.

There was no use hiding it from him.

"I mean there's something wrong with her. She's coughing up blood," I explained, having gotten a little more of the story from Aelfric after we'd bonded over Poetaster's passing. I was speaking of Frances Keats. I'd learned the full story before I left Aelfric, as we worked to burn Poetaster's body. "She vanished for a few years and came back ill."

Aneirin was at his writing desk, and I was seated across from him as if I were having a consultation. Behind him were rows of jars filled with curious fluids, assorted maps, tinker toys, and more unidentifiable books and objects of worth.

He rubbed at his throat. "I feel renewed, but perhaps I am mistaken."

"You needn't blame yourself," I said.

"Oh, then I shall stop," he said with a sarcastic sneer. "Perhaps I can learn from you. You are exceedingly good at self-absolution."

I continued. "The children have already lost their father. Do you think you could have a look at Frances?"

Aneirin rubbed the bridge of his nose with his ink splotched fingers, sighing at me in exasperation. "Once, perhaps, I could have done something. Now? My mind is a mire, a kingdom of brambles run through with thorns of thought. In all likelihood this is part of Miriam's curse. My dear, I'm afraid I wouldn't survive it."

The daylight gave him a slightly brighter aspect, but he was still haggard by his standards. And I could have been mistaken, but I thought I caught the glimmer silver growing on his temples through the short russet curls.

"If you'd get your head out of your arse and stop worrying about Verta so much, maybe you'd be a help to people you can *actually* reach," I said, standing and shoving the chair.

Aneirin felt it too, but only sighed wearily. "She isn't well."

It was the understatement of the millennia. "Did you expect her to be?" I asked.

"I didn't expect anything. Especially you." His eyes were pools of regret.

"I thought you said you could see things."

He chewed his lip for a moment, then studied his fingers. "Where Verta is concerned is rather an echoing gulf. I have never been able to anticipate anything about her. Perhaps that is what has kept me so damned allured. She remains just out of reach, always. I can sense her in the moment, but never in the current, to use a metaphor you'd find more familiar."

I no longer wanted to speak of Verta. "Can you help Frances? For me."

Aneirin gazed at me then and I knew the answer. He didn't want to say the words, especially since it was a continual recognition of his own diminishing ken. The great healer, the sun, was fading.

He cleared his throat, averting my gaze. "I'm afraid, short of moving heaven and earth, there is little I can do. But I will try. Once Verta is a little more settled. If you can be patient with me."

GETTING Verta more settled was a far larger challenge than either of us were up for. Her transference was not so easy. She wandered a great deal. Most often she was incoherent between fits of lucidity. She was having a hard time arranging the past and present. We often found her wandering the house in the middle of the night complaining about the water in her bones or the brambles in her hair.

To keep ourselves from despair, we read together a great deal. Aneirin's library was a wonder to behold, taking up an entire floor of the townhouse. Many of the books were familiar, from my initial tutelage.

I began the habit of taking Chapman's Homer with me on walks. The language was more archaic than what was now spoken in Britanniae, but not by much. It had a musical quality that I enjoyed and had committed many of the passages to memory.

After a bit of cajoling and not a few nights of passion, I was able to encourage Aneirin to visit Frances at the Swan and Hoop. Verta was stable, now that we had given her the penthouse, and as she slept most of the day, we decided to risk the short trip and leave her in Amos's care, which was mostly large quantities of opium.

When we arrived, I could not bear to go inside the Swan and Hoop proper.

"Are you certain you don't want to see her?" Aneirin asked me.

"I am a coward," I replied.

He gave me a piteous look. "My dear, you could never be a coward. You are merely wounded by dark magic. And heartbroken a bit, I think."

"I could not stand for her to see me again."

"Very well. I will do what I can."

So, I waited outside for Aneirin, meandering around the roads and alleyways, muttering to myself to bide the time. It was early evening, and the hustle and bustle of the closing day was somehow comforting. Humankind kept moving while the weight of the word shifted in the hands of godlings.

I kept thinking about Miriam, and thinking about Verta, and John, and all our godchildren. I thought about curses and wondered how they could be so powerful. And I thought about how, even now, I wanted John to win the boast. Deep inside me, some ancient cogs moved in spite of my better judgement, nudging me along toward that mad game.

After almost an hour of waiting, I noticed the presence of two young children leaving the stables hand in hand. It took me no time to realize who they were—the youngest two Keats children, Fanny and Tom. They had the look of their mother, with her more robust build. Fanny, in particular, looked very much like John did in the vision I had seen, her hair in braids and the edge of her frock covered in mud. There was a rather clever look to her, but her brother was very pale and small.

I was trying to blend in with the general crowd, but Fanny noticed me right away. Her curious little eyes rose up and up some more, and instead of cowering in fright or running away, she simply laughed, tossed her head right back, and cackled.

Tom looked mortified and tried to explain something to me about her being so young and lacking manners entirely. The sight of her made my heart ache, for she had the same joy I'd seen in her mother years before.

"I'm sorry, sir," Fanny said after her brother insisted, she make an apology. "It's only I've never seen a man so tall, and I was having such a long and strange day, and upon seeing you it seemed that it was the most wonderful, perfect thing."

Tom rolled his eyes, pressed his small hand to his chest, and spoke for her: "What my babbling sister means is we've been on errands all over town today, with quite a few disappointments, and she found some comedy in you."

He spoke like a little poet.

"It's quite fine. Though, to tell you the truth, I used to be taller," I said.

They giggled, little Tom in spite of himself. "We meant no offense," he said.

"I am not offended," I said after a moment. Staring at the children I felt as if I were getting a glimpse of my own godson, so close they were to him. I knew he was my spiritual child more than corporeal, but it didn't make their bearing less dear. "Though it is true. My height is one of the reasons I avoid hats whenever possible."

They both giggled.

"What's the book you're reading?" Fanny asked, bravely poking at the volume in my hands. "It's quite pretty. The pages are gold!"

"The edges, yes," I said, finding myself rather enjoying speaking to the children. I couldn't read them as well as most adults, and yet they weren't as complicated. They spoke and acted without as much concern for social regulations. They reminded me of myself, I suppose. When I was new. "I'm not sure how it's done, come to think of it."

Fanny grinned wildly at me and proclaimed, "My brother John would know. He knows everything about books."

My stomach slunk to my feet and I tried to appear nonplussed, but just hearing his name made me nervous. I wanted to ask them a thousand questions about him.

"This is a very special book," I said with some effort. "It's about war and gods—it's full of history and magic. I quite like it."

Tom's eyes widened at my mention of war and magic. "What's it's called?"

I told him the name of the book and he nodded as if he'd heard of it. "John reads us stories when he's home. He and George are both away at school, but they might come home now because mother is ill."

"I'm sorry to hear," I said. "Perhaps you should take this book and read her the stories. Or get your brothers to."

Little Fanny's hands were on the book before I'd completely let it go and I had to laugh at bit. Tom looked mortified.

"Truly?" he asked me.

"Truly," I said.

Just as the children were leaving Aneirin returned, his wide-brimmed hat slightly crooked on his head. I could tell he didn't want to look me in the eyes, could sense the news was not good.

"Joss..." he started.

"Tell me," I said.

Aneirin looked back at the inn, as if it would tell him another story. "She is sick in two ways. In her body and in her soul. Two separate ailments, and yet inextricably connected. I have given orders for some tinctures that could help—blast Calvinius and his hiatus from Londinium! —but I do not think her prognosis is optimistic."

I took his arm, squeezed his shoulder. "But?"

"You want my true opinion?"

I nodded slowly. "There are two options. If you recall, I mentioned a certain potion recipe, lost in Ancyra. Miriam wants it, but that does not mean we cannot use it if we find it. It could help her."

"Ancyra is a long way," I said.

He looked thoughtful, his eyes searching mine before speaking. "It may also help me," he said quietly. Touching his throat, he leaned his forehead on my shoulder just a moment, the intimate and beautiful expression warming me to the soles of my feet. I felt hope kindle.

"And the other option?"

"You go to her and try and fix what you've broken," he said softly, his hand now at my side. My breath caught. "I think she would like to see you."

"No," I whispered. "I cannot show my face. But if I may find this potion—if there is hope for you both."

"I didn't want to bring it up before. It's too much to ask."

"Nonsense," I said. "We shall speak of it again in the morning. For now, I have had enough of this place."

We dared not draw more attention to one another, and so we stepped apart, both feeling our own powers rising to meet each other. Once, in Londinium, love between two men was not such a strange thing. But now the Marians felt different. Miriam herself had no objections, but she did not speak to her followers directly. She did not care how they went about their worship so long as she was their focus.

"I will meet you back at the house," I said. "I need a little time to myself, I think."

When I came home that night, I found Aneirin sitting on the stoop of his house, elbows on his knees, staring out vacantly across the street. He had a confused expression on his face, baffled bemusement.

"She's gone," he said, the most puzzled tone in his voice. He hadn't looked up to see me.

She. Of course.

"You sure she didn't just nip out for a cup of tea?" I asked.

He shook his head. "She's back at the temple. What's left of it. Wrote that it was time, and I ought to understand."

"Which you don't."

"Of course, I bloody well don't!" he shouted, then faltered, his voice going hoarse. He put his hand up to his throat, wincing. "I have given her everything, and yet time and again…" Aneirin began coughing, and I sat down next to him, rubbing his back until the fit passed.

It was getting worse.

"You need to get some rest," I said.

There was fire in his eyes, and for a moment, I thought he would argue. He whispered, "I worked so hard getting her healthy again. Restoring her diminishing sight, maintaining sensation in her limbs and…"

He tried to stand, but I had to help keep him upright. I reveled in the weight of him against my body, in my arms, how he leaned into me.

"I shouldn't have sent you to see Frances," I said, smoothing back his hair. "I was being selfish."

"Perhaps, but aren't we all?"

Verta had taken her departure seriously. Half the house was emptied.

I had to carry Aneirin to the basement sick room, the very same we had seen Verta arise in her new, stolen body. Some of the potions had been rifled through, a few taken. Aneirin made a quick stock as he got comfortable upon the pallet and let me have a good look at him. He surmised she had taken the ingredients to make the same potion he'd been giving her; eventually she would be back for more, or else have to find the components herself.

I unwound the scarf from his neck to see that the blue blotch of his wound had spread considerably since the last time he'd allowed me this close. Then, the act of undressing had been so different. Now it felt perfunctory.

Still, the sight of the wound set my teeth. Little tendrils were making their way across his neck, and then again down his chest. Each rivulet had a dozen offshoots, and I knew in time the pain would grow too much for even a godling as brilliant and bright as Aneirin.

He gave me a weak laugh, but no explanation.

"Avoiding your own health while tending to Verta serves me no good," I said. "You're both useless to me if you're dead."

"Ah, but we never die, Joss," he muttered as I glared in frustration. "We find each other again and again."

I would wait another godling's lifetime for him if he could be mine. But there was no time for such romantic professions.

I looked around at all the labeled bottles, the drawers full of tinctures and powders and ingots and specimens. I had no idea how any of it worked.

"You've got enough ingredients here to poison the Queen's regiment. What do I need to give you?" I asked.

"Well, nothing here will do me any good in the long term, I'm afraid. It will allay the pain, perhaps stop the progression for a small time, but it won't cure me."

"Tell me, and I'll mix it for you."

The mixture included ox gall, quicksilver, hawthorn, laurel, opium, and a few other bits I'm not sure I can quite recall. It stunk to high heaven. When Aneirin instructed mixing the paste together and adding water, I, of course, took the liberty and did it myself. There was no need to turn on the pipes or fetch it from the well. It was an intimate gesture, truly, but honest too. The water I could provide, while snatched from the air, I felt would add a level of purity the rest could not. Even if the water in Londinium was considerably cleaner than it had been before the war, water was still my ken, and I wanted to take control where I could.

Aneirin was silent as he drank the stuff, not in one gulp but in small wincing sips. The color slowly came back to his face, and he regained a bit of his glow, that slightly more than human tinge he always seemed to have about him.

He saw the look of pity in my eyes and gave me a wan smile.

"Diminishing is hardly as glamorous as I imagined it would be," he finally said, holding up his hand and turning it this way and that, as if its sight was somehow unfamiliar to him. "But I suppose I hadn't noticed it until now."

"I've opinions on such matters," I said. "But I can help you. Like I did before."

He closed his eyes, blue veins on his lids a mirror of the tendrils upon his neck. "Would I could tonight—I fear you have spent yourself too much already."

"I would so again and always, Aneirin," I said, whispering his name. As so often when I said it aloud, he inhaled sharply as if I were giving him a new breath.

"I know you would."

He took my hand and drew it to his mouth, kissing my palm with his warm lips. My whole body shivered, wanting more, but suffusing with the familiar pulse of his power. Late summer erupted in my heart.

"Would you help me to my bed? I do not think I can manage the stairs on my own," he said softly.

Once I finished putting him into his bed, an ornate carved oaken structure of such elaborate proportions that I even wondered how it had made it up three floors, he looked a little better but was still tired.

He did not push me away when I gently moved the hair from his forehead, grown back but never so long as it had been. He didn't have enough energy to keep the glamour up, but he needn't have with me. His beauty lay all along his fault lines, every wrinkle and out-of-place hair, and I wondered if it was a sentiment he would ever learn to accept.

"My heart is breaking," he said.

"I won't let it break us," I said. "I swear to it. I will find Trita, and we will make a trip to Ancyra. I only wish there was more I could do for you now."

"Oh, Joss, you are too bold for your own good."

I kissed him on the mouth, slowly and thoroughly, and he returned with drowsy, sweet pressure. I traced his nose with my thumb when I finished, gazing into his bright eyes, drinking in his rare silence. I knew, looking at him then, that I would never love anyone as completely as Aneirin. No godling, no mortal. His pain was my pain, his suffering mine, his pleasure mingled in my very blood. For him to refuse my body, my power, chilled me.

I was about to close the door when he raised his hand. "Isabella Jones. Find her. She may be able to help us."

22

I did not fancy querying after Miss Jones all throughout Londinium, so I went to the waters to find her. Unlike Aneirin, my own powers returned slowly, drip by drip—and stronger every day I was further from Verta.

I knew I could locate godlings this way; I figured a mortal would be significantly easier.

First, I needed water that had been through the city, through its people, still reeking of secrets and stories.

It wasn't going to be pleasant, though. While Londinium had no dearth of tributaries flowing through it, those many rivers had been rerouted and diverted during her growth and expansion. There were many places I could go to start my search, and truly I just needed one good foot in the water, far enough from the salt and the Tamesis.

I chose Westbourne. Hyde Park would be the ideal starting point, at the Serpentine. There was a good bridge there and going in the evening would afford me little in the way of passersby.

There were plenty of water features in the place, and most of it molded to the eyes of man rather than given to nature. It was relatively free from the bones of aqueducts above, affording an unshadowed view of the park.

The Serpentine was made a lake by virtue of a dam, with a sluice gate upon the eastern side. With the fog still thick upon the city, it wasn't difficult for me to slip through undetected.

I'll admit to feeling a bit concerned once I got there, though. Standing at the balustrade and looking down into the lake I could feel the amulet at my chest bearing down, warning me. I kept it there night and day and had never thought of taking it off until that moment, sensing the rumbling of the Tamesis not far away. It promised me an ocean. It promised me escape. And I hardly realized that my hands were wrapped around the feather and heart until I felt something lick my hand.

I looked down to see the face of a dog, black and nondescript, looking up at me with expectant eyes. In but a moment came his friend, brown and dappled, shaking his thick mane with earnest. They'd both been in the Serpentine for a swim and seemed well-fed and happy. Not the sort of scrappy mutts I'd so often seen during my trips through the city before. They both sat, one on each side of me, waiting expectantly.

Their energy was warm and friendly, free of fear. I needed that. It calmed me in the way, I suppose, I had once been able to help Poetaster. It felt surprisingly familiar, important, and I took note, leaning down to scratch the dark one behind the ears and then the speckled on under the chin. Did they have names? I suppose they must, but they didn't for now. Just Dark and Speckled in my mind.

When I hopped over the balustrade, they followed after me, clearly thinking we were in for some adventure. They hopped through the shallows and, after chasing one another for a few moments, settled down next to me again, little trails in the mists around them closing up.

I reached down to the water and the dogs sniffed at me then let me to their business. The water wasn't deep enough for swimming, but they seemed curious to what I was doing.

Certain no one but the dogs were about, I took a deep breath and put both of my hands into the water, kneeling down. At first, I could only sense the Serpentine itself, and it was angry. It was cold, for one, and full of strange fish in the depths. But there were stories in it, too, stories that it wanted to tell me. Of things that were and things that were to be. I saw the face of Aneirin's scion, Percy Shelley, come to mind, and I couldn't fathom why. It was, I realized later, a message of something yet to come. Aneirin was not the only prophet, though my glimpses into the future were considerably less predictable.

I pushed out further, over the dam and beyond, deeper and deeper still.

The Westbourne stretched out and upward, then down and again. I felt the amulet tremble at my chest, knowing I could pull even more energy if I so wished, but concentrated instead on the subtle rising and falling of the water. All the water. It was bliss, falling into that flow. I felt my body slip away, felt all the aching of hunger and desire, of pain and of exhaustion, flit away meaninglessly as I rejoined the pathways that had made me. Oh, there were plenty of shit-plugged sewers in the wake, crumbled aqueducts. Bloated bodies. Rat carcasses. Never-ending detritus. I had to push through and think not on the filth but on the spaces between. Even the most offending water is purer than it is poison. To an average mortal the difference is pretty startling; for me, it's just a challenge. But there were points of brightness, marvelous brightness, and they guided me through.

Deeper I went until I became aware that the rivers—so many crisscrossing the city—were not just connected, but they were also bubbling up at intervals. The first was at Bayswater, not far. A well. I hadn't ever thought of it before, that the wells, kept since before the Romans converted the Briganti and other Celtic tribes, would serve a purpose other than religious sentiment. But I felt how powerful they were. Like the famous gates around they city, they held secrets. Secrets I would learn in time.

I thought about the name, Isabella Jones. And then I knew. Of course, I knew. The water. My first evening at Verta's temple. Isabella had been one of the women in her employ, a woman I had pleasured and known most perfectly.

It was not difficult to locate her once I understood. She wasn't even far. From what I could tell she was near the World's End inn near Knightsbridge Green. And someone else was with her: Trita Oya.

The World's End was dark and nondescript in the Brittanic fashion. Unlike so much of the city center it was built of timber, wattle and daub, with creaky wood floors and a constant murk of smoke and sweat. I liked the old Brittanic design of things and wished that Londinium had preserved more. There were still plenty of outliers, but the new, Persian-influenced style was becoming all the rage. And that favored more stone, sharper angles, and need to festoon every corner with glass and gilding. I didn't need cushions and footstools and high, wing-backed chairs to be comfortable sitting and eating and carousing. A plain bench or a booth would do just fine. Especially if it was worn smooth. Something comforting in that, I think.

It had been years since I'd seen Isabella, but she had not changed. I had taken her for a priestess in Verta's temple, but as I approached the table where she and Trita sat, I began to wonder. She was dark haired and dark eyed, with a small soft mouth and a dimpled chin. Her face was open and high-browed, her lashes stark against her pale, lightly freckled skin. She wore the height of fashion, her curls neat and tidy, her dress puffed about the shoulders and high cut below her breasts. She was not dressed in finery and yet possessed a kind of innate elegance which spoke to good breeding, or else knowing the semblance of it.

Trita was the first to see me, and she took me in, her eyes flitting to the amulet about my neck. She relaxed a bit. She was back to the same garb I'd seen her in that first meeting: trousers and a suit, her hair cropped short, her ears pierced with gold and silver hoops. She did not look surprised to see me, but she did not look happy about it either.

"Not a turn of the sun in Londinium, and you've already found me," Trita said as I approached their table. "I figured I'd have at least a fortnight before you came asking me for favors."

I bowed to both of them, and then said to the godling: "I wasn't looking for you, Trita. I was looking for Miss Jones, here."

Isabella's eyebrows went up slightly. "Joss Raddick," she said, and my name never sounded so good in anyone's mouth. "It's been some time since we've crossed paths. But it is, for all intents and purposes, Mrs. Jones, if you so please."

Ah, but the very air she breathed felt sweeter. I remembered that about her. There was a sweetness she imparted to the whole business, and I found myself yearning for it again.

Married. I doubted it.

"Mrs. Jones, now," I replied, taking a seat and scraping it across the floor before sitting down. I wanted to show off for the woman. I wanted to make her laugh again. I remembered it, from before. The golden, shining sound coming from her throat.

I could feel Trita's eyes boring into my head.

"What would you ever need with her?" asked Trita, rolling up the pieces of paper she had spread across the table, keeping my eyes from them.

"La Roche sent me," I said. "Specifically, to you, Mrs. Jones." I kept emphasizing her moniker, watching her dark eyes as I did so.

"I wonder why that would be," Isabella said, her head tilting lazily to the side. She thought about it for a moment, and then the merriment was gone from her eyes.

Trita understood. "He's getting worse."

Mirth departed the room and I felt a chill. It was the way Trita and Isabella exchanged looks that concerned me. They, too, knew his secret. And Isabella...she wasn't a godling, no. But she wasn't a mortal. For one, she had not aged a moment since I'd last seen her. There were no new wrinkles, no sign of grey hair. She exuded a constant sweetness, and more. She didn't breathe the same pace most mortals did. Slower. Her heart a third as fast, her eyes too clear and lovely.

"Yes," I said, tearing my gaze from her. "And Verta has left him. She's back at the temple, I imagine. What's left of it."

Trita shook her head. "As I knew she would."

At last, ground upon which we could rebuild our friendship.

"You fear what I fear, then," I said to her.

Trita nodded. "Yes. We can speak of it on the way. You've a carriage?"

"No," I said. "I walked."

"Well, we've a conversation to finish. You can tell Mr. La Roche we will be with him presently. We'll meet you back at High House, Mr. Raddick. If that's amenable," Isabella said.

It was more than amenable. I felt a shimmer of hope, like the unexpected flash of fish scales in the shadowed corner of a brook.

ANEIRIN WAS asleep when we arrived, but he looked a bit better than he had when I left him. His room was warm, as it always was when he was within. Amos was in attendance and reported that he'd had some wine and a bit of fruit but was otherwise uninterested in eating. I wondered at the man. From what I could tell he was entirely mortal, not a whiff of anything otherworldly about him.

But he let Isabella through without so much as a general query and made his exit politely.

I watched her set up beside Aneirin, pulling a small box out of her purse and looking for something within. I couldn't see but didn't want to interrupt.

"I admit, I was doubtful at first that Verta was truly reborn," Trita said. "But only she would behave this way. How did she manage to escape from under your nose?"

"We were otherwise occupied," I said.

"I'm sure you were."

"I've had other concerns since returning."

"I've no doubt. Perhaps your 'concerns' contributed to her departure."

"Trita."

"Yes, Joss?" She still had not forgiven me. I was no longer a monster, but I would always be monstrous.

"If you two are ready, I would like to examine the patient," Isabella said.

She produced a series of lenses from her box, and rifled through them casually, tossing the ones she didn't want on the bedspread. They were a variety of shapes and sizes, and even opacities. A few had ornate settings, but most were simply glass.

I must have been staring hard enough to get her attention because Isabella turned over her shoulder and asked softly, "Did you think I spent all my days in a brothel? You seem perplexed."

"Not sure I've ever seen such implements," I said, taking a step back. I had been looming.

"Ah yes, the *implements*."

"That's what I said."

She didn't smile outwardly, but I thought she might. "These are lenses. They allow me to see a little better in to the situation at hand. For our friend Andrew La Roche here cannot be healed by human means, nor can he be understood with human eyes."

As if guessing my question, Trita explained, "Godlings aren't the only unusual people about, you know. Though fewer and farther between. She's the last of the *Meliae*."

The word was vaguely familiar, but Trita continued, as she was wont to do. "Healers of Zeus, purported. Very old. Very rare, and very helpful for our cause when we're in dire circumstances."

"What's that got to do with the lenses?" I asked.

"Absolutely nothing," Isabella said, frowning through the lens and then putting it down. "Except it helps me peer a little more accurately into the source of the issue. As you know, his wound is expanding. And faster than I've seen in a long time. His power has its own signature, and I can capture it within these lenses, see how it has shifted since our last session."

"You've tended to him before."

Isabella gave me a tight-lipped smile. "It seems a lifetime ago, but yes. I was there when he initially performed this rite. He always knew that there was a chance it would expand."

"You don't have to talk about me as if I'm already dead," Aneirin said, stretching and then squinting at all of us with one eye. "I feel much better, thank you. Good to see you, Isabella. I hope you weren't too difficult to track down."

He did look better. But then, his smile always hid myriad troubles.

"Not at all," I said.

"Good, then." Aneirin winced, sitting a little more upright. "What's the prognosis?"

Isabella took his hand. "You're sick, you rogue. And you made yourself sicker, faster. You've expended yourself too much."

"You haven't got a way to fix it?" he asked, though I didn't think he sounded convinced.

"I do, only I do not have the correct ingredients. And perhaps 'fix' is too ambitious of a word. Can I give you more time? A little. Can I ease the pain? Most certainly," Isabella said.

Trita sighed. "She needs more honey."

"I thought you had a store," Isabella said to Aneirin.

"It was depleted. For Verta," Aneirin replied.

"For now, I can help a little. But I will need ash tree sugar," Isabella said. "And not from here. From the South."

Trita frowned deeply, rubbing at her temples. Aneirin did not look pleased but put on his best smile for Isabella.

"It's a lot to ask of you," he said to her.

"I won't be doing the travel," she said, then stood and addressed us both. "If you'll please, I need some time with Mr. La Roche. I will rejoin you both when we're finished here."

TRITA and I sat by the fire in the parlor, speaking in low voices as if we'd wake a child. Rain pattered upon the high windowpanes and drafts moved through the room, but neither of us was much affected by the chill. There are more similarities between Trita and me than I used to think, indeed I often wonder if some of the strain of our friendship was simply due to the fact we held so much in common.

She looked tired, I thought, in the way only godlings can. A kind of weariness of the spirit that transcends the flesh. She declined wine but accepted when I mentioned tea, and I had the maid fetch us some cookies as well.

We had exchanged pleasantries, but little else, when Isabella returned with Aneirin not far behind. He was pink-cheeked and dressed well, his hair brushed and soft. Aside from the blue tinge to his neck—he hadn't bothered with the scarf—he looked the picture of health.

Trita did not look surprised.

I must have, for Aneirin laughed at me.

"I hope you weren't writing my eulogy," he said, clapping me on the back as he passed me by. "We've an adventure to begin. As it happens, ash tree honey is conveniently located way to Ancyra."

23

Making good on promises to Miriam was not high on my priority list, but as Aneirin explained the situation it made better sense. In their tenure together, Calvinius and Aneirin had sought out many famed spells, incantations, and potions. They were somewhat limited to their travels, however, due to the unfortunate situation of Achaemenes in Old Rome and beyond. But now that trade was opened once again, and the immigration to the New World was beginning, there were fewer issues.

Well, save for one man. And a man with enough power, godling or no, can prove a direct challenge.

Miriam's war may have ended, but it didn't stop some of the godlings —and indeed many empowered mortals—to continue to fight. It was rumored that Miriam was behind the repopulating the settlements over the Atlantic in the West, many of which had been started and then abandoned for centuries. Little walled cities, constantly at war with the native population, a fierce and proud race with their own gleaming fortress cities rising from enormous forests and remarkable culture. Little of them was told to the people of Britanniae, save for a few infrequent visitors during the centuries of peace two hundred years hence, but there were enough rumors and whispers that even I knew them to be formidable enemies. Achaemenes would join them, and Miriam, it seemed, wasted no time.

But our aim was not yet on the West, though it would be in time. I felt an inexplicable tug within me to visit that alien coast every time Aneirin spoke to me of it. He, himself, had never been, but he had done a great amount of research on the subject.

No, our focus, for the time being, was Miriam's most decorated general, and indeed, now declared Emperor of Gaul, Rome, and beyond. Bonaparte. His eventual victory against the great Padişah Selim had ensured the Persian threat was greatly mitigated, pulled back out of New Italia, through Greece, and beyond the great city of Constantinople. While Bonaparte's war had been won primarily on two fronts—diplomacy and conversion—there was no doubt about his military prowess. His fleet of ships, it was rumored, had been the only ones spared during my great transfiguration, now attributed to Miriam.

Though the lands were placated with the gentle heart of Mary the Mother, there were still pockets of unrest. Bonaparte's current campaign was in Ancyra, some miles east of Constantinople, in an attempt to run down the new emperor of the Persian empire, Padişah Mustafa. He'd had some luck with an initial campaign but was falling low on supplies and morale. They'd been at war for the better part of the last ten years and, I suspected, even a warmonger like Bonaparte was growing tired. I could hear the cries of the ships if I listened hard enough, like orphaned whales from their pods, their sides creaking with strain and weathered beyond reckoning.

"Ancyra is our goal," said Aneirin, gesturing to the placement—unfathomably far away—on the map, his great magical map, in the drawing room. "An ancient, resplendent city, awaiting our arrival. Ripe for the picking."

Isabella showed no surprise at Aneirin's spellcasting. It was still astonishing to see on my part, how he manipulated the topography and geography in exquisite detail, his hands molding land and sky, bringing life to storm systems, armies, and cities. I could watch it for hours and never cease in my amazement.

I had been as far as the Akdeniz, but the lands beyond Greece were foreign and strange to me. Land was drier there, the people speaking in languages that had only come across Empire through the Moorish invasions and been absorbed. Arabic. Hebrew. And Marianism had begun with them, after all; a small, Semitic sect originally, it branched off from the Hebrews quickly but never took fire against the great Zoroastrians. In Gaul, missionaries shook violently during their sermons, preaching of the

Messiah and his great Mother, Mary, called Quakers by the lay people. It was not until the 1400s, however, when the Marians broke off yet again, desiring a deeper understanding of the Mother of the Messiah, arguing that the Scriptures painted her as the most perfect of beings, and not the son, a prophet called Joshua, on whom the Messianic Hebrews focused.

"None but Achaemenes has been to Ancyra," Trita pointed out, pushing aside a roiling cloud bank on the map to get a better look. "Your lead took you there?"

Aneirin replied, "The Celts had quite the society in Ancyra, flourishing until nigh on a thousand years ago. It has never been the center of life that Constantinople was, but it is an old city with ancient roots and deep ties to our kind. It is said one of my predecessors, a fellow who went by the name of Boduognatos, sent this treasured recipe in advance of a rather horrible battle he lost to Julius Caesar. The tale says after his tribe was hewn down by Caesar, he was driven to madness, and then to his end. But! The druids of the Volcae Tectosages, the tribe that rose to prominence in Ancyra, had developed a potion to give to him should he require. They knew of his special abilities, just not his fragility, it seems..." Aneirin fell silent, his eyes unfocused on the map as if he were able to see something which we could not.

Trita added. "When Rome fell and the Legion spread West, there were many left behind. The Persian Empire grew in strength, and had times of peace, but as a strictly secular state there were many struggles."

"It is not all secular in Persia," Isabella said. "Not as it once was. There exist alongside them the Hindu, as well, and even further to the East, the followers of Buddha. And then there are other pantheons, and even those who believe in a single All-Father. The Hebrews are tolerated, and the Marians were, too, until they pulled their coup. The Persians did not seek to destroy the Roman faith, but to assimilate it into their own beliefs. And now, there is yet another cult, one that believes the Amesha Spenta are bound to walk the earth again. The six great bounteous immortals."

"Sounds familiar," I said. "But there are eight."

"There will be six here soon if we don't move quickly," Aneirin said.

"So," I said. "We go to Ancyra, find this recipe, and make the potion for you."

"When you put it that way it's so beastly boring, but yes," Aneirin said, leveling me with a stare. "We did promise Miriam we'd be on our best behavior."

I leveled him with my gaze. "My oaths to her are ash. I do this for you."

"It's not how oaths work, nor how our kind functions. You can't tell me you don't feel a compunction to see the city and retrieve the relic and taste the honey."

"Only if it will help you," I said.

"I can stay here and keep an eye on things," Isabella said. "La Roche, if you remain in your bird form, I think you could make the trip. But otherwise, the risk is high you would fade before ever reaching it."

"It seems a fool's errand," I said with a sigh. "But I am willing to go if it means hope for La Roche."

For my love.

"How does this fool's errand different than any other?" asked Aneirin, smiling already because he knew he'd won me over. "You've punched me over far less."

I relented. "Then I am your fool."

Aneirin grinned. "Good. Because the *Hoel Reborn* is getting bored. It's time we take to the seas again."

I WAS RELIEVED the moment I walked aboard the *Hoel Reborn*. Whether it was my ken as Aneirin insisted, or something more, I felt more connected to the ship in ways I never did in a house. All the parts of me, so often thrashing against one another in continual tumult, felt at ease as soon as I stepped foot upon her and felt the rolling tide beneath. The flapping of the sails, the smell of pitch and fresh hewn wood. She had sailed with us and shared our stories, weathering the best and the worst of it. I knew her like a lover.

As for quarters, I was to share with Aneirin. No room in an inn, nor in a home, had ever felt as comfortable as this. Deep within the ship, the captain's room, the beating heart of the place. The linens were fine, the fruits and nuts and cheeses presented for me of my liking. I had good clothes to wear, and plenty of them. I had supplies to write letters, maps for perusal, and even a well-stocked library. And a good amount of whiskey, should the fancy hit upon me.

And I had Aneirin.

For Trita's part, she preferred to stay with the crew, many of whom were seasoned veterans to our affairs. Aneirin called them "ancillaries" to distinguish them from regular human beings—they were not entirely unaware of our abilities and yet, somehow, yet resistant to the idea that we were behind such occurrences as my kraken awakening. I suspected it had something to do with Aneirin, whether by potion or charm, but I had not the mettle to argue or pursue it.

We set sail and I kept below decks. I did not want to watch Londinium retreat, did not want to think about my godson there, living poor among the festering folk. I suppose I could have done more for him at that time. Trita and Aneirin were compelled to reach out to their children in ways I never was. Now, as I look back, I see it was mostly out of fear I kept my distance from young John Keats. Fear he would reject me. Fear is a wild, powerful thing. Maybe it's the horse in me. I'm a strong being, a powerful one. Capable of deeds even my peers did not understand. But perhaps I have always carried within me an equal measure of fear.

After dinner in the galley, I joined Aneirin in his quarters. He was dressed in his night robe, his scarf absent. His wound was still startling, but it had not spread since Isabella's application.

"Do you really believe this is a fool's errand, Joss?" he asked.

I sat down next to him on the narrow bed, and he reached up to touch my back, tender and familiar. There was no mistaking his need, his attentions.

"I fear it might be," I said after a moment. "I fear what I would do if you—"

Aneirin took my hand, and I turned to face him. He smiled his sunbeam grin, amber eyes flashing. "Look around you. Look where we are."

"I know where we are."

"I have fond memories of a place nearly identical to this. You, coming to me, your roaring sea and my impertinent sun."

"I took you, in a bed like this." We so rarely spoke of our acts but giving voice to our passion made my loins simmer.

Aneirin's incandescent smile set fire to my soul. "Once again, your astute observations astonish me," he said, his hands slipping down, fingers hooking under my belt, the leather creaking in response. "I am making some of my own observations." He punctuated his own observations of my person.

"Aneirin," I admonished, swallowing on a dry throat, feeling my world spin as his magic filled the cabin, warm and welcoming and full of promise. "You are not well."

"I am living in the present, my dear," he replied. He observed a moment more, fingers plying then grasping, sliding to make contact, skin against skin. I gasped. "And you are clearly at attention."

My mind emptied as Aneirin pulled me closer, his hand still working me while his tongue danced across my lips. Passion uncoiled at the base of my spine, my own power rising along to his call. I knew, despite my protestations, I was powerless against the pull of his tide.

"Heaven's fire, Aneirin," I breathed against him.

"And Hell's roiling sea, Joss."

WE LAY NAKED, side by side, later that night. The moonlight streamed through the small window, and the room smelled of brine and sun-warmed wood. We breathed together, quiet in the comfort, bodies limp and damp with exertion. For all the joy I found in our lovemaking, I treasured holding him the most, when he trusted me to hold him, and he relaxed in my arms.

"I do not want to go," he said softly.

"What about Verta?" I asked.

He was silent long enough I began to worry he was offended by my bold question. We rarely spoke about her.

"I do not know her any longer, Joss. I have lost her, what was left of her. I cannot keep her at High House. I cannot keep her at all. She has rewritten the rules of life and death; you were right. I let my love blind me to it. I do hope, if we are able to find this recipe for godling restoration, that I might have enough to help her. If she wants it."

"I don't know why she holds on," I said.

"She must have business to finish, my love," Aneirin said. "For now, I wish to think not on her machinations, but on the lines of your body and the marvelous whorls of your hair. We will speak of darker things when the sun is out. It is too much to bear now."

ANEIRIN FELL ASLEEP, but rest eluded me entirely. I kept worrying about what we would find in Ancyra, and the price we might pay. So, I took one of Aneirin's history volumes and meandered my way up to the deck, nicking whiskey from the cook.

I sat alone, drinking and reading, until Trita came to me.

For her part, she looked a bit tired, but otherwise well. She wore garb of the highest legion rank, the Imperial Legate. I may have been a captain, but she was a General of more renown than I could ever muster. Captain suited me well enough.

"You're drunk," she said slowly, as if taken aback by the discovery.

"Yes." I wiped at my mouth.

"I just didn't think it was possible."

"With whiskey, anything is possible." I shook the glass at her and waggled my eyebrows. I was very, very drunk, indeed.

"Lessons on the history of the world are not exactly at their best whilst you're slurring," she said, wrinkling her nose at my display.

"It's just all echoing in my brain. This campaign. The Persians. The Romans. The Celts. The Oued. The Cretes. Even your people, I found them in here," I said, thumping a large volume, well-worn green leather lined with use. "How many fled in the last century?"

"As many as could walk, run, crawl, or drag their bodies away from the monsters," Trita said, both her face and voice losing any remnant of amusement. "Joss, this is not the way to spend your trip, and I'd rather not be reminded of what my people have endured."

I frowned and pressed on in spite of my better judgement. But whiskey.

"Well, of course. Everybody kills everybody. War after war after war after war…*and* after war. If I'm not mistaken, perhaps there is something beautiful about the Yoruba being pursued by fucking *monsters* rather than *people* because *people* are the worst kinds of monsters. They're the ones that should *know* better."

Trita's gaze became unfocused. "They say the heart of Kpelekpe is a man's and walks in daylight as a friend but compels the children to him at night where he feasts on their flesh. We built great cities, gleaming palaces, but in the end, we were driven out by Kpelekpe, whether by fear or by power, I do not know. Is Kpelekpe truly a monster, or an excuse? I was not there. I did not live that life. But someday I will return to those haunted cities and I will track him down and I will call my people home."

Her words were tinged with fire, and it sobered me a good deal. "You have a people," I said. "I am alone."

"You are a godling of godlings," she said with a shrug. "We are your people."

"But why do we care about them, Trita? Why do we care about any people? Why don't we just burn it all down, start anew?"

I was shaking. I had never given voice to those deep fears, those whispers inside of me. The ones that told me nothing of humanity was worth preserving. Black tendrils around my heart, wiggling into my dreams and pressing on my doubts like raw bruises. Perhaps it was the remnants of the monster I had become, still lingering.

Trita shook her head, then took a few paces toward me. She knelt before me, putting her hands on my knees and looking me in the face. She just watched me for a while before picking up my amulet with one finger. Her face spasmed in pain as she held it, but she kept it firm.

"I know your pain. I wounded you," she said. "We forget that part of the exchange. Long after I diminish, you will still know my pain. My memory. I will have forged myself anew in your heart, in your mind. You will carry pieces of my wisdom, my pride, my anger…"

I went to say something, but she shook her head. "La Roche's head is filled so full of light that he forgets to welcome the shadows. He believes he can drive out the doubt, and he can save the people from themselves. I have not lived as long as he, nor have I seen the world through his eyes, but I have thought on these questions many a time in the dark. We tell our tale to ourselves, that we are fractions of a pantheon, scattered to the Eight Worlds. But what are human beings? We can be born of them; we can mate with them. We can awaken, as I did, as small children with new eyes. What are we if we are not them? If they are not but fragments of ourselves? I fight for them, Joss, because I have seen one small shift in the winds of a life go on to change so many others—in ways we never can as godlings. I cannot kill you. I cannot save you. Your life is your own. But I can watch over the people of Londinium, my second home, as I never watch over my people, those who clothed me and fed me before I knew what I was; those who did not judge me or scorn me, but accepted me and loved me, gave me books to read and a spear to wield."

I looked at her, and saw the tears streaming down her face.

"Why do you keep fighting?" I asked.

"Because I love them. I love them for their stupidity and their vanity, for their damned short-sightedness and their passion. I love them for their words and their deeds, for their broken oaths and flaws in every line. For each scoundrel I have met, I have found another soul so full of truth and beauty that it broke my heart to pieces. And when I could assemble it again, I could think of nothing else more worth my time than delving deeper for the good of them. Of all of them."

I sighed like the bellows, unable to answer her eloquent words, her deep understanding of herself and her purpose, with anything other than whiskey fumes.

"Love is like a hook in my heart," I said. "It pulls at me and tears at me, but I cannot shake it."

"I know," she said, standing and placing her hand on my head, as if in benediction. "So do not fight it. Build yourself about it, make your body a sanctuary for it."

"You sound like Verta used to," I said.

"Someone has to now."

PART III

24

We reached the Propontis and, at last, I saw Constantinople. Once the seat of Byzantium, for years it was called Dersaadet or Istanbul. A city at the center of the world, a literal land bridge between cultures. It had been the jewel of the Roman Empire, a glorious moment in their history, claiming the once-Greek city as their own. Of all the outposts of Rome, it had lasted the longest, mostly due to its highly defensible state. But eventually, as the rest of Rome fell, so it did as well. I have read accounts of the great battle, with Emperor Theophilos at the helm. It was true that he secured the city while Sicilia then Rome fell to the power of the Ottomans. But once he was too old to do so, his son, Emperor Michael III quickly whittled away the city's money and, by extension, their ability to support themselves.

It had been almost precisely one thousand years since the golden eagle flew above the great spires and domes of the city, but oh how they fluttered now as we passed on our way to Libyssa. Aneirin did not elucidate on the history of the place, and while I did not feel a rush of pride to see the Roman colors—I was a Briton, after all, even if Rome ruled the island —there was a sense of awe.

Fires still burned on the shores, and Trita told us there were thousands of displaced people, many of whom were simply bystanders to that long, strange war. With Achaemenes no longer there to protect them, to guide them, to inspire them in his strange way, there were lost to the winds and the sea. I wish I could tell you the new Roman rulers, those dark-robed Marians, were kind and just to the locals. But they were far from that. All the men were conscripted into the army or sold as slaves, as this was considered a suitable spoil of war according to their laws. It had been a long time since such a boon was granted, as the world had moved on beyond such things to the North. But here, where the victors desired to make a statement, there was no better method to bring shame upon a people.

When a slave ship passed us by, Aneirin spat into the water. He did not approve either.

But our course was not for Constantinople, and I was glad not to see it from the ground. Libyssa would be our port, and then we would travel by land to Ancyra. Or so I thought.

When I set foot upon the ground of this far away land—called Anatolia by some, and Turkey by others—I abruptly fell to the earth like a puppet divested of his strings. All my strength and energy, all my power, ebbed away from me as I watched the men go about their duties preparing the ship for its long docking. I could hear and sense everything, though still muted by the amulet I wore, yet it could not stop me from retching all over the ground.

Trita was by me quickly, pressing her hands to my forehead and looking up at me with concern, Aneirin moving too slowly still behind. With her help I was able to at least get myself off of the main throughway, having collapsed just at the point where the docks met the ancient cobblestone roads. We found a patch of soft earth, rocky and grown with moss, where I waited for my strength and sense of orientation to return to me while Trita sang an old song in a low voice.

"It's the amulet," Aneirin announced once he joined us again and I explained to him the sensation. "This land was held by Achaemenes for time out of mind—the soil is drenched with the blood of his people. And you carry a powerful magic upon your breast."

"It's just a feather and a heart," I said, looking down at where it was beneath my shirt. The feather had never shed so much as a single barb and was black as oil. The heart remained cold regardless of my temperature or the temperature around me.

"You know it isn't so simple," Trita said. "Verta and La Roche performed important magic to give you great protection, but it is against your nature. He is many things, Achaemenes, but his ken is all about the flow of power and creation. You know, your kind is often a co-creator of the world in myth. A brother to his sort. The land remembers, Joss."

Aneirin stroked his bottom lip for a while as we watched the endless procession of men coming to and from the boat, carrying load after load of cargo. Dried Brittanic eels, I was told, and medicinals besides. Thistle tea. Honey. Primroses from Ecosse.

"Not exactly comforting," I said. Breathing was easier and I wasn't so worried about losing consciousness, but it still felt as if a heavy weight was bearing down on my chest and shoulders.

"Well, we all have limitations, Joss. Even you," he said, not looking at me but staring off into the distance. "We've some miles to go, but I think it's time that the three of us break from the crew and begin the ascent."

25

There are two very important lessons you are going to learn today," said Aneirin, pacing back and forth beneath the bent cypress trees. The shadows fell across his hair and shoulders, dappling him as he strode, reminding me of a cat stalking in the jungle.

"And of course, you're going to teach me," I said.

"Not entirely," Trita said, licking her finger and holding it up to the air. "First, I'm going to teach you how to fight."

"I already know how to do that," I said. The mere assumption to the contrary made me flush with embarrassment. What kind of godling did she take me for?

Trita shook her head, her eyes merry. "You fight like a man. But we're going into the forest. And there you may meet foes—and others besides on this land—who will test you and break you if you don't learn some basic lessons. It's also much drier here. And you're at a disadvantage because of your amulet. So, we will teach you what we know."

"Last time I 'fought like a godling' it didn't end up so well," I reminded her.

"You didn't fight like a godling then, Joss. You fought like a *god*," she said.

I looked over at Aneirin, who was somber and did not offer me any assistance on the matter. He clearly agreed with Trita.

"And what's the second thing?" I asked.

He perked up. "Well, that's my job. Joss: I'm going to teach you how to *fly*."

We trekked south and east, avoiding the main road but keeping not far from it. The forest, they told me, was on the way to Ancyra and it would be a perfect training ground for me. The region had seven lakes and a hot spring, an auspicious number according to Aneirin. The first night we camped together but there were no lessons. Aneirin himself was tired and Trita had correspondence she had to work on—considering that we were taking her far from her work, of which I was never quite certain in those days—and so I slept under a canopy of elm trees, listening to the far away burbling of a brook. My amulet continued to press down upon me, so heavy upon my breast that I could hardly sleep.

And when I did sleep, I dreamed of John Keats. I dreamed of him sitting by a candle, writing words upon a page, tears in his eyes. I dreamed of him in pain, his face contorted as he gasped for breath. Then I dreamed of him married, holding a babe in his arms, smoothing away the soft brown hair from its forehead, a look of pride and wonder on his face. Then lastly, I dreamed of him walking through a decrepit old manse, wandering room to room as I followed behind, just out of view. He walked from one bright room into another, which darkened considerably. He tried to read a book in his hands by the light of the window, but it wouldn't give him enough to make out the words. He cast the book away and then noticed the doors to another room were open, into which he walked slowly, finding that he was surrounded by dark pathways about every side, going deeper into the house, but impossible to see where. John fell to his knees, weeping, and I rushed to his side and put my hand on his shoulder. When he turned to look at me, he had the face of Khasma, bulbous eyes full of my greatest fears.

Then I awoke shouting.

Aneirin helped me find my bearings, speaking to me calmly as he stroked my face. The forest came into view around him, then his voice to my ears. But the world felt unreal and distant as if I had awoken into a badly wrought painting.

"You've never been so far from him before, your godson," Aneirin said. "Your spirit remembers, it feels the gulf between you. But I promise you, it will pass."

"What if he's in danger? Surely, I could help him."

"You are helping him, now. Imagine what we could do with a recipe. For his mother. For their family."

Aneirin didn't even have to argue with me, he saw me slump forward and shake my head. The dream still lingered in my mind, vague and painful, yet still powerful enough to truly scare me.

"Sometimes I wish I'd never left Crummock Water. All this…it hurts too much," I said softly, staring down at the leaf-strewn ground near where I'd awoken.

"Surely not everything is so terrible," Aneirin said. He was watching me, but I dared not look at him in the face, not when I felt so raw. I felt his hand on my knee, warm and welcome.

"When I think of what happened, what I've done to his family…"

Aneirin sighed and was silent while I stewed about in the shadows of my dream. At last, he said, "There is a chance, you know, we find this famed honey. And we find the recipe. And then, perhaps, I will be well enough to think beyond the next horizon; there is even a chance we can heal Frances, and perhaps right the wrongs."

"And if not?"

"I do not want to go, Joss. I tell you that in as true a manner as I have ever told you anything. I feel unfinished, unresolved. I want to see the great things you will do, and I want to make peace with Verta."

"How do you feel?" I asked, taking his hand in mine and kissing it.

He shrugged. "The pain comes and goes. It mostly comes. I will not make it to Ancyra like this," Aneirin said, gesturing to his body. "Isabella didn't think I'd make it this far, but I have. The waters were restoring for me."

I tried not to smile. "I could still give you more."

Aneirin laughed, a deep sort of chuckle full of sadness and regret. He took my hand and held it fast between both of his. Mine were so much larger than his, that just covering one was a challenge. But unlike my heavy, thick ones, Aneirin had the finest hands of any I'd ever seen, so long and agile, the nails like perfect half-moons, the skin just touched with a fine down of hair. They were the hands of a musician, a healer, a lover. Skilled beyond compare and wrought with an expert understanding of the capabilities of our human form.

It was different when I touched Aneirin, not like the energy I got from Trita or from Verta. There was no threat there, not even due to the wound. My side did not twinge. Instead it was as if my whole body was filled with warmth and light, and all the shadowy worries flitted away and were gone from me.

"We love in such boorish, meandering ways, Joss," he said to me, and I had to look at his face, now. I marked every line. "The most powerful beings in the world, imbued with remarkable strength and insight, magic and might...and yet we flail about with our hearts as susceptible to those slings and arrows as any other. Perhaps even more so. I have lived a long, weary lifetime and my only regret is failing to realize that earlier. In believing another person—a godling in my case—could make me a better man. Could love me back the way I loved her. I wanted, so badly, to be good in her eyes. To redeem myself. Alas, such trust and hope has rather ruined me, I'm afraid."

"I want to help you," I said, watching his eyes in the shadowy light from the trees. I had never seen them so dark. All hints of the amber turned to black. "I cannot be Verta. But I can do more."

He looked at me with pity, the same look a mother gives her child when she finds him disobeying her, his hand in the pot of sweets or his face smeared with the remnants of a forbidden berry bush. Then he leaned down and kissed my hand.

"Oh, you lout, love is the *problem*. Love is the answer. Love is the magic and the madness and the mire of it all," he said. "It is our driving force. Without it, we falter. With it, we're impaired and unable to make the right choices. Love the trees, love the waters, love the damned horses and the waterfalls and the oceans. But do not put your love to another godling so completely—it will kill you in the end, as it is doing to me."

"I can't change the tide of my heart."

Aneirin stood, brushing the front of his shirt and shaking his head. "No, I suppose it's foolish of me to suppose you would. But I will refuse your offer of that deepest magic, a thousand times over, because I cannot bear the thought of you spending yourself to preserve my life. You are too precious, Joss."

"Tomorrow you will be a bird," I said, breathing hard.

"Tomorrow. Or the next day."

I rose to kiss him, felt the heat in him blaze in reply.

Never had I commanded him, but I would not waste what little time we had. "Then come here. To me."

Oh, by every sacred feather, the look upon his face. He began to speak, lashes batting, but I grabbed him by the back of the head, instead, feasting on the taste of him, luxuriating in the sounds of surprise as I picked him up, and pushed him against a tree.

We came together in that place, fierce and brief and ecstatic.

THEY ATE RABBITS AND BIRDS, I foraged for what fruit and nuts I could find, and then we walked some miles to the ancient hot springs within the Forest of the Seven Lakes. It was good to be near such a pure water source, and without any discussion I stripped and waded into the blue lagoon and plunged beneath, breathing deeply of the hot water and learning what I could about the place. The waterfall on one end churned the water beautifully, air and sediment mixing together, blending the minerals and particulate from miles and miles away, giving me release from the talisman on my chest.

The water did not connect to the ocean, and while Trita and Aneirin spoke to each other in low voices above me, I soaked in the perfection of such a place. I felt safe, protected. I did not want to leave. But I noticed flickering lights above the surface and, after an hour of sulking and weeping beneath the waters, I rose.

Trita and Aneirin were squared off against one another. The flickering light had come from Aneirin, who was twisting a column of fire up in the air above his hand. It was roughly the shape of a bird—a phoenix, perhaps—and it was half his size. He smiled, the firelight catching in his eyes, and then commanded the bird to rise, spin, and twirl its tail. Showy and, for the moment, absolutely harmless, the phoenix stretched out its neck and then began spinning in a circle until I realized it was headed straight for Trita.

In a moment, she was prepared. She had been born prepared. Trita did not need bright fire to fight. Instead, she held out her hands and twisted her wrists in concentric circles. In one hand appeared a silver spear, bright as the moon. Across her opposite forearm a shield appeared in layers, but it had no solid substance. It shimmered about the edges like a scalloped shell, but I could still see her body behind it.

When the rush of fire came down upon her, however, the shield protected her well. Making contact, the fire dissipated into a thousand little rivulets and then was extinguished.

Except that Aneirin was preparing already for another assault.

The bird was just for show, because in a moment he fired an arrow from a bow of flame and smoke, which took Trita off guard. But not long enough to get hurt. It hurled past her and sizzled in the greenery.

I had never seen anything like it, nor imagined my friends were capable of such shows of magic. Aneirin moved like a dancer, throwing arcs and fans of flame at Trita while she deftly played the defense, stepping perfectly and avoiding his most earnest assaults. She let him go on about his business for a few minutes more until she began to slowly gain ground. The spear shrunk and grew as she needed it and did something else. It emitted a sound, high and whining, sometimes low and booming, and it appeared to alter the air around Aneirin. He would try to conduct his flame creatures and find they had skittered off into another direction. He would cast his body to one side, only to find Trita was behind him, ready to knock him down.

And she did just that.

Sweaty and laughing, she helped Aneirin stand, and he brushed off the front of his shirt which was covered with ash and soot, and looked at me, pleased as a bird glutted on fat worms.

"Why've you never shown me all that before?" I asked. "And I thought you were conserving energy, La Roche."

"Your tender ministrations always invigorate me," he said, out of breath.

"There were too many mortals about; besides, you missed most of the war," Trita said with a shrug. "Though I did perform some of those techniques during my stint in Londinium—before I lost the spear of Mnemosyne."

That was my fault. I frowned.

"So, he's got fire and you've got, what, air?" I asked.

Trita shook her head. "It's more like frequency. Sound waves. Vibrations. It's a reaction between the spear and the shield, a kind of music, I suppose."

"Deadly music," Aneirin said, rubbing the side of his head. "I feel like a resounding gong."

"It's particularly difficult for him to endure," Trita explained. "He says it insults his musical tastes."

"The word is *dissonance,* and anyone with half an ear can tell it's an abomination," he sneered.

"Ah, but it *works.*"

I looked down at my hands. I noticed they were shaking, noticed that my heart raced. I was nervous; I was threatened, too.

Aneirin knew my thoughts without having to ask.

He approached me and put his hand on my shoulder, looking up into my face. "We are safe out here. There are no homes, no settlements, no roads for miles. There are few places in all of Britanniae we could say the same for. But out here, the earth is older. The ground remembers us as we once were."

"The ground makes me ill," I said.

"You know it's the amulet; you don't have to wear it. It's been long enough," Aneirin said. "A lot of magic there to hold you back. And Verta's besides."

"I'm not taking it off."

"Not asking you to, just providing a hypothesis. But you can't tell me you aren't curious as to what you could do."

What a honeyed suggestion.

Before I could answer, Trita came at me fast, a high whining sound from her weapons knocking me off guard. I was big enough and strong enough to make a good go at things without a magical weapon, but she was brutal with her attacks. Aneirin had deftly stepped aside, his smile widening, and stood back to watch. At least, I figured, he could rest.

Trita was not intending to wound me, I knew she was restraining herself. But the threat of it was in the air. It was possible that she *could*. The amulet started thrumming at my chest every time she came closer, pressing down and reminding me of what remained inside of me, what had once been. It fucking hurt. As I buffeted her blows, forearms, knees, back, any way I could, the amulet followed with a resounding *thunk* against my ribs, making me catch my breath. A hammering cadence, both pulling me along and preventing me from getting the higher ground. If such a thing was possible with Trita.

Then, I understood what she was up to. It's hard to explain how I knew, except I suppose it was due to her wounding me. But as she came down with her spear and I raised up my hand to meet it, hoping to grab it, I saw in my mind her tearing the amulet from my chest and it falling upon the ground.

The spear came up in a grand arc and I grasped it with both of my hands, stalling its descent with alarming certainty. I stomped on the ground and felt my anger boil, and indeed the earth shook. Not enough to knock Trita back, but enough to frighten her and cause her to rethink her approach.

I stared at her as she seethed and threw her spear to the ground. It vanished, then materialized again in her hands. Magic weapons are considerably more difficult to get rid of than the usual sort.

Anger welled up in me. I wanted to kick her. Hard. About the head and in the stomach. Then pin her to the ground with her own spear. I shook off that sensation and fought the urge to throw up.

Aneirin strode between us, his hands linked behind his back, looking as if he was about to lecture an entire room of students.

"You anticipated her," he said, almost impressed. Maybe.

"Fucking...*woman*," was all I could manage. "You rip the amulet from me, and I could burst a crater in the center of this forest so deep, we'd all go plunging into the fires below."

"Doubtful," Trita said, wiping at her mouth. I had drawn blood, at least. Which made me feel marginally better. Thankfully, godling blood didn't stir madness in me like mortal blood. So, there was that. Small consolation.

"She has been researching, Joss," Aneirin said. "Making significant calculations regarding your age, your provenance, and your...unfortunate transformation."

"La Roche has explained our power is finite, correct?" she asked me, spinning her spear in a half-circle, and then stowing it behind her back.

I grunted, nodded.

"I've run numbers. Quite a few times. Consulted with some old tablets, done a few more advanced calculations. I don't think such a show is possible for you, actually. I think the amount of power you had to expend that night—even with your age and relative closeness to the original—was so immense, now you're left with very little. And the amulet, though well intended, is only dampening your abilities more. Cutting you off from what makes you, well, *you*. And I'm fairly certain you won't be able to do anything of our caliber until you are free of it. You fought well, for a mortal. But you have no connection to your element," she explained.

I looked over her shoulder at the mineral springs, and I could smell the water. "I've done some things," I said. "I found Isabella."

"Did you have to submerge yourself in water?" she asked.

I nodded.

"It's not that the connection is gone, but it's a weak tie. You should be able to use the water in the air to divine such a thing," she said. I must have looked dark and unimpressed because she continued, "But if you think you've got the capabilities, then by all means, Mr. Raddick, we have no shortage of water here in the Forest of the Seven Lakes."

Aneirin smirked. "Why else do you think I chose it?"

I approached the mineral springs, stomping like some ogre out of lore. I was cold, afraid. My chest was sore from the constant percussion of the amulet, and the more I thought about moving the water the more my ribs ached. Verta and Aneirin might have once been lovers, have once been as close as the hawthorn and hazel, but it very well might have been their last act together. At least their last act in harmony. And it reminded me of just how much Verta had crossed me and how much it had hurt when Aneirin refused to see eye to eye on the matter.

Deep breaths. I tried to concentrate. The water was full of lime and calcium, I could taste it in the air as I got closer. It was warm, too. Warm from somewhere deep.

"Just like when I first brought you to Verta's, yes?" asked Aneirin. "Surely you'll be able to rise a pillar of water easily. Or are you so out of practice?"

I reached out, my hand trembling comically, and tried to pull the water to me. Not much, just enough. It began to rain lightly, but that didn't count. For time out of mind, my mood had turned the weather and I had no more control of it than a man does of his shadow.

I pressed my consciousness forward, and yet the amulet pushed back. I tried to ignore the pain, the sense it was actually boring into my skin, but it would not relent. I glanced down at my shirt to see the base of Verta's metal heart burrowing into my flesh, making little circles and separating the skin. A trickle of blood began, and then I vomited.

I hadn't so much as managed a ripple in the damned place.

26

We camped, and neither of my friends dared speak of my failure. I think I disappointed them even more than I disappointed myself. We were storming a great city, hoping to pass through heavily guarded walls and enter a deep, forgotten chamber, without spilling too much blood. Our approach had to be right. It had to be right. For Aneirin. For Frances. All for ash tree honey and a cuneiform tablet he believed was still there.

And if it wasn't…

"I'm sorry," he said, sitting down beside me by the fire. He'd provided it, and it was a crackling good one, sending sparks up into the sky, merging briefly with the stars before going cold and falling back down as ash. "I haven't been fully transparent with you, Joss."

"I don't want to know," I said.

He lowered his head, hands folded. "Joss, if I die—if I fail while you still wear the talisman, the bond will break."

I turned to stare at him, startled by my own slow brain making the connection. "That's how you knew Verta wasn't dead."

He nodded slowly. "Her magic still persisted. It allowed you to help me." Aneirin's voice cracked, and he turned his face away, hiding tears or shame I could not tell. "But then she came to us the next morning, and you were diminished again. You used your power, while you could, to help me live. Joss, I don't think I would be standing here if you hadn't."

"It wasn't just *helping*," I said. "It was more than that."

Rather than say a word, he held my hand. As always, his skin was warmer than any mortal could endure. It was wet, too, with his tears.

"The feather is the stronger part of the two. It is a piece of my body, my essence. The heart is but her craft, a kind of bond between the three of us," he said softly. "I am the stronger, in the spell and as we are now. As much as she wants to endure, I do not think she will manage long. Not in the form she now resides. She has gone into hiding and taken my heart."

"But I can help you endure the sickness," I said. "I promise I can."

He drew my hand to his lips and kissed it softly. "The only way we can arrive, undetected, Joss, is to fly there. As birds."

"I can't be a bird."

"But you were a fish. And fish and birds aren't so different. We're all birds, Joss. In fact, I would hazard to say that we are not yet complete if we cannot fly."

"But I cannot fly with this," I said, holding up the amulet with my free hand. "I wouldn't know how to try."

"No, you cannot, now. But when you do, you will rise, and you will change. It will begin in the very core of you, and just when you think you cannot rise any further, you will sprout wings. But if you avoid this, if you continue to let yourself be held captive by the amulet, when I go—and it could be at any moment, Joss, I wish I could say otherwise—you very well may do something you regret. Best to face it head-on, on your own time, surrounded by your closest friends than alone and surrounded by innocents."

I began to weep, unable to keep the fear from bubbling up any longer. Why did the man always inspire such tremendous emotion in me? Passion, hatred, love, sadness. I suppose he had the heart of poetry, of all poets, woven into his ken like a brilliant tapestry.

He took my head in his hands and let me cry upon his chest. He smoothed the hair of my brow and sang lowly to me in his perfect voice until I had no more room for fear. Until I felt, for the space of an hour or so, that there was another in the world who knew. Who understood.

"We come into this world wild, Joss," he said, at last. "And we are monsters. We have to work backward to find our humanity. It is the best part of us. But it's the monstrous bits that hold us, we godlings—we human-shaped beasts—together. In the end, our long lives make it impossible to avoid the creatures we become, but if we have each other, if we share a common story, it stings a little less. We all let go, we all eventually fade. But it's the connection, between us, that makes the long years worthwhile."

I sat up, wiping my face. "I don't think I can bear it when you go." I did not say "if" for it felt so pressing, so inevitable.

He leaned forward and kissed me, just as light as a bird's wing. He did not bring me comfort or tell me not to be afraid, but the kiss was enough

"If I am to rid myself of this," I said when I pulled away, touching the amulet. "You should be the one to remove it."

"Let us wait until the light, Joss. Even monsters can fear the shadows."

I STOOD between Trita and Aneirin, submerged to the waist in the mineral springs, the next morning, like some strange baptism. Trita had vanished the night before, but Aneirin had stayed with me all the long night, curled up in my arms.

Aneirin had a small knife with him, and he leaned over toward me. His hand shook slightly, and I steadied it with my own. He would not be able to keep his shape for long, but I needed him now. Trita wore her shield and her spear, at the ready, should I go mad again.

But with them by my side, I was no longer afraid. Not in the way I had been before. I would always be a monster, but I was a monster with a conscience at least. A monster with friends who shared the burden. Who understood. I considered myself a most lucky being, to have these two friends.

As the knife cut across the leather lance the amulet fell into the water, I felt my senses return in a rushing tide. The iron heart sizzled as it made contact, and then turned red as blood and dissipated. The feather remained, floating atop the water until Aneirin plucked it up. It burst into flame and then he breathed deep as if he had been holding his breath for a century. It returned to him and made his cheeks flush.

I vomited. Such are the sordid details of my most impressive existence.

"I think you're right, Trita," I said. My voice shook. "I feel—"

Then came the water. Like a dam awaiting bursting, the mineral springs rose into the air, and I along with them, a geyser of tremendous proportions. The waterfall went backward. The fish flitted in the air like confused confetti. Aneirin laughed, fire sizzling through the water and making a mist everywhere, until I let it all come down and sat, wheezing, upon the shore.

It appeared I had finally worked out the bird part. I knew what to expect, that the rising would come.

I shook my head, my beak. I rustled my feathers. Aneirin was high above me now. I looked up, and made a sound that was not elegant or worthy of song. No nightingale, no phoenix.

Aneirin laughed, and it resounded across the trees.

"You're an albatross," he said, between breathless laughter. "Of course, you are."

I SUPPOSE, were a mere mortal to have looked up into the sky they might have marked our strange little collection. Might have wondered what such odd birds were doing in concert with one another. An African wood owl, a black-browed Albatross, and a rook. But we traveled at night and in the early morning, and we made impressive miles together down to Ancyra.

It took a little adjusting to life as a bird, but it soon seemed to me I had never been in the shape of a man. All the extra weight and worry, the heft of my body before, seemed a strange dream. And how had I ever bothered to walk anywhere? With the sea far below and all the moisture in the sky I could ever want, I felt more like a dolphin or a seal flitting through the skies than a bird.

And I could out-fly my companions. I was large enough that, should the situation call for it, I could put them upon my shoulders and let them grasp with their talons—which I decidedly did not have—and go some miles before the dawn. My wings had remarkable qualities which my friends did not share. I could root my tendons in such a way that I could keep my wings wide and glide without having to hold them consciously. Like a glider of my own devising.

After flying on and off for two days we came into view of Ancyra. We had no need to speak to one another, for as birds we communicated without voices. But I think even Aneirin was amazed at the sight of the great walled city. For almost two thousand years it had flourished as a center of trade between the Far East and Persia, and it shone like a jewel even with all the holes in its walls. Now the flags of Mary, Queen of Heaven, and Bonaparte draped every pinnacle and parapet in red and blue and white, but the whole castle—all forty-two towers along the central fort and another hundred besides on the outer wall—spoke of another culture, another lifetime, lived within.

Everything smelled different. Even as a bird I could sense just how many people lived there beneath the towers, how many moved within the narrow streets and crawled up and down the hills. Their food was spicier, and contained large quantities of rice from the Far East. There was more wine to be had, and rice wine too. Beer, as well, and other spirits. Not to mention the large quantities of meat. Meat everywhere. Stewed and ground, roasted and turned on a spit, flame-kissed and let out to dry for days at a time. In Britanniae there was some meat from hoofed animals, and Aneirin enjoyed it. But he could afford it. Most ate fish, eel, and poultry when they could get it. Here it was heady: camel, horse, mutton, and pig.

The city was not entirely taken by Bonaparte, though. No, I noticed as I watched with more care that the highest part of the city, the central castle fort, had no banners.

The fort was our focus. Inside was a vault of some sort, with the cuneiform tablet.

"He cannot turn back into his human form," said Trita, her voice cutting through my thoughts.

We stood on the outskirts of the city, and she had transformed back into her human form. She wore the clothes of a soldier, her hair tied up neatly below a flat cap, the buttons on her jacket burnished bronze. She cut a smart figure. The only grave difference between her and the other soldiers in Bonaparte's company was the distinct lack of a firearm. Outlawed entirely in Londinium, I had not many occasions to see them outside of the fight upon the Akdeniz so many years before.

"I can speak for myself," the rook said, clicking his beak at Trita.

"I didn't say you couldn't. I was just observing," she replied. "And while I think that carrying a rook upon my shoulder may go without notice, I cannot say the same for an albatross."

I had not found my voice yet as an albatross, but I was loath to reveal myself as a human—and without the amulet.

"Seriously, you'll draw more attention than a screaming naked whore running down the street tied with roasting meat," Aneirin intoned.

"We're both here if you get out of hand," Trita said more seriously, "And truly, La Roche, how do you manage to be even more insufferable in bird form?"

"It conserves energy," he said, hopping to her shoulder and flapping his wings. "I suppose it gives me more time to think of elegant repartees."

There wasn't much to it when changing into a bird, but I found as I sat beside the main road, trying to keep a low profile between my friends, that going back toward human was significantly more difficult. The rising part was easy. But after flying for so long, I wasn't particularly fond of the idea of going bigger and heavier. I knew I'd be hungry and full of desire, and those two things were of no good to me in a place this bustling with humanity. And war.

I was about to give it a go when I heard a sound like thunder, and I crouched on my webbed feet, hiding my head in my wings.

Cannon fire.

"Do you know what albatrosses eat?" Aneirin said, swooping down from Trita's shoulder and hopping around beneath my legs.

I did not. I hadn't thought about it.

"They eat squid, you imbecile," he pressed. "Don't you see a kind of beautiful irony there? The thing you fear most you will become—you eat. Of the nearly ten thousand species of birds in the entire world, you turn into one that *eats squid*. It's rather beautiful, if I may say."

"You can't go on your whole life being afraid of what you are, Joss," Trita said, more direct. "And if you can't help me, I can't get what I need from in there. And we can't help Aneirin. Or Frances."

Then it struck me. I was going about the whole business wrong. I was thinking of falling down to humanity's level, of making myself massive and bursting from the bird form. But it wasn't like that at all. My body wasn't bigger or smaller, regardless of what it looked like. It was energy, and energy alone.

And what made me sing? What single thought made me gladder than all else?

But my scion.

John.

Everything that was good about me, everything human about me, was in my love for the child I had inspired into the world. However badly and tragically, however mistaken my intentions were. Even if he never had the chance to know me. He was my greatest tie to the world of mortals, and though I had only seen a glimpse of him through the memories of his brother and sister.

I let the sensation grow within me. I breathed deeply and expanded my wings, felt my body grow and change, the framework within shifting and accommodating my new form. It hurt, but it was a good kind of hurt. Stretching beyond the boundaries of my being.

When I stood at the right height again, I shook with the power of it.

"Oh, well, that's *marginally* better, I suppose," said Aneirin from somewhere below me. "Not near as conspicuous as an albatross, and significantly more refined."

Trita sighed. "A horse. He's a fucking horse."

27

I have told the story of my becoming a horse before, but I have always shifted the details. It's a bit too much of an embarrassment otherwise. There's a challenge in being a bit too candid, I suppose. But if there was ever a time to set the record straight, it's here in these words.

So, we began the ascent into Ancyra together. Trita rode upon me, having easily procured the necessary components—no one doubted her flawless accent or her rank—of a saddle and bridle, though neither were used to their full extent. I wouldn't have let her. In fact, if we wouldn't have drawn such attention to ourselves in the first place, I'd have suggested none of those accoutrements at all. Aneirin rode on Trita's shoulder.

Night deepened as we climbed through narrow streets. The stink of the place rose, making it difficult for us to make progress. I didn't need to be told what it was. I had smelled carrion before. But human corpses needed no description. Even as a horse the overwhelming power was beyond measure. Trita had to cover her mouth, and Aneirin hid under his wing, shuddering against it.

The streets were flooded with wounded men and women. Prisoners were tied together in long lines, their necks clasped with irons, their long black beards distinguishing them from the other soldiers. Some were plaited, others forked. There seemed, even in their rough state, a rather impressive array of beards.

It was the first time I'd seen the faces of the people I'd killed. They did not look so different, really. Perhaps slightly less varied than the faces I was accustomed to in Londinium—there did not seem to be so many of African descent. There were some faces that reminded me of Achaemenes, narrow eyes and flatter faces, paler skin. For the most part, none of them carried tattoos, which were fairly uncommon in Londinium. Aneirin said it was a carry-over from the Gauls and Picts, but I had always thought it an amusing practice.

Part of me wished these men looked different. That I could see monsters in their faces. But whether it was because I was seeing through new eyes, or else I was tired and afraid, I saw the same reflected back at me. Men whose lives were forever changed. Who did not want to bow to Mary. Who were prisoners in their own city, a grand place that had been a pinnacle of learning and lore for over two thousand years. Now the streets ran with blood and the stink of corpses. Why? Because Miriam wanted progress, and Achaemenes was too tired to fight.

We came at last to the blockade and Trita dismounted, leading me to an area a bit away from the shouting commands and the cannon smoke.

"You're going to have to try again," she whispered to me, patting my nose as I had once done to Poetaster. "You're much more handsome this way, I have to admit. But there's no way you can sneak with me where we need to go."

"Do you always make a habit of speaking to horses, General Oya?" came a voice from behind us.

I tried to avoid responding like a human might, turning my head to the source of the sound. But I did catch a glimpse of a figure, cut smartly. A sharp chin, deep eyes, a very Roman nose.

"Emperor Bonaparte," Trita said, falling to one knee.

Falling to one knee? I was grateful I was a horse, for I'd never have done such a thing. I suppose we've never had to fear mortals, not really. But an innate desire—and promise—among our kind to remain cloaked meant that revealing our abilities before them was somewhat problematic. And being cornered or followed would be a very big kink in our plans.

"Quite a magnificent horse you're riding," he said, walking past her and coming toward me. He smelled of sage and cedar. "What is it—an

Ardennes? And silver dapple too. Tell me where I can go to find such a specimen."

I had never seen Trita truly at a loss for words. Aneirin was nowhere to be seen, but I had the suspicion he was laughing into his feathers.

"It's an obscure breeder," Trita said at last. "By way of the frozen North."

It was the wrong thing to say. I could tell by the way the man looked at me he wanted to own me, and now he knew I was difficult to attain, well, he was even more interested. That day was my only experience with the man Bonaparte, but I will tell you that he had something in him that most humans don't possess. I would have thought him part of one of Aneirin's boasts, perhaps, though he never took credit for such a man. I suppose that there are wonders we godlings can't take credit for, and in some way I find that a comfort. We're a bitter, broken bunch, and often think ourselves as the center of everything.

Bonaparte reached out to touch my neck, smoothing the dark hair there. He was not a hateful man, I don't think. I didn't sense evil, per se. But he was a prideful man who loved power, and sometimes those are echoes of the same corruption.

"Pity," Bonaparte said, tearing himself from me and paying more attention to Trita again. "Were you anyone else, General, I'd insist the horse be spoils. But you have bailed me out from the depths one too many times to be considered common. And so, I will let you to your magnificent beast."

"My thanks," said Trita stiffly.

Bonaparte made to go, but then stopped. We all tensed, and I noticed for the first time that Aneirin was flitting about behind me, hopping in and around my back legs. I playfully stomped a foot at him and heard an errant squeak.

"But while you're here—and I don't recall your summons, but it has been busy—you could offer me your expertise on the subject of Ancyra. We are almost there, you see," he said, pointing upwards at the great hill. "Yet it vexes me. The people within, these men and women. They must have enough food for years, or else elaborate tunnels beneath, for they show no sign of waning in spite of our most sincere efforts."

"That does sound most vexing," Trita conceded.

There were not many mortals to whom Trita would feel so indebted, nor many godlings, truly. I could see she needed to attend to him, and so I nuzzled her gently, trying to get the point across. Aneirin and I could listen for clues. We needed to get to where Bonaparte was aiming, so it wasn't all ill-timed. Though my current form proved a little bit of a challenge.

Trita followed Bonaparte down and to one of the larger makeshift tents, from which flowed yellowy light. She joined a group of larger shadows and then faded into the fray as more soldiers crisscrossed our view.

I was not going to be able to move around as a horse, not easily, anyway. But I was stuck. And extremely visible. We could not have stopped in a busier location. And I drew attention even as I tried to back up slightly.

I was beginning to panic, and Aneirin knew it. He pecked at my flanks a few times as I began stomping the ground, especially when a young soldier came up and started speaking to his friend about what he wouldn't do for a horse like me. When I flinched at his hand, he cackled cruelly. I don't think there was true malice in the man, but my perception of the world was skewed a bit through my new form. Unfamiliar with changing shape, or at least grossly under-experienced, I had not yet learned how to temper the fears and thoughts of the animal with my own. For isn't that every shape? Just another animal? Perhaps we've always tended toward humans simply because they have the most power, at least on the surface.

Then the man prodded at me with his gun, and my mind went blank. When it came back again people were shouting and running in every direction and pieces of Ancyra castle were falling down around us. Not big enough bits to kill a person, but large enough to wound them significantly if they were caught in the crossfire.

Trita came rushing out, guessing at the source of the earthquake, and Bonaparte was understandably distracted from his work.

"You could have been more subtle," she hissed in my ear, taking the opportunity to shuffle me out of the fray and down a narrow street.

The earthquake hadn't lasted long, but it had felt good. That arsehole had what was coming to him. I'm pretty sure if I knocked his head hard enough, and scared him well enough, he might think twice about being so cruel to a horse again.

"It was rather impressive," Aneirin said, landing on Trita's shoulder. "And certainly not advisable. But when do you ever listen to reason, Joss?"

"It's not fair to tease him when he hasn't found his voice yet," Trita said. "He probably still thinks he has to talk with his mouth."

I did, but I didn't let on.

She turned to me, putting a hand on either side of my long face. "Listen, Joss. It's time for you to be Joss, the godling, the person, the human. This horse business was helpful to a point, and you're quite the fine specimen, but we've got to move—and fast—while there's a distraction."

"Which we can thank you for," intoned the rook. "You forgot to point that out."

"We're wasting time." Trita sighed. "Even supposing we can get both elements, and even supposing that the tablet is intact..."

I looked around the alleyway. There weren't any people around and I couldn't sense anyone else of power in the vicinity. I huffed a deep breath and lowered my head, noticing the narrow rivulets of water coursing through the cobblestones from further up ahead. It smelled vaguely of wine, which was curious. I had expected something else. Blood, maybe? Still, it had a calming effect on me, just to see it. It made me think of all the water all around us, in the air and in human bodies, swelling in the wood and hissing as fire roasted it. Ancyra was dry compared to the places I had lived before, but I hadn't really taken the time to understand the flow.

I had a flow too. How could I have forgotten? That framework under my skin. It wasn't a rigid structure like a tent, it was flexible and ready to be arranged if I just gave it the right coaxing. If I just followed my own source.

The ground stilled as I changed, finding my voice almost immediately so I thought it was right. I did not forget to knit clothes, though they were rough and far from the splendid sort Aneirin and Trita wore. At the very least I was not naked.

I found my voice, I say. What I mean is I made a very loud noise. A kind of great howl, a resounding cry. I was lucky in the aftermath of the earthquake there was enough chaos to drown most of it out, but the reflex was not particularly my finest moment. The truth was that the change hurt, pained me. I felt stretched and changed.

When I opened my eyes, I realized that I was significantly lower than I should be. I could see Trita's waist, but that was about all.

"A wolfhound. Quaint," she said.

I was aware of Aneirin shifting behind me and turned to see an amber-eyed dog with a short golden coat and a curly tail.

"Not my preferred standard," he said, walking in a circle and giving me a sniff. "But it'll do. Don't think I've ever tried transforming into a dog before. Am I pretty? Tell me I'm pretty."

Trita was not amused. "Are you sure that's wise? Birds conserve energy."

"I'm well aware of my limitations, Madame Oya. But if we're to move about and get where we need to go, a woman being trailed by two very well-trained dogs is significantly less confusing than a woman with a bird and a dog. Non?" asked Aneirin.

"Oui," sighed Trita. "Now let's move, shall we? Before *talking* dogs really draw attention."

I just whined and followed along, complicit and still decidedly not in my human form.

ANCYRA CASTLE WAS BURNING. As we crawled toward the main keep dodging fire was an important step. Thankfully, even as a canine, I wasn't entirely useless. I could command mists from my breath that allowed us further entrance. My sense of smell was heightened, and I could tell the direction of the flames, sense the right motion of the air currents. More than once I was able to reroute our small group to a better alleyway.

Climbing proved to be the biggest challenge. Aneirin went back and forth from bird to dog, but I was incapable of turning into anything else. I was no small dog, either, and Trita had to hitch me to her back to scale walls when there was need—and there was, often. Doorways that might once have been direct were barricaded; sometimes they were just jammed full of bodies.

"They fought long and hard, here," said Trita, as we came yet again upon a door held fast with bodies on the other side. "This is one of their last bastions of hope, and it is crumbling around them."

"We need to get to the center of the keep," said Aneirin. "There's an antechamber below the throne room. If the recipe is anywhere, it is there."

I wanted to ask Aneirin how he knew such things, but I did not have a voice. I huffed and shuddered as one of the walls to our right came crumbling down, the ancient stone laid by Romans of antiquity turning back to dust and dirt. I wondered if Ancyra would last the hour. We would, but there were plenty of others to concern ourselves about.

"They're desperate," said Trita, rubbing the side of her face. She was tired, flagging. Even godlings need sleep, and it had not come to us in a long while. But Ancyra was burning, and if we weren't careful, so too would the cure for Aneirin's illness.

Aneirin padded ahead of me, pausing to listen at the wall. The Cretan hound suited him. An intelligent outline, spry and clever.

"Something is not well within," he said, his voice low.

The ground shuddered.

I could feel it now too. Maybe I hadn't been the cause of the quake. Something lurked within the walls, heavy and strong in a way nothing I had ever encountered before. The ice furies had been of a similar ilk, but they did not have the weight that this creature did. The pads of my feet were wonderfully sensitive to the sounds and feeling around me, and I could feel the footfalls when I concentrated.

Not far.

Trita motioned for us to move in, and so we did. The blast had revealed an inner circle of the castle, allowing us entrance into the main keep which we otherwise would have had to gain through brute force. Luck? Felicity? I couldn't say. The air was so thick with smoke I was glad to be lower to the ground, but the lingering power within made me uncomfortable. Godlings, I could measure. Other celestial creatures, I wasn't so sure. Especially if I was still attacking as a dog.

There were a few unlit torches in the walls, but Aneirin quickly brought them to full brightness. He paused, at the head of our little group, and then started running forward. Toward the creature of power.

The castle was comprised of layer upon layer of stone, going back a thousand years and maybe more. At the base was the Roman and pre-Roman structure, with thick walls and wide stones. But as we made our way deeper into the castle there was a change. Sometimes it was in color, the stones going black or red. Other times in composition. Narrow window slits or high arches peaked to perfect points. As I ran behind, I couldn't help but wonder what sort of wonder the castle had once been. My feet passed mosaics and paintings of Roman make, geometric leavings of the Persians and others, and more besides. Grand frescoes, rooms full of musical instruments. What terror had been wrought on this place, and how had we let it happen?

At last, we came to an immense wooden door, a masterwork of design; a dizzying combination of woodwork, mosaic, and inlay. The gilding was present in each and every angle, the geometric complexity far beyond any piece of art I had beheld in my life. It was a jewel in gold and blue, a remarkable and utterly unfathomable work of human hands.

And then it was gone.

What had been waiting for us expanded and then exploded, sending the door and the jamb out in a thousand directions as if from cannon fire.

When the dust settled, we remained unhurt but shaken. Above us stood a creature, twelve feet high, its skin the color of coal ash and its eyes burning with an unearthly blue. The jaw was large, offset, the head barely a consideration atop the immense shoulders. Every arm—all four of them —was as thick as my waist, and the legs thicker besides. Where its belly ought to be was a kind of furnace, burning with more blue fire. And abject fury. At its existence. At its power. At its orders. I could tell it was caught between worlds, a creature bound to sorrow and desperation. I did not want to kill it, but it had just one order.

To kill us.

Behind the monster, I could see a throne and an old woman clad in white robes. Her face was tear-streaked but free of fear. Whatever had caused her to cry had burned away. I knew she was behind this creature, for she looked upon it with wonder and gladness. It was not impossible for human beings to call forth magic, though mighty rare.

"Joss!" shouted Aneirin, "Beneath the throne! We'll keep this fellow busy."

I skidded between the creature's legs, just barely singeing my fur as it passed above me. It smelled of lightning and pain, and it shrieked as one of Trita's spearpoints contacted its side. I glanced back, cowering slightly, to see Trita standing, twice as tall as she had once been, burning with a bright light, purple and regal, and her eyes blazing against the creature.

And Aneirin too. He was a bird again, but more. He was wreathed in flame, the fire falling off of him like molten metal, filling the floor and dissipating up the sides of the walls. Letting out a huge cry of anguish or challenge, I could not tell which, he drove his wings forward into the face of the golem while Trita continued her assault.

Trita did not move fast and smooth as I had seen her in our time together, fighting to keep the streets of Londinium at least marginally safer

Four arms were difficult to account for, but Trita was ready when the golem came at her, more annoyed than threatened by the firebird. She countered its attack, ham-fisted and blind, and severed one of the thick arms from its body with the edge of her shield. It fell to the ground and lay listless for a second, but then began writhing like a snake. In a moment, before I could reach the robed woman, I saw it begin to take form—another smaller golem.

That approach wasn't going to work.

Aneirin tried fire. He flew to the top of the high peaked ceiling, fanning the flames from his wings, melting down marble and mosaic, wood and metal alike, raining down drops of lava and chunks of fresco below him. It annoyed the golem, but it did not stop it.

I had to move.

Wresting my view from my two friends I finally reached the priestess. She kicked me, hard, in the ribs, and I realized immediately the limitation of my form. I skidded across the marble floor and regained my composure, but when I came toward her again, she had a long staff in one hand and a look of death in her eyes. She was not a young woman, no. But she possessed more power than I had ever encountered in a human being before

"You come to take the book from me," she hissed, addressing Trita and not myself. I was just a dog, after all. "But I have consumed it. And it has consumed me."

For a moment Aneirin went bright blue, but then pressed on. Those words meant little to me, but their impact was large upon him.

"Don't kill her until we're done with this!" shouted Trita, buffeting a blow that would have felled a small house but somehow left her standing. Her feet left trenches through the marble as the golem's angry fists came down upon her shoulders. She skidded back at least six feet and came to a screeching halt by sinking her spear into the floor and screaming.

Being a dog was proving to be a most inconvenient endeavor during this fight. And killing her was unlikely.

I bit the woman as she came closer to me, but mostly got a mouth full of her robes. I pulled and tugged and managed to get her to one knee. But still, she laughed at me.

I was afraid, I knew that to my bones. The amulet was gone. If I let go of my power now, what's to say I wouldn't destroy all of Ancyra—what was left of it, anyway—along with Bonaparte and the rest of humanity in the general vicinity?

The priestess was laughing at me again, kicking me in the ribs. She took her time punishing me, and that was her undoing. While I was pushed to some distance from her with that last kick, she was far too enamored of her golem to pay attention to what was happening to me.

If I didn't transform, Aneirin could fade entirely. And it would be my fault. I couldn't bear such a thought.

There was no sense of stretching or changing, really. It was more like a subtle pulsing, a kind of gentle expansion of myself until I acquired the borders I'd been born to.

As soon as I stood the entire world felt different. And it wasn't because I was watching the most sincerely astonishing fight of my life, a giantess and a phoenix wreaking havoc on a golem of massive proportions, but because the amulet was gone. I could smell and sense everything around me tenfold—a thousand-fold. The men and women screaming outside the walls of the castle, the children in their arms too afraid to make noise. I tasted blood in the air and fear upon every breeze. But it did not stir me to fury, not as it had once. I had not known humankind as I now did. I had not seen and felt love; I had, at the time, near nothing to lose.

When the priestess turned to see me again, her smile evaporated like a morning mist. Her eyes rose higher, higher, until she beheld me. Clad in scale mail, I stood glimmering like Poseidon of old, my hair burnished like silver and my eyes afire. I was a little late in summoning a weapon, only because I wasn't sure what it should be, so when I pulled a bright trident out of thin air it appeared far more theatrical than I meant it to be.

She cowered before me, and though I wanted her dead for her mockery, I restrained myself. I pulled chords of ice from the air and braided them around her arms, holding her tight. She struggled a moment, still trying desperately to piece together the most recent events. Hadn't I just been a dog at her feet? Hadn't there been laughter, victory?

I would have told her more, have shown her just what cruelty meant to one as I, but I had a purpose.

Just as I stepped forward Aneirin found himself clasped in the golem's arms, snuffed out, going dark. What was left, when cast across the floor, was a poor, singed creature with wings and a beak, crying out in pain to the darkening world around him.

The golem rounded to see me, near matched in size, and I turned the trident in my hands as I had seen Trita do with her spear before. Snow and mist issued forth, cooling the stiflingly hot room and freezing the melting walls and spent frescoes.

Fury was in its face as it stomped closer to me, then swung out with an arm, making contact against the trident with surprising force. It rattled my teeth and set my jaw to feel that kind of blow. Large though I was, the impact was not without note. The golem let out a strangled sound from its mouth, but I realized that it was shut by some mechanism of magic. As it cried out and came at me again, I saw something within, a slip of parchment or paper, flapping up against its grated teeth.

Trita took the opportunity for a stunning attack, slicing across the open ribcage of the creature with her spear. For a moment the golem stopped its attack upon me, dropping its hands. Then it shuddered like a great engine, shaking its head and then re-assembling its middle. It was both made of stone and clay, a viscous and unyielding material that meant any attacks were going to leave us exhausted and spent. Spending more of our power, again and again, until we were simply beating our heads against walls, draining our limited capabilities over this creature.

Both of us knew that slicing was not the way to go, else we risk more golems. Small as they were, we were barely keeping a handle on the situation without any more added difficulty.

As the golem turned toward Trita, I pointed to my mouth and signaled her as we had done during our days fighting in Londinium. It was a coordinated approach, meant to position the defender into a more submissive position. She would get her spear between its legs, and I would twist to get the head in position between my own hands. The challenge was twofold: we had never done this before with a creature so large—even at our size, we were just barely matched to it—and never had we done so to one burning blue flames.

Trita's movements were precise and flawless, as I ought to have expected. The error was in my way, so when the golem's arms came up over my head, pulling me down and burning me, I knew I had miscalculated. So yes, perhaps there were three challenges—a second set of arms is a considerable and unusual complication when it comes to a physical confrontation.

The golem broke free and, before I could fully regain my composure, hit Trita so hard across the middle that she spun out and crashed into a column, sending dust and debris all around. Her larger form diminished as she made contact with the ground, and I could tell she was dazed. Spent. She had been doing most of the fighting now, while I had been idle.

I could still hear Aneirin whining pitiably. It broke my heart and fueled me onward.

When the golem charged at me, I feinted and then sent a chain of ice toward its middle, where much of its fire remained. Whatever made it go, it was stoked within. It took three tries and not a little blood on my side of the equation, but I was able to freeze what power there was. Judging by the frenzied cries of the priestess, I was going about it right.

Just in time for Trita to regain her composure. She grew, great tendrils expanding from the side of her head. Snakes, I realized, twining around her cheeks and slinking down her chest. Then her body changed, feathers and wings, innumerable and the color of blood. When she opened her mouth, her teeth were sharp as daggers and her eyes wide with a perfect kind of madness.

She charged forward, the golem unsure where to attack now that his power was somewhat diminished. She did not need a spear to knock him free, and this time I did not fail. An extra twist was all I needed to get a grip on its head, five times the side of a man's, and pry my hands deep into its shuttered maw.

I shouted, and the ground trembled about me as I pulled and tore at its head. Chunks of it flew off, hitting the floor and hissing. Still it writhed, still it bit and tried to destroy us. It was a worthy adversary, but a sad creature breathed of nothing but hate.

My hands were slick with blood and seawater when I finally found the small slip of paper, lifting it up above its head and screaming.

Yet still it flailed and thrashed, and the priestess laughed her raspy, cruel laugh. Again, she shouted: "I have consumed it. And it has consumed me."

That was when Aneirin took to the sky again. A simple rook once again but with fire in its wake. He swooped down and grabbed the slip of parchment in my hand and tossed it up above its head where it was consumed in a holy nova of flame.

For a moment, the entire room was bathed in white light, so pure and intense that I wondered if, somehow, I was dying.

But then the golem turned to sand in my hands, littering the ground with pebbles and rocks and hissing hot stones.

Trita wiped at her bloody face, no longer a gorgon. I looked at my bloody hands. Then we searched for our friend.

Aneirin was pecking out the eyes of the priestess while she screamed silently, still chained with my magic.

We scrambled to stop him, but there was no use. It took a godling to see it, perhaps, but he was doing more than wounding the woman. He was taking something from her, within her. The knowledge from the book, whatever it was, transferred to him. I tried to interrupt, but Trita stopped me with an arm across my chest and pointed beneath the throne.

There was a stone, lifted slightly by the fray. I crawled, feeling wearier than I had ever felt in all of my life. Once again, I was as human as I had ever been. But the noise around me was lessened a great deal. My lungs burned in my chest, my hands so slick from blood that it took three times to pull aside the stone.

There was a jar of ancient make, the wax still sealed on the top. I knew what it was. I could smell the honey, and in my mind, I saw Isabella standing before me, naked and resplendent, her long hair stuck to her body like the branches of a tree. Then I opened my eyes and I was again in the carnage.

There was a tablet and a residue of wax—beeswax—but the marks were gone. And another tome, from which all the pages were gone.

I stumbled to Aneirin who now lay at the dead priestess's feet and opened the tiny jar of honey. Not just any honey, but honey of the gods. *Manna meli*. I brushed it on the end of his beak, and he at first looked as if he would not take any. But then, once the smell roused him, he began eating again. There was a goodly amount in the container—more than I would have thought—and it restored him in that moment.

I wept as I watched him take again his human form, such perfection and symmetry. We stood, all three, weeping and holding one another, though the failure of our mission hung heavily about our hearts. There was much that I did not yet understand. But we had survived, broken but not irreparably. And judging by the cries of victory and chants in Latin, Bonaparte, too, had taken the city.

28

The *manna meli* restored Aneirin a great deal, but not entirely, and was far better than ash honey, though we did collect what of that we could. There was enough, he said, to keep himself from fading for at least a decade or two, but no further.

As to the ancient recipe, he assured both Trita and me, with the most enduring oaths, that he had gleaned the contents of it from the priestess, but the production was considerably more difficult than he had anticipated. He insisted, once we returned to Londinium, he would write it down and get to work. But it would require a great deal of research to complete.

We returned in March of that year, and though Aneirin brought some of the *manna meli* to Frances Keats, there was no change in her.

When he returned to tell me the news, he looked despondent. "I tried," he said. "But I think it would be best if you went to her. She does not have long in this world, Joss."

I did as he asked. Aelfric saw me coming, and I never had to ask to see Frances. He just brought me to her room.

Years before I had stood in that room and brought Frances Keats back from the dead. I had held her child, John, and blessed him with poesy. But as I entered it this last time, knowing in my marrow that I would be done with the Swan and Hoop forever, it was as if I was in a mirrored nightmare. Frances lay upon the bed, sunken and shriveled well beyond her years. Her mouth was riddled with sores, and it stunk of shit.

Little Fanny Keats sat on a stool, whispering words of comfort to her doll.

"The doctor's come and gone," Aelfric said. "Said it's just a matter of time."

I had broken Miriam's law. But the damage had been greater than anyone could have guessed. I'd broken Frances Keats, and then I had run from her, from my duty to fix her. And now, she was gone beyond my power to heal.

"Joss..."

She said my name, and I fell to my knees by her bed.

"I thought you'd never come."

I took her hand, closed my eyes.

"No," she said, perhaps sensing what I was about to do. "No, it is enough. Let me go this time, will you?"

"I should have come sooner."

"You should have let me go then."

That was all she said to me before she slipped away. I made myself stay and watch her body grow cold, brought the pain deep into myself, and accepted my sins.

TEN YEARS SEEMS a great stretch of time to mortal minds; I know, I have spoken to them of it. For the gods of Londinium, it was not so. Aneirin and I lived a quiet life in the city while he worked to perfect the potion we hoped might prolong his life, or else rid him of the pestilence in his throat. We lived as lovers do, and there were many soft, perfect moments, and brilliant, bestial ones too.

I cannot say we were entirely happy. Verta, what was left of her, weighed on our minds. She never left the Temple. She sent no word. I could only sense her, in a most distant way, and I knew the separation was painful for Aneirin. We are jealous beings; even though Verta would never have prevented Aneirin from loving another, loving a godling was another story altogether. Verta's shadow hung darkly over Aneirin, especially on the days when he was ill, which happened with more frequency as the years went on.

As for John Keats, he had his own godmother of sorts: Isabella Jones.

After what had happened in Ancyra, and the ensuing failure with Frances Keats, she agreed to help steer young John in the right direction should he need it. She would function as his patron, if needed; she would ensure no one harmed him.

It gave me more time to focus on Aneirin.

"I worry about you, Joss," Aneirin said one night at dinner. We had begun our time at High House with formal dinners, but that soon diminished. Now, Penny made us food, and we served ourselves in the dining room or, sometimes, just in the kitchen.

"You've no cause to worry, love," I said.

His eyes narrowed a bit, taking me in. He was having one of his better days, the color high in his cheeks, but his hair had gone almost white in the intervening years. I worried about *him* constantly.

"Your work with the Vintners is appreciated, the aqueducts have never risen so high nor given such clear water to so many, but even I have found ways to check in on Percy."

"I haven't had the courage to meet my godson."

"You had the courage to fight off a golem the size of the tower of Londinium. You had the courage to lose your talisman and walk unfettered."

"It's different with John."

"He's a mortal. Yes, he is blessed. But he also has your essence within him. I know you think about him; you say his name in your sleep."

"I'm not even certain where he lives."

"Bullocks. You know precisely where he is. He works at Guy's Hospital. He's an apothecary! How's that for your dose of irony. Taking after me, after all." Aneirin paused, sipping his tea. I could see the missing finger stark against the deep blue china. "Unless you want me to check in on him for you."

He had never offered. Since Frances Keats's death, I had not ventured anywhere near the Keats family. John was a man now, his brother Thomas too. And little Fanny would be nearly marriage age by now. There was another brother, if I recalled as well, named George. All orphans. All poor. In spite of my work with the Vintners, and continued work against the tide of crime in the city—even with corporal punishment as the rage, crime never ceased—the Keats children, like so many others, barely made ends meet.

"Joss, you must find some joy beyond these walls," he said softly. "It will do you good. You live with a ghost, and it is not fair."

"You said you'd made progress on the recipe."

"Progress," he said, snorting ruefully. "Nothing that will save me. Nothing that will heal me. Mostly burned fingers and a bruised ego."

"It's been almost ten years," I said softly.

We were running out of time.

"If Calvinius was still here..." he trailed off, the color of his cheeks rising.

We had heard nothing from the Spaniard, but Miriam had reported seeing him in Rome once or twice. He had cut off communication with Aneirin and me, and his hands were the most talented in the art of alchemy.

"I can try and write to Miriam again," I said, having taken up a loose and perfunctory correspondence with her. "She is also set to return to Londinium in a few weeks. Perhaps she'll have word."

"Even if we were to find him, Joss, I doubt he will have any desire to help me."

"He was your friend."

"He was my apprentice. That, he made clear."

We had thought Calvinius's disappearance was due to the war, that once the world found a more peaceful way that he would find his way back to Londinium. But whatever the godling of Chaos was up to, it was beyond our sight.

"We'll keep trying," I said, taking his hand and kissing the bony knuckles.

AT ANEIRIN'S INSISTENCE, I arranged to visit Guy's Hospital. I decided I would make it a casual, coincidental greeting.

Getting around Londinium was easy for me. Indeed, since returning to Londinium I'd found a most convenient way of traveling that didn't require the use of typical transportation. Throughout the entire city were wells of a marvelously ancient make. Therefore, I had my very own pathway, anywhere I wanted in the city. I could simply touch the side of one of the wells and then find myself across the town at another well with the right concentration. A map within my mind.

Magical transportation or not, meeting John was still enough to set my nerves afire. I went through a thousand different soliloquies and introductions but finally resolved that I would watch him first and then, if the mood suited me, I'd speak to him.

The rain was a comfort, and as I waited near the hospital, I kept an eye on the various men and women going about their work. The fashion this year presented in blues and grays, an aesthetic I rather liked, but amidst the dark skies the contrast was glum. Melancholia was written on every brick and cobblestone, and the world was hushed.

I marked the faces, wondering if there was a chance I would mistake his features. I had only seen him in visions and as a babe. Perhaps he had already walked by me and...

I knew John Keats the moment I saw him. He was neither tall nor short, but strong of body. His face flushed red in the cold, his clever hazel eyes twinkled with an impish sort of merriment as he was discussing something with a companion of his. I could hear his voice over all the rest, and it was sweeter and deeper than I had imagined. I felt as if I would explode from pride, watching him as I did.

Even if I had tried, I would not have been able to avoid following him. Upon seeing him I felt myself pulled as if by an unseen hand. Before I even had time to consider where I was walking, I was moving behind John and his friends, trying to look inconspicuous

They chose to stop at The George, a galleried pub of decent repute, and went to ordering their drinks. Unlike his other friends who preferred ales and harder drink, John ordered a claret and, even though the rest of his company were gathered together in one of the larger rooms within, found himself a seat by the window. His companions made no issue with his withdrawing from them, but I knew the moment was mine if I wanted it.

Yet, I became overwhelmed with self-consciousness, painfully aware of my bearing and my ineptitude. Every word I had thought of saying to him evaporated from my mind as soon as I tried to put the words together. So, I ordered a whiskey, drank it, and walked back home.

Aneirin was in the parlor of High House when I returned, and he looked expectantly up at me, knowing what I had planned for the afternoon.

"You look worse than I feel," Aneirin said upon seeing me. "Did it go that badly?"

Tea had been put out, but he had let it go cold.

Aneirin took a sip of the teacup and scowled in response. I knew the brew had gone cold before I sipped it. I could have warned him.

"I didn't speak with him," I said, taking a seat in the wingback monstrosity that Verta had procured for her parlor and left as a reminder.

"It is intimidating, the feelings they arouse in us. It is why Miriam has imposed such rules… Can you imagine what you'd feel if we'd sired a child together as godlings? Goodness knows some good things come out of her rules. There are enough monsters among us."

He asked it casually, but I reddened at the thought. "I don't know," I said, "I could imagine a fine child between us."

"Alas, we godlings can no longer do such things," he said with a sigh. "But you will miss out on the opportunity to meet your godson, and you will regret it for the rest of your life. Joss, I will not be here forever. You need your own future."

I stared at him. I hated when he spoke in such a way, it made my insides squirm and my body ache. I could not live without him.

"Talk to him," he insisted. "Be brave. He is but a mortal, even though he is blessed. Londinium is a dangerous place to live and die."

29

The following day, I was up in the highest aqueducts, inspecting some of the new pipes, when I felt a stab of pain in my side, clear and sudden. I nearly fell off my perch, and scrambled down, in my panic changing my shape—no one was near enough to see, but I scolded myself for letting my guise slip.

I was an albatross again, and so I flew to High House as quickly as I could, my heart thrumming with fear that I would find Aneirin dead.

I landed on the stoop of the house, but when I tried to change back to my human form, nothing happened. I was thirsty enough to drain the river itself, and exhausted from the trip, but there was nothing I could do to make the change. My side, under my expansive wing, stung like I'd been shot. Unable to ring the bell, I flew up to the third story, where Aneirin's room was, and tapped on the window with my beak.

There were voices inside, Trita's and someone else's. Then the curtain moved, and I was met with Trita's teary eyes. Her hair was cropped short to her skull, and there were white symbols painted on her eyelids. I had only seen her on and off over the last ten years, but I was relieved to see her.

It was difficult getting through the window, large as I was, but I managed it.

"Silly lout can't…even get himself…in decent shape to see me," I heard Aneirin say, halted and weak.

Relief. He still spoke.

Aneirin was as pale as the sheets around him, his lips cracked. There was blood beside him, and on the sheets, purple and fresh.

I transformed slowly back to my human form. Trita came to me and embraced me; I let her. I was shaking, exhausted from the trip and beset with emotion. She soothed me, rubbing my back and arms. It was like holding onto the trunk of a tree, branches waving over my body.

I craned my neck to get a better look at my dying friend. His throat was swollen and blue from the chest to his chin. Tendrils of blackening rot reaching out, marring his smooth skin. He was wracked with pain. Now and again he would shudder against it.

"Don't be angry," Aneirin said to me as I shook myself. "I fell down the stairs to the laboratory and…I don't know. Trita was not far; we were going to surprise you with her visit."

"Surprise?" she said.

"It's good to see you, Trita Oya," I said. Aneirin's fingers were so cold.

"Oh, Andrew," Trita said, "You are like Shiva swallowing the Kalakootam poison in ancient times. I only wish we could undo it."

"But the recipe," I pressed. "Surely we can keep trying,"

"It won't work," Aneirin said. "I can't make it work."

"Nonsense," I said. "You are gifted in these matters."

"He's tired, Joss. He needs his rest."

"I have seen it written in blood… But keep me warm, let me rest, and I shall come to you again…" he said, his voice faint yet firm. He was delirious.

Aneirin fell into a deep sleep, and Trita and I retired to the parlor when we felt we could do no more. When I went to fetch him more *manna meli,* I saw that the pot was almost scraped clean. The last time I had checked, there was so much more. It appeared he was worse off than he let on.

I almost threw the jar to the ground but restrained myself. Instead, I stomped back upstairs and shook it at Trita.

"Verta should be here," I said. "Why in heavens isn't she here? I cannot do this alone."

Trita looked so sadly at me I thought she might burst into tears. But she did not. She took my hand and said, "We could find her. Try and speak with her."

"Not today," I said, firmly. "If he doesn't improve then…yes, I suppose we can go to her temple together."

The sorrow over Aneirin's illness was so great I couldn't keep track of human time, so great was my grief. It ate up everything around me. It colored every branch and flower, it sat upon my shoulders.

For weeks, I wandered around in a daze while Aneirin slipped in and out of consciousness. He was only lucid for brief moments, and even then, there was no course to his narrative. Trita and I took turns watching over him, and in between I had gone through much of his laboratory but found nothing remotely resembling the cuneiform tablet we had taken from Ancyra.

I began to wonder if he had lied to me about his progress, and darkness threatened me on every side. He had it, I know he had the knowledge. But he kept it from us. From me, especially. He said he retained the information but would not tell me where. Damn, the man. Damn him.

Still, the darkness of the matter hung over me. Made worse by my continual avoidance of John Keats. I relied on Isabella for any and all information, and none was good. Even though she tried, bless her, to disguise the tone in her letters. John was, she said, every bit my child. A free spirit yet trapped within a mortal body. But melancholic. And prone to fits of fever. She was inquiring after his health.

Aneirin was dying, no wonder pestilence began seeping its way back to the world.

And then two things happened to wrest me from my sorrow, at least a bit: I met my godson, and Verta came back.

"Pardon me, sir, but do you happen to be Mr. Joss Raddick?"

The voice cut through my melancholic stupor, and I looked up toward its source. Her eyes. He had her eyes.

I was out in the street, not far from the Londinium Bridge, hoping to get a bit of fresh air and reset my mind. It was raining, as it had been for weeks, and John Keats stood before me, his skin pale and his cheeks flushed, his auburn brown hair clinging in damp curls to his forehead. He was shivering hard enough that his teeth chattered.

I must have gawked at him, for he asked the question once again, more tenuous this time.

"Yes," I said, ducking under the eaves of a building to get us both out of the rain.

He looked at my shirt, confused. I was dry. But he was too polite to say anything, and I presented him with a handkerchief which he took without question. He was drenched through to the skin, and judging by the smell of him, sick with something. It was the same smell that permeated the entirety of Londinium by the Tamesis, and I cringed inwardly. And there was something else about him, too. A strange, metallic odor I hadn't sensed before.

John had a hard time catching his breath, and as we weren't far from the George, I took him there, ordered him food and claret, and he didn't argue with me once.

His lively hazel eyes took in everything. He was an observer of the world, and he missed nothing. With John, the world seemed to move around him, and he watched like a stranger, absorbing every detail. He acted a great deal like me. Like a fish in a man's world.

"I didn't mean to call you out so," he said over our drinks. "It was rather rude of me."

"Not at all," I said. "I'm used to it."

"Yes, I suppose...my mother described your likeness to me, you see. But I did imagine you'd have aged more, if you don't mind my saying."

I shrugged. "My hair has gone white," I said. "You must only look closer."

"I do wonder how I ever could have missed you. Have you been in Londinium long?"

"A while yet, yes."

"Striking."

"Well, you've found me," I said. "Was there something I could help you with?"

He smiled, but it was all too fleeting. "Yes. I'm grateful for that. You see, Mother told me that if I were ever in need of anything for our brother Tom, who's been ill for some time, that you had a friend, an apothecary or doctor of sorts, who you'd spoken of. A Mister La Roche. I haven't got much in the way of funds, I'm afraid..."

I must have been unable to keep the sorrow from my face, for I saw him falter when he saw my expression. For a moment I had considered hiding the truth from him, claiming that La Roche, my dear Aneirin, was gone or on a trip or simply indisposed.

"I'm afraid, I fear that, as much as I would wish it different, your search is in vain. Mister La Roche is too ill himself to be helpful," he said.

The look in John's eyes spoke of his hope, dying there before me. So, I continued hastily, "But, I have access to his papers and research. There is some chance that I might find something useful."

John sighed, nodding. “I’m so very sorry to hear of this. There’s been a blight on this place, and I fear it hasn’t gotten any better in the last months. My brother Tom, you see, has ever been a sickly child. But now the doctors don’t know what to do for him, and I’ve been staying with him…” He trailed off, wiping at his damp brow with shaky fingers.

“You’re sick yourself,” I observed, for the first time, saying the words as they reached my mind. The smell of sickness was about him, the color from his cheeks had never faded, even after we’d come in from the cold.

John’s eyes shot open, white with fear, like Poetaster meeting a stranger for the first time.

“I pray the gods spare me from the sufferings of my family,” John muttered. “But if you find it in your heart to look through the work of your friend, I would be indebted beyond words. Here is where I’m staying. You may write me or call on me there if you so desire.”

“I’ll do all that I can,” I said.

30

Since moving to High House, I had left Aneirin to his business, only meeting with him a handful of times in his office. I had the keys, always had, but respected the space as his own. Our intimacies extended to almost every other room in the house, and it was important that he had his space. Seeing as I had exhausted the search in his laboratory, the office was the most logical next step: perhaps the tablet recipe was there, and it could help both Aneirin and Tom Keats.

Now I was left to go in, without his express permission, and root through his things. The weight of that intrusion weighed so heavily on my soul that I had to walk around the front of the house, pacing, to gain my strength.

So that was how I was found the next morning standing outside High House, blinking up at the door as if I had no idea how to open it.

"You do live here, I believe," said a voice beside me. "At least, someone used to inhabit these walls of your general description. Which I've yet to see repeated in all my life."

It was Isabella Jones, and she was wearing a fetching dress of aubergine and a wicked smile.

"Unless I'm mistaken," she added, "and you are, in fact, not the Joss Raddick of my previous acquaintance."

"I am that, more or less," I said. "Good morning, Mrs. Jones."

She took my arm and squeezed, and I felt momentarily full of sunshine.

I couldn't stop looking at her. I wanted to fill up the world with the image of her, to wrap her in my arms, to stroke her face and run my hands through her long, dark curls.

I felt immediately guilty. Aneirin would not be jealous, I didn't think, but as his bodied crumbled above, I was having thoughts of Isabella in a most pointed manner.

"You look puzzled, Mr. Raddick," she said, drawing closer to me. "I'd ask if you'd lost your keys, except you have them in hand. I was hoping to see you, my dear. All this time in Londinium, and I've seen you but once. I had a question to ask of you that might be best put to words and not pen and paper."

"Oh?" I asked.

"Verta. Have you seen her?"

"She's not in. She hasn't been in…not since oh, years back," I said. "It was abrupt, but I could not find the strength to see her. And I do not think Aneirin has, either." Unless he had not told me.

"Strange," she said, almost absently. "Perhaps I am misremembering."

"Would you like to come in?" I asked.

She nodded and squeezed my arm. My body filled with light. "I thought you'd never ask."

"It isn't as if she writes to me often," she explained to me over wine and soft biscuits, "but typically she replies at least within the year. I'm no longer promised to her, as she let me go of my vow years ago, but we are friends. She's gifted me with many things, and I feel it my debt to repay her in kind when I can."

"She changed after the incident with Shanna. La Roche knew it," I said. "I always believed there was something unnatural in it—but La Roche…"

Isabella looked somber and stroked her bottom lip. "Unnatural. Yes, it is. I focused my study on other areas while at the temple, but I know Verta is ancient. She has always had knowledge far deeper and darker than anyone suspects. And that she hasn't returned, in spite of La Roche's condition is…distressing."

"I thought so, too," I said. "Trita came all the way from wherever the hell she was, damned woman. Said Aneirin's pain was pulling at her like a hook in the lip."

"Curious. And when did La Roche start falling ill?"

I struggled to find the right words. "We had ten years where the change was subtle. Bad days, strange fits, but we were happy. When he wasn't trying to work out the tablet recipe we found, he was scribbling in his diaries, and..."

That's when it occurred to me. His diaries. Perhaps I never wrote much down, but he had. Diligently. Even when we were in the middle of a bloody war, that man always took time to put his expansive thoughts to paper. It's how he'd gained my trust in the first place. There was power in those words, and I'd always assumed he'd been cataloging his life story for his own amusement. Then it occurred to me he might have had an ulterior motive for all of it.

"You look as if you've figured something out," Isabella said to me, giving me her half-smile. Her chin dimpled, and I had to stand up and walk about the room to prevent myself from putting my own fingers there.

"Well, I was trying to steel myself to go into his office, thinking I might find some information about the medicine, but then... I think I've been looking in the wrong place the whole time," I said.

THE ROOM SMELLED OF HIM. Like sunshine on daisies. The threat of death had followed me since I left the lake, but it had never been so personal and so lingering. I had never been forced to walk around in the emptiness left when someone is dying, and I was glad Isabella was there to prevent me from slipping again into the dark brambles of melancholy. I felt a rather daft need to keep face, but she could see through me. Now and again she put her hand on my elbow or my shoulder. Her touch was an anchor.

"He was working furiously on the potion, and he promised he had the recipe," I said. "There were multiple recipes, including the one he claimed to have extracted from the priestess as she died. It was a gruesome thing, but he was filled with hope on the subject."

Isabella took in the room with her dark eyes. "It really is a magpie nest, isn't it?"

"A rook, but yes," I said. I frowned. "Though it isn't usually this out of sorts."

I was looking for his journals, but the state of his room was utter disarray. The way the papers had been strewn about led me to believe someone had been through them. He was never organized to say the least, but there was a sense of order to his chaos. The shelves that were once lined with his trinkets and collections were all moved about, the harmony disturbed. Statues turned to the side, scarves spilled out of a chest, lamp shades tilted.

"Does someone else live here with you?" Isabella asked.

"Trita is visiting. Penny, the maid. Amos, our doctor. But they are not allowed in here. Only I have the key."

"Perhaps he was in here looking for something," Isabella noted. "Before he fell so ill."

"It isn't like him," I said. A decanter of claret had spilled all over half of his desk, long dried and sticky from evaporation. But there was enough moisture to tell me the story. He had been drinking it, judging from the glass nearby which had rings of red in it left behind. "Or he was accosted."

"Do you think Verta knew of the *manna meli*?" Isabella asked. "Do you think they were still in contact?"

I didn't think they were. But I couldn't very well ask Aneirin.

"Which would explain how fast our stores have been depleted," I said darkly.

Isabella sighed. "Joss, I'm sorry…"

I held up a hand. "I will refrain from judgment until I know what I am judging. That is why his journal is so essential."

We rummaged about the room for almost an hour until I finally found what I was looking for. The volume was the same as it had been years before, when Aneirin had first opened its pages to me in order to gain my trust. I'm quite certain now the book itself had magical properties.

My heart leapt to my throat as I pulled the journal from its hiding place, stowed behind a painting of a landscape with a brook; it was by a painter he'd loved named Turner. The painting itself was slightly askew, but the scene spoke to me. It was water and sky, light and darkness. Like the belly of a trout.

Still, I hated looking up into Isabella's expectant eyes to deliver her the dark news.

"It's blank," I said. The first half of the book, approximately what I'd read before and a little more, was filled in his flourishing script. But it stopped abruptly. "Every damned page is blank. And this whole room is fit to bursting with nothing."

Isabella put her hand on my shoulder. She had to reach up a good deal, but when she got on her tiptoes, she was able to kiss my cheek. The brush of her lips on my skin gave me pause and space to calm myself down.

I looked into her eyes, and I felt myself smile with a kind of relief.

"Thank you." I barely managed it, my throat thick with tears. "For being here with me. For this. I need the strength right about now. I've been strong for long enough that I'm going brittle."

"Well, I am no lady of iron. Not like Verta was."

Isabella went to the window, measuring her words. "I can't pretend to know what business you all have, and what pulls you to it, but I am worried about Verta. I think she may have answers."

THAT NIGHT I returned to Aneirin's study, calmer and with more resolve. I needed answers. The book might have them—perhaps not in the empty pages, but in what he had written before. I just needed to read the passages again.

Exasperated, I sat down at Aneirin's desk and again opened the journal, reading every last inked page, until I came again upon the blank pages. I had thought perhaps a spell would reveal itself to me, and the words would leap off the page. But they remained blank.

I shouted at the page, loud enough to wake the house. I paused and listened, but Aneirin did not stir. Trita knocked on the door to ask after me, and I sent her away.

Fury proved to be useless, and in despair I let my head fall on the open pages.

Then I took a deep breath in and realized my stupidity. My inanity. It would have taken Aneirin mere moments to figure out such a puzzle, yet I was left in my dimness. It wasn't that he'd stopped writing in the diary—he written in salt water. Salt water! Something he knew I'd notice and likely no one else would.

I couldn't see it with my eyes, but when I ran my fingers over the pages, I could taste every word.

And there were many things for me to learn, and not all will I share. For Aneirin bared his soul for me to see. There were secrets not for me to divulge, confessions that I will take with me to my grave. But for the purpose of my tale, I will share what I can.

31

Joss. If you are reading this, there is a great chance I am no longer walking the earth. Or I'm dying. Or I've gone off on a tirade and you've gone curious and snooped around my things. Living as long as I have, I think I've tended to dramatize the events of my possible demise. Sometimes I dream of a long line of lovers, dressed in black, mourning my loss, dabbing their pale faces and wailing as my body is wheeled on by. And then they all, in their grief, turn to one another for solace, kissing and licking and tearing their clothes off. Other times I think of a grand send-off, full of fantasies that I will someday achieve the status of a king or emperor, pistols and banners at the ready, my guards weeping and singing songs to the heavens, unable to live without me and running each other through in grief.

But as you know, I will never manage such a thing. For all my desires of comfort and pleasure, I am a man of the people. At heart, I am a prophet and a healer, and these vocations put me forever in the clutch of those who need me, not those who desire me. There is a world of a difference between those two sentiments, no matter how much I have tried to rally against that.

But now, now. You have found my scribblings. You'll notice that for all intents and purposes it appears I stopped writing sometime after our adventures in the South, those heady days of ribaldry and adventure. You are looking for the famed recipe. It is at the end of this note, but I ask that you do not use it. You will know, when you read it, why I decided against making the potion, and instead, chose to live out my last years with you, quiet and loved.

We all must go. We can live ten thousand years and still go. Yes, we can change and expand, we can move mountains and raise armies, but we still go on. My time is coming, and I have seen it and railed against it for so long. I am finally giving in. I will come back, though different. Another Apollo, brighter than the firmament, curious and bawdy and brave. Perhaps you will find me, and we will share more adventures. You have just begun to live, and I love you too much to see you in such pain.

I kept a rather impressive catalogue if you'd like to recount them at your leisure; my book is yours, as it has always been, a testament to my openness with you. I am not a brave creature, I fear. I never have been. But I am trying to be honest. If not for the first time, for the only time, and the last. Among all the people I have met, those godling and human alike, I have never felt such a kinship as I have with you. A friendship beyond the bounds of reason. A love that transcends. So, before I discuss any further, you must know how much I treasured our time together. How, in spite of the boast that nearly rent us asunder, and my continual foolishness, we remained friends. We could not be more different in bearing or in personality—you, such a quiet, lumbering creature, and I, a man of light and reason and conversation. And yet, still...you have given me hope. And passion. And purpose. You gave me a love unblemished by time and jealousy, pure and ecstatic.

First, to the Boast. See to my godson. I will never know his greatness but see it in the stars. Perhaps I am there, in his mind, that great Ozymandias. I like to think so. Take care of him if you see him. Protect him. Guide him. His life will be short, but a time will come when you will know what to do.

You see, my death has been foretold for a very long time. When I was but a child, a brilliant young godling in the body of a Gallic boy, I knew. I knew what Verta was when I met her, understood what loving her meant, and yet still gave her my heart. I do not regret it. Nor do I regret the years I tried to change what ultimately would be inevitable. I hope that through the telling of this you will realize why I made the decisions I did and know that, regardless of how it has all played out, to love as I loved—even as briefly as it was—was the greatest joy of my life.

I loved you freely, but Verta shaped me.

After I raised the dead in my village, Verta gave me a way toward redemption.

"I can show you a way to cleansing," she told me, "and a way toward penance. You will save a thousand times more than the lives you took, and you will bear only one scar."

So, I did. I cannot tell you how, but she guided my hand. We traveled the world and I ate the ills of mankind, holding them within my body. The pain never left me but became a part of me, yet I could continue on knowing that I had saved more human beings than I had destroyed.

I was afraid of her. I loved her. I trusted her. I was jealous of her.

I continued on.

She asked me for my name.

I did not tell her. I did not yet know it.

We traveled the continent together, and I healed, and I healed. Sometimes it was at Verta's bidding, but other times I simply found myself wandering on my own, attracted to sickness and disease like some confused bee about his business. I would be lying if I said I never took advantage of the situation, occasionally convincing grateful wives and sisters and daughters, sons, husbands, and lovers, to come into my bed. I thought of it as righteous payment. I rationalized to myself that I had earned it for saving their lives, and as they had no power to rebuke me, it made the experience so much easier. Though it is not that it didn't take its toll; years of it left me empty and angry and looking for something else.

She asked me again for my name, but I had not heard it. So, I remained La Roche.

Monogamy was never a consideration between Verta and me. We run too hot, the two of us, and though our appetites for each other never slaked, it was still not enough. I went about my business, yet always came back to Verta, and it took me a very long stretch of time to understand that my dalliances made her jealous. It was ever so with you. I think you were her only true rival, and had I been healthy and hale perhaps our stories would have been different.

We were living in southern Gaul, by the ocean, in a seaside manor that we had decorated to our liking and lured many an individual to. We had left the ruins of the Northern Reach after the locals had begun making ridiculous assumptions about us. That we drank the blood of our lovers, we didn't age, that we had fangs, and we could not stand the sight of the sun. Such petty and boring imaginations. It was but a taste of what we were and though we never partook in any blood-drinking, we could have fangs if we wanted. And while the sun gave me strength and called to me during the day, I found it easier to treat and find my sick flowers in the evenings.

It was 1346 when she told me:

"I knew you before. Before you were remade. Not terribly well, but well enough."

It was somewhat of a surprise, but I didn't quite realize the gravity of the situation. "Was I as handsome as I am now? Or—wait! Perhaps I was a woman. Did I have large—"

"Andrew," she cut me off, looking hurt. "That isn't what I mean."

"I love you," I said, trying to reach around and grab her breast. In my defense, she didn't usually resist. She had tried many times to speak to me of serious things and I had convinced her otherwise. This time she was in no mood.

"You don't know me. Not really. You know the person I have shown you, but not who I truly am." Her words were sharp.

Somehow, she escaped my hands again, and it was as if she turned into a mist and then formed again. One moment her flesh had been hot and yielding to my touch, the other moment she was standing in front of me and frowning, her dark eyes like a coming storm.

She'd never displayed such an overt show of power, and even then, I wasn't an imbecile. I knew she was older and far more powerful than me, and there was no reason for me to press the issue. Especially in a moment of such gravity.

"Verta..." I said, whispering her name.

"Your predecessor. He died. He..." she shook her head as if dispelling images before her eyes, "He was not a virtuous man. Not like you. But he did one great thing—one truly great thing—that until recently, I thought, still remained."

"You're not talking sense to me," I said to her, feeling sulky and jealous.

I knew there had been a godling before me, but I had not been aware that Verta knew him. It had taken some time for that fact to permeate my consciousness, and then as any male of a certain age (or any age, I might add) does when he discovers an acquaintance of his lover afore unknown, I began to seethe.

My first thought was that she was speaking of my manhood, of my abilities as a lover. That he was better than I was at pleasing her. But then, in my ignorance and arrogance, I decided such a feat was impossible. I was the embodiment of Apollo, perfected by the heavens; she'd never had better than me between her thighs (or so I believed).

But she did know I was feeling jealous—which, let's be honest, is just about as predictable as rain during a Monsoon—and it dampened her spirits even more. She looked at me in a way that spoke of my ignorance and childishness and selfishness. All of which was true.

"Could you be a better man than he was?" she asked me, her voice low, almost as if she didn't expect the answer.

"I would do anything to prove it to you," I said.

"I know. And that's why I'm asking you to do this. It isn't just for me. It's for all of us," she said. She must have seen a shred of fear in me, because she softened for the first time during our conversation, reaching up and brushing back my hair from the side of my face. "My Adonis."

"What would you have me do?" I asked.

"You heal," she said. "You can bring pestilence into yourself and keep it from hurting others. It is the most remarkable sign of your kind. If you choose, you may prevent illness. I had thought that the one who was before you, that his sacrifice was enough..."

And this, of course, is how I learned the rather sobering truth about my predecessor. He had taken a great pestilence into his body after centuries of life, and in the process given up. The pain had been too great. He had tried to keep the sickness within himself but suffered such intense torture from it—which he claimed was trying to find its way out—that it drove him mad and eventually he simply slit his throat.

I have a row of freckles right across the center of my throat. I've always wondered if it's something he left behind to remind me of that desperate knife.

"If he had told me his true name, I could have helped him," she said softly.

"I still do not know my name," I said. It was true. But she was furious.

We grew together, we grew apart. Time passed, and we came to Londinium, and helped usher in a golden age.

Then I met you.

I saw you, Joss, and I knew it: I knew my name.

And then you gave me of yourself, and you came to my bed, and you loved me without question.

But I knew then I was losing the battle with the poison in my body. You have given me more years, and I have treasured every breath with you.

I am being torn apart by this. The matter that makes me a godling is rending apart beneath my flesh. I spend all day trying desperately to hold everything together.

And Verta.

The manna meli was not just for me. I have been sharing it with her, and she comes to visit when the moon is full. She is changed. I had to see it for myself. She only comes for the treatment, asks me my name, and leaves. She wants to break me. But now she has stopped coming. I cannot stop loving her. It rips me apart from the inside because I know, had I not been so ruined by her love, I might have spared more for you. What a life we could have had.

Heavens, Joss, I have been such a blind, selfish creature. I have loved her more than myself. And while I learned every inch of her over the years, I also learned to permeate every crack. We have played games with each other's hearts for so long I can't remember when the last time I looked at her and did not want to make love to her and kill her at the same time. I have kept parts of her locked within myself, and I have made it almost impossible for her to go.

She needs to leave. I do not know why she has held on. I fear she wanted me to believe she would diminish. I fear she has another plan. I fear I will never see it to fruition.

And so, I must let go. Of Verta. Of myself. Of my own life. Though I consign millions to die along with me, perhaps my life has just been to delay the inevitable.

Disease and war? Which is the palest horse? I only hope that when I appear again, when I am reborn—if that truly happens, and all our histories prove to be more than fantasies, he will know love, and healing, and trust. For all the love I have given, all the hearts I have cured, and all the words I have trusted, I have found so few with those traits.

Live well, my love.

My Sight dims.

32

Then came the recipe. The potion. The ingredients were not difficult to find, save one. Written in his script, but not nearly as neat as the rest: "Blood of my blessed."

I put down the book. It had not felt as if I had been reading in the slightest, but as if Aneirin had spoken the words to me directly. My ears were ringing, and I turned around, the hair on the back of my neck rising, expecting to see him standing there, laughing at the joke of his grandest hoax yet. I saw nothing but the wall, plain and unremarkable. Nothing at all like Aneirin.

No wonder he couldn't make the potion. It would require the blood of Percy Shelley, and he would not sacrifice his child.

But I might.

I sat down at the desk again, pouring another whiskey. Aneirin had a good store, and I had made quite a dent in it since he'd fallen ill; he had given me permission, after all. Some were centuries old and likely could have fetched a fine price if I'd any need for money. Vintage or not, it all burned on the way down. In another time I'd have stopped and tasted every place within that whiskey, felt a connection to every grain of barley and wisp of peat. But in the moment I felt painfully human and only in need of the dulling effects, even if it took a good bottle to do the trick.

Verta. I had to find her. Before I decided to bleed Percy Shelley of his life...I had until Midsummer, and it was December. There was a little time, but not much.

And Trita. I couldn't tell her about the potion. I knew the three scions were together in the Alps, but if she knew I was even considering...

Still, I dared not reach Verta alone. Not with Aneirin so ill.

I'd have to lie to Trita. And I'd have to lie to Isabella to get her to stay with Aneirin.

But it was his only chance.

Oh, how ruthless the Wheel. Damn it all.

LYING to Trita was not easy, but I found simply omitting details about my other plans the easiest course of action. Besides, we had agreed that confronting Verta was of the utmost importance. I knew, in my mind, once we understood what Verta was up to, I would seek out Percy Shelley and try and complete the potion. I needed a good deal of blood.

We would go, along with Isabella, to the Temple of Venus, and discuss matters with Verta. We would ask her to reconcile with Aneirin, in hopes that it would give him a little more strength.

It all seemed to be going to plan until Isabella did not show up on the day agreed upon.

"You think she suspected?" I asked Trita as she frowned at me, then at the door. We had waited for almost an hour.

"Of course, she suspected. You're truly a shit liar."

"Not all of us have as much practice," I said.

"You wound me," Trita said, putting her hand to her heart. It was one of Aneirin's sayings, and we both smiled a little sadly.

I found Amos in the parlor and asked after Isabella.

"No, I haven't seen Mrs. Jones," Amos said. "But I assure you I'll keep Mr. La Roche comfortable."

TRITA and I walked side by side, her long legs easily keeping up with my lumbering pace. If there was rain, I didn't notice it. We were of a mind and neither asked for direction or purpose. We'd fought long enough and hard enough together that speech felt superfluous in such situations.

I tried to convince myself Isabella was out of harm's way, that she went in knowing of the danger, and if anything had surfaced, she would have told me. Delusion is a strange drug. It kept me relatively calm until we crossed the bridge and arrived at the ruins of Verta's old temple by the Tamesis.

The front of the building had been destroyed during some part of the war, and unlike most of the houses adjacent to it, it was still in a state of disrepair. The once flawless marble carvings were crumbled and decrepit, the windows shattered and hung with fragments of cloth. The great statue was just a pair of legs, broken at the knees.

Once, the Temple of Venus had been such a decadent palace, and now it was full of shadows. I wasn't sure if Verta had managed some glamor we could see through, and therefore the house was invisible in its pitiable state to passersby, or if people simply didn't care. Regardless, it was a heartbreaking scene. It didn't take much to see the parallel between what she had become and what she once was.

"The front is barred," Trita said to me. "We could change shape."

"No. I don't want to face her in such a way."

"When was the last time you spoke?"

"I don't remember. I wish I did."

"And Isabella. You can sense her?"

I closed my eyes. Nothing.

"The water is strange here," I said. "It is unreadable."

Before I had much of an idea of what I was doing, and with time of the essence, I hit upon the front door with a blow so fierce, the rubble and the door cracked and split before me, parting as if at my command.

The room beyond I knew well enough, but it was a shadow of its former self. The rich tapestries and hangings were threadbare, eaten to nothing but rags by years of vermin and insects. It smelled like a tomb, long forgotten and forlorn. Once brilliant paintings had been split and torn by the force of knives, paint and canvas littered the ground. Broken pottery lined the floor, molded food desiccated to the point of mummification.

"A side effect of the Marian uprising," said Trita sadly, picking up the remnants of a chalice, once with two women holding up a phallus and a broad cup resting atop it. I remembered it. It amused me, seeing it them. "You remember the riots?"

"Not quite. I'd come back from war. My mind was elsewhere," I said.

"Verta's temple was a magnet for unrest in the Marian uprising. A symbol of everything antithetical to what the Queen of Heaven represented. Purity. Chastity. Loyalty. I understand, on some level, how easy it was to misinterpret the facets of Verta in such a way. But they forgot her greatest gifts. Comfort. Healing. Pleasure. And deep, abiding love. Love that runs deeper than any well."

"And what if the well is poisoned?" I asked, walking deeper into the room, searching my memory. They were below. In the baths. But I didn't remember how to get there. It had been so long. So many years. The time in between, the madness, had erased so much. I remembered the beauty, the pleasure. But the location, the pathways, vanished before me.

I laid my hand on the floor, feeling the cool marble. I needed to center myself, to make sense of things. Presumably, with the water below, I could detect something. A confluence. A connection. It shouldn't have been difficult. But it was. The water was there, but as to which direction it flowed, or of what it was made, I was utterly baffled. It was as if I'd put bread in my mouth, seen it and felt it with my hand, but had it dissipated when touching my tongue.

Trita seemed to sense my confusion and took the lead. Neither of us had the need to light a torch, for we both had heightened sight. Perhaps it was a residual of our bird forms, or else it was a gift given to the godlings, but neither asked when we plunged into what most humans would find impossible darkness.

Things were cast in shades of blue and white as we moved deeper into the house, chamber upon chamber. We tried the wine cellar first, surmising that would be the first to house a stair below. But it turned out to be nothing but a long, broken table, mummified figs and apples, and hundreds of broken bottles. The tang of wine and spirits was still on the place, but distant, like strange whispers.

"Some of the more enthusiastic truants broke the into alcohol, feeling it was against the call of the Marian church. A shame. Save for La Roche's store, I doubt there was any rival to this collection in the world," Trita said, her voice even and cool, oddly free from too much judgment.

"You don't sound angry," I observed. "That surprises me."

I could almost hear her smirk at me before I saw her teeth in the dark. "Regimes change, Joss. It's the way of the world. Kingdoms rise and fall, and I've seen so many. Very little surprises me."

"But why can't I sense the water, then?" I asked.

"Verta is older and smarter than you. No doubt, she's expected you. She's probably cast a spell, or else poisoned the spring. She's capable."

"This doesn't feel like godling magic. It feels like poison."

"You must always think ahead of your opponents, as in the game of Mad Queen's Chess."

"I hate to think she's my opponent. But perhaps I have made her so."

Without speaking further, we hunted about the ruins until the moon rose to its full glory. A few times, we thought we'd found the correct way, only to be let out on a porch or into an anteroom. I had no idea the temple was so large. It had felt mysterious and vast to me, but I could only describe our descent that night as positively labyrinthine.

I was beginning to feel angry, baffled. Concerned. I wished more than once Aneirin was well enough to accompany us. We three were unbeatable together, and now he was wasting away abed in the house he'd made with Verta. He'd have considered something I'd have missed, or else remembered above all where the rooms were. He'd frequented her rooms more than anyone. He wouldn't have been fumbling around in the dark.

"I feel ill." I shivered. More than ill. Dizzy. Chills. "Maybe we shouldn't have come."

Trita held up her hand. She was staring ahead of us at the wall, smeared with soot and the sad last bits of a tapestry. I couldn't even remember what it had been, but wisps of gold thread still remained in spite of the ruin.

Moving aside the tapestry, Trita then wiped the wall. Her hand traced a path through the dust and mire, showing the beautiful carvings beneath. There was a shell there, simple and unadorned. A scallop shell. Most would have missed it, to be sure. It was unassuming and hidden amidst a thousand other reliefs in the wall. But of all the gamboling cherubs, defaced and dancing figures and ornate trees, it stood along as the representative of a watery realm.

"There isn't any water there," I said.

"What do you feel, then?" she asked, her hand pausing above the shell.

"Heaviness. Sorrow. Emptiness, and yet…substance," I said, trying to put into words what was confusing me. "It makes me nauseated. Confused. I sense Isabella, but it's as if she'll buried beneath a mountain, and there's no way in."

Trita snorted and pushed the shell. "There's always a way in, Joss. It's the way out I always worry about."

The portion she touched clicked slightly, and then the wall itself moved an inch or two inwards, then parted along an invisible seam. The smell rising from the depths made us both recoil. That sense of sickness, of being unwell, spread to my bowels. I had to steady myself on the threshold. If Trita noticed, she didn't say. She simply moved forward, pulling a dagger from her belt.

The walls dripped and oozed with years of mildew and growth, slick to the touch and perilous on food, even for godlings. We moved slower than we wanted in order to save ourselves from too much noise. Injury was less than a concern but falling headfirst into what might be an unexpected visit would likely put at risk our entire plan.

But the element of surprise was never ours to have. Halfway down, we began to hear it. I knew it was Verta, because I knew the song. She had sung it to me once, in a graveyard in Londinium, what felt like a lifetime ago. It was that night I had decided to trust her. To be her friend.

She knew I was coming. She had planned this.

She and her lyre were rarely parted, and when I visited her in my first years, I often found her bent over it, humming lovely hymns in accompaniment. She was connected to that instrument, like a mother, holding close her child.

Except now, I could not hear the humming. But I could hear moans. Strange, strangled sounds, wet and weary, punctuating the beautiful music which resonated throughout the limestone passageway, down into the deeper dark.

Candlelight flickered, casting our shadows along the wall. I tried to say something, but Trita gave me a cautious glance. Perhaps she could see something I could not. Figuring her bird form was an owl made me wonder. She could likely hear what I could not, as well. Bloody albatross.

I will say, I had expected a fight right away. My heart throbbed within my chest as we turned to the great bath, and I was assaulted with the memories of a thousand loves and a thousand battles. My blood boiled with readiness. I don't know what I expected, but it was certainly something of an epic scale. Perhaps Verta, adorned in battle armor, commanding demons. Or surrounded by a harem of her most dedicated priestesses. It was certainly far grander and less gruesome than the sight I beheld.

Trita fell back against me, seeing it first. And I knew I was in for something truly harrowing.

The baths ran with quicksilver. At first, I didn't know what it was, but recalled Aneirin's writings on the subject. He had worried it might cause me some discomfiture, since it was a liquid I couldn't control and had a certain level of poison to some of the godlings. We had experimented with small amounts of it, which gave me headaches—but on a level this vast, it explained how utterly baffled I was.

The spring beneath the temple had been poisoned on a massive scale. All the water now ran with quicksilver, and at the center of the pool sat Verta, poised on a pedestal shaped like a broken scallop shell, her feet dangling into the liquid metal and her face tilted up. Her hair was gone. Her teeth were gone. Where her fingertips were remained only bones, worn through by her incessant lyre playing. And she did not stop. Even when we stood there, staring, she would not cease her nightmarish music.

I had forgotten her face. Not just her physical face, but the true face of her godhead. That was long gone.

Verta's skin was pallid and streaked with blood, and I looked up to see the source, understanding though not wishing to. Above her, dripping steadily in time with the music, was Isabella. Or what was left of her. She had been tied upside down, her long hair undone and some of it pulled out in clumps, the scabbed bits left behind on her scalp. She had no clothing on to speak of, and most of her skin…

I don't know how to say it. There is a word for it which the Romans used: *excoriatus*. Every inch of her had been peeled and she looked like some strange bleeding flower. The damage had been done so deliberately, so measuredly. It was not the hand of an unskilled knife—it was practiced, purposeful. The work left behind was almost beautiful were it not so inhuman. And she pulsed with power, channeling energy, down into the very root of Verta.

And there were others, sucked of life and blood, hanging like macabre chandeliers. Their faces wrinkled past recognition, their skin paper-thin and fluttering in the air current, charms and trinkets tied around what remained of foot and finger. A mad nightingale, nesting in the bones of her victims.

I was horrified to find it so beautiful.

Of course, it would be beautiful. It was Verta. Nothing she did was without thought of beauty. Not even death and destruction. She sat there amidst the macabre as if it were an orchestrated piece. Meant for me.

The quicksilver began to bubble was we approached, the smooth surface rippling and changing. A smell like sulfur and burned blood rose up around us, and I coughed. I felt unsteady on my feet. I'd never been seasick in my life—if anything I'd been landsick—but this was as close as I imagined I'd ever been.

I was going to speak to her, but I lost my words when out of the quicksilver rose a metal horse, frothing and rippling in the tide. It sprouted wings, sprouted fangs, and opened its mouth and spoke:

"Water and wisdom, be gone. There is only madness here."

The words were whispered, yet harsh. I felt my skin crawl. From its mouth came black breath, a mist that was darker than the dimness around us.

Squinting, I looked up to see Isabella. She breathed, still. But her pain was palpable. She was the only living creature left.

"Verticordia!" Trita shouted. "Enough!"

The black mist seemed to laugh at us from every direction. Then it said, whispering from every corner, "There is never enough."

"Can't you see? I did this for him." Verta's voice danced between moaning and singing, ringing off every corner of the cavern, echoing new sentences.

"He threw me away."

"He would not touch me."

"I made him a new body, I gave him my soul."

"I made a new womb. And I must feed it."

The voices bounded off the walls, and none of it made sense.

"La Roche is dying," I shouted. "Please, Verta. Listen to me."

The horse reared and Trita launched a flurry of daggers forward. They flew true and straight, and I felt my hope go with them, frozen as I was in fear and fury. But just before they were to make their mark, tendrils of quicksilver rose from the pool and snatched them down like errant flies. They disappeared into the molten before so much as a thought.

"You can't kill us, Verta!" shouted Trita, her voice rising and threatening, enough to strike fear into my heart. "You're too weak to wound us."

I remembered what it was like to fight beside Trita, how she reveled in the tactics and discipline inherent in battle. But now all of that faded away. She was frightened by what she saw, and I couldn't blame her. The wrongness of the scene was beyond reproach.

"My body grew old and he did not love me."

"Only loved the water man."

"The new body was not enough, was broken."

"I didn't love him enough."

"Must repay my debt to Father. To Father."

"He wouldn't tell me his name!"

This last whisper ended in a shriek, and it sent my head spinning.

There was no water in the room. What little there was remained within the body of Isabella. I could move her blood, manipulate it, but in the process, I would kill her. And I knew, instantly, that it was what Verta intended me to do. She had played my love against her loyalty, and Isabella's vow was stronger.

The mercurial beast flapped its wings and charged at Trita. The swift godling of wisdom and war knew better and darted out of the way, but another horse rose from the pool, just as fast, taking Trita by surprise. She twirled fast enough to break a human's neck, and fell badly, her arm twisting behind her. She grunted and transformed, taking her owl shape and rising up to one of the hanging corpses, flying crooked and lame. Wounded.

I found my voice after some moments of breathing in and out. The part of me that depended on water was spent, terrified along with Trita. Two horses now circled around me. I knew looking into their furious faces would break me from my focus. I needed to reach Verta, or whatever was left of her in the husk of a body in the middle of the pool.

The air was thick with vapor from the pool. How long she had been there, I will never know.

I tried again. "Verta. My friend."

The horses reared. They could wound me, it was true. She had yet to do so. I carried wounds from Trita and from Aneirin, but not from her. I could withstand it.

I saw teeth and heard the pounding hooves, and I felt myself change.

Quicksilver pooled around my feet, but I floated inches above it. I had changed, I had transcended my oafish human body to something truly magnificent. No bumbling bird, no slippery fish, no scraggily dog. I was a black horse, grey of mane, twice as large and wild as Poetaster had been, but infinitely stronger. Dappled and confident. My heart beat with newfound courage, and I saw the liquid metal dimple and change around me.

Verta had not expected that. And what I commanded was not the water. This horse, it was part of what I had been in my madness, years ago, when I'd inadvertently won a war for Miriam. I felt the power in my blood, electric and full of fire. Lightning. Thunder. The rumblings of the earth.

Power. Lightning.

Another ken, one I had long forgotten.

The whole room reverberated with her frenzy. I saw from the corner of my eye, my new sight somehow longer and more sensitive than before,

Trita working on untying Isabella. And giving her what strength she could spare, pecking away at some of the more vicious ties.

"Verta, please," I begged. "For La Roche's sake."

"He abandoned me."

"Wouldn't touch me."

"I shaped for him a new body."

"Tell me his name!"

"I must feed."

I charged forward as the quicksilver rose around me in sharp peaks, no longer equine but simply a force of destruction. I knew what I had to do, sensed it on a deep, dark level. The world in all its mad violence seemed strangely simple to me. The power was in my hooves. It had always been there. I had just forgotten. And I had enough power to push Verta to the edge, to let her, at last, let go.

I felt my hooves connect as I came upon Verta's form, colliding with the platform. I overtook her. The current from my hooves arced up and around, igniting the air around us, dazzling and bright. It pulsed, again and again, like some celestial heart. The hanging bodies, flayed and dried above us, caught fire and blazed.

Too much, I feared I had destroyed Isabella. Hearing a strange, singed crackle from where Verta had stood made me worry even more. But one glance to the ceiling and I saw Trita Oya had grown wings—immense, blue-black wings, which shielded Isabella from the blast. She blazed with her own fire, adding a charged, spicy note to the diminishing flames.

The fire burned brightest where Verta had been, and the quicksilver which had once flowed about us and under us, was gone. All that was left was an empty bath. While Verta burned upon her pillar, I drifted down to the bottom of the limestone bath and breathed into the source. I felt the water rise before I saw it emerge, clean and clear and blue, into the baths. Feeling it trail around my hooves and dampen me from tail to tongue filled me with energy and hope. I was more than a horse in the water—I was a water horse. My back legs relaxed, changed, twirled and scaled.

A hippocampus.

Drawing my hands up, I commanded the water to quench the fires about Verta, but it took some time. She was laughing a strange, wet laugh again, and I took a moment to propel myself up to Isabella and Trita.

"Joss..."

Verta called to me from her pyre. In spite of my efforts, it would not stop burning. Whatever power I had summoned had set her ablaze in a way I never wished.

I felt myself slip back into my human shape, and I walked slowly across the water to her. The flames about her burned bright white, and I could see her form, writhing and trembling at the center. Trita landed on my shoulder, deep talons piercing my flesh.

Verta's words became garbled, and she began to scream. She continued to repeat, "He promised..." over and over again.

Trita alighted on my shoulder, clicking her beak. "Let go, Verta."

"I stayed. For him. I could not serve two masters."

"You broke the law," Trita said. "You twisted yourself into an unnatural creature."

"Trita Oya!" shrieked Verta, her face swimming out of the flames a moment, a floating skull with sapphire eyes. "Cursed will be your children! Cursed will your child be, and the babes within her womb...wither and die...and wither again, even after they draw breath a thousand days."

Rather than reply, Trita nuzzled the side of my face. This was something she understood, this risk. And she wanted me to know she was dedicated to the cause.

"I will burn forever!" Verta shouted from her ever-burning pyre. "I will burn forever and you will tend to my undying fire!"

She would. In her fury, she would. But there had to be something. Something I had, which she did not that would quench her fury.

Then it came to me.

"I have his heart. I have his name." I spoke quietly, knowing what that must feel to her.

In the cinders of her body, I saw her heart kindle a moment, red as ruby and heard her voice—the very voice she'd had when I'd met her, before she'd been changed and warped by blacker magic—and she said: "Joss...tell me his name."

"I keep it in my heart."

"Tell me his name!" Verta howled, and the walls shook with her fury.

I said only one word: "Never."

"Tell me! I will give you every power! I will give you everything! I will save your godson!"

"Don't listen to her, Joss," Trita said. "She doesn't know what she's saying."

"I can save him," Verta said. "I can give him protection."

Verta showed me a glimpse in her fire, John Keats in profile, sunken and so young.

"There is nothing you can offer me, Verta, that will change what you know is true. You will never know his name, Verta. Never. And only I will."

And that was all she could take. What wounds had riled her body I will never know. What pain and madness had driven her to such a place, only she understood. She had lived lives beyond my knowledge, even beyond Aneirin's. But she had broken laws, she had twisted life and death, and now I saw Miriam's curse was not so much given, but simply a consequence. As were those I had put in motion when I had resurrected Frances Jennings.

The red spot of Verta's heart went black. Then all that was left of her was a pillar of smoke and flame—and even that could not stay long. Her arms drew up, her head leaned back, and with a sound I will never forget nor wish to describe, she was gone. She vanished inward, leaving nothing but a singed pillar behind her, and the smell of opium and earth.

A voice began singing: *Ovidus Fasti IV.*

It was Isabella, and she fell back into her dreams once again, clinging to life in an improbable, gruesome, and cruel way.

33

As Trita and I walked the dark streets of Londinium, gently carrying Isabella—what was left of her—I sensed the lack of Verta in every sound and saw it in every passing face. The Tamesis no longer stank, for one, and that was a blessing. It had been cleansed. But tied up within her mad nest of emotion and pain there had also been bright things, bits of joy and love wound together. Until she was fully gone that brightness remained. But now the world felt less full of color.

I could only imagine what would happen when Aneirin left.

We did not speak of the worry between us, and together managed to get Isabella situated at home in one of the spare rooms. Her once smooth body was a mass of scars, changed and melted to her skin like strange tattoos. We couldn't save all her skin. Some was cut off to prevent infection. Her aethereal body was surprisingly strong, but the wounds were deeper and stranger than through her body only. I could not imagine that she would never again be restored.

We wrapped her in bandages. I put some lavender and rose petals into the basin of hot water, and then decided to look in on Aneirin. Trita promised to find me if anything changed.

I HAD TO TELL ANEIRIN.

I opened the door slowly, not expecting to see the scene altered. For weeks upon end it had been the same thing. Aneirin asleep, Aneirin dozing, barely able to make a coherent statement. Holding on to some imperceptible sliver of life amidst all this chaos.

He was awake, though, and looked confused when I walked in.

"I dreamed you died," he told me. "It felt so real."

"Aneirin, I need to tell you—" I started, but he held up a hand to hush me.

I should have known he'd have felt her death. How foolish to think I'd be the bearer of the news.

"I awoke for the first time in weeks hungry," he said, taking my hand with his. So slight and bony he'd become, but I refused to be frightened by it. Death was a daily event among humans, and I promised myself I would become its welcome friend. "I do believe she was holding me down a bit. It all seems very dim to me now."

"You were sending her *manna meli*," I said, unable to tell him what I had read, what I knew about their relationship. Yet I sensed, somehow, he was aware and we were speaking in doubled language.

"Of course, I was, Joss. You understand. But there should be enough for a little while, at least. I have mourned her for ten years, and yet I was not capable of truly letting go. I should have been there, in the end..."

I could not tell him everything Verta had said in the bowels of the temple, but I told him what I could. About the bodies, about Verta and the quicksilver. He listened, patient, lucid, and still. And it seemed to quell his feelings of guilt.

"I would not have wished this on her," he said, "even at my most furious."

"She was a creature of her own making," I said. "Now, you can stop fretting about her and focus on your own healing."

"I will always fret about her," Aneirin said, sadly. "I do not know how else to live."

"We have a little time, yet," I said, kissing his forehead. "I will fight for you, my love."

"I know," he said, and held my hand, taking a deep breath. "But there is only one course forward, Joss."

I SLEPT on and off for three straight days. Aneirin seemed better. Isabella was healing slowly, and Trita and I spent much time perfecting potions and performing cleansing rituals. She might yet live.

One morning, Amos handed me a scribbled note from Aneirin.

"You've a guest coming today, love. I hope you will forgive me, but I have given John Keats your information. We have corresponded for some time, he and I, and I have told him you would like to interview him about becoming a patron of his work."

An hour later, a dark carriage came to a stop by the front door. It was a little past noon, and two young men walked out. One was John, and the other was a darker-haired, more intense lad I had never seen before.

My initial thought was to barricade myself in the house and pretend not to be at home. They'd leave, wouldn't they? But in spite myself, I found myself walking to the door and opening it, and looking down into John's hazel eyes, inquisitive and searching.

I could no more have refused him than stopped the course of time.

He recognized me, and started to say something, then stopped, smiled, and tried again. "Why, I hadn't realized it was you."

"Keats the poet, is it?" I asked, having no idea of what to say to him in the least. "I'd been expecting…"

"Someone else?"

"No—I expected you. It's only I've had a trying day, and my mind has been elsewhere. Mr. La Roche sent you, didn't he?"

"We should come back another time," the second man said, bowing politely and making to leave.

"Not at all, Mr…?"

"Leigh Hunt," the friend of John's said, following behind me as I walked through the front door. "I'm a publisher, sometime poet, and…" He had a lot more to say, but to be fair I wasn't really paying attention. He struck me immediately as the sort of man who primarily gets his excitement from connecting to other people, rather than creating anything useful himself. He mentioned about every famous poet in a fifty-mile radius in half a dozen breaths, and I found I tired of him in half that time.

Regardless, he was with John, and as such I knew I had to be polite. I was already feeling ill with jealousy, and it didn't become me.

I was about to apologize for the state of my parlor, when I opened the doors to find an expensive and impressive tea spread out. It was the custom for the upper classes to have tea, now, since the routes to the East had been reestablished. But it was expensive.

Thankfully I had help. Another servant, this time a young man with flaxen hair I thought I recognized yet couldn't place. He averted his eyes but poured the tea into black glazed cups with expert care and served little pickle sandwiches. I did not eat nor drink, and when Mr. Hunt began talking again, I waited patiently.

"I hear we are also mutual friends of Isabella Jones," Leigh Hunt said, leaning back on the sofa.

"I...ah, yes," I said.

"I was sorry to hear she is unwell," said John. "Mr. La Roche informed us. It appears your friends are sadly afflicted."

He did not know the half of it.

Mr. Hunt gave me a skeptical glance, warmed by an ineffectual smile. "Well, Mr. La Roche said you were an avid appreciator of poetry. You have, no doubt, read from Mr. Keats's first volume, *Poems*?"

I had read extensively the words of both Shelleys, and of Byron—of Blake and of Wordsworth. And others besides, like the great Charlotte Smith. But my own scion, I had not.

"I'm afraid I haven't yet had the pleasure," I said.

They both appeared surprised, but John more crestfallen. He blanched slightly as Mr. Hunt searched for something in his jacket. It was a slim volume, somewhat tattered, but rather handsome in its simplicity. He held it out to me and indicated I ought to turn to a page.

"I believe Mr. Keats will agree with me when I say much of it is far from sophisticated. But there are a few gems. That one there, in particular, still moves me every time."

I turned to the page and read in the type-set print, pristine and perfect: "On First Looking Into Chapman's Homer."

"Much have I travell'd in the realms of gold,
And many goodly states and kingdoms seen;
Round many western islands have I been
Which bards in fealty to Apollo hold.
Oft of one wide expanse had I been told
That deep-browed Homer ruled as his demesne;
Yet did I never breathe its pure serene
Till I heard Chapman speak out loud and bold:
Then felt I like some watcher of the skies
When a new planet swims into his ken;

Or like stout Cortez when with eagle eyes
He star'd at the Pacific—and all his men
Look'd at each other with a wild surmise —
Silent, upon a peak in Darien."

Some "watcher of the skies" indeed—islands to Apollo.

"I've never heard it read so well," said Mr. Hunt.

I hadn't realized I had spoken aloud, but when I glanced up there were tears in John's eyes. My first thought was that Aneirin would love the poem, not the least of which was because he'd been cited in it. But it was about the things he loved most. Knowledge and enlightenment and discovery—potential.

I straightened myself in my seat, remembering I was a hulking mass of a man, and handed the book back to Mr. Hunt. I cleared my throat.

"It's impressive," I said. "I am moved."

"Tell him the story of how you came to Chapman, John," Mr. Hunt said, elbowing John rather rudely. "I never tire of the tale."

John smiled shyly, stroking his chin, but I could see he had the fire of a storyteller in him. As unfamiliar we were with each other, he was no simple child. He thought me someone to make an impression to, and so he cleared his throat and told me the story and I wondered what would become of him, how he had been made, how he would be broken.

"Well," John said. "It starts out rather somber. My brother, Tom, recalls that we had the volume ages ago, but I do not remember seeing it until the death of my mother. She left us painfully little, but there was a slim volume in her things and I, not thinking much of it, threw it into a trunk. I was at school when I discovered it again, among my few possessions, and thought to give it to a teacher of mine, Mr. Clarke. He saw it and shared with me that it was worth a great deal more and ought not be given as a gift. And so, we read it together, spending long evenings bent over the well-worn pages. It was a welcome connection, but moreso, the volume simply spoke to me...in a way until quite recently I thought entirely..." he drifted off and shook his head as if dispelling strange memories. "Regardless, I wrote it for Clarke. That poem. I gave it to him the morning we finished our first reading of Chapman's."

"What do you think of the poem, Mr. Raddick?" Leigh Hunt asked me.

"If you want my opinion of the poem, it's exceedingly good," I said. "But I am hardly a literary figure of worth."

"Have you any connections?" Leigh Hunt pressed. "I had hoped you might know someone to review the volume."

"I fear I have little influence," I said. "But I could always offer some financial support…"

The money was appreciated, but I could sense John was disappointed. As Leigh Hunt made his way to the carriage, John lingered at the door a little longer.

"I apologize for this. I feel like a beggar, and it pains me. But, you see, my brother, he's…he's died…" the poor boy finally managed. "I was just hoping to speak to Isa… Mrs. Jones," John said, dabbing his eyes with his kerchief.

"She is convalescing," I said. "I'm sorry to say. I will let her know you called upon her, however."

John looked doubtful, then worried, then was unable to speak for tears.

I was empty. Looking at my suffering child ought to have made me weep, to have stirred my emotions. But since losing Verta, I had been haunted.

"I know what it is like to lose those you love," I said. "And though I am no poet like you, Mr. Keats, there is some power in simply telling the story rather than letting it consume you. It has been a cruel winter, but there are yet some things of beauty to be seen, or so I try and tell myself."

John composed himself, apparently finding my words more meaningful than I did. "A thing of beauty," he said. "Yes, I suppose so…"

"Life is brief, no matter how long we live. We always want more, I think. Your brother Tom was blessed to have you in his."

He took a deep breath. "I feel as if the last few months have torn me to my marrow. I am restless. I spend far too long agonizing over every word, haunted by my very own existence."

"John, I…"

"My apologies, Mr. Raddick, but Mr. Hunt is awaiting and well,—I am moving to Hampstead, you see, to share a house with my friend, another poet. If you do hear from Mrs. Jones, tell her she can call at this address." He handed me a card, the location scribbled in blue-black ink.

"I will tell her in my correspondence."

John paused for a moment, staring blankly at the space beside me, as if he saw someone sitting there. Then he looked confused, and I felt not a little bit discomfited.

"I have a letter for her," he said softly, reaching into his jacket pocket and standing. He took a few paces toward me and handed it to me. It was as close as we'd ever been.

And in a moment, he was gone again. Excusing himself, going to the door, leaving, as I stood dumbly holding the note.

34

That afternoon, I looked in upon Aneirin, and he still slept. I took a minuscule amount of the *manna meli* and put it on his lips, kissed him gently, and departed to sit by Isabella.

She lay as she had, and Trita was glad for the break. Keats's letter burned in my pocket, and I know I ought not to have opened it. It was not my business. But I was weary, and lonely, and admittedly more curious than I should have been. And, by virtue of the whiskey, even a little sauced.

And perhaps jealous too.

He loved her. He had been with her. Tasted her flesh when it was still sweet, devoured her. She was more than a lover to him, she was his Muse.

I crunched the letter in my hands.

"He's sent me so many, burning one won't change anything," Isabella said from her bed.

"You..."

Isabella was smiling at me through the gauze on her face, trying not to wince through the pain. I went to her, slowly and dumbly, taking her hand gently as she gave it to me. She reached up and gently removed the gauze, revealing the pink, puckered scars below.

"You're a fool, Joss Raddick," she laughed. "And I'm a fool twice over for bothering with you."

"You shouldn't talk. You need sleep," I said.

"Sleep. No, I've had enough. I need to press on, else I will..." she gasped in pain as she tried to move her legs. Isabella was being strong. For me. For herself. But she was a ruin of a creature, and she knew it.

"Or else you'll fall to shreds," I said. I reached down and touched the hair at her forehead. There hadn't been much left after her imprisonment, and she still looked faded, aged. But the soft lock was silky and dark brown, the color of the most exotic tea.

She closed her eyes and I noticed the lacerations made their way even to her eyelids.

"Can you open the window?" she asked, her voice barely a whisper.

"It's freezing out there," I said.

"Please," she said. "It will help. In a week, I will wake and we will speak again."

I walked to the window and opened it, wincing against the chill. In the distance I could see a few enthusiastic Marians preparing the holly and ivy, lighting blue lanterns, and hanging silk lilies. I envied them in their simple understanding of faith, in belief. I knew, watching them play with their children and sing hymns together, that I would never feel such a way. Miriam had won Londinium, too, in her quest for purity. The last vestige of Venus was gone.

Lost in thought, the buzzing took me off guard. At first, I thought it was something out the window, but then I realized it was coming from inside. Not just inside the room. Inside of Isabella.

Her head tilted back, and she opened her mouth. Her chest began heaving, and I was certain she was going to perish there and then. Except she was smiling. I began to fret but found I was so captivated and horrified by what I saw that I could not change the course even if I tried.

A single bee crawled out of her mouth, then a swarm. They flew about the room, tangling in the drapes and bedcoverings. They went into my beard and down my shirt. But most of them stayed upon her as she lay back down. They spun and spun, making honeycomb and rebuilding her. They covered her eyes in wax, sealed up her lips, filling the room with the sweetest perfume.

I had never taken much time to think of insects. I'd eaten plenty of them in my time as a fish and then as a bird but seeing them now was something altogether older and stranger than my magic. Had they not come from her, I'd have thought they were harming her.

In an hour, she was completely encased, and out the bees went. Not a single one of them had stung me, or really bothered with me much. The few who'd found their way into my beard easily caught up with their fellow workers. Were I a mortal man and unused to such things, I'd have tried to lead them away from Isabella's body. But as she was, one of the *Meliae,* and older than me by scores, I felt no compunction to save her. She was not a woman who needed saving.

I leaned over to her and stared at her casing. So perfect. It was a shallow network of combs all about her, lending her body a most beautiful, geometric curiousness.

One week.

"Trita, I need to make a short trip," I said to her.

The godling of war and wisdom looked at me and nodded. "Of course. You could use a break."

"I won't be long."

"I'm not arguing with you, Joss. With everything that's gone on, I have no desire to leave Londinium. I will keep an eye on Andrew."

"Trita..."

"Just go, Joss. Before you change your mind. If anything happens, I will find you."

ANEIRIN WAS AWAKE, reading a book on his lap. He wore glasses now, a strange necessity as his body continued to change. Gone was the glow of his skin, the luster of his hair. And yet, he was ever beautiful to me.

"Good morning, love," he said, not looking up.

"Aneirin," I said to him. "I need to leave for a few days. I think I will go to Crummock Water. To speak to Scale Bottom. If she'll listen."

He glanced up at me, a look of mild confusion on his face. "I suppose I cannot judge you for your selection of friends."

"I don't have to leave. If you wish for me to remain, I will."

"Love, you know I hate my condition leaves you here, haunting High House like a ghost. Please. Go."

I wanted him. But I was so afraid of hurting him. I sat down beside him on the bed, and he took my head in his lap, putting aside the book. We rarely sat like this any longer, but it reminded me of our first days together. He ran his fine fingers through my hair, pulling out the tangles and running the strands across his palm.

"Your hair is white now," he said softly. "I suppose we are a matching pair."

I chuckled. "No one would ever mistake us for a match."

"Perhaps not. But then, I think it is what gives us our unique strength; we are incongruous, and yet..."

"I miss you," I said.

"I love you," he said.

"I know."

I ARRIVED two days later in Switzerland, finding rest by a rambling Persian mansion. It had been whitewashed since the Marian occupation, but remained every bit as ornate and breathtaking as it might once have been. The pointed arches, the branching, fractal blossoms of organic art even made my eyes dizzy, and I had to stop to admire it before I transformed again into human form. There was something about the shapes themselves that seemed to be a clue. The white paint was an attempt at hiding those mysteries, but not for long. No, not for long. I vowed to find out more when I could, as soon as my deed was finished.

Three of our scions were together. From my outcropping high on the wall of the mansion I could see them in the distance, gathered near the edge of the great Lake Geneve. There were other people I did not know among their ranks, an official-looking man in a turban and a wispy woman who paced back and forth along the beach.

The most striking figure was Noel. He was Verta's child, without a doubt. He burned green in my vision, limned in light and strength. Uncommonly attractive, he was strong, and his voice boomed across the water when he laughed. His sweat was thick with alcohol—mostly wine—and sweet with fruits.

Mary Shelley, the blessed child of Trita, stood with her arms crossed, looking a bit perturbed as Noel fussed with the boat. She wore a white shift in the new fashion, tied with a brown sash about the middle. There were no shoes on her feet, and her hair was loose about her shoulders, a wild look in her wide, brown eyes. The strength of her mind was palpable, even at such a distance.

And, as his godfather before him, Percy blazed like the sun. It was hard for me to concentrate on him with my bird sight but looking slightly away I could make out his features. He was far smaller than I thought he'd be; appropriately birdlike, I suppose, a jumble of energy and excitement. He spoke animatedly, flapping his hands as he described things, eyes blinking and his auburn hair blowing about his face. When he smiled, it was a brilliant thing, but it was rare. And fleeting. I sensed in him a man full of energy and yet unable to channel it.

I didn't want to have to hurt him, but I felt it was my only choice. Aneirin had this one last chance. I had hurt human beings before; I had destroyed them. Surely this one would be no different. Or so I told myself.

There were many approaches I could take in such a situation, but I decided I had neither the focus nor the discipline to do what Aneirin would have done. He would have walked in the front door, fresh as a spring breeze, and made friends with everyone and all, then slit Percy's throat in the middle of the night and be gone before the sunrise.

It was with such evil thoughts on my mind I decided to frighten Percy Shelley first. To tear him down, to make him afraid. I had heard he was an atheist. Well, I would change that. And when he was frightened enough, I would take his blood.

So, I decided to haunt him. I began subtly, with sounds throughout the house over a few days. Ripples across the water. Birds in the air flying at strange angles. Then I started appearing by the windows, moving objects in the house when least expected—a book here, a glass there, a ream of paper now and again. I could tell by the housemaid's screams that I was indeed doing my job.

I needed the blood of Aneirin's blessed.

It was one night in the kitchen that my schemes came to an abrupt stop. I was rearranging some loaves of bread, cloaked as I thought in my camouflage, when I heard someone descend the stairs and cough politely.

I turned slowly, expecting to see Trita or else another godling, but finding myself equally surprised to see Mary Shelley standing there in her nightgown, frowning at me.

"I don't know who you are, or what you are," she said, "but I would like to ask you leave the premises."

I just gaped at her. "You can see me."

"Of course, I can see you," she said. "You're one of the most enormous men I've ever seen."

"You ought to be afraid of me," I said to her, knowing that she wasn't.

"You haven't hurt us yet, exactly, but you've been entirely a nuisance," she said to me, clipping her words with impatience. She reminded me of Trita in that way, though her appearance could hardly be more different. "And I'm tired of cleaning up after your mischief."

I raised my eyebrows to her and wondered what to say. I felt like a child caught with their hands in the pie chest. That sense of guilt was rather overwhelming. For a moment I wondered if Trita had imbued her daughter with some extra sensitivity toward godlings.

"I apologize. My mischief wasn't meant for you," I tried a bit lamely.

Mary almost smiled. "I mentioned you to Percy, but he promises me he doesn't see you. My rational brain tells me you must be simply unusually stealthy, but part of me wonders if you might not be some sort of apparition."

"I am no ghost," I said, picking up a salt shaker and placing it on the table. "Ghosts, as far as I know, aren't capable of altering the physical world."

Mary squinted, crossing her arms defiantly. "Whatever you are, you ought to go."

"I mean you no harm..." I said, then followed her conversation back a few paces. "You said Percy doesn't see me."

"Apparently not," she replied. "Polidori claims to have—Byron and Claire, too, though they believe practically anything. I'm glad to hear you speak, I admit, lest I am having a strange dream—which is possible. Quite possible."

"Percy doesn't see me. I suppose he doesn't believe in ghosts, then."

"The only thing he believes in is himself."

That made more sense to me than anything had in years. I stared at her and wondered at her grace and poise, but I could tell that she was growing impatient with me.

"I'm sorry," I said, then changed to vapor and departed through her in a cold mist.

There was no time.

I needed to get close enough to Percy to pull his blood out of his body. All I was doing was dawdling. Because I was afraid.

Percy couldn't see me, so my ridiculous attempts at haunting him had no effect other than to annoy Mary, which had similarly little purpose at all. But she had unintentionally given me the key to frightening him, to giving me a chance to take his blood, or else kill him. I feared I wouldn't be able to control myself, but it was a risk I would have to take. I had followed him long enough to know him a pale imitation of Aneirin, filled with all the negative features and none of the positive ones. Arrogant, foppish, entirely self-centered…

I waited two more days and then staged my misdeed. The days in between my meeting with Mary and my haunting were spent changing my own shape, watching Percy as closely as possible and then rearranging my body to look like his. It was exhausting work, I tell you. Should you meet anyone who tells you such magic is easy, I suggest they're lying. It's one thing to turn into a familiar—like my horse or my albatross. In that case it's natural, simply an extension of my deepest being. It's only a matter of learning. But changing one's visage and bearing to look like another—to look like a mortal—is a painful, precise art. And perhaps more of a perversion than an art.

It was not good magic, if I believe in any true difference between good and evil. Perhaps it was simply corrupted magic, going against the strange, natural order of the godlings. I couldn't say. I can't say. I know it was wrong and I paid for it.

Once I was able to convince the staff that I was indeed their own Mr. Shelley, I picked a good dark evening in the midsummer. A world away, John was falling ever more deeply in love with Fanny Brawne, and his body was breaking down day by day, his illness seeping into his bones. This potion, perhaps, would give me the key to his healing, and Aneirin's.

He was alone, young Percy. He had a fevered, mad look in his eyes as he looked out upon the water of the lake. I hid there, waiting for him. Then, just as the sun began to slip behind the mountains, I rose. In his visage, I stood above the waters and stared at him, pointing. I said nothing.

"What are you?" he cried, seized with fear. Oh, his fear tinged the whole world around me with triumph.

I pointed to him again.

"Mad vision," he gasped. "Are you the same I saw in the garden?"

I was not. And that was a strange thing to say. But I lied and shook my head in the affirmative.

Abruptly, Percy fainted. I could sense movement in the house above, so I moved as swiftly as I could, shedding my disguise. I called a vial to collect his blood, and I knew the task would require a great measure of control.

If I killed him too fast, the blood would be no good. It would spill, there would be panic. I might even lose myself.

I was prepared to lose myself if it meant saving my godson. And saving Aneirin.

When I got next to Percy, face down in the mud, I paused, heaving breaths, knowing I'd have to turn him over. I'd have to touch him. Had I had more time I would have stopped myself, considered what such an act meant. Touching this child of Aneirin's no doubt would move me in ways I had not intended. But through my utter exhaustion I half forgot my place.

I touched Percy's shoulder and turned him over and yes, I wanted to kill him. To destroy him. Every muscle and nerve in my body told me to do it. To take his light and drown him. To slit his throat, or else just take his heart in my hands and twist it until it ceased to be nothing. But when the last ray of the setting sun—how moronically poetic—fell across his fair features and turned his hair to fire, like his father's, I was unable to do the task.

Aneirin had wrote to me of Percy: *Take care of him if you see him. Protect him. Guide him. His life will be short, but a time will come when you will know what to do.*

...A time will come when you will know what to do.

I need not kill Percy. Not now. I saw through the waters what would happen. And soon. I saw Noel and Mary, destroyed by the loss of their friend and husband. So much sorrow would befall them. The mountains would shudder at the loss of young Percy, and I could not change that. It was not his time. His fate was not mine to take, though I wanted it. A greater tide than me moved my hand, and I was able to control, to take just a small amount of blood from the wound at his cheek, a scarlet gash amidst the pale skin and freckles.

When I stood on shaky legs and hung the vial, corked about my neck, I half expected to see Aneirin standing there, smiling at me. But there was nothing but the evening star, judging me with her harsh green light.

I took flight, just as Mary came into view. She came at a good pace down the hill, her dress billowing about her like the trail of a spectre. I know she saw me. One last time. I felt her eyes upon me.

And in that gaze, whether it be from my strange state or my mental weakness, I knew Trita had won the Boast. Mary would be the victor.

35

"You are almost too late."

Trita.

As I walked the stairs up to Aneirin's room I felt the weight of each step, the pain of the moments reaching out between us. Between eternity and the abyss. A thousand emotions ebbing around me at once, threatening to cast me down the stairs, crippling me from doubt and cowardice. I could leave. I could let him to the deed alone.

But it wasn't what he wanted.

Even godlings, long lived as we are, desire nothing more than to be near one another. How else would such a motley group of us have endured together in Londinium for so long? Even Miriam was not far. Only Achaemenes remained on the fringes and he, for reasons I still did not understand, was treated as an outcast.

Trita Oya. Joss Raddick. Andrew La Roche. Verticordia. Calvinius Pardo. For a breath of our lives we had all been friends. Now one by one they were falling away from me, curling up and dying as I still was unfurling my wings. They had befriended me and saved me, loved me and betrayed me, but they were my people.

The door felt so heavy as I pushed it away, and Amos bowed and departed as soon as he saw me.

Aneirin did not look ill, not to the eye. He had good color to his skin, though it had an ever-present blue tinge beneath his jaw. His eyes were bright, amber and clear. Even the smile on his face spoke of warmth and cleverness.

But I knew better. He was putting on a show for me. The heat from his body had diminished so much that it almost seemed a chill came from him.

I dragged the chair over to his bed, unable to hide my tears.

"You made the mad dash, didn't you?" he asked me. "I could have stopped you, but I wanted you to tell me what you thought of him…I wanted to hear what he looks like now."

His voice sounded so strong. It was unfair.

I could only nod.

"Yes," I said. "I'm sorry, Aneirin. I thought that I could do it."

"He's beautiful, my Percy. And headstrong and…doomed, I fear. You know his first wife drowned herself in the waters of the Serpentine a few years ago. But he will not live long. He is too much like me."

"Aneirin," I whispered, "we can keep you a little longer, still. I can help you, I can—"

"Joss, you would keep me for yourself. I had fight in me. I promise you, I did. But it slips from me, and I cannot hold on any longer," Aneirin said, face twisting in pain again. His eyes, I could see the light leaving his eyes.

"Please, love, don't go," I said. "I have a little…we could try with…"

"Not enough," Aneirin whispered. "You know it is not enough for me. And I never would have let you."

"'Twas all for naught, then. The boast. The plague—your sacrifice—the war?"

"On the contrary. You have loved, you have lost. You have become a man; you have become a god. And you gave me hope, and love, and passion; ah, but there is nothing so much as I love as those."

"I was going to heal you. I could have, but I failed."

"Make the potion but use only a tenth of the manna meli. And the small bit of blood. If you can get it to your John, if he is felled by any of the ills I have prevented, it may cure him. No disease will maim him."

I was afraid to voice my doubts, but I knew I would never again see this oracle, this blessed Apollo. He would never know me in this way. "And what if it doesn't work?" I asked.

"Get him far from here. Far from Londinium. Back to our ancestral home. To Rome, where the waters run deepest; perhaps there you can give him some peace. If he stays here, his fate…I cannot see it through the mists."

Ah, such a blessed and cursed gift.

I took his hand, and it was like ice. "I love you," I said, so quiet it was more a rush of air than words.

"And I, you. And were the fates with us, perhaps our lives would have been different."

I made some protest, and he chuckled lightly.

"You will love again. Boldly and brightly. And you will lose again. And you will find your way, then again find it fallen by the wayside. You will stand by giants and be counted among them, and then flow again to the sea until you, at last, lay down your head to rest and bring another into your place."

"Aneirin..."

"Good night, my love. Do not make this more difficult than it needs to be. Now, let Trita in, if you please."

Trita stood at the door and came to sit on the other side of him. She took his other hand, and I could tell by the way she looked at him that they had also had words. Of other times and other lives, other loves and strifes.

"I have no words," Aneirin said, wincing against the pain. "No parting wisdom. I am emptied out. It's a strange feeling. I fear I have outlived my stay and now must make a most untidy exit. No pomp and circumstance, but rather a withered bow."

He changed back to a rook. And I wondered, not for the last time, if he had been born as such. Without a word between us, we became albatross and owl, and curled about his cold bird frame as the night deepened. Time slowed, his small breaths our only measure of it passing.

Then, at dawn, he simply passed. All of him. Feathers and all melted into a kind of glimmer, the very color of the flashing dawn.

And he was gone.

TRITA and I sat together in silence and drank whiskey the night before she left, in what was left of High House. It was rather the opposite of my experience with Aneirin. The closer I'd drawn to him, the more words he'd shared. But I enjoyed the quiet between Trita and me, the silence of understanding. It was a sense of absolute neutrality, perhaps listing toward true friendship.

"His name was Aneirin," I said to her.

Trita's eyes brimmed with tears and she slogged back another shot. "It's a beautiful name."

"It was. And he gave it to me."

We fell quiet again.

"Whiskey has a habit of clearing my wits," she said, holding up the amber liquid in the delicate glass. One of Aneirin's, of course, but one of the last. I had taken the liberty of breaking many of them that afternoon. I had broken a good deal of what was in the house. "I am unsettled. I keep thinking… A line, from a play I once inspired: 'What see'st thou else in the dark backward and abysm of time?'"

She reminded me of Khasma.

"Joss?"

"Powerful words."

"Words are all I have. Here are some more:

There's nothing ill can dwell in such a temple:

If the ill spirit have so fair a house,

Good things will strive to dwell with 't."

"Heaven's fire."

"Verta corrupted her temple. These bodies," Trita said, pulling at her hair, "they're not really us, are they? They're like clothing we wear. Temples we build to hold our real substance."

"Indeed," I said, wondering at the way her eyes moved when she came upon ideas. "Perhaps that is why Miriam has given us these rules. Not as a demagogue, but as a caring parent. Her rules are meant to prevent us from the pain we will inevitably engender."

"All roads lead to Rome. I hear it is quite good on the constitution," she said.

"Trita?"

"Yes, Joss?"

"Thank you. You have been a patient teacher. A steadfast friend. You stayed with me through this…and I…"

"You've never been good with words, Joss. Don't try now."

We held each other, whiskey on our breaths wreathing about us, until the dawn. I watched her fly away into the rising sun, glad that she would move to a new life, a new adventure.

After Aneirin's death, I truly became the ghost of High House. I kept an eye on Isabella, but her state did not change. For two months I rearranged the furniture of and kept a fleet of ugly cats, wandering in from the street. I called the two largest ones Shit and Puke, for that seemed to be their most defining characteristics. As much as I disliked the creatures, I simply had no strength to cast them out.

I broke through a few walls. I screamed a great deal. But the sorrow I felt weighed down on me heavier than the amulet ever had.

Then, one afternoon--many weeks, and not the one--Isabella woke up.

I was changing the flowers in her room, something I was wont to do, when I noticed her stir beneath the waxen shell she had woven for herself. I startled, terrified at once that she was dying, and went to try and free her from the encasing.

I didn't quite know what to do, and while I was pondering whether or not she was alive, she stirred beneath again. The shell collapsed around her, sticking to her form more closely. It remained there a moment, casting her as if in bronze. Then the wax melted off her lips. Then her eyelids. The skin left behind was golden, smooth, free from the marring caused at the hand of Verta as she left the world in madness and pain.

But there were changes. In her hair, a streak of white. A scar, just below her lip. Still, as she revealed herself to me, smooth and naked and covered in wax and honey, I couldn't help but consider myself a lucky man. I carried her in my arms, helping her to stand.

"I've got a feeling you've been through a great deal more than you let on," I said to her softly.

I set her down and she took me by my face. "It was my last swarm," she said softly.

"Bees. And all I had was a school of sullen trout."

"They have come to my aid six times before. They are my sisters, my little priestesses. I am a *Meliae*, and we are above all, worshippers of the Tree of Life. They knit me back together, though it is a gift I can only give once. As I did when you returned with La Roche so long ago."

"He..."

"I know," she said. "I felt it. As I slept."

I didn't often say her name. I thought it. But when I said it, it somehow made me happy.

"Oh, Isabella..."

"Can it wait?" she asked.

She drew closer to me, relief and a flicker of desire in her eyes.

I had forgotten the sensation. Though smelling her, being around her, cast my sorrow to the shadows, Isabella and I had had our moments together, but it hadn't been about that kind of intimacy. It was deeper and more profound.

But now.

Damn, she was a fine woman. But damn, my sorrow was too deep for her.

Isabella sat down softly beside me and put her head on my chest, took my hand in hers. Her fingers looked as tiny as a child's in my big, ugly hands, but it felt right. Her hair still smelled of honey, and wild dreams, and open fields.

And I could taste happiness, just out of reach. But there, and therefore, attainable. Eventually. But not now.

36

I sent Isabella to look after John, to keep me apprised of his movements. Part of me wanted her around, but then I knew I was not yet capable of loving again. If ever. I knew she loved me, and I could not curse her with unreflected love.

My focus was on John Keats. Preparing the medicine for him would take time, and we would only have a short window in which to administer it. I had a single chance. I had failed Aneirin and could not abide failure yet again.

"You look horrible," Isabella said, when she finally met with me at the house, months later, bringing news of John, her first report. As ever, she was most pristine, bedecked in bluebell-hued silks and a beautiful bonnet laced about her sharp chin. To the naked eye, she was unchanged. "And the house smells of rotting meat. Have you even bothered taking a bath?"

"I sent the servants home," I said. "Nuisance more than anything. I've got no interest in having people take my coats or pour me water."

Isabella sighed. "Must you make a great effort to remain so uncivilized, or does it simply come naturally?"

"It's as natural as barnacles on the bottom of an oyster," I said. "And I've no mind to change it, if that's what you're implying."

She pulled off her gloves one at a time, grasping the tips and then slipping them from her long, strong arms.

I gestured to the parlor, which was hardly welcoming. The shades were drawn, it was covered in dust, and the remains of my last meal—crackers and pickles—was strewn about the pillows. I'd have been ashamed if I hadn't felt so sorry for myself, so instead of cleaning off the sofa, I offered her another chair after evicting a cat.

"I didn't know you liked cats," Isabella said, taking the seat without complaint.

"I don't," I said. "I can't stand the mangy creatures. They chased away all the birds, piss everywhere, cough up the vilest smelling concoctions. But they keep the mice at bay, and every time I kick them out, they find their way back in, sneaky little bastards. I suppose I'm making peace with my demons after all. These are just furrier than usual."

Shit and Puke arrived, as if on cue. Honestly, they were both black with jade eyes, and I had no idea which was which. I'd thought for a few weeks they were one single cat, and I'd briefly marveled at their size for all the excrement and vomit. It seemed a magical feat to me. Until, that is, I saw them rutting in the pantry. Then it made more sense.

I supposed there'd be more little Shits and Pukes in the days to come.

"How many are here?" she asked, watching Shit and Puke make little circles by her feet.

"No idea. A dozen, at least. I've let them have run of most of the house, though not in...not in his rooms." I felt the tide rising in my eyes and cleared my throat. I should have been more concerned about the smell of cat earlier, but I'd become rather immune to it in my melancholy. Isabella was being polite, but I could tell it was an effort for her.

In a bolt of horror, I saw the filth of my house from her perspective.

"Quite a pride," she said.

"Indeed."

"We should go for a walk," she said gently.

Puke meowed loudly and pissed a stream by the fireplace. I suppose the horrid creature agreed.

WE STROLLED TOGETHER for a while in silence, and the air cleared my head. I'd been living too long in the piss-drenched house to think straight. I'd been spending a good deal of my time poring over Aneirin's journals again and again, studying maps of Old Rome, reading John's *Endymion*.

"John is sick. The time is coming," she said at last, squeezing my arm as she spoke. Her touch calmed me, helped me anchor myself back to reality. "I wouldn't quite go so far as to say he's ailing, but our last few visits have been strained. He's well situated in Hampstead, but he's...well, in love."

"Oh," I said.

She sighed, her eyes resting on my face a moment before looking again in front of us. "Yes. He feels an urgent pull to finish. To write. To improve himself. But she is a distraction too. I fear he burns too brightly."

"What do you want me to do?" I asked.

"Go to Hampstead. There, perhaps, you can do what you should have done so long ago."

"What's that now?"

"Become his friend."

There was wisdom in the advice.

IN THE CHILL of February 1819, I left High House. I could find neither deed nor bill of sale and left the majority of the furniture and decorations that Aneirin and Verta had collected through their lives. I never did go back, but I have always wondered if the cats took over. Shit and Puke didn't leave the house, even when I tried to convince them otherwise. I like to imagine they turned it into a great pride between those walls, propagating and infesting every nook and cranny. Perhaps even now they preside over a great and powerful kingdom of black cats with green eyes. It would be almost poetic if not for the stench.

I went to Hampstead. In the night, in a low-riding chariot of simple profile, Isabella and I slowly took the western way and left the bustle of the city for the fields of Hampstead.

As we moved north and west away from the waters of the fetid Tamesis, which once had called me so strongly, I felt a lessening grasp around my heart. The pain I had been carrying around with me had been so rooted in Londinium itself, so embedded in every moment of my being, I forgot what it felt like to be free of it. Not that the rivers and tributaries of the north were without pollution—indeed, the Wells River, much of which ran underground, was hardly more than a stream—but the air seemed to mitigate it somewhat.

In Hampstead I found a new landscape of rolling fields, sprawling houses, and ponds. I felt again the power of river water. The pulse of tributaries gaining strength in the hills, springs and wells moving all around.

I had to find a more suitable place to live, a place where I could impress John and his friends to a greater degree. Where I could serve him the drink I hoped would save his life—claret with Aneirin's potion. Money was not an issue, since the bills and bullion I'd found at High House could buy me half of Londinium if I wanted it, but I had to find a house that kept me in close proximity to John but was stately enough. Isabella let me to my business while she insisted on at least ensuring the house had a good garden. She promised she would look in on me from time to time, as she could. But she needed to be in Bath, she said, to keep up her strength.

I didn't think I would miss her so much, but I did.

After some looking about and speaking with locals, I was able to attain a small homestead with a good amount of land and a stream. And good gardens. I'd purchased the whole farm, including all the furniture, by promising the current lord—who was on most unfortunate financial legs due to his falling out in the Senate and his daughter's bad reputation—that after forty years the house would return to her estate. He thought me mad to make such a deal, especially considering the amount of money I paid for the house. But he did not argue.

"Your time is running out," Isabella wrote to me, but I did not listen well. "Invite him to the house, give him the drink in some strong claret. Then go to Rome. Take Miriam's protection."

I knew what I had to do, but my rationale was muddled, to say the least. As I had with Percy, I felt unable to approach John. Even though his life was at stake. Even though I had all the elements of what I believed would be his cure. He was a human child, touched by godling magic, and yet it was as if I were the mere mortal.

At last I decided I needed more knowledge of John, and so I hired myself a spy since Isabella could no longer do. Before I'd left for Ancyra, I'd met a young painter named Joseph Severn at the World's End. He was a reserved man with a head of curls and vivid, deep eyes that reminded me of a mountain loch. We got on rather well, and I promised to look him up should the need ever arise.

So, I did as gentlemen did in those days, and called Joseph Severn to meet me. I saw immediately that he misinterpreted my request and, as he exited his carriage, he brought with him a tube of sketches and two paintings.

To say the man was foppish was an understatement. He was not blessed with grace or with wit, and he seemed more concerned with the knot on his cravat than anything. But I still sensed a man of good heart. And a man who needed money, desperately. I promised him a good weekly sum for information regarding John. And to buy some of his pictures. He would befriend John, I would get him to drink the potion, then talk to him about leaving for Rome where the weather was better.

37

It was February 1820, frigid and disagreeable, by the time John and Severn at last came to dine with me.

Having no idea how to set a table, let alone run a house, I put Severn in charge of hiring the right staff and ordering the correct food. He did a passable enough job, but after seeing the lamprey pie he ordered, I decided to take the drink into my own hands. I'd have to get John to drink the claret, anyway. I'd have to give it to him. I'd been keeping it with me for more than a month and thought of a thousand ways to slip it into something of his without his notice—but at the end of it all, I didn't think I could stomach more in the way of treachery. There's only so much a person can take, even a mad godling like me.

Keats was punctual, and Severn and Charles Brown were with him. I could tell by the way that Keats walked he was feeling ill. He was not a large man, and each time I had seen him before I wondered at the ease of his walking, how smoothly and carelessly he managed a graceful gait. But as they scaled the front stairs to the manor, I saw him pause and press a kerchief to his face. Hunt's features pinched and Severn removed his glasses and polished them distractedly.

By the time they were ushered in to see me, sitting in the parlor, Keats's cheeks were crimson and blotchy.

"Ah, only could we get such tempestuous climate shifts here in Britanniae," Keats said to me when I could not hide the look of concern on his face. "Terrible for the constitution."

Keats extended his hand in a friendly manner, and I took it without thinking. I had thought of that moment since the last time I'd felt his skin, the tender moment I could feel him closer than I ever had. My godchild, my blessed one. My heart was thundering in my chest as I reached out for his hand, but I couldn't hold it for long. As soon as the flesh of our hands met, I felt an overwhelming desire to vomit. A metallic taste rose in my mouth, and I had to cough and look a fool in order to let go and maintain what shred of my dignity was left.

"I'm sorry," I said, confused.

Sweating, I quickly greeted the other guests and made myself appear busy while the young men took their tea and cakes.

Aneirin would know what it meant. I glanced at my face in the mirror above the mantel, and not only did I look a ghastly pale, but my eyes were blue. All of my eyes. Not just my pupils. My whole body had reacted to Keats's handshake, a strange defensive response.

My back still to my guests, I poured myself a glass of whiskey—waving off the well-meaning servant trying to do it for me—and drank it quickly. Another glance in the mirror told me my eyes had returned to their natural, dark brown, and what hints of monstrosity I had seen there had dissipated. If I could be called any less than a monster.

"You've really done quite some impressive work with the house," Brown said, affecting his smile and doing his best not to notice my frazzled state. For his part, Keats was focusing on his tea. "I never saw more than the outside, I'm afraid, with the previous owners, but that alone is spectacular. Quite tidied."

I cleared my throat and nodded as a gentleman ought when his estate is complimented. "It was all a matter of water," I said. "Just some good scrubbing of surfaces."

"Well, it is quite impressive—as I was saying to you the other day, Mr. Raddick, it's quite a welcome sight in Hampstead," said Severn, smiling at me with trembling lips. "With so many changes in local politics, old families falling out of favor—and some even packing up and going back to Rome after so many centuries here—why, it's hard to know what to expect. Belsize is practically run amok with weeds—and while I enjoy sketching them, there's murmurs about town as to the unseemly folk gathering there."

"Wouldn't that include you?" Brown teased. "You do seem the expert."

"There is a wild beauty to it," Keats interjected, measuredly. The words were dreamy, but his tone was not. "I've seen it, myself. After so much progress for so long I like to think there are places full of savage beauty left in the world. It's too much to think that the world is so bereft of mysteries."

"Oh, there are plenty of mysteries yet, Mr. Keats," I said, finding my words faster than Mr. Brown could manage a reply.

Keats looked at me, a glimmer of hope in his gaze. Up until now he'd had no reason to like me. I'd banished his hopes of saving his brother Tom, failed to support him as he should be. And if only he knew what had befallen his mother Frances on my account, or his father by way of Poetaster, he would never look at me again.

I wanted him to look on me with love. But I had spent his entire life trying to save him, and never thinking of curating a friendship.

"Mr. Raddick," said Severn, pleased beyond belief to play his part. We had rehearsed this. "You should tell us about your visit south, and your time in the war."

"I don't talk about the war if I can help it," I said, "But I can assure you all that there are wild, weird worlds out there, still. You just need to get out of the smoke of Londinium."

"I've been to the Lakes," Keats said with a sigh. "But even there…I feel as if it's tarnished. As if there is yet a veil between me and what I can truly see."

"Some veils exist within us," I said.

Then the room went quite silent, and I saw Keats's expression. It was then I realized that I hadn't spoken the words aloud, but he'd heard me. And he hadn't spoken the words aloud, either. With trembling hands, he drained his claret and continued on the conversation, which had changed toward the bearing and form of some of Brown's more recent female acquaintances.

The evening proceeded with little else in the way of distraction, and I encouraged Severn to keep the conversation light. I wanted the opportunity to be alone with Keats if I could, to give him my gift. But he already guessed at something strange, and I was terrified as to our conversation.

When at last I found myself alone with him, Severn and Brown some paces away talking over an old volume of mine, some illustrated Arthurian nonsense, Keats was the first to talk.

"I met you once, in Londinium, and you were dry."

"Dry. It's not a word people often use to describe me," I said. I could smell the same harsh, metallic sick on him as I had that first time.

"And when I met with Shelley, he told me of a man he'd seen in his dreams. A wild creature who seemed to control the waters, born of some strange, ancient power. I thought him a bit mad, and he even laughed it off after he spoke of it. But I can't help but wonder if he was talking about you. You do keep showing up, don't you?"

"Would you like a drink?" I asked. "It's a good vintage. A claret. 1782." The platter was laid out just so. I had arranged every step in this dance.

It was strange, having actually followed Aneirin's recipe, I discovered the potion was not a liquid at all, but a powder. It was the color of rust when it was complete and smelled of grass and open fields. There was a small amount of *manna meli* in it, but it was enough to add a singular note of sweetness. Once stirred into Keats's goblet, it was undetectable even to my sensitive nose.

"I suppose, but I've already had a bit..." he tried to protest, but his eyes were hungry. He no doubt knew the pleasing release.

"You're in pain. It will help," I said. He took the glass. The right glass. Honeyed with the last of the manna meli gift, adorned with a few precious drops of blood from Percy Shelley. It was a presentation worthy of Shakespeare.

He looked at me doubtfully and then sighed. "I want to trust you. But then, part of me protests aloud. I do not know your part in our family history as I ought."

"And I am too little of the man I used to be, I'm afraid," I said, taking one of the large chairs by the fire. "Please, join me."

Keats hesitated and then swallowed half the claret, sitting down across from me in the matching chair. I admit I watched him for a good twenty seconds, waiting for some transformation to occur. Worried, I reasoned to myself that such magic might take some time, and the effect would be complete once he'd finished.

He coughed politely into his hand, going rigid as he did so. When no more coughing came, he continued our conversation.

"Did I hear right you have been to Rome recently?" Keats asked me, leaning forward a bit. There was a deeper, more lost look in his eyes than I remembered. Not just a look that was brought about by claret and merriment. And not the source of the metallic smell I always caught around him. Something else. "Or, perhaps I misheard..." Keats said, when I did not reply in time.

"Yes, yes. The Alps, at least, and then down to Rome," I said. "And it does stand up to Byron's adulation. It is a massive, marvelous place. The air tastes different. The earth feels...well, I'm not terribly good at describing things. But it feels oddly familiar to me."

I was seeping words in my nervousness. I hadn't felt any of those things about the Alps at all. I could hardly remember any of my visit there, so clouded I had been with thoughts of destroying Percy Shelley. I had left in such a state of disarray there was hardly time to consider the scenery.

"I'd like to go," Keats said with a sigh. He took another sip of the wine and gave me an approving nod. "It's only..."

"Miss Brawne," I said. Severn had filled me in, copiously, on Keats's love affair with the woman. His neighbor in Hampstead.

"We are engaged, you see..."

"I see."

"She is my Muse. My heart. My Beauty and reason." When I said nothing, he continued. "Have you ever loved someone so much that their absence is like being pierced with a sword?"

Nodding, I drained the rest of my glass. At the suggestion he did the same, and I felt a trickle of dread mingled with excitement make its way down my spine.

I nodded. Poured myself another drink. Stronger this time. I tried to hide the guilt in my eyes, knowing I had dosed him without his consent. That I had gone the coward's way. Such a thing was even beyond Aneirin. What if it killed him? And why had my body reacted so badly to his touch? If only Isabella hadn't left. If only I wasn't so damned alone.

I filled up the space with words.

"It has been my experience, Mr. Keats, that every great love must come to an end. We strive to love, to be loved, to make love, all as often as we can. But it is only because such passion and delight is so fleeting. What is endured with patience and dedication, even of the most honorable and valiant sort, will eventually be sundered. While we mourn the parting before it has even begun, there is yet a power in being able to choose the precise moment we can shatter the dream. There is no greater sorrow on earth than a love which dwindles. I have seen it, and I fear it like nothing else."

"I feel the same about death, Mr. Raddick. About dwindling. I'd rather choose it, but I am too much the coward and the fool, so I press on in hopes of achieving some greater ken," he said. "Love for Fanny keeps me from choosing darkness each and every day. Yet I see nothing but thorns for the future."

"The darkness lingers, whether or not you turn your eyes there," I said.

I am certain I thought I would surprise him with my speech, but he looked at me and shook his head. "Your eyes are like black pearls," he said, "and they stare at me with the truth I run from."

"A change of climate would help," I suggested. "I've heard of the spas of Rome. You will be cared for there. The weather…"

"I know. I have heard Shelley speak of it. And countless others. The climate is much more agreeable than it is here, even in the country," Keats sighed. "Severn tells me time and again. I simply feel I am not yet ill enough—the doctors have told me that I'm surprisingly fit, all things considered. I haven't had a hemorrhage yet. I do not want to consign myself to such a change of view unless I know I have no other choice."

I watched him. Surely, he must feel different. Surely the magic would be working by now. I began to feel panic well up in my throat.

"Perhaps…perhaps miracles can happen," I said, hating myself to give him such hope. I scanned his face for any indication the medicine had worked, but there was no change. He still smelled of illness, of metal and decay. It hung about him, pervasive and cloying.

The rest of the evening passed, and still there was no difference in Keats. I went over in my head again and again, to make sure I had given him the right claret from the right bottle in the right cup. But I knew I had. My mood darkened even more, and it began to pour outside; I did nothing to stop it.

Unable to keep them any longer, I helped Keats and Brown to the front of the house, giving them each a bottle of spirits to take with them. It was when Keats took his, a whiskey older than the building itself, that he collapsed in a coughing fit of the likes I'd never seen. The spittle from his lips was flecked with blood, and in horror I grabbed him and put him to the sofa, propping up his head. Again, I felt ill touching him, but I was still strong enough to put him abed.

"I told him to stop exerting himself," sighed Brown, coming up behind me. "Damned the man."

"Can you blame him?" Severn asked. "He's had such marvelous progress writing—it's a shame."

"I'm here…you idiots…" Keats gasped. He rolled his eyes and then winced against the pain, flapping his hands in the direction of the door. "Get the damned carriage. I want to go home."

Brown and Severn looked at me doubtfully, but I beckoned them to go. "I think the worst of it has passed," I said. "I'll keep him comfortable."

When they left, Keats blanched a shade paler and his entire body relaxed upon the pillows. Tears streamed down his cheeks, and he shook his head. "Dying wouldn't be so bad were that it wasn't so painful," he said. He rubbed his hands on his chest, "It feels as if there's shards of metal floating around in my…in my lungs…"

"I am so sorry," I said, and I meant it deeper than anything I had ever spoken.

"My mother died of this. My brother, Tom. I am but another useless minnow," he sighed, and this brought on another cough. I handed him my handkerchief, and he gasped and sputtered for another minute before falling back to the pillows. "I hate…I hate my weakness…I cannot be the man Fanny needs me to be…I cannot provide for her…not while I'm dead…"

"Hush, now, John," I said quietly, dabbing his forehead again. "You'll feel better on the morrow. Soon will be spring, and the fields will blush green and the birds sing their songs every morning."

"Yes, but it's the nightingale which calls me most," Keats said, choking back tears again. "And I want to dwell with her in the dark."

They took him away, and John pressed my handkerchief back in my hands. I watched the carriage depart, and then looked down to the bloodied cloth in my hands. The nausea I felt I attributed to the sorrow but took no more thought to the handkerchief until I returned to the parlor.

In the dim light of the fire, I noticed that, mixed with the flecks of blood, was something else. Something metallic. A metal that was liquid. Only the eyes of a godling could recognize the small amount present but notice it I did.

Quicksilver. He was poisoned by it, through and through.

He was not ill from a disease; he was sick with poison. No wonder I had reacted so badly to his touch.

As Aneirin died, many new illnesses arose in Londinium. Many of them, as a cruel irony, were spread in the brothels. And the most common human treatment, quicksilver. John was an apothecary. He would have had access to such a metal, in good quantities… And he would have wanted himself cured for Fanny Brawne.

Rome. Miriam. My last chance. I had to get Keats south.

38

I decided I had to encounter his most trusted friends to convince them that John needed to go to Rome. I ran into his steadfast companion Mr. Brown at the Spaniards. He was half his way to a drunken stupor, but his smile was convivial enough even if his eyes were sad. I hadn't had much of an acquaintance with the man, but the tall Scot was the sort of many I had an innate respect for. He seemed to bluster into life without thought, all emotion and sensation and desire. He often spoke inappropriately, harshly. I didn't always agree with him but admired his lack of restraint. I was surrounded by far too much of it.

Brown was drinking at the bar, staring down into an empty glass. He reeked of it, but the man could hold his liquor—I remembered how easy he was on his feet the night of Keats's collapse.

"Mr. Brown," I said, coming up to him and ordering a drink myself. "I trust you're well."

The look he gave me could have withered a fresh lily. "Enough with the 'Mr. Brown'—call me Charles, if you must call me something. Your life's as much of a jape as any, so I hardly see it having any matter."

"Harsh words for so early in the evening," I said to him. "I am sorry about Mr. Keats."

"Are you?" he asked. "Are you truly, man? It's hard for me to parse out from all the meddling you're doing."

"I've nothing but his good health in concern, I tell you."

"And why is that? You're no man of letters. Or politics. Or breeding." Brown sneered the last bit at me.

"You've no idea of my breeding, Charles. And were I to tell you, you'd never believe it for a day."

"Try me."

I could not tell him. Looking at him I saw a man mortal. A man who would die on the shores of another land, far from Britanniae.

I missed Aneirin. He would have liked Brown. He'd have allayed my fears and anxiety about the whole situation.

"I'm admirer of Mr. Keats's poems, and know his—" I tried.

"You don't fool me. You want the praise when he dies. When he spills his blood all over the ground, you're the one who wants to be there! To snap up the glory in your jaws!" Brown shouted.

He was getting rather angry, and the patrons didn't like it a bit. Nor did I. Having been drunk and angry a good part of my life I knew what destruction it could wreak, godling or not. It was in this very place Keats had written his Nightingale poem, as I'd heard, and indeed I thought I heard it in the weary silence that fell upon the crowd after Brown's explosion. It brought me to my senses a little.

"Take him outside," the barkeep growled at me. "Surely, you're capable of that, Mr. Raddick?"

I nodded and moved, with some effort, Mr. Brown. He cursed at me the whole way, but halfway to the gardens, he began sobbing into my arm. His tears reminded me of home.

"He's just a young man," bawled Brown. "Just a young man. And so full of promise. I didn't mean to snap at you; it only seems so unfair."

Then he was sobbing into my shirt in a most unseemly way, drunk and full of mucous. A pitiful human being in every which way, but with a broken heart. What he felt for Keats was clear to anyone, but he had kept it locked away under a very rigid exterior. A little anger and some libation were all it took to lose it to the world.

Once he was done, he straightened himself out a bit and blew his nose in his handkerchief.

"I'm sorry, Mr. Raddick. I'm protective of him. As if he were my brother," Brown explained to me. "But he's more than that. He's special."

"I know he is," I told him. "But he's dying. And there's nothing we can do here."

Tears came again to Brown's eyes and he only nodded miserably.

"You know if he goes to Rome, his health will be vastly improved. The waters there are imbued with minerals, and the air is drier, fresher. He could live longer, brighter—perhaps not for another lifetime, but long enough to be more, to write more."

"I know. I've told him as much," Brown said. "But he won't listen to reason."

I'd not expected that. "You've told him to go to Rome?"

"Of course I have! Do you think I want him to die here? Every day there's news in the paper of the wonders of Rome. Healings and miracles. Praise Mary!" he mocked, holding up his hands in mock prayer. "Meanwhile, there he is, gasping like a fish plucked from the river. Gods, man. He's a marvel, Keats is. And I'd never forgive myself if I didn't try to get him to a better place."

"Then you and I are of a mind. I can finance his trip. He only needs to consent," I said.

"He won't budge."

"Of course, he will."

"Not while Fanny Brawne breathes."

WHAT TO DO with a man infatuated? With Brown and Severn now my accomplices, I worked steadily to arrange for Keats's trip. Each passing day his health deteriorated and, as was reported to me, his dependence on laudanum increased more and more. And there was the matter of the quicksilver. It was likely he was dosing himself, as it was a common treatment for many ills. But the amount he had must have been overwhelming. And expensive. Perhaps it was finding its way to him otherwise. I asked Severn to check to see if he'd seen a physician any time recently and to check for strange bottles.

I had a few other thoughts. One was to kill Ms. Brawne. It wouldn't be difficult, and with so much disease and pestilence about there would be little suspicion. But I doubted killing her would diminish her in Keats's eyes, regardless of how much I wanted to do the deed himself. Severn reported that as Keats's health continually fell, he wrote more and more furiously to Fanny, often passing notes to her many times a day rather than penning poetry.

I wish no ill thought on Fanny Brawne. You may think I paint her as a dullard and a distraction. She was certainly not the former and somewhat the latter. She was a pleasant enough girl, and she was kind to Keats. Kind in a way I don't think any woman had ever been. Isabella was welcoming to him, but not in a soft and yielding way; she had been a force of nature, quite literally. She had schooled him and let him worship her. But not so with Fanny. She was a true woman of the earth, coy and proper and very much in love with John Keats. I knew going through her would do nothing.

But her mother. That was another story. Surely her mother had thoughts about this young, dying poet, and his continued infatuation with her daughter.

The thought occurred to me as April dawned bright and cold. I had not visited Brown's house, where Keats lived in half while the Brawnes inhabited the other. White and square and unremarkable, I approached it with trepidation, straightening my cravat. On the rare occasion I had to leave the house I did my best to dress in a way I thought would make Aneirin proud. I had often had conversations with Aneirin in my head as if he were there. Though he was no longer among the living I was conversing with him and consulting with him more and more.

Madness? Perhaps. Most likely. But a madness I wouldn't give up.

Mrs. Brawne came to the door and blinked up at me. The nostrils in her hawkish nose fluttered as she did so, and she had to adjust her bonnet a little to get the whole view.

"Mrs. Brawne," I said, extending the basket of honey and wine I'd purchased for them. "I'm Mr. Raddick."

"Yes, I see," Mrs. Brawne said, her voice half a whisper. She smelled of elderberries and something warm and welcoming. Bread, perhaps. In her form there was nothing in the least bit appealing, but I thought her hands rather lovely. It is my experience that even the homeliest of people have good qualities.

She took the basket and stared down into it for a moment.

"May I come in?" I asked.

She laughed a little maniacally and nodded, gesturing me into the house with rehearsed grace.

Within minutes I was seated rather uncomfortably on a green patterned chair, sipping weak tea and politely nibbling on some of her sandwiches, unable to speak for Mrs. Brawne's incessant chatter.

My expectation was, upon mentioning Keats, she would be rather polite and demure on the situation, considering she had no idea who I was. But it was just the opposite. My stature—and her knowledge of where I lived—must have informed her decision to prattle on for an hour about that "most grievous" Mr. Keats, his shortcomings, and his long-standing infatuation with her daughter.

"Oh, Fanny won't say it to me outright," Mrs. Brawne went on, waving her hands about. "She doesn't think I know. Doesn't think I can see it. How could she be so blind? I'm her mother, I raised her from a little thing. Even Samuel sees it. The look in her eyes she sees Mr. Keats isn't *love*. It's pity. She fanned his flames and now he's burning up, and she doesn't want to be the one that kills him."

"Perhaps she is—"

"No. She isn't *anything*. She is wasting her time, and her best years, meddling with that man. Oh, he's kind enough to me, and I wouldn't mind him so much if he didn't send letters so constantly and sit by the window and pine after her. I'm not an imbecile. I know my Fanny's not the comeliest girl in the world, but she's smart. She's too smart to be sidled with a poor man."

"Yes, that poor man," I said, inflecting differently.

Mrs. Brawne blushed. "He is dying, isn't he?"

I nodded. "He is."

"Well. You know. Since Mr. Keats had his episode, Fanny hasn't seen him at all. I don't want her catching. And she doesn't want the catching, either. We have to worry about these things now, in cursed Londinium. She permits him to write her, and often passes by the window. But to be true, sir, I think it's vanity. Vanity of the young, and vanity of the pitiful."

Mrs. Brawne was beginning to wear on me, so I made my point as clear as possible. "I am trying to do what I can to finance Mr. Keats's trip to Rome. I believe we can help prolong his life there, in such a climate. But he does not wish to stay on account of your daughter. If, as you say, she is merely pitying him and feels no true affection, then I agree with her—she ought not tell him. But, if she is true, she ought to encourage him to allow me to pay his passage. Would you not have done the same for your husband?"

She frowned, looking into her teacup. Her shoulders slumped and I could smell the tears in her eyes before they fell. It isn't hard to tell when a person has lost a spouse or family member. I could smell the lingering sickness in the house, noted the prominent paintings and miniatures, sensed her mourning even amidst all else. She had raised her three children and lost two before they could speak. She did not need a mourning shroud for me to see the loss draped about her shoulders.

“I understand,” she said, choking back the tears and fingering her mourning ring.

Romantics. A pox upon them all.

MY PLAN WORKED. Charles Brown agreed to take John to Rome when he was ready, and as the year progressed and Keats's health deteriorated it became clear what had to be done. And as it was, there were not many days to be had left at Wentworth place, and not just due to Mrs. Brawne's insisting. There were more than a few times I spotted Fanny Brawne on the arm of a soldier or a merchant in town, especially once Keats was removed to Londinium proper when new tenants came to Brown's house. I kept a quiet distance and helped Brown in his planning, using Severn when I needed him but, by and large letting him do as he wanted. Now that it was decided Keats was to go to Rome, there was little left for him to do.

Perhaps I could not save him, but I could give him comfort in his last days while I hoped for a miracle.

39

The day Keats arrived in Rome I returned home to pack what little belongings I had. I would follow them, of course, by a few weeks. I would be there for the last few months of his life, or years, if I had to. I would make for myself a new face and a new name and be a friend to the man I never truly knew as my godson. I felt the plan was sound, and one Aneirin would be proud of.

In preparation I read all of Keats's work again and purchased a special volume of Shakespeare for him. I would board a ship as a man would, and join him, prepared for a new chapter of my life in the land of power.

I tell you, hope blinds people. Godlings and men alike. And I was not prepared for such a horrible fate to fall upon me.

I was tidying up my baggage when someone rang at the door. When the butler returned to me, it was with a letter. From Calvinius Pardo.

"Achaemenes is in Rome. Miriam will see no one. Come find me."

I TOUCHED down not far outside of Rome, and the sight startled me enough to break through my rage. I admit to never having had much of an eye for things crafted by human hands. The artifice flies in the face everything I find beautiful and inspiring and right with the world. But

Rome was not Londinium. Rome was something beyond what I had expected.

I know, because I have traveled since then to other worlds, that Rome is always a place of wonder. But then I had not been to the marble steps. Here, in the world I was born into, it was a sprawling wonder of light and marble, statues and pointed arches, as far as the eye could see. And at the very center, the highest building of worship I had ever seen. I knew my Homer well enough, knew my Virgil. I understood the importance of this place. Achaemenes had lived here for thousands of years, commanding his forces until he could hold the walls no more.

It was approaching Marymas. There was no snow, but the air was chilly. And since much of the war was waged from within—Achaemenes's own armies converting to Marianism and rising against him—Rome itself had been rededicated to her. I could smell the flowers in the air before I landed, knew to expect the decoration, the ships floating on the water.

But I had not expected the lanterns. It was the day, on the Marian calendar, in which she had been visited by the King of Heaven, and upon when she was conceived. I've no idea why such a strange thing should be celebrated, but her virginity and purity have ever been at the center of her appeal—though her true form, Miriam, is far from it. I suppose we're all capable of wish fulfillment should the opportunity arise.

I saw them rise from the Tiberius, and at first, I thought they must be weapons of war. Some strange exploding device. But then I could smell the burning wax, beeswax, as the lanterns took flight. A thousand thousand of them, rising high and reflecting in the waters of the Tiberius. An offering, a remembrance, a gesture for the Queen of Heaven.

When I entered the waters of the Tiberius, I became a fish. It had not been on my mind, but the moment the cool waters covered my skin I reverted to a fish for the first time since I had left Crummock Water. And with that transformation came a perfect calm and clarity and vision.

The water wound for miles. Part of my fish mind worried Achaemenes was aware of this, knowing I would seek the waters first—but the other part of me, the godling part, was not so worried. Beneath Rome ran a million tributaries and rivers, aqueducts and cisterns, and I could feel them all. That vast network I had once tapped into without so much as a second thought was given to me again, lighting up in my mind like a great glowing net. And the people within were like the lanterns, bright and moving across the grid. All of Rome and its inhabitants.

It did not take me long to find the location of Keats and Severn. They were directly to the west of where I had set down, in the shadow of the Mausoleum of Augustus. The city was remarkable from a water perspective, and I knew more about it in a few hours that I ever would in a lifetime as human being. The food, the worship; the vice, the celebrations. I knew where the wineries and distilleries were, where the brothels were kept, where the clothing was made. Everything humans do leaves a trace in the water, and in a way as I never had before, I studied.

Breathing in the water through my gills, I swam back and forth, noting the subtle shifts of the days and nights. Achaemenes would be waiting, and I had to get to John—but not if I was going to put him in danger. I had to wait until I could sense Achaemenes, with precision. I had lived too long as a trout to avoid traps, but it didn't mean I had to go blindly.

Then, I saw him in a burst of violet light.

Calvinius.

In the water map of my mind I knew he had landed in Rome, not far from where John was sleeping peacefully after a prolonged hemorrhage.

With clarity and rage, I went to meet him. How had he hidden from me for so long? And why was he revealing himself to me now?

Traveling in a bank of fog, I slipped across the Mausoleum of Augustus and through the city streets, pouring myself through every crack and crevice, learning again to breathe air. I rearranged myself as a gentleman dressed in gray, brandishing a sword.

As I approached the Spanish steps, whereupon Keats was sleeping in the pink house, I realized how much I had missed. Calvinius was not even trying to hide from me, not really. The Spaniards Inn. The Spanish Steps.

The Spaniard himself, wearing the clothes of Joseph Severn.

The blackness of night obscured much from my vision, but not Calvinius. He stood with his hands folded across his chest, his eyes taking me in with mild curiosity.

"A sword," he said. "It's a nice touch. I wanted to warn you. Achaemenes is on his way."

"I am here for my godson," I said, walking up to him until I towered above him. "He is ill. He should not be mixed up in all of this."

I thought a look like sadness flickered across his features. "Hello, Joss. It's good to see you again."

"You know if I could I would smother you to pieces," I said to him, and I felt the earth tremble beneath my feet.

Calvinius put up a finger of warning. "Ah, ah, Joss. Don't go expending yourself. You haven't got much left. And truly, this is just a sad side-effect. You know, John wasn't really ill, not in a way the medicine could have helped. It was the medicine killing him."

"I don't understand."

"My dear, did you not notice he felt strange to you? I suspect you were near him."

"Of course, a few times..." I recalled the ache when John was in my arms. That wrongness.

"Mercury. A prescription often given to treat syphilis. And something easily attainable by a young, shy alchemist, who wanted nothing more than to impress the new love of his life," Calvinius explained. "Though, I do admit, what I gave him was higher than the typical dose, but, alas..."

Rage prickled at the edges of my vision. "How could you?"

"It was a matter of necessity. His body was Perfect for the ritual. Any of the children of the boast would have done—I had tried with Blake, of course, but he proved too strong. You hate me, I see that, but I did this to better preserve our future. Miriam is going mad, you must know. But with Verta's help, I was able to concoct a new way to be reborn, to preserve our memories from one incarnation to the next."

"Calvinius, no..."

"The mercury experiments with Verta worked to some extent, though her own transference was rather disastrous. Still, she proved useful: her rather curious menagerie went so well. They helped preserve the bodies, and with one blessed, well. Now, I can give Achaemenes a new, better body. We tried with Verta first, but the naiad was a failure. But I had already set the boast in motion. We knew one of them would suffice, and yours came to age fastest, poisoned by his own hand."

"What monsters," I whispered. "I will not let you."

"But you already have. You are too weak, otherwise, to fight us. And why should we be barred from the magic of life and death? Oh, I could not get La Roche to see, no matter how hard I tried. And I knew there was no getting to you if he was not in agreement. So, I built trust, I fed Miriam with tales of Ancyra—they were not lies, but they gave you something to believe in."

I could say nothing. I could barely breathe.

"When we realized Keats was sick, we had to ensure you came here with us," Calvinius said. "His transference will be even more potent that way. And Achaemenes will lead us to a new land once he has a strong body. We will be free of Miriam, free of the burden. I hope you will see the right of it and understand what gift a gift this is, how right and true!"

"There is no wrong, and there is no right, Calvinius. It's just a mess of mad monsters rutting in the dark."

"If you say so."

"And Miriam?"

"She's grown too large. She cannot see past her own nose. Once we leave here and make for the New World, we will be out of her reach."

"No war is ever won, it's only delayed," I said.

I didn't know how long Calvinius had been masquerading as Severn. I didn't know if the man I knew as Severn was alive or dead or had ever been. I simply understood there had been signposts all along the last years of my life, and I had missed them. For worry about my friends, for my fixation with healing Keats, for my failures.

For my love.

We were all pawns. We just took turns playing King and Queen while it was convenient.

I burst open the door and quickly made my way to where Keats was. The building was eerily quiet. I could feel the empty rooms about me and smell the sickness and quicksilver all about us. In the distance, Keats's voice whined and wheezed every now and again.

I have told you a great deal about my madness, but I can say it was never stoked so much as it was when I stepped foot into that house and knew my godson, my scion, was dying. His poisoned blood and body furiously working to keep alive while he was played as a pawn. I don't know what I looked like when I swept into the room, and I have never asked. But of what a mother feels for her endangered young, so I felt. Blood rage.

And when Keats's eyes fell upon me, he was surprised, but feverish and alone.

That look, so full of fear and pain, cut through me as a sword would. Before I knew what I was doing, I had him in my arms; so poisoned he was with quicksilver that the very pressure of him on my flesh was almost unendurable, but I would not let him go. Every moment with him I knew I was diminishing my own power, but I could not give in.

All this, and he was alone and dying. I had trusted Brown to be with him, and instead I had left open the door for Calvinius and Achaemenes and their conniving.

I would not let him die. I could do nothing to prevent it, though. My own godson was poison.

Even as I felt Achaemenes grow more present around me, a heavy red fog encircling me, and as my body fought against the quicksilver still now taking John's life and making him gasp his last, like a fish out of water.

A minnow. Just a little minnow.

"He's coming, Joss," Calvinius said, waiting in the doorway. "There's nothing to be done. Just the mist."

John looked up at me, tears flowing down his cheeks.

"I did not expect…this would be…the end," he said.

Helpless. I was helpless.

Unless…the tears. They were enough. I set my hands to the side of my godson's face and breathed in, deeply as I could. A storm, a raging wind and rain, and let it all into my body. Everything made of water about him. The pain of the poisoned water ricocheting through my veins and limbs brought me to the point of losing consciousness, and only through the pleading in his eyes could I be brought around.

I spoke to him without words, told him everything he needed to know. As the quicksilver moved closer and closer to my heart, the world did indeed begin to slip from me. The connection between us grew stronger as I slowly started to turn the tide, to fill him with purer, better water. I wrote his name again and again on the walls of his heart and in his mind, to help him remember, to help him know.

But it was not enough; I did not have enough within me. For all the times I had tried to ignore the power inside of me, all the years I had pressed on with the amulet around my neck, now that I had need of the power it was gone from me. There was simply no more water in the well. I felt Achaemenes's presence press down on me, heavier than thunderclap, and the bond between John and I was broken. Quicksilver spilled out of my mouth, my hands, streamed down my face, dappling the ground beneath us.

Keats slipped from my grasp, and Achaemenes reared and plunged, not toward me, but into John.

Achaemenes did not want me. He never wanted me. He needed me to do precisely as I had done. I had, in effect, purified John's body as perfectly as any godling could.

Keats's body twisted, changed. His limbs shook, and his neck snapped back. Those perfect hazel eyes clouded white, and then filled again almost black. Like my eyes. Achaemenes, godling of creation, refashioned the body of my godson as only he could. A blank canvas upon which he could draw. The walls of his heart and his mind were purified by his magic, the vessel wrought by godlings to make room.

But it was not without cost. It was raining in the room, and everything had been torn from the walls—every picture and even the paper. I was weak, but not without fury. Yet my legs would not move.

I only watched as Achaemenes remade my godchild, and I felt my heart grow cold as ice in the wake of such unfairness and despair.

Calvinius still stood in the doorway, confused when he met my glance. Achaemenes had kept things from him too.

"Yes, I am John," Achaemenes said, staring at me, answering my unspoken question. "You may call me Iosheka. And I am far, far away from home."

"This is unexpected," Calvinius said from behind me. "Do you remember me?"

"Chaos, I always remember you. But I am not as I was. I am transferred," said Iosheka. He touched his face and blinked down at me, confused. "This is not as I expected it to go. I feel feeble."

My head was so heavy I could not do more than loll it to the side and groan.

Iosheka's body, the one he had woven from my scion's, was taller than Keats had been, and far darker. His hair was black and straight, falling evenly around his high cheekbones. But the brow and the jaw were the same. Watching him move made me feel disoriented.

"This is not my home," Iosheka said, looking over to me helplessly. "I shouldn't be here."

Calvinius sighed, frustrated. "You don't remember anything?"

"I didn't say I don't remember anything. I remember everything. But it is shadowed and strange. Faces, details, they bleed together..." Iosheka moved closer to me, knelt down, and put a hand on my forehead.

Calvinius said: "His name is Joss Raddick."

Iosheka gave me a sad smile. "That is one of his names. He has almost died for this. And I, selfish and strange, have taken away the one thing he loved. I will begin this life cursed and end it so. I am sorry."

I went to swat at Iosheka, which is when I realized I was half a squid. My right arm, which had been draped across my field of vision, was well enough still a man. But the left was deep blue and streaked with pulsating suckers.

"No wonder he can hardly breathe," Iosheka said, tears spilling down his cheeks, splashing upon my tentacles and malformed face. "He has gills."

40

Kindness was the last thing I ever expected. Kindness and understanding. Iosheka was not the monster I wanted him to be, nor was Calvinius, for all his trickery. Pawn though I was, yet another instrument in the war between Achaemenes and Miriam, I was broken and warped from taking the quicksilver into my body and wracked with such deep sorrow that I did not want to wake.

They took me to the Tiber, down from the city, though I don't recall the method of my transportation. I only had one power left to me as they moved, trailing the name of my godson on the cobblestones behind me as they dragged me bodily. His name, over and over, upon the streets of Rome. So much so, that when they erected a grave for him, they wrote: "Here lies One whose Name was Writ in Water."

The water of the Tiber again did its magic, and though I wanted to die, the healing powers would not let me. They both stayed with me, nursing me, speaking to me, even when I did nothing to help them. Even when I tried to let myself go. But in spite of myself, there was too much in Iosheka I recognized as mine. Glimpses. Memories. His voice. John's voice.

A week passed and still I was not strong enough to leave Calvinius and Iosheka. My body healed, eventually, and I reverted back to my human form. Though there were scars, great scars. My heart felt empty; my purpose scattered. There was nothing I wished for more than death, yet while pieces of my godson still lived on, I felt it impossible to sunder the ties. I had not saved him. I had transformed him, transferred him. Aneirin had told me that he could see John only in a mist. So, he had been.

Then I heard a familiar voice at my side. I was not yet strong enough to travel as a man, nor manage for more than a few hours at a time, and so I sat astride the river in my albatross form.

"I should have seen it," said the voice to my side, the owl I knew well. Trita. "What Verta was doing. I suppose she had a debt to Achaemenes. For you and I, younger than the others, it may be we underestimated the power of the many lives we can live in one incarnation."

I shivered, going closer to her. "I am only glad La Roche did not know."

"Joss, I overflow with grief for you. I cannot imagine what this must feel like, after all of this. Your scion…"

It felt raw, to think of John again. As if my entire heart were exposed. But I had grieved as a god for so long that there seemed no room to grieve as a man.

"He is not in pain," I replied after a long moment. "He lived in a great deal of it; pain of body, pain of mind. But he did not die suffering."

"Your blessing saw him through, though, helped him attain his greatest gift," she said. "I do know that for certain."

"He will be long remembered," I said.

"Shelley wrote him a poem, did you know? And the name John Keats has been much praised. A light which was never so much appreciated as when it was snuffed kindles anew."

"How strange it is, Trita. My soul is awash in this grief and yet poetry, somehow, makes it better. In the way rocks retain a bit of the heat when the sun goes down. It does not banish the dark, but it is a reminder there will yet be life again." My body spasmed, and I gasped with the pain, letting out a mournful sigh.

"You should rest more."

"I can't bear to right now. There is too much darkness on the horizon."

"Yes, there is. For our blessed godchildren, the damage is not yet done. The hour draws near on Percy Shelley's demise," Trita said. "It would be fitting, I think, if we could be together. On the 8th of July."

"La Roche told you?" I asked. I didn't use his true name; I felt I could never speak it aloud again.

"He did," she said softly. "As his godfather, of course, he knew these things. Please, consider joining me in Geneva."

"I may not be strong enough," I told her. "But I will try."

CALVINIUS AND IOSHEKA left for the Americas shortly after, and though I considered joining them again, I knew I had more to do in Britanniae. In time, I would go to those shores. But my body was too weak, my power too dimmed.

For a few years I returned to Belsize and tended the gardens there. Isabella came to me often, and we spent many quiet nights there as she marked my progress. She was no physician to the gods, but she knew enough of our sort to project my healing. After her measurements and observations, she noted I was indeed gaining in strength, but almost imperceptibly. It could take more than a hundred years, she surmised, for me to have even a shadow of my strength back.

That was well enough for me. I found myself in the small streams, in the rain-covered afternoons, in the morning mists rising from the fields. I slowly began to put myself together. I could not do much, but I could change into a bird.

So, when the time came, I joined Trita to bid farewell to Percy Shelley, the last of Aneirin remaining on earth. I couldn't have intervened at the time, even if I wanted to; Miriam's curses taught me enough in my life, and besides, I was much diminished.

We met, as birds, and awaited Percy Shelley.

I could not help but notice the rising storm, but it was not a storm I knew. It felt unnatural, brought about by ill omens and strange winds. I was far too weak to command my own water, let alone water on a surface as great as this, so we simply watched. And when the ill-shod boat carrying Shelley and his friend came into view, I saw the horror unfold before me.

Then she spoke, her wise owl eyes never leaving the scene before us.

I had never felt so alone in a storm, so helpless. My feathers ruffled; my vision blurred. Nature herself had us all in her mercy. Unknowable, unfathomable, immutable.

The air went cold, the boat struggled in the surf, and then I felt Percy Shelley's life vanish.

Trita nestled up next to me, and we sheltered one another as the storm passed over us.

I had never seen a storm like that. I had always been at the eye, a calm and furious center.

And then, the sun broke through the clouds. It showered the boat with golden light and I felt my soul rise anew. Without a doubt, I knew Aneirin had been born again into this world. Perhaps not the same, but a light, still. In the years since his death, I had been walking in the dark, unable to see the sun for the wonder it was. But now...hope. Unexpected and as sharp as a needle to the heart.

"I see now," I whispered to Trita. "I see now."

And she spoke the words Shelley had written for Keats. But I know now they were not for Keats. They were for his godfather, for Aneirin.

Peace, peace! he is not dead, he doth not sleep
He hath awakened from the dream of life
'Tis we, who lost in stormy visions, keep
With phantoms an unprofitable strife,
And in mad trance, strike with our spirit's knife
Invulnerable nothings. — We decay
Like corpses in a charnel; fear and grief
Convulse us and consume us day by day,
And cold hopes swarm like worms within our living clay.
The One remains, the many change and pass;
Heaven's light forever shines, Earth's shadows fly;
Life, like a dome of many-coloured glass,
Stains the white radiance of Eternity,
Until Death tramples it to fragments. — Die,
If thou wouldst be with that which thou dost seek!
Follow where all is fled!

TRITA, my true friend, left the world without a word to me. Some say she was fighting aside Noel, Lord Byron, when the Persians rose again, however briefly, and he with them. Others say at the death of Mary Shelley, she fell to darkness in grief. Either way, she was battling, whether inside or outside.

As I sit and write this, she has not returned.

Calvinius, I never understood. I know he faded completely not long after Percy Shelley's death in a remote New World village. Perhaps it was the death of Blake. I do not know. I try not to think on it too much. Years of hiding his face from all of us—even Miriam—must have expended his powers beyond measure. Lies build a hollow, fragile house, and he has always been prone to madness.

As to Iosheka, he made himself a home in the New World among the great tribes. He had lost the Continent, but he would forge a new one, and he had no hope in colonialism as Calvinius had. As Miriam was populating the coastlines, for of course, she had to follow her old rival, he would mobilize his new troops from within. They had been expecting him. They would remind him of what hatred and malice were. He would spend lifetimes fortifying his borders and keeping out Miriam's encroaching forces.

I would see him again. And I did.

EPILOGUE

It took fifty years for me to regain enough strength to travel over the seas again. Oh, many stories could be told of those days in between, but they were mostly lived as a mortal man in the mountains up north. I loved a little, and when Isabella left for the New World, I threw myself in deeper with humankind; with pestilence again rampant, there was need for clean water, for healers, for wise men. I found widows and widowers, and I helped them where I could. I hunted. I traveled. I told stories of Aneirin—some of them true, and some of them lies. But the lies were my favorite, because I know he would have loved them most.

Then, an unexpected letter. From Isabella Jones.

She was in Boston, and she asked if I would join her if I could. She described a great new city to me, where buildings rose higher than in Londinium, and new marvels appeared on the street every day.

How she found me I do not know. But knowing she would be there, awaiting me, I faced my last challenge and crossed to the New World, myself. Iosheka was not a friend, but he was a connection. Perhaps the only godling connection left in the world. I felt I might need to make peace with him before I let go entirely. I should like to know other rivers before the end. I should like to learn to be a fish again, if I ever could. My body was compromised, and it was unlikely that the kind of power I once experienced could ever be manifested again. But I wanted to learn, at last, how to be a man without the burden of such loss and sorrow.

I lived in a constant state of agitation on the ship, and a persistent nagging in my side. A stitch, the sort of ailment a mortal worries about. I thought it had to be seasickness, and so consigned myself to the barracks. But when that did nothing, I found myself pacing the decks, muttering to myself in the cold wind, trying to banish thoughts of Aneirin, but not really.

And that was when I saw them. Their silhouettes shone dark against the starlight, and their breath billowing about them in perfect mist. And I knew.

He, somewhat slimmer and fairer than he had been; she, pale and wan, though no less beautiful. I knew them, though they did not know me.

"Pleasant evening for a stroll," said the man with a smile as I stood gaping at them. He wore spectacles and had a more professorial look about him than Aneirin had. The grit and brawn I had recognized in him before had faded as if he had been traced with charcoal. But brilliant still, brilliant as ever. The sun. Apollo.

"Oh, Randall, must you talk to everyone you see?" asked the woman. She looked at me and for a moment I thought she would recognize me and welcome me as Verta once had. But instead, she just seemed confused. "I'm sorry—are you well, sir?"

"My apologies," I said. "I didn't mean to interrupt you."

"No interruptions, at all. We've honeymooned quite enough," said the man, Randall. My Aneirin. Reborn. "It's about time we met someone new. You—you're headed to Boston as well?"

"I suppose I am," I said, astounded at this miracle of rebirth.

I had a purpose, just there, a breath away.

"I'm Randall Roth," the man said, extending his hand. "And this is my wife, Matilda. Roth." The introductions were halted and strange, and what silvered tongue Aneirin had once possessed was gone in this incarnation. But I could not miss the cleverness in his eyes, that familiar intellect.

I shook his hand and said, "I'm Joss Raddick."

When Randall touched me, his hand flared brightly for a moment, and his eyes widened. The gold rims of his spectacles kindled, and he laughed. "Why you...you're..."

"Yes," I said. "Yes, I am. And I'm here to teach you."

I ARRIVED in Boston in the deepest winter and the air was scented with lilies, fresh lilies. And chill! Tears streamed to my eyes as I looked down the row of houses and out across the river. Everything shone. The gas lamps and candles of the city shone on the Charles River and turned her to fire—for she was frozen solid with ice. Just as the Tamesis had once been.

There were people, simple people, everywhere, celebrating as I had never seen. They crowded the streets and streamed from the shops. They danced on the river, walking on it with unsteady feet, casting flowers, singing songs. I could smell roasting nuts in the distance, and noted the great bowers of holly and ivy, twined together in great shapes: fantastical representations of enormous peacocks and cuckoos. And over everything, the smell, always the smell of lilies.

Feeling drawn to the river, I meandered my way through the crowd, startled when a comely young woman dressed in white with holly about her temples, offered me a garland of mistletoe. Protection, a blessing of the Virgin. She kissed my cheek and danced away, leaving me to wonder after her.

Would that Aneirin could see it! He'd have laughed. We knew Mary for her true self, as Miriam, the powerful, vengeful, jealous, and protective godling. But perhaps that was what her followers found so endearing. More than a thousand years under Roman rule, and now free to find inspiration somewhere else on other shores.

I remembered my first Marymas, sailing down the Tamesis in victory with Aneirin. We were coming down the river in our great warship, and it was nighttime. The edges of the river were lined with lanterns and candles. Every bridge was illuminated by the glittering lights of men and women standing vigil.

"Mister Raddick, is that you?" came a voice from behind me.

It was Isabella Jones, wrapped in white ermine. Her black curls stood out in perfect ringlets, and her dark eyes shone when I caught her gaze. I had not seen her in many years and had forgotten how charming she was.

"Mrs. Jones," I said.

"I hoped you'd make the trip," she said, catching me about the waist. "Did you meet them?"

"You are a curious, scheming woman. How did you know?"

"Ship manifests. Gossip. Innate cleverness. How are they?"

"They will learn," I said. "They are very much in love. I thought I might be jealous, but it isn't such a thing. Randall is not La Roche, not really. But they both have such potential."

"I'm glad it's worked out," she said.

"It's been a long time, Isabella," I said, her word like honey in my mouth. But this time, lingering. "I'm sorry it's taken me so much time."

"You really ought to dance. You are not quite the bulk and brawn I remember but will still draw attention to yourself if you stand here like a bewildered bear."

She linked her arm in mine.

"I don't stick out."

"You do. Especially when you fold your arms like that. You look like some strange statue. And there's snow all over your beard."

"I don't know how to dance," I said. "I've never tried."

She laughed. "Take my hand. Put one there, at my waist. Now we're on ice, so you must tread lightly…"

"You forget who I am," I said, bolstered by her forwardness. My hand upon her curving back centered me, focused me. I smiled in spite of myself. "I won't slip."

Isabella grinned, raising her brows. "Are you going to surprise me?"

I nodded and began to twirl her about, commanding the ice beneath our feet to slip and resist just perfectly, so we slid about with ease. The band playing music nearby caught our theatrics—how Aneirin would have loved it—and started a happier tune, punctuated by Isabella's laughter.

And as the snow fell around us, swirling in patterns more artful than any human eye could see, I forgot about the darkness plaguing me. I only saw the light in Isabella's eyes, and the joy our dancing gave to others. I felt a gift bestowed and a gift begotten, and my soul, for a time, was eased and full of laughter.

Yes, it is true what they say. All of it, and more: I am a savior of ships, a commander of the seas, the child of a fish, a wielder of lightning.

But more than those great epithets, there is one I prize above all. I was the great, deep ocean wave who rose and dared to touch the Sun. And, heavens above, how we shone together in that brief light of dusk; how we danced, and lived, and loved.

ACKNOWLEDGMENTS

This is a book about grief. It was not an easy book to write, but it was a book that changed me as a writer. While you may be holding this in your hands after its 2022 publication date, I began writing this book in 2013, shortly after my daughter was born, and abruptly lost two people dear to me whose loss impacted me greatly. One, gone before he turned thirty; another, well into her 80s.

Sometimes you have nothing you can do but sit with grief and listen. And so, in this framed story (if you take *Pilgrim of the Sky* and assume Joss is telling his story to Maddie), it is about sitting with grief, examining it, and changing from it. Initially, Aneirin's death was swift, and Joss spiraled, unprepared. But then, the longer I sat with this manuscript, and particularly their relationship, I realized that even godlings linger. That death, and grief, are not always so sudden. That in those final weeks and months and years you are reinforcing the last of your love for each other while holding out hope for just one more day.

Joss burst into the pages of *Pilgrim of the Sky*, and I knew there and then I would write his story, his *bildungsroman.* Initial drafts were even lengthier, with early chapters featuring William Wordsworth, Samuel Taylor Coleridge, and Dorothy Wordsworth. Instead of dallying in a kind of Romantic poet fanfiction, however, I opted to re-examine the relationship between Joss and Aneirin, as well as the relationship between Joss and Trita. These three held up the pillars of the tale, and their adventures in Ankara became some of my favorite chapters to write. For we had never really seen godlings living like historical superheroes before.

But none of them are easy characters to like. As I've revisited both this book and *Pilgrim,* I suppose I am most proud of the consistency among godlings, who balance on the razor's edge of holiness and the profane. Like all good heroes and villains, each of our godlings believes they are doing the right thing. I suspect I could write this same story from the point of view of Calvinius, for example, and it might show Joss in a very different light.

That said, after over a decade I am very glad to share Joss's story with you all. For those first fans who followed Maddie through the looking glass in *Pilgrim of the Sky,* thank you. Ten years after its initial publication, I'm thrilled to find readers still discovering the book. *Gods of Londinium* is a drastically different kind of story in some ways, and for the first time I was able to really open up Joss's world as a fully realized godling.

Thank you to Michael for trips to the ocean where I could listen to Joss whisper across the reeds; to Sam and Kendra Montgomery-Blinn for their continual support; to Jennifer Hansen, my selkie sister who always reminds me to heed the call of the sea even when I'd prefer to run to the trees; to Kate Sullivan, my first editor, who glimpsed this world first; to John, Emily, Tuppence, and Kristen and the whole Falstaff crew; and finally, to all of those who have loved against the odds, against expectations, and against the tides. Love is love.

ABOUT THE AUTHOR

The award-winning author of *Queen of None,* a feminist Arthurian retelling, Natania Barron is preoccupied with mythology, monsters, mayhem, and magic. From medieval-inspired tales to Regency fantasy romance, her often historically-inspired novels are lush with description and vibrant characters. Of her first novel, *Pilgrim of the Sky, Library Journal* wrote: "Barron's debut is an sf adventure that mixes high action with exquisitely detailed depictions of everyday existence in these alternate worlds."

In 2021, *Queen of None* won the Manly Wade Wellman Award for speculative fiction.

She is represented by Stacey Graham at 3 Seas Literary.

ALSO BY NATANIA BARRON

Wothwood

Rock Revival

Frost & Filigree Series

Frost & Filigree

Masks & Malevolence

Time & Temper

These Marvelous Beasts - The Complete Frost & Filigree Collection

Queen of None

Pilgrim of the Sky

FRIENDS OF FALSTAFF

Thank You to All our Falstaff Books Patrons, who get extra digital content each month! To be featured here and see what other great rewards we offer, go to www.patreon.com/falstaffbooks.

PATRONS

Dino Hicks
John Hooks
John Kilgallon
Larissa Lichty
Travis & Casey Schilling
Staci-Leigh Santore
Sheryl R. Hayes
Scott Norris
Samuel Montgomery-Blinn
Junkle

www.ingramcontent.com/pod-product-compliance
Lightning Source LLC
Chambersburg PA
CBHW030538310726
48979CB00010B/1954/J

* 9 7 8 1 6 4 5 5 4 1 7 9 0 *